HUSBANDS, INCORPORATED

Our Business is Your Pleasure.

By Elizabeth Ann Atkins

Book One of the
Husbands, Inc. Trilogy

Celebrate life & love!

Elizabeth Atkins

12·31·14

HUSBANDS, INCORPORATED

Book One of the Husbands, Incorporated Trilogy

First Edition: February 2014

eBook Edition: February 2014

Printed in the United States of America

ISBN-10: 0-9821415-2-1

ISBN-13: 978-0-9821415-2-6

Cover Photos by Clarence Tabb, Jr.

Cover Design by Marylin E. Atkins

Published by Sea Kingdom International LLC

The Husbands, Incorporated Trilogy

By Elizabeth Ann Atkins

Book One
HUSBANDS, INCORPORATED

Book Two
HUSBANDS, INCORPORATED
Under Siege

Book Three
HUSBANDS, INCORPORATED
Happily Ever After

Dedication & Acknowledgements

Words cannot quantify my infinite gratitude to God, Jesus, Daddy, my beloved Angels and my beloved Ancestors for your Divine guidance and support while I was creating the Husbands, Incorporated Series.

Likewise, I lack words to express my immeasurable gratitude to my mother, Marylin Atkins, my son, Alexander, and my sister, Catherine Greenspan, for your loving encouragement and support while I was writing the Husbands, Incorporated Series.

THANK YOU to my friends and fans for cheering me on while I was composing the Husbands, Incorporated Trilogy.

And here's LOUD APPLAUSE for writers everywhere. Keep writing and bring your books to life!

HUSBANDS, INCORPORATED

Our Business is Your Pleasure.

By Elizabeth Ann Atkins

*Book One of the
Husbands, Inc. Trilogy*

Prologue. A Last Attempt to Keep Love Alive

A shiver danced over Venus Barker's bare skin as she slipped into ivory satin lingerie.

"This won't just put a *spark* back in our marriage," Venus whispered as the winter wind howled against the bedroom windows. "I'm about to ignite some *dynamite*. I hope."

Any minute, John would walk into the master suite of their dream home, and she would resuscitate the passion that had fizzled so many years ago. She hummed as a playlist of their favorite love songs lulled from the sound system throughout the house. She ached to tingle as she had during their first wedding dance, when John had twirled her in his arms.

I will. Tonight. Because it's just the two of us, for the whole weekend. The twins were on their high school's annual Valentine's Day trip to Chicago. So all 8,000 square feet of this brick colonial were about to become a cozy love nest.

She had stocked the house with finger foods for them to nibble during long, fireside chats that would reignite his interest in her mind. They could make love for hours by candlelight, and get back on track to living happily ever after.

Another icy bluster rattled the panes of the bay window, whose white sheers billowed slightly inward from the darkness outside.

Stop kidding yourself, Venus. He doesn't want you. Hasn't for a long time…

Goosebumps rippled up her thighs as she fastened the tops of her opalescent stockings to the garter belt. But she was not cold.

She was burning up — aroused, aching for the hot, rockin' sex that she and John used to have every day back when they first met. But 17 years of marriage, two kids, his legal career and the sad truth that "familiarity breeds contempt," had annihilated their sex life.

After years of neglect, Venus was so hot, she wanted to get down and dirty. Nasty. Raunchy. Completely hedonistic. Fucking like animals until dawn.

She did that every day — in her imagination. Her partners were muscular young men she'd see, bare-chested and glistening with sweat, as they jogged past their lakefront home in Grosse Pointe Farms, Michigan. Other times, make-believe trysts were superb with handsome guys on TV. And she'd enjoyed countless, multi-orgasmic romps in her mind with the suntanned men on the summer landscaping crews who cut the lawn and blasted their long, thick leaf blowers up and down the flowerbeds.

Now, Venus forced herself to smile so she wouldn't cry. The heart-shattering truth was that she shared a bed with a man who was having equally erotic adventures — in real life. He'd presented plenty of evidence, and a litany of lies, straight to Venus' face, to cover it up.

I am so tired of being sexually repressed, oppressed, and depressed! I can't take this much longer...

The hardwood floor was cold under her stockinged feet as she approached the orange glow of the crackling fireplace. On the mantle, the silver clock said 5:55.

As she lit small, vanilla-scented candles in crystal holders spaced across the mantle, the clock made her pause. A wedding gift from her parents, it was shaped like a seashell. Its inner curve held the mother-of-pearl face with black roman numerals, while its scalloped edges fanned up and around it from a rectangular silver base engraved: *Venus and John, Eternally Yours.*

Their favorite movie had also inspired the large, black and white photograph beside the clock in a matching silver frame. Venus gasped. The current reality of their marriage was the exact opposite of their sizzling passion in that picture — embracing as waves washed over them on the beach during their Hawaiian honeymoon.

"I want that back," she said, savoring the heat of the fireplace on her lower body. "From the hell of now, back to that for eternity." That thought threatened to unleash the sadness and loneliness that were her constant companions. No more! Tonight would change everything.

She quickly lit candles on the nightstands and on the dresser. Ice cubes shifted as she adjusted the chilled bottle in the silver champagne cooler beside the bed, which beckoned with its cashmere comforter and piled-high pillows.

This was supposed to be the heart of their home. Where love was celebrated and strengthened. Where adoration was whispered. Where bodies were shared in the sanctity of blissfully bonded souls.

It will become that again tonight. In just a few minutes…

Venus entered the dressing room, which was lined with cherry wood drawers and cabinets. Rows of John's dark business suits and bright-colored golf wear led to cubbies full of sweaters and shoes, followed by racks of Venus' dresses for the frequent dinners and black tie events that she attended with him. In the center stood two gold racks. One held his tuxedo that she'd picked up from the cleaners today. The other displayed her cream-colored satin dress that she'd wear to the Valentine's Day Ball tonight with him.

She stepped into the bay of three, full-length mirrors.

"Wow," she sighed. Melancholy glazed her eyes, despite the sexy dark liner and black mascara. Her blue eyes were dull from the pain of looking into the windows of her soul mate everyday and seeing a SORRY, CLOSED sign flash back. And that was when John actually made eye contact with her.

Tonight, she would give it a final try. Her sad pallor was hidden under a pretty dusting of bronzer on the sharp point of her little triangle of a nose and the high mounds of her cheeks. And rose-colored lipstick glossed her lips that once, long ago, had inspired John's compliments and kisses.

She turned in the mirror. Though she hadn't worn lingerie for years, she now looked better than ever, thanks to running, bike riding, kick-boxing and strength training. Toned and firm in all the right places, her physique made it all the more heartbreaking and baffling that John had lost his lust for her.

"If this doesn't get his dick hard for you," her best friend Raye Johnson said in the lingerie boutique as they shopped for this ensemble, "then you either need to get a Boy Toy on the side, or leave hubby in the dust. 'Cause I guarantee, if he's not doin' you, he's doin' some young hottie. You deserve better, girl. I got mine, and look at me."

Venus wanted to say, "No, marriage is forever." But the sparkle in Raye's eyes, and the exuberant glow on her cinnamon-hued face, announced that replacing a cheating, emotionally absent husband with a young stud would make her feel alive again. That thought made Venus ache with arousal...

But no, she had to make John see her as the desirable woman whom he'd vowed to love and cherish forever. Marriage wasn't supposed to be easy, and it wasn't just about sex. Even though their lack of a sex life symbolized the void of emotion and interaction on every other level.

Yes, tonight would end all those silent meals when John's laptop created a literal wall between them on the table as he read the newspapers online. No more of his six a.m. to midnight workdays, even during trials, without a single phone call to say hello or to tell her when he'd be home. No more failing to tell her about his courtroom victories that she'd instead learn about on the six o'clock news, alone in the kitchen, while preparing dinner for the kids while he went out celebrating until two in the morning.

No, tonight she would make him fall back in love with his beaming bride, the mother of his children, his partner "'til death do us part."

I want us to be like my parents. Married 42 years, they were still as passionate and enthralled with each other as when Venus was a child.

Now, she bristled with the irony that her life's earliest memory was her parents clapping as she donned a veil and toddled through The Bliss Bridal Boutique & Wedding Chapel. Growing up in her parents' popular bridal business had been every little girl's fantasy. She had loved watching brides choose from racks of poufy gowns and glittery shoes, then speak dreamily about the groom, the ceremony, the honeymoon and the happily ever after.

I grew up believing the dream! My own marriage cannot fail...

As Venus stared at the honeymoon picture, she ached to hear John speak to her as he once did:

"Venus, darling, what do you think about the president's speech tonight? Venus, my love, a new restaurant downtown specializes in your favorite, sea bass. I made reservations for Friday night. Venus, I'm calling you first to share the good news — I won the trial! Come to the office now, we're celebrating. Venus, my lovely, join me on the couch so I can hold you and breathe you and bury my face in your hair. Venus, let me kiss you and love you for eternity..."

Venus' heart fluttered. This 48-hour marriage make-over would even enable her to banish all suspicions about John and that young associate at the law firm, and his weekend business trips, and his overly attentive behavior around his best friend's teenaged daughter.

Yes, tonight would save their marriage.

And my sanity. Thirty-six is too young to suffer from dead love.

Because her body had never felt more alive. Most mornings, she awakened with an ache for John to extinguish the fire between her legs. But despite her sensuous writhing against his nude and aroused body, he'd leap out of bed, hit the shower and go to work, or mutter about being tired and achy from golf. After tonight, he would crave her in the morning, at night, and even in the middle of the day.

Barking... Yes, their German Shepherd was barking downstairs.

John is home.

Her heart hammered. She slipped on the cream stiletto sandals that she would wear to the Ball tonight — after interlude number one. A final glance in the mirror...

Confidence — or was it desperation? — glowed in her eyes. Her adventurous spirit and optimism radiated like a shimmery aura around her. She tucked a tendril of her straight blond hair back up into the high twist that, with the pull of a clip, would tumble into a seductive cascade around her bare shoulders.

Her pulse raced as she adjusted the straps on her three-inch heels. She was five nine, but even in these heels, John would still be a good three inches taller.

The music changed to one of their favorite love songs. She poured champagne into two crystal flutes — the ones they'd used on their wedding day. Then she stood in the orange glow of the fireplace.

Excitement electrified her as John opened the double doors. The soft light illuminated his navy blue suit, starched white shirt and yellow silk tie. The thin mustache that he'd been sporting in recent years gave him a debonair flair, especially when he parted his light brown hair on the side and let the natural wave swoop over one ear. The firelight caught a few of the silver strands at his temples;

his forty-ninth birthday and the Kensington case had ushered in the gray.

Bewilderment flashed across his face.

"Hello John," Venus said with a sultry tone. She held out a glass of champagne. "I have a surprise for you."

Annoyance twisted his mouth. His blue eyes narrowed to slits. He shook his head.

"The roads are terrible from the snowstorm," he snapped as he darted into the room. "We need to dress and go. Or we'll be late for the VIP reception."

Venus' cheeks stung. "Oh, honey, just sit down and relax," she cooed, handing him a glass.

He took it, standing in front of her.

"A toast, to you and me, all weekend," she said, tilting her glass toward his. But she missed. Because he was chugging the champagne like it was a whiskey shot. His smooth, winter-paled cheeks puffed out, then he gulped.

"Ah," he said. "I needed that." He handed her the glass and removed his suit jacket.

She set both glasses on the mantle, then sauntered close to him.

"Honey," she whispered, holding his tie, "let's—"

"No, let's not." He yanked his tie from her grip, then fingered the knot loose.

She cupped his jaw in her palm. "Honey, I want to make love," she whispered, nuzzling his ear. "Before *and* after the party."

"What else is new?" he shot back. With it came a gust of his cologne — and perfume.

Hot pangs of anger burned through her.

He doesn't want me because he already gave it to somebody else...

Venus glimpsed herself in the mirror over their dresser, across the room. She looked like she'd just stepped out of a lingerie catalogue, but John was looking at her like she was a grotesque ogre.

"Venus," he said, sitting on the bed and bending down to remove his shoes. "I couldn't get it up right now if you brought a crane in here to do it for me."

Stunned, she stared at him. Her cheeks stung as if his words had smacked her.

John exhaled, annoyed. "And don't tell me you were so busy with all *this*—" he frowned at her lingerie without even looking in her eyes "—that you forgot to get my tux from the cleaners."

*　　*　　*　　*　　*　　*　　*

Divorce. Divorce. Divorce.

It flashed in her head like a neon sign as she sat with perfect poise in the passenger seat. John let out another exasperated sigh as his big, black Mercedes inched forward in the long valet line. Taillights on a limousine ahead of them cast a red tint over John's brooding expression.

"Venus, why would you pull a stunt like that when you knew we had to be on time? You *knew* the weather was bad. It's your fault that we're late."

His lips pursed as he stared forward as the windshield wipers whipped away giant snowflakes. To their right loomed Chateau D'Amour, a huge, pink stone estate built by an auto baron. Venus had attended countless awards dinners and galas in its upscale restaurant and chandeliered banquet spaces. Tonight, over its castle-style façade, a banner announced "Welcome Michigan League of Lawyers — Valentine's Day Ball."

John cast a warning look her way; she did not look at him as he ordered, "And when we get inside, do *not* tell that joke about the exotic male dancers. The wives always laugh, but the men, we just don't appreciate it."

She plastered a pleasant expression on her face and said nothing. From now on, her body would robotically play the well-practiced role of "perfect wife" while her brain strategized the smartest way to escape.

It's time to just do it.

As if it were a crystal ball, Venus stared down into the sparkle of her three-carat, diamond wedding ring.

"Christ! Why the hell are they going so slow?" John gripped the steering wheel, grinding his teeth. "This is the most important event of the year, and you scheme a little temptress scenario."

His words pinged over the icy shield around her mind and heart. Yet the heat blazing between her legs was a reminder that she still had so much living to do.

I need a plan and some leverage, to make sure I get my share when I leave him. I gave him everything. My youth. My body. The kids.

Christina and John Junior had been the only reason that she'd stayed this long. Now 17, they were accepted into college, and were finishing their senior year with A's at the private Arcadia Academy of Detroit. In September, J.J. would attend the University of Michigan, while Christina would study acting and dance in New York City.

Sometime between now and September, I'm out. And Raye will help me—

"Venus, if that hellion in heels named Raye Johnson is here tonight with one of her boy toys," John said, finally pulling up to the front door, "don't go traipsing off with her. Ever since she left her husband — a good man! — she's been a disgrace to the institution of marriage."

Venus bit her lip to stop from laughing. Disgrace? Clearly John and his friends hadn't looked in the mirror—

"Any respectable woman," he ranted, "especially with a business of her caliber, should be married, not gallivanting around town like a jezebel with some stud of the day from her male harem—"

Venus' laughter shot out in a cough-like gag.

John glared at her. "I don't care how long you've known her. I want you to end that friendship. She is a terrible influence—"

An explosion of expletives danced on the tip of Venus' tongue. She wanted to scream at John about all of his sexual indiscretions that came to light when she took his clothes to the cleaners and found make-up and long hairs of every color on his dress shirts, and even in his boxers when she did the laundry. She had seen the scratch marks on his back, and the hotel charges when he left his business credit card statements in plain view on his desk in his home office.

She even suspected that something was going on between him and his best friend's teenaged daughter, because once John was careless enough to send Venus an email that said: "Em... Butterfield 336 @2."

If Venus hadn't been out of town on a college visit with the twins, she would have scoped them out. But when she returned, she had fallen into her comfortable coping pattern of denial by telling herself:

Surely that text was for Emilio, the new lawyer whose Hispanic heritage gave John boasting rights that his firm promoted "diversity." Yes, and the lawyers must have been meeting in conference room 336 at the Butterfield Hotel at 2 p.m.

Venus always explained things away, because she didn't know what else to do. Married since age 19, she had exchanged her chance for a bachelor's degree for an M.R.S. degree from a man whose legal future was paved with gold.

"All that glitters is not gold," Venus' father had always warned.

Now as she watched fancy couples streaming arm-in-arm toward the grand entryway, she wondered if her father's warning applied to one couple in particular. As a 40-something woman clutched the arm of a tall, slim, silver-haired man, she was decked out in a full-length, white fur. Her gold satin gown swished around sparkly heels.

Were they happy? Or were they pretending, too? Was he faithful now that she had wrinkles and the wisdom of a mature woman? He was very handsome; did he keep a few chicks half his age for sex?

"Venus, I'd appreciate it if you could at least pretend to be nice to Ted's wife today," John snapped. "When Emma and Marla come to stay with us next week, I want Mary to know you're happy about it."

Venus smiled as her brain lit up with the A-bomb that she would someday drop on John to blast out of this marriage and keep him at bay forever. Now all she needed were a few of those secret video cameras that detectives used—

"Of course, honey," Venus said sweetly. "Christina and J.J. are so excited to have the Pendigree kids stay with us. What a way to end senior year."

The valet opened his door; John threatened: "Venus, I will leave this party alone before I look all over kingdom come for you and that vixen Raye—"

Venus smiled. "My cell phone number is 313—"

"I know your number!" John snatched his black leather gloves from the dashboard. "Where are the tickets?"

"You have them, darling."

"I gave them to you!" he barked.

"You took them from me—"

"You are simply useless!" He turned to get out. "You don't understand how hard I work so you can sit there like a queen in your fur coat. Christ, you didn't even finish college."

But I got my M.R.S. degree. And look how far it's gotten me.

If only she could rewind to that fateful day during her first year at the University of Michigan, when that handsome young lawyer had visited campus for career day.

If only she had declined Prince Charming's invitation to whisk her off in his white Porsche. He was 13 years her senior, and their whirlwind courtship had led to pregnancy — with twins. So he put this sparkler on her finger, asked her to take a petal-strewn trip down the aisle in her custom-made fairy tale dress, and even bought her an ivy-covered house behind a white picket fence. There, she could raise their babies while he worked to build their American Dream.

But somewhere between the diapers and long hours at the firm and grocery shopping and homework and business trips — it had all started to feel like a big, white lie.

Now, the valet opened her door, so she could step into the masquerade that had become her public life with John. He offered his elbow to escort her inside. As passing lawyers nodded in recognition, he donned a cheerful expression, but maintained a biting tone: "Venus, don't ignore Mrs. Snead like you did at the New Year's Eve party."

The governor and his wife appeared beside them. "Hello John and Venus," the governor said. "Lovely coat."

"Thank you," Venus said, smiling with a nod to John. "A gift from Santa."

John grinned.

The governor said, "You're a lucky lady."

Oh I'm about to get very lucky. Venus smiled.

The governor winked at John. "You're a lucky guy yourself."

"Thank you, sir," John said proudly as he beamed at Venus. "Married to this beauty, I happen to think so, too."

Venus wished this were a costume party, where she could wear one of those sparkly, feathered masks from the Italian Renaissance or Mardi Gras. At least then, the pretending would feel honest. But as they ascended the foyer's sweeping staircase to the second floor ballroom, her heart ached with the reality that the smile masking her pain was mirrored in the faces of so many wives, especially those over age 35.

Many stayed married for the children. Or for the husband's professional status or political ambition. Or for the money. That was especially true for the women who would have nothing without the grandeur of being the "and Mrs." after their husbands' titles of Dr. and Judge and Congressman.

All that glitters is not gold, Venus thought, as she surveyed the hundreds of women in sequined gowns and diamond jewelry. The men were pillars of tradition in black tuxedoes. Amidst the romantic glow of twinkling Valentine's Day lights, flowers and balloons, the crowd was eating hors d'oeuvres, sipping cocktails and chatting over live jazz.

"This way, darling," John said, leading her into a velvet-roped area where his colleagues and their wives stood around one of dozens of cocktail tables. Bursts of lilies on each table perfumed the air, while tiny candles cast a soft glow.

A chorus of "Hello, Venus and John" rose from a cluster of couples at the table marked with a sign that said: RESERVED FOR ATTORNEY JOHN SEBASTIAN BARKER & ASSOCIATES.

"Venus, tell me your secret," gushed Tammy Jacobs. She stood beside her husband, Karter Jacobs, a lawyer at John's firm who was president of Michigan's African American Bar Association. "How do you stay so svelte?"

Tall, trim and mahogany-hued with rimless glasses, Karter wore a bowtie that was the same hunter green as Tammy's chiffon dress. It cast an unflattering tinge over her almond complexion as the dress' floaty fabric danced around her thick midsection like leaves on a round bush. A string of pearls peeked from the bulge of fat at the base of her throat. Her hair had turned totally gray since this event last year.

"Exercise," Venus said. "And no processed food."

"Well your discipline certainly becomes you." Tammy speared another gravy-drenched meatball with a tiny silver fork from her plate on the table. "I'd like to look like you, but I'm afraid I love chocolate cake far too much."

Venus laughed, aching to help liberate Tammy and all these women from this miserable charade.

Maybe after I escape, I can help them...

"I'd like some fresh fruit," John said, glancing about 20 feet away at the buffet table. Three large ice sculptures of Lady Justice stood amidst sumptuous spreads of tropical fruits, cheeses, crackers, gourmet breads, and carving stations with turkey and beef. "Venus, would you like anything?"

Yes, a steady stream of lovers to make up for your neglect. An exciting career of my own that takes me all around the world. But first, a divorce.

She flashed a mischievous smile and said, "Actually, I'm craving a really big piece of meat. But I can wait."

She turned away from his annoyed expression and focused on their friends.

"Karter," Tammy said, smiling at her husband, "he runs his five miles every morning at six. You could set your watch to it."

"The fountain of youth," Karter said, patting his white tuxedo shirt over his flat stomach. With a shock of silver hair and surprisingly few wrinkles for a guy who was pushing 60, he eyed Venus' chest and smiled. "Yep, the fountain of youth."

John's fingers fanned over the small of Venus' back. A sizzle shot through her. Not because it was John. But because it was the first time she'd felt a man's hand on her body for—

I can't remember how long. Tears burned her eyes.

"Venus amazes me everyday," John said proudly, with the same panache that he reserved for performances in front of juries who awarded millions of dollars to his clients. Why couldn't he just *pretend* to love her? Why couldn't he just put on an act like this in the bedroom tonight to reward her for being a good, faithful wife for 17 years?

"My wife is the most disciplined person you'll ever meet," John boasted. "You could put the best cheesecake in front of her, and she wouldn't touch it. Don't know how she does it."

He beamed down at her, basking in the admiring gazes of their friends.

"Johnny-Ace!" the deep voice of John's best friend announced the arrival of the family whose portrait graced billboards and posters all over town, under the slogan, *Theodore Pendigree for Congress: A Return to Wholesome Family Values.*

"Let the party begin!" John exclaimed as he and Ted exchanged their fraternity's hug and handshake. "But everybody be good. The prosecutor is here!"

"Soon to be Senator," Karter said. "You've got my vote!"

Their friends erupted in greetings as John kissed Mary Pendigree's china doll cheek. Talc white with pink blush, her childish face belied her 35 years, as did her doe-like eyes. Her powder blue dress, cinched at her waist with a satin bow, covered her chest and arms. Upswept, brown hair with wisps down her thin neck made her look fragile.

The opposite of their daughter, Emma. The 17-year-old wore a sleeveless black dress with an over-the-shoulder strap that hoisted the bodice upward, to showcase her recent upper body growth spurt.

I would never let my daughter wear that dress.

Emma reminded Venus of the *Growing Up Skipper* doll she'd had as a girl. With a turn of the doll's arm, two breasts popped out of her chest, so she could join her friend Barbie in all the grown-up fun. Emma certainly was growing up. Too fast.

"Venus," Ted said, taking her hands and kissing each one. His sharp brown eyes contrasted against colorless skin that was so clear and smooth, it looked waxy over the sharp boniness of his nose and cheekbones. "You are radiant tonight."

"Johnny-Ace," Ted said to John, "I'd say we've got the prettiest wives in the place."

John smiled as he hugged the Pendigree girls.

"Venus, you do look lovely," Mary said. "Your dress, yes, white is definitely your color."

"It's winter white, Mother," Emma snapped. "Cream, cashmere, French vanilla. *Not* white."

"Yes, dear." Mary giggled and turned to Venus. "The fashion designer has spoken. She's taking a style class, so she thinks I'm a bumbling idiot about clothes." Mary imitated her daughter's snippy tone: "'It's not plaid, Mother, it's Burberry. They're not pumps, Mother, they're Manolos.'"

Emma cast a disgusted look at her mother. "Mom, get it right for once. I don't want to be a clothing designer. I want to be a rich, powerful lawyer, just like Dad, so I can have anything I want in life, and buy my own designer clothes. And if I ever get married, my husband will be gorgeous, but I'll be the boss, like Dad!"

Mary let out a nervous laugh as sadness roiled in her eyes. "Oh Venus, what *are* we going to do with these teenagers?"

Venus wanted to say, *"You need to slap the sass out of that girl's mouth. And cover up her chest."* Because all the men, including John, were ogling it. They'd take a quick glance around the room, or look down at their drinks, then steal another look at the girl.

"Pushing limits," Venus said. "That's what growing up and finding your place in the world is all about."

The Pendigrees' other daughter, 16-year-old Marla, who was Christina's best friend and so smart that she had skipped the ninth grade, wore a conservative black velvet dress with a high ruffled neck, long sleeves, a full skirt and patent leather flats.

"Mrs. Barker," Marla gushed, "we can't wait to stay with you when our parents go to Asia. Two whole weeks! Christina and I plan to do each other's hair every morning before school."

"And I'll pick your outfits," Emma said.

Venus cast a reassuring smile toward Mary. "And *I'll* give final approval before they walk out the door."

Mary's small, baby-soft hand grasped Venus' fingers. "We really appreciate this, Venus. If it weren't for you and John, I'd have to stay home and miss the trip of a lifetime. China, Japan, Thailand, Korea."

Ted nodded. "Couldn't be any safer place on earth than with you and my fraternity brother. I trust you like I trust myself and Mary."

Appreciation washed over John's face. "That means everything, Teddy. It's what friendship is all about."

Ted smiled at John, but their eyes followed a young woman's behind as she walked past in a snug black dress.

Mary seemed oblivious. Did Ted and Mary ever have sex? Was Mary a pistol behind closed doors? Did she play naïve in public, vixen in private? Did they leave their wholesome family image at the bedroom door, then don studded black leather so she could whip him into submission?

No, Venus was sure that Ted was getting his groove on without his wife. In fact, Raye's client said he'd witnessed Ted kissing a gorgeous tennis instructor on a sailboat on Mackinac Island. John and Ted always attended the springtime gathering there with political, business and civic leaders while Venus and Mary stayed home with the kids.

That annual weekend was one of the many "business" trips that John and Ted took. Their frequent travel out of state always inspired Raye's warning about her now ex-husband's penchant for hiring expensive call girls during his extensive business travels.

I can't wait to see her! Venus scanned the crowd for Raye, who would be bringing her Hunk of the Month.

"Venus," Mary said, "get ready to visit us in Washington, when Ted gets elected."

Venus faked a smile, imagining Ted in a city notorious for its high ratio of women to men. As a Congressman, Ted would have his pick of the chicks, while Polly Anna here continued to dutifully tend to her homemaker duties.

Venus' heart ached for Mary and all the women around them.

This is the last time I'll have to attend this event with these hypocritical men. I can't wait to escape this painful pretending — and change my name back to Venus Roman.

Venus remembered a women's studies class she'd taken in college before dropping out as a pregnant sophomore. She had read Betty Friedan's book, *The Feminine Mystique,* about how middle class housewives of the 1950s and 1960s were miserable — despite living the American Dream. Now, Venus felt like the modern-day version of that.

But if the reality of married life were a secret nightmare for some women, then what would be the dream?

"Saw your new toy at the golf club," Karter said to Ted. "Shiny as a new dime and fast as blazes, I bet."

Ted grinned. "My reward for years of hard work," he said, inspecting his immaculately clean, trimmed fingernails. "Had to stick with black, though. Photographs of me zipping around in a red convertible would not bode well for my Congressional bid."

"Dad lets me drive it sometimes," Emma boasted. Since Venus had last seen the girl at their families' traditional Christmas Eve gathering, Emma's teeth were not as white and her cheeks were not as dewy — thanks to her secret smoking habit.

She had better not even dare to light up at our home.
Venus' already sour stomach cramped with disgust. Because John was eyeing this girl like she was a big, juicy steak. He masked it well in front of her parents and their friends. But he was slick: his gaze whizzed past her, and he stole glimpses when others turned away. Venus smiled at John, thinking, *You are gonna be so busted…*

She turned to Emma. "Emma, you know John has a two-seater—"

"The 550 SL?" Emma's eyes grew wide. "That is my favorite Benz of all!" She bounced up and down, like a child asking for ice cream, which made her tits jiggle for all the ogling male eyes. She turned to John. "Please?"

"Of course you can drive it—" John glanced at Ted "—in the driveway!"

Everyone laughed.

"C'mon, Marla, let's go raid the appetizers," Emma said, flitting away with her sister.

At the same time, Doc Whittier and his wife, Suzanne, joined them. Their passion for tennis kept them slender and suntanned year-round, thanks to a winter home in Palm Beach, Florida.

"Doc, you look different," Tammy said. "Your forehead is smooth. And that crease between your eyebrows, it's gone."

"He got Botox," said Suzanne, his office manager, who looked glamorous in a silver, 1920s flapper dress and small, feathered hat. "So did I."

Mary looked puzzled. "Is that safe? Injecting botulism in your face?"

Doc shrugged. "We're still standing. A cosmetic surgeon and his wife have got to look good. Ask my patients." He smiled as a bald, sixty-ish man walked past with a young woman in a blue mini-dress. Her boobs mesmerized all the men at the table; Venus was sure that if the fire alarm went off, they wouldn't look away from that chick's chest.

"That's Mia," Suzanne said. "She and her sister came in for enhancements together."

"Poor thing looks like she'll topple over," Tammy whispered as the girl walked on four-inch stilettos and stick-thin legs past a group of mesmerized men. "She's not even *half* his age." Sadness darkened her eyes; her face was haggard, splotchy. "Forty years with Helen, and he tosses her out for that floozy?"

Mary's eyes widened with dismay. "It's like his wife was an old clunker and he traded her in for a new car."

"There's the other one at the buffet," Suzanne said. "Tia."

The sister's tight, pink dress was so short, the bottom of her ass showed as she bent to reach the fruit display. Lust blazed across John's face; he looked like he would bend her over the buffet table and fuck her — right here, right now, if given the chance.

"Excuse me," John said, stepping toward her. Animal hunger shimmered in his eyes as if he were a wolf moving in for the kill. He stood beside Tia, taking a plate and serving himself grapes.

Tia smiled at him; he cast a lusty grin down at her face, then her big, fake tits. They shook hands. He gave her a business card. Then the girl used silver tongs to place a huge strawberry on John's plate. He leaned in close enough for his lips to tickle her ear, and for her hair to obscure his face as he whispered something. The strumpet immediately looked at Venus, then raked her gaze up and down Venus' body. Giggling, she turned to John and whispered in his ear. He roared with laughter.

If John could make Venus tremble this hard with orgasms, she'd be in paradise. But right now, her insides were registering a 15 on the Richter scale of zero to 10.

She was red-hot to her core, and rage was cracking the foundation of her very soul.

If he's this brazen in front of me, what does he do when I'm not around?

Outrage exploded inside Venus; she curled her fingers into her palms to hide that she was shaking so hard. All she had to do was let years of rejection, disrespect, humiliation and despair surge down to her right fist. She would lift it up, cock her arm, like a spring attached to her shoulder. Thumb tucked in, knuckles squarely facing the target, nose level. *Pow!*

But violence was not the answer. Nor was revenge.

I need to just get away from John and create a life that's more fabulous than he or anybody here could ever imagine.

Someday, somehow, Venus would savor power and pleasure and independence. She would never look back, because she would be so busy having exquisite orgasms with beautiful, interesting men who treated her like a queen.

Until then, she would don a new mask — one of numb compliance with the status quo — while she secretly orchestrated a plan of escape.

Now, as John walked back toward Venus and his friends, his erect penis made a distinct outline in his black tuxedo pants.

I guess he found a crane to help him get it up.

Doc gave John a congratulatory pat on the back and asked, "Does she put the smokin' in smokin' hot, or what?"

"Johnny Ace!" Ted exclaimed.

"Don't tell me she wants you to sue her plastic surgeon," Doc teased.

Tammy popped another meatball into her mouth. Suzanne sipped her wine. Mary dashed toward her daughters. And Venus squeezed her fists to stop from—

"Girl, there you are!" Raye Johnson's toned arm swept Venus away from the table. "Vee, I got news!"

"You've got perfect timing," Venus said, loving the comfort of her best friend's arm around her as they strode into the crowd.

As Raye smiled, her skin shimmered; her red dress hugged her trim, toned curves and her black hair was curled and swooped up to show off dangling ruby and diamond earrings.

Looking into Raye's face roused instant relief and consolation. Her almond-shaped brown eyes were ringed with Cleopatra-style black liner, while fire engine red lipstick showcased her full lips and straight, bright-white teeth, thanks to the braces that Raye's ex-husband had insisted that she get. Her radiant, cinnamon-hued skin always looked perfect. With foundation, powder and impeccably arched and waxed eyebrows, her face looked almost air-brushed.

But the intelligence and zest for life sparkling like diamonds in her eyes left no doubt; Raye Johnson was far more than just a pretty face.

"Raye!" exclaimed Bill Carlton, CEO of a restaurant and sports dynasty. His mustached face glowed with boyish exuberance as he air-kissed Raye's cheeks. "I love what you're doing with my portfolio. You're as brilliant as you are beautiful."

"Thank you so much, Bill," Raye said with her deep, raspy voice. "It's my pleasure to help you prosper. Gladys, you look lovely."

The man put his arm around an obese woman in a blue muumuu. Her eyes were dull despite her smile, and she shifted laboriously on swollen ankles and low-heeled shoes.

"Bill and Gladys," Raye said, "this is my dearest friend in the world, Venus Barker."

Bill chuckled as he looked at Venus. "I hope some of this lady's business savvy rubs off on you. The world would be a dangerous place if we could clone the likes of Raye Johnson."

Raye smiled and said, "I'll take that as a compliment."

"Raye, don't you have an escort?" Gladys asked with a condescending tone.

"He's getting my champagne right now," Raye said, "while I catch up with Venus. Gladys, enjoy yourself tonight. Bill, I'll see you at our meeting next week."

As they walked away, Raye whispered, "She looks like his mother. Shoot me if I ever get like that."

"You won't," Venus said as Raye led her into a columned hallway lined with statues of mythological gods and goddesses. "You saved me, Raye!"

Venus cherished how Raye's positive, confident energy had always been an elixir of fun and happiness. Even as kids, Raye had this same pizzazz when they'd met at Albert Einstein Elementary School in the Detroit suburb of Oak Park, then attended Clinton Middle School and high school at Arcadia Academy of Detroit. After that, they roomed together at the University of Michigan.

When Venus married, Raye was the maid of honor, and went on to earn an MBA from Michigan's Business School. Meanwhile, as Venus raised Christina and J.J., she lived vicariously through Raye's success at using her Midas Touch to help wealthy clients multiply their wealth exponentially.

Now, Venus asked, "Raye, what's your news?"

"Lead story on the news tonight," Raye said. "'Venus Aphrodite Barker did NOT body-slam her husband at Chateau d'Amour this evening, despite his outrageously *disrespectful* behavior."

Venus seethed and smiled all at once.

Raye crossed her arms. "Girl, I saw the whole scandalous PDA! Public Display of Asshole. I wanted to come over there and jack him up myself. But I have too many clients in this crowd. Nobody wants to see their financial advisor go *Charlie's Angels* on one of the most popular lawyers in town."

Raye made pretend karate noises as she lifted her fists to her nose and did a quick kick — with her red satin stiletto sandal.

Venus smiled. "I'm ready."

Raye's eyes sparkled. "You need a plan. Monday morning, come to my office. We'll hook you *up!*"

EIGHT YEARS LATER

Chapter 1. Going Global with the Erotic Empire

Venus clawed the sheets as the young stud's ferocious thrusting blasted her toward yet another orgasmic convulsion. She was on her knees; he was behind her, gripping her hips, pounding his nine inches into her to the sexy bass beat of hip-hop music.

"I'm gonna keep you cumming so good, you'll crave this dick every minute of the day," he declared with a cocky baritone. "Yeah, a goddess like you needs a dude who can take control of this pussy and make you shiver all over this mother-fuckin' bed."

A raspy moan escaped Venus' lips. Behind her closed eyelids, her mind was a red-orange-gold swirl of fire and sparks shooting up from the friction of his rock-hard rod inside her; he had already gifted her with three earth-shattering orgasms during the past hour of this exquisite dick-ramming.

"Yeah, take it," he ordered as the song's tempo quickened; he thrust with bionic speed. "Think about all the times you needed it so bad—"

Venus smiled slightly, remembering that humiliating night eight years ago when John had rejected her one final time. Now, every thrust shattered that bad memory into a billion tingles of pleasure.

Soon, thanks to Husbands, Incorporated, women everywhere will enjoy this kind of unparalleled indulgence and power. Our revolution will change the world!

She opened her eyes to behold the paradise that she and Raye Johnson had built. From here on the huge, round canopy bed in her master suite, Venus focused beyond silvery sheers billowing around the open French doors to the balcony.

Below it were the crown jewels of this erotic empire: beautiful men, hundreds of them, wearing only black shorts with HUSBANDS, INC. embroidered in red over one thigh. Those sexy superstars were lifting weights in the grassy gym, jogging, playing volleyball on the beach, splashing in the pool and sunbathing on the sleek white yacht.

All under the enchanted observation of 200 women from around the world. Half of them were American, seeking Husbands. The remaining women had invested millions to open the first-ever Husbands, Inc. International franchises in their homelands.

Together we are creating heaven on earth.

In about two hours, Venus would join the women for the ribbon-cutting ceremony to launch the week-long orientation to officially set this global revolution in motion.

But for now, she needed to get her power-glow on. And she could best do that by enjoying the decadent fruits of her labor as CEO and co-founder of this luscious fantasy that had catapulted both herself and Raye Johnson onto the *Forbes* list of the world's 50 richest women.

And I am loving every second—

Suddenly the music stopped playing on the built-in, state-of-the-art sound system. Though this was her favorite playlist for sex, a few tunes had brief silence in-between. Now, the room was quiet, except for his groin slapping against her ass — and the noisy pandemonium out on the street.

Sirens blared. Engines roared. And a huge mob chanted: "Venus Roman, wicked omen, shut her down, outta town!"

The protesters had been multiplying outside the mansion's huge, wrought iron gates for the past week. They had shown up after Venus began appearing in local, national and global media for the first time since the company's inception.

Until now, the business had operated quietly and discreetly. No website, no advertising, no media interviews. Just word-of-mouth referrals.

But she and Raye had agreed that the introduction of Husbands, Inc. International was the ideal time to initiate a promotional campaign touting the benefits that the company was providing for thousands of men and women across the United States and the world.

"Men for sale, go to jail!" the protesters roared. "No fake wife! Marry for life!"

Her hunk *du jour* kept thrusting as he declared, "Those jealous motherfuckers *wish* they could come inside the gates of this paradise."

Venus chuckled. Another sultry song began to play, blocking out the bedlam. But a flash caught her eye; her cell phone was silently lighting up with a call. Again. She usually never brought it into the bedroom, but with so much going on, the phone was within reach, just in case.

"Kimberly Lee" flashed across the screen. Her assistant would only interrupt for an emergency. Either the media, the protesters or John needed to be checked immediately. Venus reached for the phone; her lover never missed a beat. Raspy and impatient, she blurted, "What."

"I'm sorry, Venus," Kimberly said, words shooting from her mouth as hard and fast as pellets from a B.B. gun. "There's a helicopter heading toward us, probably paparazzi for the wedding, but our Air Patrol had a problem and was delayed—"

Venus stiffened. "Tell me it's fixed."

"The captain said the fleet might not arrive fast enough to avoid an interruption for the Montague wedding—"

"Get them there!" Venus ordered with a steady voice despite the delicious pounding.

"Another thing," Kimberly said. "The police just arrested ten protesters from that deranged group, Men for Traditional Marriage. One was holding a torch and threatening to burn us down, and the others were trying to climb the stone wall out front. All the news stations are out there, broadcasting 'breaking news.'"

Venus half-smiled, savoring the sensations that were tantalizing her flesh. She couldn't thank the protesters enough for their superb timing. They would be silenced soon enough, after the global media had given her a fortune's worth of free publicity.

"And," Kimberly warned, "the police chief and sheriff want to talk with you. Again. They're worried about security. I reminded them that Husbands, Inc. is in a *castle!*"

The grounds of Sea Castle were impenetrable, according to Husbands, Inc.'s security chief, Gus Piper, who had provided an overview of orientation safety measures during this morning's briefing. Gus now stood outside the bedroom doors with bodyguard Mario Meyers. They were part of a ubiquitous foursome of former Navy Seals who kept constant watch over Venus. The other two, Derek and Decker, were guarding the upstairs hallway leading to her master suite.

Round-the-clock bodyguards, a high-tech surveillance room and dozens of live security cameras enabled her staff to monitor every inch of this 200-acre waterfront property east of downtown Detroit. The compound included The Inns at Sea Castle where her American clients and international guests were staying, as well as the cottages housing the Husbands Academy where the men were trained. Vigilant security had become necessary after the founding of Husbands, Inc. had roused an onslaught of threats from angry ex-husbands, ex-boyfriends, and vicious critics.

"Last thing, Venus," Kimberly added. "John just called again. He's so ridiculous! He's on this tirade, threatening to launch a federal investigation to put you in prison for prostitution. He said if you keep ignoring his calls, he'll have everyone here arrested and thrown in jail today."

"You're right, Kimberly. He's ridiculous. Thank you." Venus hung up. Her phone said "three missed calls."

She loved how her lover's fingertips were digging into the flesh of her waist, so he could hold her in place to fuck her with gusto while she listened to John's voicemail rant: *"Venus, I'll shut you down! No ex-wife of mine will prance around the globe as a brazen pimp, peddling gigolos—"*

Venus laughed, sliding the phone across the bed. What a poor, pathetic loser. All bark and no bite. *I have the power! He has none.*

As her lover hammered harder, she gripped the sheets and admired the sparkle of her three-carat, heart-shaped diamond ring. She'd bought it for herself after the divorce, and wore it on her wedding ring finger — before, during and after each marriage here at Husbands, Inc. The ring symbolized that she was wed to this decadent dynasty that was bringing joy to womankind.

"You're the boss, baby," the stud declared. "Boss of the world! Venus, the Roman Goddess. Greek Goddess Aphrodite. All that shit! Queen of the fuckin' universe, in my book. All those other motherfuckers can kiss your pretty little ass."

Venus closed her eyes, smiling. Her lover's verbal swag was so sexy, she could almost cum by listening to him talk. But even with the orgasmic euphoria engulfing her mind, she acknowledged that Husbands, Incorporated was operating squarely on the good side of the law, and John knew it.

He was just rabidly furious that she had created the sexiest business empire the world had ever seen. Not to mention, John was foaming at the mouth because she was enjoying a steady stream of young studs. Meanwhile, his gold-digging wife — the twin bimbette named Tia whom he'd met at the Valentine's Day Ball right before Venus' eyes — had "let herself go" after using sex appeal to secure her financial future as Mrs. John Barker and mother of his small children.

"My ex-husband," Venus had said during recent interviews on countless television programs that were featuring her revolutionary alternative to traditional marriage, *"and all of my critics, are outraged that I'm freeing women from the oppression and sexual deprivation of marriage and monogamy."*

Venus had concluded each interview by saying, *"Our critics will be silenced by the firestorm of romance and passion that will blaze across the globe under the auspices of Husbands, Incorporated."*

Now, she arched her back so her lover could pleasure her deeper. He had been trained so well at the Husbands Academy; she didn't have to tell him how to blast her into another one of the mind-blowing orgasms that rocked her body every day.

"I got somethin' else for your sexy ass," he said, reaching around and pressing his middle fingertip to that juicy berry between her legs. It was covered in cream, and swollen, ripe to the point of bursting. With one stroke—

A tiny starburst ignited under his touch. At the same time, he was hammering her insides hard, like a match striking, over and over, setting off sparks up and down. He rubbed, he rammed, and that starburst let off a flash of light behind her eyelids. A ripple of heat shot up her abdomen, down her thighs.

Venus bit the sheets. Clawed the bed.

"Yeah, you need a dude who's not scared to do you like a raw-dog, roughneck motherfucker," he groaned over the sexy music. "You need a dude who can take you to a place you've never been before."

Goosebumps danced across every inch of Venus' skin, including her face.

"Oh, hell yeah," she moaned; he had just achieved her ultimate measure of good dick.

If a man had the right girth, length, ferocity and endurance to make her *face* feel like it was shimmering with diamonds from the inside out, while goosebumps tingled over her entire body, then the man ranked on her elite list of extraordinary lovers.

But even they were off-limits while married to clients here at Husbands, Inc. She had only hooked up with Mike over the past month, while he lived on the grounds during his training. After his wedding, she would have plenty of other men to satisfy her needs. However, she would not choose another Husband until after the global launch was complete.

For now, Venus glanced back at beautiful Mike Rivers. His bronze skin glistened with sweat; his bulging pecs and the muscles up and down his arms rippled. His long, straight black hair formed a cape that swayed around his broad shoulders, down to his waist. The vertical cuts of his lats framed his washboard abs, which crunched every time he thrust.

And thrust. And thrust.

"You love gettin' dicked like this, Venus." His big, dark eyes smoldered down at her. His face was model-perfect: clean-shaven, with a wide, angular jaw, prominent nose and full lips. Mike Rivers was straight out of central casting for a Native American hero in a Hollywood movie.

During his first interview two months ago, he'd shared that he was raised by his Puerto Rican-born father, after his Italian American mother died during childbirth. Catholic school had kept him out of trouble, but walking there and back home every day amongst hoodlums in their northwest Detroit neighborhood had endowed him with street smarts, toughness and urban "swag."

As a result, Mike's ability to speak the King's English, as taught by the nuns, as well as nasty talk that he learned in the 'hood, were excellent qualifications for a Husband.

On top of that, his breathtaking beauty would prove invaluable to meet the demand for one of Husbands, Inc.'s most popular wedding packages: *The Native American Dream.*

Venus knew exactly who would claim him today. Down at Orientation right now was a new client named Jane Collins. She had echoed the essay on her application by telling Venus at last night's welcome reception that she had always craved the exotic sensuality of the Indian men she'd seen in westerns as a girl and read about in romance novels as an adult.

Now, Venus cast a lusty smile at the 28-year-old; he smiled back, proud that his bedroom skills were off the charts.

Not only were applicants' penises required to measure a certain size, but they were also mandated to stay erect for a minimum of 30 minutes for each act of intercourse. Candidates also underwent intense training to perform all sexual techniques with expertise and to behave with super sexy machismo, unless the client requested otherwise.

"Venus, baby," Mike said, "tell me you love to get hammered with young, hot dick that won't quit."

Venus' eyes twinkled at him with lusty agreement; his hips moved faster, faster, harder, harder. She pressed her hot cheek into the sheets. Just as she closed her eyes, his fingertip set off an erotic explosion.

All she saw were golden sparkles. Her hips jerked up and back. A primal scream shot through her lips. Lightening bolts jolted her shuddering limbs. Then she whimpered, gripping the sheets, savoring the sensory extravaganza.

Suddenly, the memory of that smirk on John's face, so many years ago when she had tried to re-ignite their marital passion, flashed in her mind. That elevated her pleasure even more as Mike pounded relentlessly.

"I'm gonna keep fuckin' you 'til you can't move," he said. "So you can't even remember any dudes before me."

Luscious sensations kept cascading through her, filling her mind with a psychedelic swirl of colors.

"A goddess like you deserves this every day," Mike groaned.

Her parents had named her after the Roman and Greek goddesses of love, to celebrate that she was born of a union that epitomized their undying passion and soul-deep unity. Now, as they marked their fiftieth anniversary, they proved that true, loyal, lasting love was possible.

But finding it was nearly impossible. In fact, Venus believed that women who yearned for what her parents had, faced the same one-in-175-million odds as folks who played the lottery.

Fortunately I've found the solution for women to win in a new way, over and over...

Mike kept pounding and stroking, pushing her way past the point of orgasm.

"Did you get enough?" he asked. "'Cause you know I can go all day."

She nodded weakly. He jack-hammered fast, let out a deep groan, then shuddered. "Damn, that was good," he whispered.

He gently held her waist as she sunk to the bed, on her stomach, because she sure as hell couldn't move right now. Facing her, he fell to his side. His still-hard dick was safely covered in an extra large Magnum; cum filling its tip looked like a tiny scoop of vanilla cream. He grinned as his eyes sparkled with pride and enchantment.

Her head was spinning, ears ringing, body still spasming. Especially when he tickled her back, from the firm curve of her ass to her toned shoulder.

"Now Venus Roman, CEO of Husbands, Inc. International, is ready for the world," he said. "You can step out there with your freshly fucked glow, as your own best advertising."

Lacking the energy to speak, she gazed up at his adoring face. He was framed by the metal canopy of swirling purple metal and gauzy silver sheers hanging from it. Above him, the domed ceiling appeared baby blue with white clouds. At night, its recessed lights glowed with rainbow pastels, one minute at a time.

"You're so fuckin' beautiful," he whispered. A boyish grin parted his full, red-wine-hued lips, revealing large, white teeth. His palm brushed over the base of her spine. "You don't need a tattoo over your ass. You already got the coolest birthmark."

She half-smiled as his finger traced the silver dollar-sized spot.

"Looks like a giant pearl exploded on your skin and stuck there," he marveled. "It like, shimmers when I fuck you. I love that shit. Never seen anything like it."

His big, strong hands kneaded her ass. She moaned, because that made her pussy throb for more, but that would have to wait.

"Hey, how'd I register today on the Venus Scale?" he asked, pressing his palm to her thigh to feel her trembling legs.

Her system for rating orgasms was similar to the Richter scale for earthquakes. This guy never registered less than 10 out of 10.

He watched in awe as her thigh muscles jumped under his hand. "Damn, I'd say fifteen, at least."

She laughed, but stopped when her phone vibrated at the edge of the bed. It was probably John again, or Kimberly calling to report protesters vowing to shut her down.

I won't let them! The planet will be a much better place when women finally get to luxuriate in this carnal indulgence — on our own terms — that men have been enjoying with harems, mistresses, courtesans and multiple wives since the beginning of time.

Mike stroked the top of her head. "I'm touching a genius, because this business is the best idea! The chicks get laid; the dudes get paid. And I'm the fortunate motherfucker who gets to enjoy it!"

His mischievous laugh made her smile. Someday he'd want a real marriage, kids, the whole white picket fence thing. It was important to experience that. And he'd know that when he — and his wife — tired of that, and the kids grew up, Husbands, Inc. could give them both what they needed.

He pressed his hot lips to her cheek, then whispered: "Want some more?"

She found the strength to raise her fingers to rake a tendril of his long hair from his damp temple back over his huge shoulder.

"She moves," he said playfully.

"I need to get ready," she rasped.

"She speaks," he teased. "Next time I'm gonna lay it on so hard, you won't move or talk for an hour! No, wait, I can't do you anymore, after I get my first wife today. Right?"

"Correct." She turned on her side, admiring the upbeat, youthful energy in his eyes. "You need to get ready, too. I want your first marriage to be spectacular for you and the client. I already know who she is, but I want to see the chemistry crackle between the two of you, to confirm it's the best match. So lift weights after you shower."

He flexed a bicep.

"Love that." She wrapped her fingers around the rock-hard hump of muscle. "Do some of those sexy pull-ups out there. You'll be married in no time."

"And *payyyyd!*" He grinned. "I wish my real fiancée could have been like you. Relaxed, confident. Laila was always so worried about her looks. I don't think she could really let go and enjoy sex. And she's like, 15 years younger than you."

Venus smiled. Next Friday, one week from today, she would turn 44, and she had never felt better.

"You don't age," people were always telling her, or, *"You look younger every time I see you."*

Because Husbands, Inc. enabled her to savor copious and refreshing gulps from the fountain of youth every day, and she planned to continue doing so for as long as life allowed.

"Younger chicks can learn a lot from you," Mike said, "about when you do your own thing, to please yourself, then people like you better. And you get *more* beautiful, from the inside out."

"Thank you," Venus said softly.

Mike shook his head. "Man, Laila was so caught up in trying different things to make me love her more, but it backfired. I just wanted her to act normal."

Venus sat up. "Sometimes it takes awhile to learn that happiness is an inside job. She'll see."

"Too late." Regret glinted in his eyes. "I'm about to say 'I do' to some lucky lady."

"Very lucky," Venus said. "Plus, you're part of our global movement to put the 'happily' back in front of the 'ever after.' One man and one woman at a time."

"Dig that," Mike said as the song ended. The noise of sirens, protesters and roaring engines burst into the room. "Sounds like we're under siege by the world."

"Revolution never comes easily," Venus said, remembering a news report she'd watched this morning. It showed the protesters burning life-sized effigies of her and a Husband. Then, as now, the hairs on the back of her neck stood up.

"Whoop! Whoop! Whoop!"

Venus startled as the deafening alarm blared. The red light flashing from a tiny box near the ceiling seemed to mirror her worries.

Mike showed no reaction because the fire alarm was ringing as scheduled, during the safety presentation that her security staff performed every morning. It was important for everyone on the grounds to recognize the alarm, and learn how to evacuate the buildings, if necessary.

The alarm decreased in volume as Gus' recorded voice boomed over the intercom system throughout the mansion: "This is only a test. During an actual emergency, you would proceed to the nearest exit to evacuate. This is only a test."

The alarm's constant drone triggered an ominous feeling that tore through Venus. It raked up a wicked chorus of John's threats, the protesters' chants, and her critics' voices.

Why did the alarm seem extra loud and long today? She covered her ears, as did Mike, who was staring at her with a playful expression.

Yes, this gorgeous man in her bed — and the sexy Nirvana on the grounds below — were tangible reminders that whatever battles awaited, the passionate life mission that she had discovered in the throes of divorce required her to win, on behalf of women around the planet, for centuries to come. She tilted her chin upward.

My enemies can bring it on. I am on top of the world. Husbands, Inc. is here to stay. And nothing will stop us.

Chapter 2. A Woman Scorned Seeks Revenge

As the Channel 3 News Chopper zoomed toward the castle-style mansion by the lake, reporter Laila Sims seethed in the passenger seat.

Her ex-fiancé was down there somewhere, among hundreds of men sunbathing on a docked yacht, playing beach volleyball and lifting weights on the huge lawn. Didn't they know, they were nothing more than hunks of meat at a man market?

And all those horny bitches were picking their male merchandise as they walked around the lush grounds behind hostesses wearing white uniforms. The pool deck was a downright brothel, with those gigolos — wearing skimpy black shorts — posing and pouring champagne for the women.

"This is like, *beyond* wrong!" Laila exclaimed, still shocked that Mike had dumped her to work *there* for that bitch Venus Roman. "It goes against everything marriage stands for."

Laila was so mad, a drop of spit flew onto the tiny black microphone attached to her headset.

"Calm down," said the pilot, a fifty-ish man named Len who'd been married half his life. "You can't report fairly if you're having a fit about it. A reporter is supposed to be objective."

"Yeah," said the cameraman, Owen. "This is *your* story, Laila. It's got Emmy written all over it. Why are you so miffed? Looks like every girl's dream down there."

The carnal compound included two ivy-covered Inns and a cluster of cottages in a wooded area. On the emerald lawn behind the mansion, a sign announced "HUSBANDS, INC. INTERNATIONAL — Welcome to Global Franchise Orientation." The sign stood beside a huge, white tent with four Husbands, Inc. flags fluttering at its peaks.

"Man!" Owen exclaimed. "Can't imagine what kind of sexcapades go on in that place."

"Yeah, it's every girl's dream, alright," Len chuckled, "and every guy's worst nightmare. Can't believe we're this close. Last time we tried, three choppers chased us away. Madame Roman doesn't play around."

Laila stiffened.

Neither do I. Usually. But this story is personal.

And nobody would ever know Laila's secret motive for obliterating Husbands, Incorporated.

Mike will pay! Everyone at the station thought her fiancé had moved back to Los Angeles to give his acting career another try. He'd even changed his name, hoping that "Mike Rivers" sounded more appealing to casting directors than "Miguel Rivera Cruz."

Holy shit, what if Venus Roman took *him* as her next Husband? What if she had already fucked him as a try-out for the job? That slut probably had a casting couch to rival the sleaziest Hollywood producer, but this was worse, because she was stealing good men and pimping them.

Laila coughed. She snatched a bottle of water from her purse and chugged, then massaged her throat with her fingertips.

"Relax, Laila," Len said. "Last time you got all worked up, you had a coughing fit and couldn't finish your live report. Maybe you need to go down there and hire a husband yourself. Ever since Mike left town, you've been so edgy—"

She glared at Len, then spun around to Owen: "You getting all this? Zoom in on the guys, too. Let's expose those gigolos—"

"Got 'em," Owen said playfully. "I'm gonna sign up tomorrow. Everybody'll be like, 'Where's Owen?' And Len'll say, 'Oh, he's got a new career. Husband.'"

"Dream on, buddy," Len said. "You gotta do a whole lotta sit-ups to make *that* cut."

Laila didn't laugh. She studied all the faces on the monitor as the camera zoomed in.

"Owen," she asked, "do you see Venus Roman? Tall, blond, beautiful. Always wears white suits and dresses."

The cameraman shook his head. "Nope. But when I get her, your story is the first to show her live in action. Hey, you should interview her ex-husband. You know, the lawyer on the billboards and commercials where people say, 'Thank you, John Barker.' Venus Roman is always dogging her marriage in the media; I bet that dude would dish some dirt on *her*—"

"Actually," Laila said, "as soon as we get back to the station, I'm going to call his secretary to set up an interview."

Len grinned. "Just promise you'll still talk to us little people after you win your Emmy Award."

Laila smiled. Yeah, this story would make her an overnight superstar in the news business. But most importantly, it would destroy Venus Roman's whorehouse, with Mike as the first casualty.

"I need the money," he argued when she confronted him after finding the Husbands, Inc. Training Manual in their apartment.

"I've been looking into this place," he confessed, "because I don't know any other gig that can pay me 150-grand in a year. It'll be a good experience for my acting career. So, Laila, I'm sorry, but—"

Dumped! All in one heartless little sentence. But Mike would soon see, in one media blitz, Laila would rise. And he would fall. That would be his punishment for dating her four years, but refusing to go through with their *real* wedding. It made no sense, because she had done everything to entice him: dieting, working out like a fiend at the gym, wearing sexy lingerie, learning how to give the best blow job, even getting bikini waxes that hurt like hell.

He always said she didn't need to do all that to impress him, because he liked "regular" girls. Yeah, right. All the women's magazines said the best way to keep a man was to do everything she was doing — or someone else would.

I should've gotten the boob job sooner. When he sees me now, he'll want me back, for my big tits alone. But he will never have the pleasure of touching me, ever again.

She could almost feel steam shooting from her ears. Instead, it rose up her throat, and she coughed. Now Mike was going to marry a stranger, and fuck her every day, for money?

Laila's cheeks burned with rage. In the mirror, her slim, creamed coffee complexion — framed by a straight, brunette bob — was still fresh and perky, despite her anger. She removed her sunglasses; the blinding sunshine reflecting off the water below made her topaz-brown eyes shimmer.

"You guys, we *have* to get exclusive video—" she coughed. This story would be her double-whammy springboard to a bigger city, or to the anchor desk, or to the networks. At 29, it was time to advance from being a local news "street slave" to the big time.

"Len," she ordered, "if those choppers come back, do not leave. We *have* to get video of Venus Roman surrounded by her gigolos."

Her cell phone rang; it was her producer. "Laila, ready to go live?"

"Ready," Laila said, putting a device into her ear so her producer could talk to her during the report.

Moments later, the light glowed red on the Chopper Cam, which was secured to the front window. Laila stared into the lens, a magical black circle of glass that would instantly put her on millions of televisions across southeast Michigan. Her report would no doubt get picked up by her station's parent company, National News Now, which broadcast worldwide.

She sipped water, and took a deep breath. The thrill of impending triumph soothed her scratchy throat.

"I'm Laila Sims reporting live from the sexiest spot on the planet," she said. A small video monitor in the dash showed her face, then a live, aerial view of the man market behind the mansion.

"You're looking at the first live video *ever* of the super-secret, super-sexy stud farm called Husbands, Incorporated," she said. "All eyes are on CEO Venus Roman as she unveils her secretive company and goes global with this husbands-for-hire enterprise that she founded with a friend... after their first marriages ended in divorce."

On the monitor, a Native American hunk — riding a white horse with a woman whose wedding veil billowed behind them — galloped along the beach past a gazebo covered with black and white balloons.

Laila gasped. *That's Mike! Already married!*

She coughed, watching his long hair bounce around his shoulders. But that tattoo down his arm — no, that wasn't Mike. He was too afraid of needles to get a tattoo.

Holy shit, I miss him so much! He was the most gorgeous man she'd ever seen; her attempts to date in the wake of their break-up had really sucked. It made her feel shallow as hell to compare every man to him, but she couldn't help that his swarthy Latin look was her "type."

Doesn't he know we were the perfect couple?

Laila used to love staring at his clean-shaven bronze skin, his Indian warrior nose, and his prominent cheekbones and wide jaw. And his eyes! Large and dark, they once radiated so much love as he gazed down at her. When he kissed her with those full lips, his long, black hair would drape around them, making her feel like the happiest chick in the galaxy.

Now he was going to share all that with some bitch who would be paying for it. Laila's insides burned red-hot; another cough exploded up her throat.

Len mouthed, "What the fuck?"

She chugged water, then said, "Excuse me."

But where was Venus Roman?

"This trend for one-stop-stud-shopping is so hip," Laila said on camera, "that today a rock 'n roll heiress is saying 'I do' in that gazebo. Claire Montague now joins thousands of women who are purchasing the perfect marriage at Husbands, Inc."

Every word scraped her throat. Was Mike among all those shirtless dudes lifting weights in an outside gym on the lawn that looked as manicured as a putting green? Was he lounging on one of those sunbathing mattresses on that sleek, white yacht? Or was he with those guys around the pool? All Laila wanted to do was stare down there and find Mike. But she had to focus on her report.

Get a grip, Laila.

Her throat felt like sandpaper as she said, "Even though Venus Roman has given dozens of national interviews and graced the cover of *Forbes* magazine, media is strictly banned from her company's hedonistic headquarters. But we're giving you the *first ever*, sky-high scoop as the virgin daughter of rocker Stone Montague—"

Laila paused, wide-eyed, as panic exploded inside her. *What if Mike is marrying that spoiled rich girl... then screwing her all day, every day...*

"Laila!" her producer shouted in her ear. "Wake the hell up!"

Laila startled and continued: "—the virgin daughter of rocker Stone Montague jumps on the biggest trend in marriage... ordering the perfect husband from a real-life catalogue of cuties at this fantasy fortress."

The video monitor showed wooden crates near the gazebo; they probably held doves for release after the wedding. Laila had featured that idea in her series of reports last year that chronicled how she and Mike were planning their wedding.

"Soon," she continued, "women around the world will have access to the same husbands-for-hire service that reclusive Claire Montague—"

A row of men jogging across the lawn caught Laila's eye. She stared at a long, dark ponytail... big shoulders... *Mike?*

She coughed, then faked a smile. "See ladies, one look and you'll be speechless, too. As I was saying, the young heiress has been so disillusioned by dating gold-diggers — she came all the way from Los Angeles to Detroit, to find and finance Mr. Right."

The video monitor showed close-ups of the men pumping iron as a crowd of women ogled their glistening muscles.

"But is this a legitimate mating service?" Laila asked. "Or a hotbed of male prostitution? I'm Laila Sims, and I'm going to expose the truth."

And shut that place down!

Chapter 3. Play By Raye's Rules, or You're Out!

As Raye Johnson emerged from the Emerald Bay Yacht Club into the warm afternoon sunshine, her Husband opened a sunbrella. He held it over her as they walked past a gold-framed sign announcing: *Financial Advisor of the Year Luncheon.*

"Congratulations again, baby," whispered Danté Wilson, kissing her cheek. Adoration glowed from his handsome face that was as smooth and creamy as gourmet milk chocolate. Raye loved feeling dwarfed by his broad shoulders and height.

She beamed, thrilled that Danté was finally acting right. Contrary to the specific requirements of his contract, he'd already had two episodes of being stingy with the dick. One more, and he'd be out.

Danté handed a small ticket to the valet as they joined a cluster of well-coiffed people awaiting a steady stream of luxury vehicles.

"Damn, baby girl, we look good together," Danté said, catching their reflection in the window of a Bentley that rolled to a stop before them.

Raye smiled at their picture-perfect reflection. Behind designer sunglasses, her flawless skin was luminescent and smooth as glass, thanks to cosmetics that she custom-ordered from Paris. Her trademark Cleopatra hairstyle — pin-straight, jet-black, shoulder-length with bangs — was so perfect, it looked airbrushed. Her custom-designed, red pin-striped business suit hugged her curves that she kept slim and firm with running, strength-training and yoga.

She laced her arm through Danté's. He looked good enough to eat in that blue and white seersucker suit that she had tailor-made for him. The 1920s style "boater" straw hat and butter-soft, white leather loafers made him delectable from head to toe. Not to mention the sexy, pro-athlete body underneath.

And I'm about to feast on his fine ass.

She glanced down at the crystal, star-shaped award in her hand. It was engraved, RAYE JOHNSON, CEO, QUEEN FINANCIAL SERVICES.

I love my life! Today epitomized Raye's definition of success. This morning, she closed an eight-figure deal with a new client. At lunchtime, she was honored at this luxurious event. This afternoon, she would revel in the pleasures of her sexy, young Husband in her waterfront penthouse that was decorated like an Egyptian palace. Or maybe they'd take her 50-foot Sea Ray out for a cruise on the lake.

"Danté," Raye whispered seductively. "When we get home, I want—"

He yawned without covering his mouth, and shook his head. "Naw, baby, I know exactly what you want. But I got the 'itis.' All that filet and lobster for lunch, and pie on top of it, I need a nap."

"You're forgetting all the rules," she accused, as their reflection disappeared because the Bentley pulled away. "Getting sleepy after you eat with the 'itis' ain't in your contract. It specifically states you must accommodate unlimited acts of intercourse—"

He laughed. "I did you so good this morning—"

"I ate a delicious breakfast this morning, too. Then I was hungry again when it was time for lunch—"

He shook his head. "Baby girl, you need to tame your appetite."

Raye stiffened; she felt like her insides were simmering with rage as red-hot as her suit. "You need to remember why you're standing here next to me—"

Her insides boiled a few degrees hotter as he poked out his lips in protest.

"Raye Johnson!" called a deep male voice. She turned to see her wealthiest client, Smitty Samuels, who was CEO of a global soft drink company. His hair matched the gray sheen of his double-breasted suit, as well as the baby doll dress on his 28-year-old wife, Peggy.

"Raye," Smitty said, grasping her hand. His blue eyes contrasted sharply against his leathery suntan and laser-whitened teeth. Smiling, he said, "Raye Johnson, we are privileged to know you, and honored to work with you."

A cool gush of pride tempered Raye's anger toward Danté as she shook their hands. "You took the words right out of my mouth, Smitty. You're my favorite client, and I want to thank you for the honor of serving you and Peggy."

"Congratulations," Peggy said, smiling, as the warm breeze tousled her Farrah Fawcett hairstyle.

"This must be the lucky new man," Smitty said, shaking Danté's hand. "Congratulations, big guy! You gotta be awfully special if this lady found you worthy of her expensive time and attention."

Raye joined Smitty and Peggy in a laugh.

"I definitely earn my keep, sir," Danté said with a tone tinged with resentment.

Raye seethed over that flagrant foul; he was required to act like the perfect, even pandering, gentleman toward Raye's clients, no matter what. But now she was the one doing the acting, by smiling up at him with a love-swept gaze and gushing, "Oh, he definitely does earn his keep."

"If I weren't a more progressive man," Smitty said with a quick glance at his buxom bride, "I'd say that Husbands, Incorporated business was preposterous. But I see how well it's working for you, and a couple other ladies we know. I just wish you and Venus Roman would let investors in on the deal. Going global and all, you're sitting on a goldmine."

Raye smiled. The privately held company had evolved exactly as they'd planned, with Venus as the face of the business, handling the day-to-day operations. Raye's 50 percent ownership meant she had equal say on every decision, as well as half the profits. From the beginning, however, she had preferred to play a lower profile role so that she could continue to pursue her first passion: money management. And because her marriages blurred the line between her personal and professional lives, it was imperative that she portrayed a perfect image of Husbands, Inc. at all times. Even when her Husband was misbehaving.

"I hope both of you get an opportunity to meet Venus," Raye said. "She would have been here, but she's hosting the global orientation today."

"I just love her!" Peggy exclaimed. "When I was Miss Michigan and I went to the Miss America pageant, us girls had a fantasy that we could custom-order a husband." She smiled up at Smitty. "I got lucky, but my girlfriends are pinching pennies so they can go to Husbands, Inc. and be like you."

"Tell them, 'Be careful what you wish for,'" Danté said with a laugh. "She's a man eater."

"That's why she's such a good businesswoman." Smitty shot a hard look at Danté. "You ought to appreciate—"

Raye took her Husband's hand and cooed, "Oh, he appreciates." She gazed up at Danté with love-swept eyes that belied her urge to cuss him out.

If she wanted all this mouth and disrespect, she could have stayed in a real marriage 10 years ago. But now that she was paying for it, she had the power. And he had just lost the privilege. Thank goodness she and Venus had taken drama classes back in college, before Venus dropped out to marry that Neanderthal named John Barker.

"Danté appreciates me," Raye told Smitty, "in ways that give new meaning to the word."

Smitty nodded. "Glad to hear it."

Raye took Peggy's hand. "Tell your girlfriends, the new Husbands, Inc. Foundation is offering scholarships for women who need financial assistance, so they can enjoy the experience."

Peggy squealed, "Oh, bless you! You will make a lot of women very happy."

Smitty grinned. "Raye, expect calls from several of my associates. I was so impressed with how you shielded my portfolio from that blasted recession, I've passed your name to my boating buddies down in the Bahamas. Some big-name guys. Real international players."

Raye basked in the genuine good will beaming from Smitty's face. She wished her late grandfather could have witnessed this moment. Having grown up in rural Georgia under the oppression and humiliation of Jim Crow,

Granddaddy had always warned her about pursuing a career in the world of finance.

"All them rich white men ain't gon' give their money to a brown girl from the Detroit ghetto," he would often say when she was in college and graduate school. Sadly, a heart attack had robbed him of the chance to see Raye dazzle clients like Smitty Samuels.

So now, she spoke on behalf of both Granddaddy and herself as she said, "Smitty, I'm so grateful and stunned by your kindness."

He laughed. "It ain't kindness, sweetheart. You're just damn good at what you do."

A black Ferrari F149 California pulled up to the valet. Danté shook their hands, then headed to the driver's side.

Raye hugged Smitty and Peggy. "You're a very lucky lady," she whispered to Peggy, "to find such a good man." Then she told both of them, "I hope your trip is fabulous."

"Raye, you'll have to join us down on our island in the Exumas," Smitty said. "You'll love it."

"I'd be honored," Raye said, making a mental note to send them something special for their anniversary.

Meanwhile, she wouldn't be celebrating one with Danté. If Smitty hadn't been watching, she would have ordered her Husband from the driver's seat, but she gracefully entered on the passenger side. Nestled into the caramel leather seat, she waved to the Samuels as Danté drove away. Danté turned up the stereo; a deep-voiced rapper blasted with a sinister beat:

"All my bitches on yo' knees, do whateva I fuckin' please; I got the dollas, makin' you holla; if a freak don't thrill, I gotta kill—"

Raye jabbed the touch-screen to silence it.

"You are so out of bounds!" Raye snapped as they pulled away from the valet canopy. "You are officially trained to comply with the rules of the *Corporate*

Companion package.   But three months in, you're a *Corporate Catastrophe.*"

Danté stared straight ahead while driving onto the mansion-lined boulevard along Lake St. Clair.

"Withholding sex, making snide comments in front of my client, and playing bad music in my car," Raye ranted as they passed the spectacular Butterfield Mansion. "I could have all this aggravation with a normal relationship!"

She crossed her arms as an onslaught of anger reminded her of how unhappy she'd been with her first real husband, who had never seemed to grasp the meaning of monogamy or honesty. He always had such a sorry-ass look in his eyes when he was lying about the scratch marks on his back after he came home at three in the morning. Even worse was his cocky expression when he tried to justify his cheating by blaming women for seducing him.

"It's just the price you pay for success," Tremaine said. "Money is a magnet for hoes, plain and simple. I got what they want, and they're offering what no dude can resist. So you and me, we can stay married, and you just deal with that. Do your own thing. I don't care."

After her divorce, a steady stream of men had reminded Raye that the rules for the dating game were written by men, to make them win every time. They won control, they won the sex, and they won the power to declare "Game Over" whenever they damn well pleased. That left their defeated female playmates out on the field, desperate to get invited into another losing game with a guaranteed winner.

Now Danté couldn't deal with the fact that Raye — and Husbands, Inc. — had fixed the game in women's favor. Even though they were receiving financial incentives and a luxurious lifestyle, it was too much of a mind trip for some men. As he drove, Danté maintained his super cool posture, with his left wrist on top of the steering wheel and his elbow on the center console.

"Put both hands on the steering wheel! That's dangerous!" Raye's heart hammered against her ribs. "I've worked too hard and come too far to be bothered with all this bad behavior."

Danté put one hand on the steering wheel and made a tooth-sucking sound, while staring straight ahead in the silence. Raye's whole body trembled with indignation.

I get awards and accolades from the top CEOs in the world, and Venus and I started one of the most innovative companies ever, yet I can't get a man to act right. Was my own father this arrogant and uncooperative?

All Momma would ever say was that she had met the handsome jazz musician named Raymond in New York City while she pursued her dream as a clothing designer. But when Momma got pregnant, Raymond fled to Paris. With a broken heart, she returned to Detroit to raise Raye in a crumbling little row house on Kercheval Avenue on the East Side. Still, Momma was always designing dresses, then sewing them without a pattern by using scraps from her seamstress jobs and the clearance tables at fabric stores.

"Someday you'll be rich enough to have all your clothes custom-made," Momma would say, holding up her newest Ritzy Diva Designs. Her specialty was mother-daughter outfits that she and Raye wore on bus outings with their neighborhood church and community center. The Detroit Institute of Arts, the Detroit Science Center, historic Greenfield Village and the Ann Arbor Art Fair were among many places where Momma exposed Raye to culture and a world of wealth.

All while modeling her fashions and building Momma's client base, one by one, because people everywhere would stop and ask where in the world she'd found such unique outfits.

Raye's favorite, when she was seven years old, was a denim skirt and jacket with glittery studs and ruffled pink leather along the hems.

She was wearing it one morning in second grade at Butzel Elementary School, when a banker visited for Career Day. The woman wore a tailored blue suit with a big diamond ring, and she arrived in a white Mercedes-Benz. Alayna Johnson was the richest-looking African American woman Raye had ever seen. With an elegant swoop of straight black hair that curved around the right side of her face and curled softly behind her left ear, she carried herself like a queen.

"This most important thing for you," Alayna Johnson said, "is to stay in school, go to college, then choose a career that's exciting and helps people."

"How can I become a wealth management advisor like you?'" Raye had asked in addition to many other questions. Alayna Johnson had answered every one, and Raye wrote down the answers, then memorized them.

After the presentation, the elegant woman confessed that she wanted to purchase the same outfit Raye was wearing, to give as a gift for her niece's birthday.

"It's a Ritzy Diva Design," Raye said proudly. "My Momma hasn't opened her boutique yet, but she takes custom orders."

"I love that it's one of a kind and so unique," Alayna said with a huge smile, handing Raye the first business card she had ever seen. "Give this to the very talented owner of Ritzy Diva Designs, and ask her to call me before the close of business today."

From then on, Raye decided she would become an even bigger, better version of Alayna Johnson. At the same time, the woman paid Momma a small fortune to create three evening gowns. And she took such a liking to Raye and her mother that she secured a small business loan for Momma to open her boutique, which made so much money the first year that Momma paid back the entire loan and bought a nice, three-bedroom, two bathroom brick home in the quiet suburb of Oak Park in 1975.

All the while, Raye earned A's at Einstein Elementary School, studied finance on her own, and with Alayna's guidance, became Momma's bookkeeper. The icing on the cake was that Momma fell in love with Alayna's brother, who owned an electrician's company. They married, and Paul Johnson adopted Raye; he became a loving, attentive father. Together, he and Momma bought a bigger house on Parklawn Street near Oak Park Boulevard.

The day they moved in, Venus and her parents showed up at the door, offering a big fruit basket and an invitation to swim in their backyard pool. Raye had never had more fun in her life than the first afternoon that she spent with Venus, jumping around and floating on inflatable chaise lounges in the pool. All while Mr. Roman grilled burgers and their parents sat at an umbrella table nearby and talked about life, love and the town's extraordinary harmony amongst white, black, Jewish, Chaldean, Asian and Russian residents.

When Raye and Venus began sixth grade at Clinton Middle School, one of their constant companions was Eden Greenfield. They joined her family for celebrations of the Jewish holidays Passover and Hanukkah. They also had great fun at the huge bat mitzvah party for Eden's thirteenth birthday. All the while, her grandfather provided a living history lesson by telling stories of the horrors he endured in a Nazi death camp during the Holocaust. He showed them the numbers tattooed on his arm and described how he was rescued from Auschwitz by Soviet soldiers in 1945.

Venus, Raye and Eden were inseparable from Zahra Wazzi, whose Chaldean family had fled religious persecution of Christians in Iraq; her grandmother introduced Venus and Raye to the delicious flavors of Middle Eastern food.

The fifth member of their "club" was Kimberly Lee, whose Filipino parents owned Sweet Dreams, an ice cream and candy shop at Coolidge and Nine Mile Road. All the boys and girls hung out there to flirt while enjoying hard-packed cones, candy necklaces and fruit-flavored Jolly Ranchers.

Venus, Raye, Eden, Zahra and Kimberly wore matching denim jackets that Momma designed and sewed, with each girl's name embroidered in metallic pink over the left breast pocket. The backs were adorned with PARKLAWN PRINCESSES in pink satin letters lined in rhinestone studs. Their "club" — with carpooling parents' help — enjoyed sleepover parties, Wednesday night ice-skating, Saturday afternoon roller-skating, movies and outings to Northland, Twelve Oaks, Fairlane and Oakland malls. Of course, boys were their favorite conversation topic.

In fact, their trademark gesture, when they liked something, anything, was to blow over their fingertips like they were sending a kiss of approval into the air.

Now, 30-some years later, Raye wanted to do anything but blow a kiss at Danté. He epitomized how the male species — whether irresistible or infuriating — had always been Raye's most decadent pursuit.

If only grown-up relationships were as simple as the giggly crushes that the Parklawn Princesses enjoyed with this boy and that boy, all through school. Raye and her friends were experts at navigating the fickle waters of adolescent and teenaged romance. But the one boy who never caused Raye's heart to waver was her little brother, Whittaker, born on the first day that Raye started ninth grade at Arcadia Academy of Detroit.

She had never seen anything so beautiful as his little face—

Screeeeeeech!

Danté slammed on the brakes. Raye's seatbelt restrained her chest as she lurched forward. She watched in horror as the front of the car skidded toward the back of an SUV that was already stopped at a red light. With just inches to spare, the car stopped.

"Pay attention!" Raye shouted. "I'm not tryin' to get whiplash — or die this afternoon!"

He looked straight ahead, bunching his lips like he was mad.

"Danté, those red lights on the back of a car mean stop!"

He turned to her and accused, "Raye, things would be better between us if you'd stop acting like a drill sergeant. A relationship is give and take, compromise—"

"You clearly have forgotten where you are and who you're talking to," Raye said. "That doesn't even merit a response. But just let me remind you, I'm *giving* you the life of luxury and a very fat check at the end of the year. And according to the document you've signed four times here at Husbands, Inc., that entitles me to keep *taking* to my heart's desire."

Raye crossed her arms and stared out the window as Danté turned down the boulevard toward her penthouse. The old Raye would have thought she'd never find another man who could lay it on as well as Danté; his big, thick dick was a perfect fit, and he had superhuman stamina, when he felt like indulging her. It was the kind of dick that could make a woman so crazy, she would stick with a man no matter how doggish he was.

Thankfully, six Husbands, Inc. marriages had proven that Raye's next draft pick could have even more talent and endurance than his predecessor.

"Pull over," she ordered.

"What?" he snapped.

"Pull over so I can drive."

"I'm driving," he said.

"Then go to Husbands, Inc."

"Why?"

"Three strikes, you're out," Raye announced. "Withholding the dick signals 'Game Over' in Raye's Rulebook."

"This ain't a game, baby girl. It's a marriage."

"It's a game, and I own the team, so I set the rules," Raye declared. "I'm going to have Venus Roman cancel our contract."

He kept driving straight.

"Danté, turn the car around, now, or you'll never have another marriage here again. You act like you don't need 150 G's."

He stopped at a red light, removed his sunglasses and looked into her eyes. His extraordinary handsomeness didn't register on her mind. *At all.* It didn't matter. His attitude was ugly. Hideous.

"You have breached your contract," Raye said. "You're supposed to pleasure me as many times a day as I want!"

He shook his head. "I don't care how rich you are, baby girl, you can't buy the right to fuck me to death. Then I'd never get paid."

Anger surged through her so strongly that her legs jerked, making her stiletto heels scrape the plush, black carpet. "Who ever heard of a punk-ass man turning down some pussy in a penthouse? After you drive a new Ferrari in custom-made clothes, eat food made by my personal chef, and chill on my yacht!"

He turned, stopped at the security gate leading into her condominium complex, and said, "I need to get my clothes."

"Your clothes?" Raye shouted. "When I picked you up at Husbands Inc., you had nothing but your big dick in your hand! Now I'm returning you the same way. So drive!"

Chapter 4. Plain Jane Finds Her Fantasy Man

Jane Collins could not look away.

That's him. My Husband.

She saw only a glimpse of his face. But if this Husbands, Inc. deal were all that she believed it was, then she'd just found her dream lover — an exotic, Native American warrior. She'd dreamt about him most of her life, read about him in countless romance novels, ached for the fantasy of savage passion—

And there he is.

A black ponytail dangled down his bare back. The rich, bronze hue of his flawless skin made her mouth water; she wanted to lick and bite every inch of him. A hot wetness throbbed between her legs.

He was doing pull-ups in the center of the outdoor gym, surrounded by two-dozen men who were lifting weights on the lawn between the mansion and the lake. The deep chopping noise of a helicopter in the distance echoed her heart, which was pounding with lust and terror.

How could a sexy guy like that pretend to love a Plain Jane like me for a whole year, even if he is getting paid?

With each pull-up, his hips swayed forward with such grace and sensuality, she shivered. Her nipples felt like they they'd poke through her new lace bra. All she could think about was him laying her on one of those exercise benches, hoisting up her dress, and giving her what she'd been craving for years.

"Good Lord, I'm in trouble!" she whispered, oblivious to the 30 women around her and the Husbands, Inc. hostess who was explaining the process for selecting a man.

"I hear you, girlfriend," whispered an ebony-skinned woman beside her. Her nametag said LaShawn Hawkins from Brooklyn, New York. Curvy in an orange dress, with long, skinny braids, the woman had a regal stature and confident eyes. "I'm 'bout to write a fat check and be a repeat customer at Husbands, Inc."

Jane smiled, but the word "customer" made her cheeks burn.

Am I such a loser in love that I have to "buy" a man? And do I have the guts to really let loose with such an intimidatingly gorgeous hunk? My head may be full of fantasies, but the real me is just too plain chicken to act on them. Cripe! What am I doing here?

Maybe her years of loneliness and two failed "real" marriages were a warning that she was simply unlovable. Maybe she was doomed to be alone and lonely. Suddenly her best friend's voice echoed through her mind:

"Live like you're dying, Jane," Pamela warned just before an aggressive cancer killed her a few months ago. Only 34 years old, she whispered from her deathbed, "You never know. The clock of life is always ticking. And when you're laying here like me, you'll want to say you lived your wildest dreams. I didn't. And now I never will."

Now, Jane stared so fiercely at her dream lover that she didn't even blink. She hoped Pamela was looking down from heaven to witness this daring adventure, because that man could have stepped off the pages of the romance novels that had fueled their daydreams about torrid trysts with Indian heroes. Jane felt dizzy with excitement that Venus Roman had figured out how an ordinary woman could do the impossible — enjoy a dreamy guy like him for 365 days.

Okay, yeah, I can do this...

Muscles popped from his wrists, down his arms and shoulders. Sweat glistening on his skin showcased every muscle fiber, which rippled down his back along the valley of his spine, then flexed around his ribcage, down to his elastic waistband. She loved that he and the other men wore black shorts with HUSBANDS, INC. on one thigh.

A shiver danced over Jane's skin. One touch from that guy would probably make her 34-year-old body explode with more orgasms than she'd ever had.

Jane's stomach gurgled. Suddenly she imagined a big plate of bacon, cheesy eggs and pancakes soaked in maple syrup. *Quit it, Jane!* That would be a surefire recipe for a bad reunion with the 30 pounds that she'd just lost to become the perfect "Wife" for her "Husband."

If he saw the real me, before the crash diet and beauty shop magic, he'd run for the hills!

Jane looked down at her black mini dress. Below her flat stomach, her toothpick-skinny legs jutted out, with a spray-tan and new muscle tone, thanks to the expensive personal trainer. The pointed toes of her black stilettos, though painful, looked so sexy.

She smiled. Well, maybe that guy *would* find her attractive. She looked as close to a *Cosmo* girl as she ever would, with the blond hair extensions falling in big waves around her shoulders. That laser treatment made her teeth shine whiter than a new bathtub. She didn't love the sensation of the contacts, but she was thrilled that they were granting her life-long wish to have blue eyes instead of her natural brown.

Breast implants were still on her wish list, but the cost would have cut into her Husband budget, so she would make do with her B-cups. Meanwhile, the fake, black eyelashes felt heavy and created a sort of dark awning over everything, but they sure made her feel as red-carpet ready as she'd ever be.

If her family in Reno, Nevada could see her now! Not that they cared, but it would sure be sweet revenge after all their years of calling her "Plain Jane" and yakking that she'd never keep a husband. Clear across the country, her parents and siblings were so caught up in their dysfunctional dramas, they couldn't care less about what she was up to, anyway. Never had.

Her two sisters had dropped out of high school, pregnant. Now 23 and 24, they worked as cocktail waitresses in the casinos to support their kids. Last she'd heard about her two brothers, ages 30 and 31, they were still unhappily married, working odd jobs and smoking as much weed as possible. Their parents were obese and debilitated from smoking, drinking and eating junk food. That made them meaner than ever, and too busy going to doctors' appointments or eating in front of the TV to ever call. Likewise, her aunts and uncles didn't so much as send a Christmas card, so Jane was really on her own.

That's why, after Pamela had moved to Detroit for work, Jane had followed, landing her current job, then suffering through the world's most pathetic relationships with men.

I really have no one in the world who gives a darn about me...

Maybe having a Husband from this place would rescue her from the solitude and emptiness that were her constant companions. She glanced around, hoping like heck she wouldn't run into Raye Johnson anytime soon.

Raye would have a fit that I've pretty much cashed in my entire life for this one last hurrah! Not that she'd recognize me without the brown hair, frumpy clothes and flubbery body.

Jane pressed a hand to her gurgling stomach; the acrylic fingernails and French manicure were so shiny and pretty. No way could she bite her nails with those things on!

Yeah, I can do this...

But her stomach was so empty, it hurt. How could she live on protein shakes and salad for a whole year? She hated every minute of those butt-kicking workouts in the gym. Without them, though, she would be one big fat, ugly whale.

One year, and I'm out. Peace Corps, here I come!
Then I can let myself go back to hell in a hand basket in the
looks department.

"Physical fitness is a requirement here at Husbands, Incorporated," said the hostess, who'd introduced herself at the opening reception last night as Eden Greenfield, Business Manager for Husbands, Inc. With pouty pink lips and black liner around her blue eyes, she wore her tawny hair in a sassy bob that bounced around her slim, freckled face.

Like the other fit, bubbly female hostesses touring groups of women around this place, Eden wore a short, white cotton sheath dress with HUSBANDS, INC. embroidered in metallic red over her left breast. The hostesses' sparkly red sneakers reminded Jane of Dorothy's ruby slippers in *The Wizard of Oz.* As if three clicks would transport every woman here into the arms of a sexy, romantic wizard. Yeah, Dorothy got her happy ending, when Glinda the Good Witch told her she already had the power within to live a good life.

But I don't think I have the heart, brains or courage to go through with this...

"Every Husband," Eden continued, "is required to maintain the ideal body weight and measurements for the duration of each marriage. Failure can result in financial penalties or immediate expulsion without pay."

LaShawn whispered, "That'll keep him in check. Girlfriend, you haven't looked away from hottie over there. I know who you'll be taking home."

Jane giggled, watching him do pull-ups. His glutes were two perfect mounds of muscle, above bowed hamstrings and sculpted calves on lusciously long legs. Like the other men jumping rope and lifting chrome weights on black leather benches, he wore white athletic shoes. Big ones. Like a size 13 or larger. They dangled in the air as his hips swayed up and forward; he groaned as he pulled his chin over the bar.

"MMmmmm hhhmmm," Jane moaned.

"Close your mouth, darlin'," whispered the woman to her right, Georgetta Lane from Dallas, Texas. She was the first person Jane had met last night at the welcome reception here at Husbands, Inc.'s world headquarters. Now, the forty-ish brunette towered over the other women in high heels and an expensive, trendy jumpsuit by the designer GiGi Gateau. Fanning Jane with the small notebook that the 200 women had received, Georgetta smiled. She whispered with a slight southern accent, "Jane, you look like you wanna have him for supper."

"I wish," Jane cooed.

Sweat trickled down his spine, into his shorts.

"Ah, mon Dieu," sighed a petite woman to Jane's left.

"I see a couple of Husbands who could have me speakin' in tongues, too," LaShawn said.

"What did you say, anyway?" Jane asked the woman, who looked rich and elegant, yet natural. Jane couldn't see a lick of make-up on the woman's smooth, sharp-featured face or around her warm, hazel eyes. Copper streaks in her brown pageboy style haircut caught the sun in a way that made it glow around her. And she wore a tailored white pantsuit with expensive-looking leather flats. She was no spring chicken, but her ageless beauty was captivating.

Beside her was a young, blond woman who turned and looked at Jane; the chick's big, blue eyes were so beautiful, Jane glanced down.

I feel so poor and ugly next to them.

She hated this familiar feeling that had started in childhood. Every morning, she dreaded when she and her rag-tag siblings would get off the bus at school, and the well-dressed rich kids would call them "dumpster divers" and "trailer trash."

Now, envy consumed Jane as she stared at the older woman. *All the stylists and make-up in the world couldn't make me look that pretty.* The woman clearly came from way on the other side of the tracks from where Jane grew up, yet she gave off a vibe like she didn't look down on anyone. In fact, Jane felt slightly giddy that this high-class lady was looking at her in such a nice way.

"I said, 'Oh my God' in French," the older woman said with a thick accent. "I am from France."

"Wow, I've never met anyone from France," Jane said. "So what do you think about this? I'm excited, but how can they make a guy be attracted to me if he's really not?"

"Look at you, girl," LaShawn said, scanning her from head to toe. She licked her finger, touched Jane's arm and said, "SSSSstttt. Hot mama!"

"Money talks, darlin'," Georgetta said. "These boys have nothing but nice bodies, time to kill and a big hambone for the highest bidder. They're a dime a dozen."

The French lady watched in awe, as did the stunning blond beside her.

"These dudes are just like the groupie gold diggers that go after pro-athletes," LaShawn said. "I know, because I was married to one. But here, the tables are turned. And it's better, because the rules are all in writing. These dudes have to go along with our program or they don't get the Benjamins. Ha! Ladies rule!"

As they shared a high five, the French woman joined in. "I am Josephine DuJardin, and this is my assistant, Coco Versailles. We are opening a franchise in Paris."

"Paris," Jane sighed, shaking their hands. "It's so romantic there. Why would you need this?"

"Because in French culture, it has always been okay for the husband to take a mistress, but not for the wife to take a lover," Josephine said. "When I was growing up, my father never came home right after work. He had a *cinq-à-sept*, a 'five to seven,' which was the time when men visited with their mistresses."

Jane gasped. "Married men?"

"Of course," Josephine said. "It was normal. But it was not acceptable for the wife, who was home making dinner and taking care of the children." Josephine shook her head. "Things have changed in modern times, but we're excited to bring pleasure to the women of our country—"

All around them, the women whistled and cheered as a dozen, bare-chested men jogged past, smiling and waving.

"Oh help me, that's Washington 'Buck' Briggs," LaShawn gasped, pointing to a big man with muscles, a bald head and a bright smile. "Let me sail away on that dark chocolate dreamboat—"

"A masterpiece if I ever saw one," Georgetta said. "I met him when he played with the Detroit Lions against the Cowboys in Dallas. He came to a party at our home, since Buck had an endorsement deal to wear the clothes and shoes that my ex-husband's company created. Poor guy, lost everything. To go from Super Bowl champ to Man-for-Rent in what, five years—"

"I remember something bad about him in the news," Jane said. "Drugs?"

"He had a turbulent love affair with Jack Daniels and Captain Morgan," LaShawn said. "Now he's about to be mine."

Jane turned to the French women. "Josephine and Coco, did you find your guys?"

"There," Josephine said, pointing as mischief sparkled in her eyes. "He has long hair and tattoos. Coco and I, we will both take the *Rock Star Dream* package. I am building a music studio and stage in my chateau near Paris, to watch him compose and perform for me. Then I will become the Venus Roman of France."

"You must be loaded," Jane said.

Josephine's expression was blank. "What is—"

"Rich," Jane giggled. She mustered up enough courage to look Coco in her eyes. She probably wasn't even 25, and her skin was clear and creamy, making her impressive cleavage even moreso.

Cripe, life must be so easy when you're that beautiful.

"Actually," Coco said with a sexy accent, "we have many investors, many businesswomen and heiresses from Europe. They are eager to enjoy marriage in this new way that liberates women from the risks."

Jane was mesmerized. "Sorry, but I'm totally confused. Why do *you* need to get a man this way?"

Coco smiled. "I have a business degree from university; Josephine has the financial ability." She cast a lusty look at a tattooed, long-haired guy lifting weights near Jane's dream Husband. Then Coco said, "It is very important for us to experience the service we will provide, so we can personally endorse it to our many influential clients."

Josephine nodded. "Thankfully, I am a divorcée, and my husband was very generous, after his many indiscretions—"

The thunder of horse's hooves drew everyone's attention. Jane joined a collective gasp as the women turned toward the water.

A bare-chested Native American man was riding a white horse toward them. With flowing brown hair and a suede loincloth, his massive, caramel-hued thighs gripped the sides of the horse. Clutching his muscular waist and riding with him was a euphoric woman whose wedding veil billowed behind them.

Jane's mouth dropped open as the horse galloped at the water's edge and headed toward a white gazebo where a couple was getting married.

"C'est magnifique," Josephine sighed.

"I'll take *him*," Georgetta declared.

"Ladies," the hostess said, "behold the *Native American Dream*, one of our most popular packages."

Jane whispered to the women around her, "I already signed up for that."

Georgetta shook her head. "Honey, I love all this man candy, but the whole operation seems too good to be true. How can it be legal to lease a husband like you lease a car?"

"Yeah," Jane sighed. "I was worried about that, but they say it's legitimate."

Georgetta crossed her arms. "What's our recourse if we shell out the big bucks, then find out it's a sham? Or illegal?"

That black helicopter thundered closer; its side was emblazoned with a yellow Channel 3 logo. The deep chop of its blades roused a bad feeling as Jane shielded her face with her hand, as if to block out the sun.

Darn it! If anyone at work sees me on the news, I'm done for! I'd be fired and homeless!

LaShawn crossed her arms. "They told me, no media. Period. Now this—" she glared up at the helicopter. "Pisses me off! Nobody needs to see who I'm about to take home to my bed."

Jane scowled. "Makes me worry about what else could go wrong here."

Josephine looked confident as she said, "I trust that it will be handled."

"Ladies," the hostess said, "now that you've seen the wedded bliss that can be yours, I want to redirect your attention to the Husbands here."

Jane focused on her Husband-to-be. Yes, he would be worth the risk of selling her house and car, and cashing in her savings to come here. Then, how lucky could a girl get, being asked to house-sit her boss' waterfront condo for 13 months while he was on a mission trip to India! Jane wanted to smile up at the sky, certain that Pamela had hooked that up, but she'd wait until the news chopper was gone.

Jane had to keep her marriage hush-hush, because she had made her boss believe that she'd be alone in his house for that whole time. It wasn't like he'd told her *not* to have any men there.

But he was the CEO of a non-profit organization that helped Christian families. And before he left last week, he'd been all over the news, condemning Venus Roman and Husbands, Inc. as "immoral."

At the time, Jane had already plunked down her money here and agreed to house-sit for her boss. Neither he nor anyone else in the world knew what Jane was planning. She hoped they never would. The organization where she worked maintained its immaculate reputation to ensure a steady flow of multi-million dollar grants for programs that helped the poor. As a result, employees were expected to follow a strict, though unwritten, moral code of conduct.

Which I'm blatantly violating right now. But as long as everything with my Husband goes smoothly, nobody at the office will ever know why I'll be coming back to work in 10 days with such a big smile on my face.

As for Raye, who would no doubt tell Jane that she was shamefully irresponsible, the response would be, *"You inspired the idea, Raye!"*

Raye Johnson was the one who, during investment strategy sessions, always talked about her latest new Husband, and how it was worth every dime to enjoy control in the relationship. The only reason Jane even had a financial advisor was because she had won a year's worth of Raye's services in a raffle at a women's conference where she'd had to staff a booth for her employer.

That was five years ago; her work with Raye had gone so well that Jane stayed on as a client, learning how to save money. She loved being around Raye, who was everything

Jane wanted to be, but wasn't: confident, beautiful, rich and fearlessly in charge.

"Earth to Jane," Georgetta teased. "Honey, you're a million miles away."

Jane tried to smile, but her stomach cramped with hunger and worry as the hostess explained how the marriage would end.

"You'll spend the last ten days of your marriage on the U.S. territory of Guam," Eden said, "where non-residents can obtain quick, easy divorces when both parties agree to the terms. It will feel like you're taking a honeymoon in a tropical island paradise to celebrate the end of your marriage—"

Jane cringed. *Oh my gosh, I won't want it to end!* She would hopefully be a million orgasms richer, but literally bankrupt. Plus, if she ever dated again, no regular guy could compare to this fantasy. And did she really want to join the Peace Corps?

Sunshine blazed on her fake hair; sweat prickled her scalp and she wanted to scratch it, but that would look so unattractive. And these darn eyelashes felt itchy, too. One touch and she'd smudge the black eyeliner and look like a raccoon. Not to mention, she would have to wear these contacts for an entire year! They were bothering her already, but once her new Husband looked into her now-blue eyes, taking them out to reveal her brown eyes — and wearing her gumpy eyeglasses — in front of that hunk would never be an option.

This is a mistake! Sadness gushed through her.

No one will ever love me as I am, and I can't spend a year starving in this glamour-girl get-up. I don't care how gorgeous he is...

"Ladies," Josephine said, gazing at Venus Roman as she approached with two huge bodyguards, and a waif-like Asian woman who was speed-talking into a headset and glaring at the TV news chopper.

"Here comes the prophetess who's delivering us into temptation," Georgetta smirked.

Jane was spellbound. Venus Roman's white suit jacket flared over her slim hips and tapered into a tiny waist adorned with a rhinestone clasp. Her long, toned legs were bare under the slim-fitting skirt. Diamonds sparkled in her ears, and her short blond hair made her look bold. Topping the super glamorous look were silver sunglasses and matching stiletto sandals.

"Ah, mon Dieu," Josephine sighed. "Her aura appears like stars bursting around her."

LaShawn stared in awe. "What I see is a woman who's gettin' it good. Really, really good."

Josephine nodded. "Yes, she is having exquisite orgasms. All the beauty creams in Paris could not make the skin glow with such luminescence."

As Venus approached, she removed her sunglasses and smiled. Her eyes glowed with the kind of passion and purpose that Jane viewed as the pinnacle of female power.

If I could have just a tiny flicker of that in my eyes...

Another hot gush of sadness overwhelmed Jane. No beauty salon could light a fire in a woman's eyes like that. All the self-help articles in women's magazines said it came from deep in the soul, from self-love. But when Jane tried to apply that idea to herself, she concluded that if she even had a soul, then surely it was dark, cold, empty and ugly. So that whole "radiant from within" idea seemed hopeless.

As her dream lover did another pull-up, the rumble of that helicopter echoed her bad thoughts.

There's no way he could love me, even for money. I can't pretend for a year, and the real me is too unacceptable to deserve a man like that—

She watched Venus Roman, who walked so elegantly, she seemed to float. A woman like her deserved a guy like him. She was probably naturally thin and loved eating salads and working out. Not to mention, she had all the money in the world to look like a million bucks all the time, with a hot guy on her arm. Just like Raye.

I could never be like them. Jane wanted to kick off the stilettos, take a taxi to the grocery store, and buy all the ice cream her stomach would hold — *after* she stopped at Lafayette Coney Island downtown to devour a mountain of chili-cheese fries and Coney Dogs oozing with chili, mustard and onions.

She wanted to rip off the hot hair extensions, fake lashes and blue contacts. The tan would fade, the fingernails would fall off, the weight would pack back on, and she'd return to her same old, despicable self.

Live like you're dying, Jane. You never know.

Jane stiffened as Pamela's voice echoed in her head. Suddenly Jane envisioned herself on her own deathbed, regretting that she had never lived her greatest fantasy. She glanced at the sky in the opposite direction of the helicopter.

Okay, okay. When I die, I want to smile with the memory of being Mrs. Him for a year, even if I have to pay for it.

𝒞𝒽𝒶𝓅𝓉𝑒𝓇 5. Claire Marries a Man for Money

Through her white veil, Claire Montague glared at the Justice of the Peace, who couldn't perform her wedding for the very reason that she'd chosen to tie the knot here at Husbands, Inc.

The media.

Madame Roman had assured her that paparazzi and reporters were banned from this place. And if they didn't take care of it now, Claire was going to stomp out of this gazebo in her white leather wedding dress, find Venus

Roman and demand a refund. If they couldn't get this important detail straight, how reliable were all the other clauses in the contract?

It had to be perfect, because this marriage meant everything to Claire and her future. In fact, it was worth $500 million. The 300-grand she was spending to have Billy Jack Burns as her Husband was an investment to guarantee receipt of her inheritance for her twenty-fifth birthday.

Mom and Dad will think I fit their definition of "normal," once and for all. I'll get paid. And I'll live happily ever after in a paint studio on the beach with my Nikk-Nikk.

But right now, Nikki DeFiore looked annoyed as hell. She was standing at Claire's left as her maid of honor in a matching white leather dress. Her adorable button of a nose was all wrinkled against her round face. Her dark eyes were shooting poison darts at the judge. And she kept running her hand through her short spray of chestnut-brown hair. All of which let Claire know, her beloved was one mad bitch right now.

Claire's groom, however, looked just as happy-go-lucky as she expected from his country bumpkin ass. When she'd put in an order for the *Country Boy* marriage theme here at Husbands, Inc., Billy Jack didn't need much training. He was a certified hillbilly, straight out of the Bible Belt. He'd never heard of her father, rock 'n roll legend Stone Montague. And Billy Jack had no clue that her secretive lifestyle was the paparazzi's obsession back in Los Angeles.

Hence, the helicopter.

"I apologize for the delay," the Justice of the Peace shouted. Behind him, the wind from the helicopter made scallop patterns on the blue lake. One of the secret service type security guards who were all over this place stepped to him and whispered something.

The Justice of the Peace nodded and shouted: "Ms. Montague, the problem is being remedied as we speak. Then we will proceed."

Billy Jack, who was tall, thin and adorable in his white tuxedo — though she could do without the four-inch, faux-gold crucifix hanging over his chest — leaned close to Claire's ear and said, "You look prettier than my momma's rose garden in July."

Claire smiled. This dude was so different than the guys in L.A. They all looked at her with dollar signs in their eyes. Or a scheme to promote themselves as musicians or actors by dating her.

She'd only dated them to try to fulfill her parents' order to marry a *man* by age 25 to get her inheritance. But she hated that the guys wanted to use her. This guy was using her, too, to get his 150-grand at the end of the year. However, Claire liked the official lack of pretense here at Husbands, Inc. Their mutual use of each other was signed and sealed in a contract that her lawyers said was water-tight and legitimate. He was in it for the money; so was she. Now if only Nikki could finally be at peace with the program.

"I'm gonna sneak in your house tonight," Nikki whispered, "and pretend it's *our* wedding night." Her eyes radiated lusty rebellion.

"You know the rules," Claire snapped. Nikki should have just been glad that Claire was leasing two houses — one for herself and Country Boy, and another one, secretly, nearby for Nikki. She could have left Nikki back in their house on Malibu Beach, but she'd insisted on coming here, out of fear that Claire might enjoy being with a man and forget her real purpose for this "marriage."

Now, Claire's challenge for the coming year was to minimize Nikki's jealousy, while giving Billy Jack no hint that she preferred girls. Most guys grooved on that idea, but he'd made it clear in the initial interview that his religious beliefs condemned homosexuality as an abomination punishable by eternity in hell. Claire had chosen him for that reason; if she had picked a Husband who'd want a threesome every night with her and Nikki, he'd be tempted to take the money in a year, and write a tell-all book about his life with Claire Montague and her lesbian lover.

Then I'd be out $500 million. And I won't play starving artist for anybody. Not even my Nikk-Nikk.

But the deepening rumble of the helicopter sounded sinister, like Fate was warning that it wouldn't be so simple. On one side, Billy Jack clasped her hand, as Nikki whispered angrily on the other side through her veil, "You're not *really* gonna fuck him tonight, right?"

Claire smiled at Billy Jack, then glared at Nikki. "You know the deal."

"I told you I don't care about the money," Nikki snapped.

"You would if you were hungry with no place to stay."

"I can work."

"Chill out and you'll never have to work," Claire said, glad that Country Boy couldn't hear them over the noise. "We can just paint and play, all day long. Forever."

Nikki scowled down at her tiger lily bouquet. "I feel sick thinking about him touching you."

"Blame my parents."

"They're such freakin' hypocrites," Nikki spat. "Maybe I shoulda stayed in L.A. Anywhere but here."

Claire cast a half-furious, half-heartbroken look at Nikki. She could still taste her, and her body tingled from the sensuous hours they'd enjoyed in a Butterfield Hotel suite this morning. Back in the Malibu house — which Claire had sold before coming here — they had talked about doing this, and sticking it out, no matter how hard it was, so they could start fresh in San Francisco. Then they would be free together forever — inheritance in hand.

"Nikk-Nikk, you promised," Claire said. "But if you can't handle it, you can go—"

"I'll try harder." Nikki's gaze softened, until she looked past Claire and shot a wicked look at Billy Jack. The Justice of the Peace watched them; his face mirrored their annoyance, which he probably assumed was sparked by the helicopter noise.

Billy Jack tightened his grip on Claire's hand. "I feel like the luckiest guy in the world. Doin' what the Lord put us here to do. Pair up as man and wife."

Claire looked into his clueless blue eyes. He was essentially a gigolo. Where would he find justification for that in the Bible? He was cute enough, with straight, straw-colored hair and a dimpled baby face. He was 5'11" according to his profile. Neither she nor Nikki hit 5'2" — so Country Boy towered over them even now in their high heels. Claire hoped that the clause in the contract that said no children would result from this marriage would mean that he wouldn't want to have sex. In the Biblical sense, sex was for procreation. And this union would have none of that.

Then again, maybe I can try it.

She smiled at him. Something about the hunger in his eyes when he looked down at her, and the way his pink lips parted over his straight, white teeth, made her wonder what it would be like. She had touched a penis once in high school, during a "make out" game at a party. But boys and men grossed her out, and she had always been so happy with Nikki and other girls that she had never wanted to sample sex with a male. Now, however, curiosity convinced her that this would be the perfect chance to try a guy under the safest, most confidential circumstances. Even Nikki would never have to know.

"Don't smile at him like you want him!" Nikki snarled. "You're not supposed to make love with anyone but me.

That's why you picked the religious dude. So he won't want to—"

"I wish my parents could be here," Claire exclaimed to both of them. The truth was, she hated her parents for putting her through this. Why couldn't they just love and accept her as she was?

Her mother was ridiculously righteous and moralistic in that convent down in Argentina, after years as a drugged-out groupie and rock 'n roll wife. No doubt, back in her heyday, Mom had had her share of girl-girl action in threesomes and orgies. Meanwhile, Claire's father had a harem of whores around the globe. Who were *they* to dictate morality?

The helicopter got louder; the gazebo rumbled. Nikki ran to the edge, and pointed a middle finger at the chopper.

Claire and Billy Jack looked at each other and laughed, cupping their hands over their ears.

Chapter 6. Venus Welcomes the Women

Venus Roman savored the post-orgasmic trembles in her legs as she strode toward 30 women who were watching the Husbands pump and flex in the outdoor gym. She couldn't wait for every one of her clients to enjoy the thrills of tailor-made marriages with all the sensational sex, romance and fun that they could only *imagine* outside of Husbands, Incorporated.

But the ominous rumble of three approaching helicopters was a maddening reminder that the rest of the world was not going to let them indulge this fantasy without an ugly fight.

The choppers were approaching the gazebo, where feisty Claire Montague was probably livid. If Venus had to make anyone happy today, it was the demanding young heiress whose future depended on her success here. This business was built on word-of-mouth referrals, and glowing endorsements from high profile clients like Claire encouraged more women to luxuriate in the decadence of Husbands, Inc.

"Make those choppers disappear, now!" Venus ordered Gus Piper, whose platinum buzz cut matched the silvery scar across his throat. Like his swarthy partner Mario at his side, he was big, dark-suited and discreetly armed. Derek and Decker were already standing amidst the women to ensure constant surveillance from every angle.

"Gus, you know I promised Claire Montague — no paparazzi!" Arrows of anger shot through Venus, but she maintained perfect poise under the watchful eyes of her clients and franchisees. "Where the hell is our Air Patrol?"

"Kimberly is in communication with Air Traffic Control now," Gus said, nodding at Kimberly, who was shaking her head as she listened to the headset attached to her iPad.

Always pixie-like in leggings, flats and a flouncy top, Kimberly hurried alongside Venus. Anger pinched her round face and glinted in her dark, slanted eyes. Her taut lips were painted the same shade of red as the tiny silk roses in the headband holding her black, Tinkerbell-styled hair.

"John Barker is like a schoolyard bully on steroids!" Kimberly snapped as she glared at the helicopters. "I just learned that he conspired with his fraternity brother — an Air Force general! — to order a secret military operation that created a 'no fly zone' over our hangar, so our choppers were grounded!"

Gus pressed his finger to the earpiece attached to a coil that disappeared in his jacket. "Water Patrol just blocked a boat full of intoxicated men who were taunting Husbands and clients on the yacht. And a paparazzi photographer was arrested. He was trying to take pictures from a kayak."

Venus focused on four Husbands, Inc. speedboats that were patrolling the lake as clients, franchisees and Husbands mingled on the docked yacht, on the beach, in the pool, near the training cottages and around the wedding gazebo.

"No more intrusions!" Venus ordered. "Now tell me a brilliant way to make those choppers disappear."

Gus leaned close. "Simple: birds and balloons." He nodded toward the gazebo.

"Superb. Do it." Venus strode quickly, telling her entourage: "John's little battle plan will backfire. I'll delight the entire planet with passion, and he'll rot in hell with his pathetic pack of bullies."

Venus walked faster, outstretching her arms toward the visitors.

"Ladies, welcome to Husbands, Incorporated, where our business is your pleasure!" she exclaimed over the helicopter buzz.

The women exploded in cheers and applause.

"I love you all!" Venus declared, kissing her fingertips and thrusting them toward the women.

Their nametags announced their home cities and states, as well as their native countries, including Australia, South Africa, Switzerland, Zimbabwe, Italy, Brazil, Mexico, Ireland, the Bahamas and Fiji.

Venus had met each woman face-to-face at yesterday's opening reception. Prior to that, months of Skype sessions had enabled her to nurture a rapport with each client and franchise owner, while learning life stories and motivations for coming to Husbands, Inc.

Now, as Venus stepped amidst the group, removed her sunglasses, and looked into each woman's eyes, she felt that she knew them intimately. For example, stunning Marena Barboza from Venezuela inherited her beloved husband's petroleum export company when he died unexpectedly four years ago. Acutely conscious of her status, and tired of attracting money-hungry Casanovas, Marena planned to take home a Husband and open a franchise in Caracas to help other wealthy, self-protective women enjoy romance and passion.

Now wearing a blue silk dress and a long, dark ponytail, Marena stood between Josephine DuJardin of France and Orianna "Joy" Ekpo from Nigeria. The ebony-hued supermodel was CEO of a cosmetics empire that she founded with her earnings from walking the world's most exclusive runways. She was "discovered" at age 14 in her family's village, by a British magazine photographer who promised Orianna's parents that she would provide an English education – including college – if the teen could also model in London. Now, Orianna's many endeavors included operating the Joy School for Girls in her Nigerian village.

Like the Husbands nearby, she joined the women in a stunning spectrum of complexions that ranged from milky white to butterscotch to black as licorice. Yet despite their disparate origins and appearances, they shared a common, colorless trait: the desire for love. It sparkled in their eyes, animated their bodies and charged the air with excitement.

Venus multiplied that by thousands of clients and Husbands over the past eight years, and that equaled a glorious surge in positive energy around the planet.

"Ladies and gentlemen, we're promoting human harmony on a monumental new level," Venus said.

Though she was smiling as she glanced up at the helicopters, she was seething inside, because John's vindictiveness had caused today's helicopter chaos. Those choppers were no doubt broadcasting live video of her, the Husbands, her guests and the grounds, right now, on global television.

"I apologize for the noise," Venus said. "The intruders will be sent on their merry way, so we can watch a wedding, and find you the men of your dreams."

Excited chatter rippled through the group as Venus ran her left hand over the muscular shoulder of a suntanned hunk; her heart-shaped diamond ring glistened in the sunshine.

"Gentlemen, please, don't mind us," Venus said, loving that Jane Collins was visually devouring Mike Rivers, who stood at attention with the others.

Beside him was a suntanned Adonis named David Valentine, one of several "display models" who were not available for marriage to clients. Instead, they were paid generously to live here, pose and perform during special events, and be available around the clock for any services Venus might need.

"Please get back to pumping and flexing," Venus said.

David crunched his six-pack abs as the Husbands resumed their exercise. The women squealed.

As Venus and David exchanged a smile, the air crackled between them, thanks to countless sessions of multi-orgasmic abandon they had enjoyed when he was her first Husband here.

"Venus," Gus said, nodding toward the gazebo.
Suddenly 10 wooden crates opened; white doves fluttered upward. At the same time, the black and white balloons on the gazebo's roof released into the sky. In a matter of minutes, the media choppers would be forced to flee.

Venus smiled.

John and all our enemies can huff, and they can puff, but they will never blow this house down.

𝒞hapter 7. Ex-Husband Vows, Attack and Destroy

A low growl escaped John Barker's mouth as he glared at his ex-wife on international television. In his cherry-paneled office, he stood beside his desk, aiming the remote at the large TV screen that was mounted amidst tall shelves holding law books.

"Today, News International is live outside the headquarters of Husbands, Incorporated," said a male reporter, standing at the huge gates of Venus' stud farm. "Not only is CEO Venus Roman revealing the sub-culture she has been discreetly building for the past eight years, but she's doing it on a global scale! Women from around the world are now buying franchises of this husbands-for-hire company. Check out this unprecedented video from our Chopper Cam of Venus Roman today with the men and women who are helping her pioneer uncharted territory—"

The rage consuming John felt like a pack of pit bulls mauling him from the inside out. He glanced at his lifelong friend, Ted Pendigree, sitting in a wing-backed leather chair, facing the TV.

"What's got me so rabidly mad," John huffed, "is the *scale* of what she's doing. All this time, she led me to believe she was running some bullshit matchmaking service! That woman is the most dishonest, conniving—"

On television, Venus appeared again, wearing a white suit, diamond stud earrings, a cocky expression and that short, spiky hairdo that she'd been sporting since the divorce.

"I am on a global mission to liberate women from the disappointment and frustration that often plague traditional marriages," Venus told the reporter. "By pioneering this innovative new way to enjoy passion and romance—"

"She'll burn in hell!" John howled. "How dare she flaunt male prostitution on television!" He aimed the remote at the TV and clicked to Channel 3. That cute little Laila Sims and her noticeably larger rack appeared. She was doing a live report from a helicopter over Venus' pit of sin. He clicked again, and again. "Goddammit! Venus is on every channel!"

Ted turned around; his face was as stiff as his perfectly coiffed, side-parted brown hair. Tall and thin, wearing a dark blue suit, a red tie and white shirt, he sat with his legs crossed. His long, elegant fingers outstretched on his top leg. On his left hand was his wedding band; on his right glimmered a gold ring, identical to those worn by John and their fraternity brothers. It was imprinted with Greek letters above 1979 and The University of Michigan.

"Johnny Ace, stop frothing at the mouth! As my campaign manager, you should be glad that she's giving us ammunition for launching my campaign," Ted pointed to posters leaning against the bookcases. They said TED PENDIGREE FOR CONGRESS with his slogan, *Restoring America's Traditional Family Values.* Below that was a picture of Ted with his primly-coiffed, white-haired wife Mary, their four grown children and their golden Labrador retriever.

"In all honesty, your ex-wife is simply fertilizing the groundswell of support for my campaign so we'll win this time," Ted said, pulling a small, clear tube of hand sanitizer from his pocket and rubbing it on his manicured hands. "I haven't even officially announced, but voters who see her as the enemy of family values have been calling, emailing, and volunteering to help elect Ted Pendigree to Congress."

Venus' picture, with all that fire in her eyes, taunted John from the covers of newspapers and magazines on his desk.

"I'll feed that bitch to the hounds of hell myself!" John snatched up *The Wall Street Journal*, pointing to a page one story. "She blames our quote 'sexless' marriage for giving her this god-blasted idea to *lease* men! How dare she!"

John pounded the desk so hard, the receiver bounced off the phone, just as Venus' deep, confident voice boomed from the television.

"Here at Husbands, Inc., we provide every woman's fantasy, without the risk," she said, standing with a bride

and groom. *"Our marriages are legally and morally respectable—"*

"You're a pimp, Venus!" John barked. "You are officially done. Done!" He glowered at the TV.

The report showed a crowd of men in front of the gates leading to the mansion housing Venus' house of sin. The men held signs that read VENUS ROMAN = MARRIAGE KILLER and SHUT DOWN HUSBANDS, INC.

"Venus Roman's sexual revolution is sparking a hostile backlash," the reporter said as video showed a man in his forties wearing a cheap suit and tie. The rage in his eyes mirrored John's feelings.

"This man, Steven Davenport," the reporter said, "formed a group called Men for Traditional Marriage. They're protesting in front of Husbands, Inc., with the goal of putting it out of business."

The man said, "When I married my wife, we promised, 'til death do us part.' Not 'til one year do us part.' What that terrible woman is doing behind those gates, is telling the world that marriage is a temporary thrill based on sexual fantasies."

John let out a nasty chuckle. "I think I just found a new friend." He watched intently as Steven Davenport shouted:

"Men for Traditional Marriage is mobilizing worldwide to shut Venus Roman down! Here, and in all the countries where she's trying to spread this. We will stop her from destroying the sacred institution of marriage!"

"Where do I sign up?" John yelled.

Ted chuckled, holding up his hands, inspecting each manicured fingernail for the slightest speck of dirt, which he never found.

John clicked to Meteor Multimedia Network, where that sexpot Sasha Maxwell was sitting at the anchor desk with her big hair and enticing tits. Her blue-green eyes and suntanned sensuality reminded him of Brazilian women he'd seen on the beaches in Rio. That made her unfit for delivering the news. How could a man concentrate on what she was saying, when his dick was throbbing to fuck her?

"I'm special correspondent Sasha Maxwell. I've spoken with some of Venus Roman's female clients and their husbands, and they praise her as a messiah."

"For Satan," John huffed. He glared at Sasha, who had only recently shown up on that liberal network, after using her radio and TV show to exploit her sexcapades with 10 men. "No wonder you're so biased," John spat. "You and Venus are both whores to the Nth degree!"

On her report, a well-dressed man said, "Women have been marrying for money forever, by pretending they're in love."

A dark-haired guy added, "Yeah, find a rich dude, get hitched, divorce him, get paid! Now we're doing it. Without the deception. Everybody knows what time it is."

A black fellow with big muscles chimed in, "Us Husbands, we get the best of both worlds. Short-term relationships, big bucks, and sex!"

Ted shook his head. "Marriage is about love. Not money!"

John glared at Venus on TV. "I hate that bitch. How dare she humiliate me. She should be like my clients in my commercials, saying, 'Thank you, John Barker!' I gave her the perfect life!"

The Sasha Maxwell report continued with a montage of women:

"Everybody's motives are clear," declared a wrinkled Asian broad who had to be staring down 60. "I get a healthy, charming hunk for a year. He gets paid. Nobody gets hurt, and we all have a good time."

A black woman, probably in her forties, grinned and said, "Wham, bam, thank you, Sam!"

A young blond with nice knockers chirped, "Control! Over something so unpredictable: relationships! It's awesome!"

Then a Hispanic woman said, "It's about time! Females finally get to play the guy's game. And we're winning! It's a fantasy, but it's reality, too. I'll never go back to regular marriage. I hope every woman in America, no, in the whole galaxy, gets to try this." She puckered into the camera. "Muah! We love you, Venus!"

John seethed. "They'll all be kissing my ass in a minute. Venus is single-handedly corrupting—"

"Enough, Johnny!" Ted snapped. "Don't give her so much credit."

John plunked into the big leather chair behind his desk.

"Now let's put some bite behind your bark," Ted said. "I say we indict her, get her prosecuted and thrown in prison. We'll make that my last-hurrah as U.S. Attorney. I step down to campaign, and her demise catapults me into Congress."

John grinned. "Genius! We need a team. The media, the legal system, law enforcement—"

Ted held up a hand like a stop sign. "Halt it there, Johnny Ace. I want everything totally legal. Honestly, no clandestine phone calls or behind-closed-doors meetings. Anything less than squeaky clean, can only end badly. Remember the Cumberland case."

That case happened shortly after he and Ted had graduated from the University of Michigan School of Law, passed the State Bar of Michigan exam on the first try and began working at Ted's father's fourth-generation law firm, Theodore Pendigree & Sons.

An older lawyer, Ralph Reynolds, who was known for winning every time, had taken John under his wing, mentoring him on "the number one rule for success: use *what* you know and *who* you know to win." As he spoke, the scent of Ralph's pipe always wafted around his impeccable suits, silver hair and pale eyes. John's gut instincts told him that Ralph's philosophy would not pass the Judicial Tenure Commission's standards for Character and Moral Fitness. Sure enough, Ralph's dirty dealings on the Cumberland case resulted in him losing his license to practice law.

Meanwhile, the first time John refused to use "who he knew" and lost a case — and the senior Mr. Pendigree put him on probation to prove his worth in the firm — John had a change of heart. For his next case, he followed Ralph's advice and called in favors from his own father's business partners. And as a result, he won a high, six-figure jury verdict!

Ralph got caught, but I never do!

Ted, on the other hand, always seemed to win by following the rules to a tee.

"Johnny, I see scheme in your eyes as we speak," Ted accused with a light-hearted tone. "Seriously, Johnny Ace, keep it clean."

"The Cumberland case was thirty years ago," John said. "Ralph took the fall. He was the one with dirty tricks—"

"Exactly," Ted said, straightening his stiff, white shirt-cuffs and running a fingertip over the dark blue monogram, which he centered precisely over each wrist.

"The whole world is already watching your ex-wife," Ted warned. "Everything we do will be scrutinized. Truthfully, John, even the slightest whiff of impropriety, and I'm out. We both have everything to lose." Ted fanned his fingers and examined them, then glanced at John. "Understand?"

John nodded. "You're right. Don't need anything coming back to bite us in the ass."

"Have you — or a loved one — been injured?" John's own voice made him turn to watch his new TV commercial. It showed him here in his office, sitting in the leather, wing-backed chair in front of his bookshelves and the American flag that hung from a pole.

Good call, wearing the custom-made, pinstriped suit with the red tie. He also liked that his trim, silver-specked goatee made him look sophisticated and stylish. Plus, the suntan reminded him to shoot his commercials during the summer months, unless he'd just returned from a vacation in a warm climate.

"I'm Attorney John Sebastian Barker, and if you've suffered due to someone else's neglect, then millions of dollars could be yours."

A montage of clients came on the screen:

"A truck hit my motorcycle," said a young white guy. "John Barker went to court, and I walked away with 800-thousand dollars!"

A gray-haired black man said, "All those years working with asbestos messed up my lungs with mesothelioma. John Barker made sure I can pay all my medical bills and enjoy life. Two million dollars!"

A 30-something blond couple, sitting beside a child in a wheelchair and head brace, held a picture of a tiny preemie. The husband said sadly, "Little Jeremy died at just two days old. Now his twin brother Henry will never walk or talk. We can't measure our loss and heartache. But thanks to John Barker, we can take care of Henry, with the six million dollar jury award that John Barker won for us."

Then the couple said in unison: "Thank you, John Barker."

"Thank you, John Barker," added the older black man.

"Thank you, John Barker," the young motorcyclist declared.

In the commercial, John sat in his chair said, "I want to get to work for you right now, so you can join thousands of my satisfied clients who are saying, 'Thank you, John Barker.' So call 1-800-THANK-YU. The consultation is free. I'm Attorney John Sebastian Barker, winning for you!"

John nodded, thrilled that the public relations firm that he'd hired five years ago had come up with the "thank you" campaign and the "winning for you" slogan. Those themes on billboards all around town, as well as on TV commercials, had attracted a treasure trove of lucrative cases.

"Ted, remember we're meeting with the PR firm next week to strategize your campaign promotions, including the TV commercials."

Teddy nodded. "Let's talk with them about a 'quit while I'm at the top' strategy for leaving my office with a bang. I want to hear their ideas *before* we tell them that my last and final case will be the globally publicized annihilation of Venus Roman's immoral enterprise."

The soft light from the sheers on the tall windows lit up Ted's brown eyes and milky skin that was so clear, he looked like wax, especially around his thin, pointed nose and ears.

John had always marveled at how Ted stayed so clean, even when they were kids. Years later, John figured it out, while showing a photo album to Venus and the kids. J.J. and Christina were around six, the same age as he and Ted were in the photographs of their first camping trip as Cub Scouts. One showed John hooking a worm for Ted's pole as they learned to fish in the lake. Another picture showed John using sticks that he'd gathered to rub together and start a campfire — while Ted watched.

"Daddy you're a messy eater!" exclaimed little Christina, pointing to the snapshot of John grinning, his cheeks and chin covered with chocolate, marshmallow and graham cracker crumbs as they ate s'mores around the campfire.

"Uncle Ted is neat!" little J.J. announced, pointing to a group photo. Ted was clean, while the other boys' faces, fingers and shirts were smudged with white and brown. Ted later confessed to paying another boy one dollar to make s'mores for him, so he never touched the sticky marshmallows or gooey chocolate.

Ted always lets other people get their hands dirty, so he

keeps his clean. Even with his long-time mistress and all the other women along the way. Likewise, Ted's team of lawyers did the dirty work while he focused on the intellectual aspects of piecing everything together to win, and bask in the glory of his success.

"Leaving office with a bang," John repeated. "I like that." He aimed the remote and clicked to another channel.

"If the ladies are winning a man's game," a news reporter said, *"they're doing it through legitimate marriages with a Husband who signs a prenuptial agreement that promises his payment after one year of marriage, which ends in a quick divorce on the U.S. territory of Guam."*

John smacked his palm on the desk. "Sounds like prostitution to me!"

Ted nodded. "That's it! We'll nail her on the Mann Act. It was actually created in 1910 to stop men from transporting women across state lines for prostitution or immorality. It's been amended to apply to men and a variety of contemporary circumstances."

"Brilliant!" John declared.

"We'll argue that Venus is clearly violating the Mann Act by bringing men from across the country to Michigan to hire out for sex." Ted shook his head, pointing to the TV. "In all honesty, what I find profoundly disturbing is that these women are so unashamedly bold about sex. A woman is supposed to save herself for the man she marries before God."

John licked his lips with excitement. "Right! Marriage is supposed to be forever. And we're about to make Venus suffer for eternity."

Chapter 8. TV Report Fuels Fires for Vengeance

One glance at Venus Roman, and Laila Sims felt like a giant fist was squeezing her chest and throat. It clamped down tighter as Owen zoomed in for a close-up, making that pimp-bitch's face fill the video monitor.

Holy shit, how am I gonna talk!? Laila forced herself to inhale.

"Check out our exclusive, live look at the queen of this carnal kingdom, Venus Roman," she rasped. "Women praise her as a pioneer who's putting a modern twist on marriage. Critics call her a pimp, brokering boy toys to any woman who can pay big bucks."

Static crackled in Laila's ear, followed by her furious producer: "Drink some water! This is the biggest story of the year, and you're fuckin' it up!"

As the monitor showed live video, Laila gulped from her water bottle. Then she said, "Take a look at all that beefcake — and the women who will spend a year feasting on it."

Owen panned the women, then the men. He focused on a muscular guy with a deep tan and a long, black ponytail.

Mike! Holy shit, that's Mike!

Owen zoomed in for a close-up; Mike's face expanded across the monitor as he cast a lusty smile at a bottle-blond chick in a black mini dress. Owen tapped Laila's arm and looked at her with shocked eyes, mouthing, "Mike!"

Laila coughed so hard that tears filled her eyes. Her face burned with rage; she was probably bright red.

"Shit!" her producer shouted. "No wonder your losin' it. That's Mike! Laila, keep it professional. You can get through it—"

Laila struggled to look calm as she faced the camera and spoke into her microphone.

"What the hell?" the pilot snapped. "Where'd all the birds come from?"

Laila ignored the pilot. Whatever was going on, he needed to fix it, because she would be supremely pissed if something interrupted her report.

"Wow," Laila coughed, "this is shocking. They say it's legal, but is it? And if it's not, is heiress Claire Montague putting her reputation and her fortune at risk by saying 'I do' in that gazebo?"

"We gotta go!" the pilot shouted.

Laila disregarded him as she coughed. "News 3 is working to obtain a copy of the prenuptial agreement used by Husbands, Incorporated, and we'll talk with lawyers about whether Venus Roman can get away with what critics are calling prostitution—"

Suddenly, a flock of white birds and all those balloons on the gazebo rose up into the helicopter's path.

"Len!" Owen said. "Three choppers, comin' right at us."

"Chopper two to base!" Len panicked into his headset. "Emergency turn-around!"

He turned to Laila and Owen and said, "We get caught in that, we're dead in the water." He quickly pulled a lever to raise the altitude.

"No!" Laila exclaimed as birds and balloons threatened to engulf the aircraft. She coughed, gasping for breath. She wanted to shout, *That whorehouse will be boarded up, with Mike and Venus Roman out on their asses when I get done with them!*

As three choppers flew toward them, Len retreated over the lake.

"No!" Laila rasped, still on the air. "Three military-style helicopters are literally forcing us away. I'm Laila Sims, and I *will* be back for the truth about the sexy, scandalous secrets at Husbands, Incorporated."

Before her live mike turned off, she doubled over, hacking.

"Laila!" her producer screamed in her ear. "That was a hideous fuck-up!"

Laila gulped water.

"You okay?" Len asked. "What a shocker, to see your guy down there—"

"No problem," Laila said, massaging her burning throat. "I got an idea, how I can get inside for the scoop of the century."

She bent over, coughing — and secretly smirking that she had a new plan to destroy Husbands, Incorporated.

Chapter 9. Scandalous Secret Riles Friends

Guilt and dread chewed at John's senses, because Ted had suddenly veered into a diatribe about his daughters' chastity.

"Quite honestly, John, the media ruckus with Venus has just appalled me as I think about Emma and Marla." Ted strode across John's office, then picked up one of the campaign posters that were laying against the bookshelves. He pointed to his smiling daughters in the family photo.

"Johnny, can you imagine your daughter being so brazen about such private matters?"

For a moment, John cast a blank stare back at Ted. Daughters and sexuality were something John never wanted to discuss with his childhood friend. If Ted looked this mad just talking about it, he'd lose his mind if he ever learned the truth.

Ah, but he won't! John cast a well-practiced expression of engaged listening as Ted continued.

"Patrick and Charles, they're respectable, married men. They know when to be gentlemen and when it's appropriate to do what men do. But Emma and Marla? If my daughters ever flaunted their sexuality like that—" Ted shuddered, "—it's just not something a father would tolerate, no matter his daughter's age. Ever."

John's gut cramped, but he nodded coolly. "Ted, I fully agree. Poor Christina, she's in New York trying to date actors and Wall Street egomaniacs—"

"Thank God Emma is engaged to an honorable young man," Ted said. "Brian shows promise to become a partner at his father's firm, and I think he'll help keep my little girl's wild side in check."

Sweat prickled under John's starched white shirt. Yes, Emma sure did have a wild side, from a very early age. John stifled an arousing flash of memories by glancing at the TV.

"Teddy, crushing Venus under the Mann Act! That idea is so delicious, I can taste it! It will ignite a provocative legal debate in the courtroom, in the media and on Main Streets across America. Then we'll be hailed as the superior legal team that restored moral justice for the institution of marriage."

Ted tilted the campaign poster, admiring his photo. "Of course, upstanding Americans will express their appreciation for me in the voting booth."

John dialed his secretary on speakerphone. "Agnes, call my fraternity brother, the reporter at Wolf News. Tell him I have an announcement about Venus Roman, and I need him to come to my office as soon as possible."

"Will do, Mr. Barker," she said.

"Teddy," John said, "speaking of fraternity brothers. Ours tossed a little monkey wrench into airspace operations at the whorehouse of Venus." He let out a malicious chuckle.

"Johnny, keep your dirty deeds to yourself. She's providing us with enough legitimate ammunition. Honestly, like I said, don't engage in any unscrupulous shenanigans."

Ted's scolding tone made John feel like a puppy with his tail between his legs.

"Truthfully, John, I've already gained supporters by promising that when I get to Congress, I'll join the conservative groundswell to make it more difficult to divorce in every state. The fifty percent divorce rate is what's helping Venus justify her assault on the most sacred institution we know, outside of church, of course."

John smiled. "Right. When more women are forced to stay married, that's less of them trying to disrupt the proper hierarchy in society."

He and Ted had always agreed that a wife should stay home with the children, taking care of the domestic front while the husband earned a good living. That was the successful family formula that they had learned from their parents and grandparents. John and Ted had emulated this ideal with Venus and Mary.

As many times as Venus had expressed interest in going back to finish college, starting when J.J. and Christina began elementary school, John had vehemently disapproved. He'd always said she could do whatever she wanted after the kids were in college. He just didn't anticipate that she'd actually *divorce* him when that time came.

Now, Venus appeared on television, saying: *"That whole 'til death do us part thing, just kills passion. But at Husbands, Inc., the honeymoon lasts twelve months."*

Beside her, a beaming woman in a white veil said, "As Madame Roman says, my every wish is his command for a year. And boy, are my wishes coming true!"

The reporter continued, "That message is earning Venus Roman the prestigious Visionary of the Year award—"

"Award?" John snickered. "She should be burned at the stake!" John jammed his finger into the phone on the desk, pressing a single button to dial Venus. He activated the speakerphone.

Venus' sultry-smooth voice — with a tone like she was laughing, echoed off the paneled walls: "Superb timing, John! I've been expecting you to call again, to congratulate me today."

Her every word clawed John's senses as she said, "Since you've been blowing up my phone all day, I just wanted to tell you to cool your pants. But make it quick. I have women from around the world, and hundreds of Husbands to match—"

"You're a world-class pimp, Venus!"

"I'm a global revolutionary and I'm being celebrated as such," she declared. "And neither your childish helicopter hijinx, nor anything else you're scheming, can stop me."

John glared at her face on TV as he shouted toward the phone: "Ted and I are going to shut you down! You're done!"

Venus let out that soft little laugh that always made him feel stupid.

"Oh John, how's Emma?" she teased.

John's heart pounded. Ted turned around and shot him a perplexed expression.

Venus knows nothing!

"That girl is so photogenic!" Venus exclaimed. "I've saved the video for a long time, but I thought you might want to reminisce about when she stayed with us—"

Ted looked alarmed. "Is she talking about my Emma?"

John shook his head.

"Thank you, John Barker," Venus teased, "for revealing your true self. And Ted would be so proud of her, just a teenager, doing such grown-up things with you."

"You're crazy, Venus! Crazy!" John shouted, shaking his head. He looked Ted in the eyes and declared: "Teddy, she's crazy, you know that."

Ted strode to the desk. Nervous sweat prickled over John's body.

"Oh, Ted's there!" Venus taunted. "Tell him he'd be so proud of little Emma, getting a head start on her trampy ways. Does your wife know you like 'em that young? I mean, now that Tia's almost 30 and Emma's 25, you've probably been trolling high school parking lots for a young cheerleader—"

John snatched up the receiver to take her off speakerphone. Ted's steely stare demanded answers.

"Venus," John yelled. "You are a virus on society! You're going to Hell!"

Venus laughed. "Hell, John? I was there, remember? When my name was Mrs. Barker. But I escaped, and created my own version of heaven."

John gripped the phone so hard, he was sure the plastic would crack. Ted's glare gave him the sudden urge to shit his pants. "Venus, do not mention our marriage again!"

She laughed. "Flip open one of your big law books, John. It's called the First Amendment. I'm allowed to express my opinions."

"I'll get an injunction. An indictment!"

"Oh John." Venus sounded bored. "I have a global empire to run."

"Empire? It's an illegal sex ring!"

"Rant, rave," she mocked. "You and your legal beagle buddy have no grounds to throw a tantrum in court. Besides, when you see the video of you and Emma—"

"You have nothing of the sort! You know nothing!"

John slammed down the phone. Rage gnawed his every cell as he glared down at Venus' picture on the cover of *Time* magazine under the headline "MESSIAH OR PARIAH?"

"John!" Ted thundered with accusation and anger. "Eight years ago, with Emma? That's when Mary and I were in Asia. And *what* video?"

John mustered every bit of acting ability that he had honed to mesmerize juries. He tried to project confusion and innocence. But he couldn't stop his mind from flashing with images of the teen's soft, smooth body, and her surprisingly aggressive moves during their trysts at the Butterfield Hotel.

If Ted ever finds out, he'll kill me with his bare hands. But he'll never know. Because together, we'll bring Venus down before she can do anything. And if she has any video, I'll get to it before Ted ever sees it...

"Johnny?!" Ted demanded.

"Venus is ruthless!" John said, as beads of sweat popped from his forehead. "This is her devious scheme to divide and conquer us with scurrilous innuendo."

Ted's eyes seemed to drill two holes of suspicion right through John's lie. "I've seen how you look at Emma—"

John patted his friend's shoulder and cast an affectionate look. "Teddy, the day you entertain that witch's lies — over the sincerity of your life-long friend and fraternity brother — is the day that—"

John's eyes glazed with tears. He buried his face in his hand, exhaled loudly, and dashed to his desk, snatching up *The New York Times.* The headline said: FORMER HOUSEWIFE GOES GLOBAL WITH MULTI-MILLION-DOLLAR HUSBANDS-FOR-HIRE EMPIRE.

Beside it, another article said, RIGHT-WING FEDERAL PROSECUTOR PLANS TO RESIGN, MAKE SECOND BID FOR CONGRESS ON CRUSADE AGAINST "IMMORALITY ROTTING CORE OF AMERICAN FAMILIES."

John slammed the paper on the desk.

"This is our ticket, Ted. Mark my words. So what if you lost to the liberals eight years ago. This is your time! One day those headlines will say FEDERAL PROSECUTOR SHUTS DOWN MALE PROSTITUTION RING AND WINS LANDSLIDE ELECTION TO U.S. SENATE. We cannot allow Venus' lies to come between us."

Ted charged toward John and stopped just inches away.

John flashed a nervous smile. "Let's see if a little legal fire and brimstone can't cure that whore of her nymphomania."

Ted had never glared at John with such violence and accusation—

John squeezed his sphincter muscle. He held out his hands for their fraternity handshake. Ted reluctantly joined him, and they recited: "Brothers in power, ruling the world! Unstoppable kings, gods of all things." Ted's hand clasped tightly around John's, as it had thousands of times during this ritual.

But now his eyes are threatening to beat my ass!

Adrenaline kicked John into overdrive to distract his friend. "Ted, I think we need to team up with other men who oppose Venus, like the guy on the news. That bitch will fry in hell when we get done with her."

Ted stared at John with the same expression that he cast on defendants while prosecuting them for unspeakable crimes.

And that made John squeeze his ass harder, so he wouldn't make a stinking mess of himself.

Chapter 10. Scrutinizing Security at Sea Castle

Venus charged through the central hallway of Sea Castle, into the grand foyer, with Kimberly and her security entourage in tow. Sunbeams shot down through the stained glass windows above the huge, wooden, front doors. She dashed toward the huge, double staircases that curved around 12-foot marble statutes of Venus de Milo and Venus de Medici. An enormous crystal chandelier sparkled two stories above.

"Those helicopters were a warning that our enemies are stealth and ruthless!" Venus trembled with urgency to get into the surveillance room for an impromptu security briefing.

She was still gripping her phone, having just hung up with John. As her deliberately mocking tone had suggested, she would *never* allow him to believe that he had any power to intimidate her. Plus, she would thwart him before he could move in for the kill. Nevertheless, his abrasive voice and threats continued to ricochet through her.

"John is out for blood," Venus said. "We need to be prepared for anything!"

As her heels clinked across the white marble, sunshine illuminated the five-foot diameter, tile mosaic in the center of the floor. Its metallic gold script letters said SEA CASTLE 1744.

"Oh my God." Venus grasped the white marble banister that was inlaid with cobalt blue stars, which matched the carpeting on the staircases.

Gus towered beside her. "Venus, what is it?"

She felt dizzy with revelation as she pointed down at the mosaic. "I believe, when the French built Sea Castle as a fortress in 1744, they were preparing it for *our* revolution. I declare right now, no matter how vicious our enemies get, we will prevail. I command it! We will remain unstoppable. Utterly untouched. We will win!"

Kimberly blew a Parklawn Princesses-style kiss as the men nodded.

"To quote Winston Churchill," Gus said, "Victory at all costs, victory in spite of terror, victory however long and hard the road may be; for without victory, there is no survival."

"Amen to that!" Mario exclaimed.

Venus smiled, then glimpsed the mosaic. It showed a beautiful mermaid and a handsome merman with emerald tails, embracing in front of a castle surrounded by blue, curling-up ocean waves. Beside them, two knights held up swords crossing above the couple's heads, in front of the castle doors. Over them in the sky, an enormous male angel held up a sword and shield, surrounded by angels playing harps and trumpets, and sprinkling golden dust over the couple and the castle.

When Venus and Raye purchased this mansion seven years ago, the mosaic was hidden under centuries of dirt and grime.

Their real estate agent had recommended that they check out this long-abandoned but structurally sound property on the Detroit River. It was far more work than the "fixer-upper" mansion that Venus and Raye had envisioned as the Husbands, Inc. headquarters. But the property was irresistible for its glorious architecture, its remote location behind an industrial area north of downtown, and its $1 price tag from a land bank.

As for the huge budget for extensive renovations, Venus and Raye received a small fortune from one of their first clients. The woman had been so satisfied with her first Husband, back when Venus and Raye were leasing office space downtown Detroit, she gave them a seven-figure donation to express her gratitude.

In addition, the woman's word-of-mouth referrals in her wealthy social and business circles helped Husbands, Inc. prosper so exponentially that Venus and Raye had easily paid to restore the inns and cottages. They also showed their appreciation by creating a scholarship in their benefactor's name for female architecture students at the University of Michigan.

Meanwhile, the design on the mosaic became the official seal of Husbands, Inc., now appearing on stationery, note cards, coffee mugs and other items at the two Inns at Sea Castle. Very soon, the franchisees would take that logo worldwide as the official symbol of Husbands, Inc. International.

And no one will stop them!

As Venus hurried toward a closed, unmarked door in the curved wall under one of the staircases, she declared, "We will not be ambushed again, in any way."

Gus held his palm over a camera lens hidden in the cream taffeta wall. The door slid open to reveal the windowless surveillance room, which was dim except for dozens of video screens and blinking monitors covering the four walls.

"Good morning again, Venus and Gus," said the surveillance manager, Zahra Wazzi. Her three staffers nodded while Venus and her team entered. Zahra wore a black blouse and slacks with her dark, wavy hair in a ponytail. Glimmering at her neck was the same gold crucifix she had worn as one of the Parklawn Princesses.

Zahra had attended Wayne State University, earning a degree in computer technology and criminal justice. After marrying, having three kids and working in corporate security for years, she joined the team here at the inception of Husbands, Inc.

"We're here," Venus said, "because this morning's absurdity with those helicopters was a jarring reminder that anything can happen at any time. As I said at our extensive meeting yesterday, we need to take every precaution to ensure that we have zero security breaches."

J.J. entered and said, "Good morning."

Venus cast a loving gaze at her son, the full-head-taller, 25-year-old, male version of herself. Eyes blazing with business major brilliance, he wore a crisp white dress shirt, brown suit pants and a butter-yellow tie.

"J.J., thanks for coming on such short notice," Venus said. "I know you're working in overdrive to process the franchisees."

As clean-shaven J.J. nodded, Venus made eye contact with everyone.

"By unveiling our empire to the world," she said, "we're pissing off a lot of people. This is already robbing me of precious time and attention that I should be lavishing on our international guests right now."

"I'm worried," Zahra said, pointing to the monitors, including one that was replaying video of men burning an effigy of Venus.

"They are sick," Venus said.

Zahra pointed to a monitor showing video from cameras that were attached to poles across from Husbands, Inc.

"You're looking at hundreds of people out there," Zahra said. "And they're getting more disorderly by the hour."

Demonstrators crowded the street in front of the tall, stone fence that surrounded the entire property. Behind the huge gates, the three-story, white stone Sea Castle rose from a hilltop.

Sunshine gleamed on the cone-shaped roofs of four, round turrets at each corner of the mansion. Also glistening were the stained glass windows adorned with faux Juliet balconies made of rococo-style swirls of dark purple wrought iron.

The castle overlooked lush landscaping that included manicured hedges of pink roses lining the driveway that circled a blue marble fountain featuring Greek gods and goddesses.

"It's like looking at a dream and a nightmare all at once," J.J. said. "We're in the dream, and the nightmare is on the other side of the stone wall."

"And we will maintain that boundary," Zahra said, as a monitor showed police erecting more barricades to contain the crowd. That enabled officers to direct delivery trucks as well as limousines that were bringing a continuous stream of new clients to Sea Castle.

"Every media network in America is out there," Zahra said, pointing to several reporters doing stand-up reports while rows of news trucks – satellite dishes and all – lined the opposite side of the street amidst police cars and an ambulance. "The police chief says the ambulance is a precaution, anytime there's a volatile crowd like this."

Gus said, "The safety briefings and the alarm drill with our guests this morning went smoothly, to familiarize them with evacuation procedures and emergency protocol."

Mario nodded. "We're also issuing reminders that photographs and social media are prohibited due to security concerns, and violation of that rule can result in immediate expulsion and prosecution."

"Zahra," Gus said, "can you show what we talked about?"

"Sure."

A large, center monitor showed three handsome men being escorted from the property by Husbands, Inc. security guards.

"Oh, what a waste!" Venus said sarcastically. "They missed their calling."

"As things escalate," Gus said, "these guys are a good reminder for us to remain extra vigilant about rooting out saboteurs. Whether posing as Husbands, clients or franchisees, our enemies probably perceive that as the easiest way to gain entrée."

Venus crossed her arms. "Should we add even more layers to our screening process?"

Gus shook his head. "Our new enhanced background check system could rival the CIA. But our eyes, ears and gut feelings about people can serve as the best lie detectors."

"Always," Venus said.

"So if someone doesn't look right, sound right or feel right, let us know," Gus said as Mario nodded. "And we'll take it from there."

Zahra pointed to one of the screens. "Meanwhile, we're monitoring the media." She turned up the volume to hear a female reporter outside the gates.

"Absolute mayhem outside the world headquarters of Husbands, Incorporated right now," the reporter shouted over a deep chorus of male protesters and the roar of engines. *"Hundreds of people are here, to both protest and support the husbands-for-hire empire—"*

"Venus Roman, wicked omen," protesters shouted. *"Shut her down, get outta town!"*

The camera panned to show police officers forcing a mob of shouting men and some women to stay behind temporary metal barricades that looked like waist-high bike racks.

"Marriage for life!" the protesters yelled. *"No fake wife!"*

"Men for sale, go to jail!"

The demonstrators wore t-shirts emblazoned with MEN FOR TRADITIONAL MARRIAGE and messages that declared:

"My wife is at home, barefoot and pregnant."

"Marriage is not for sale."

"Man: the dominant sex."

"100% Caveman: Return to the Stone Age."

"Meanwhile," the reporter said, stepping across the open driveway space, *"over here we have counter-protesters, cheering on Venus Roman and the hundreds of women and men inside."*

A vast swarm of motorcycles — all driven by women — roared behind the barricade opposite the male protesters. The reporter approached a woman wearing head-to-toe pink leather and asked: *"What brings you here today?"*

"We've never met Venus Roman, or used her services," the woman said as the sun glistened on chrome all around her. *"But when we saw all these dudes out here rallying against the good things she's doing for the sisterhood, we had to take action."*

The woman waved to the female bikers, who revved their engines. The thunderous noise drowned out the men's shouting.

"We're here to show love for Venus," said the woman in pink. "We think Husbands, Inc. is amazing. And we want the world to know, what she's doing is long overdue. Venus, if you're watching, YOU ROCK, BABY!" The woman grinned into the camera, holding two thumbs up. *"We love you and we're here for you!"*

Venus smiled. "Kimberly, have the caterers deliver refreshments to those women." As another report showed the hostile picketers, Venus shook her head. "They're just mad that their ex-wives and girlfriends are here, waiting for the real bliss to begin."

Zahra switched channels. "Venus, here's a replay of the reporter from that first helicopter."

It was Mike's ex-fiancé, Laila Sims, on Channel 3 News, coughing rather than talking as video showed Mike pumping iron for 30 adoring women.

"Poor girl's got her panties in a bunch," Venus said. "No wonder, losing a man like Mike Rivers to us." Aside from Mike's pillow talk about his ex-fiancée, he and all Husbands were required to disclose information about prior relationships and marriages during the application process. Sometimes past relationships posed conflicts of interest that disqualified men from becoming Husbands.

Kimberly shook her head. "Either that just came as a big surprise to her, or she thinks viewers forgot those reports about her wedding plans with Mike."

"Either way," Gus said, "I'll keep an eye on her, and file an official complaint with Channel 3, citing their reporter's blatant lack of objectivity."

Venus pointed to a center screen. "Now everyone, please focus on the monitor showing the front gates."

They were open as one of the company cars, a black-windowed SUV, entered. Then, as the gates closed, they linked gold, script-style letters that said, "Husbands, Inc. at Sea Castle." Gold, arrow-like points adorned the curving top of the gate.

"Imprint that image on your minds, ladies and gentlemen," Venus said. "Literally and figuratively, the protective gates of Husbands, Incorporated are closed, locked, secure and ready to withstand the likes of them—" she pointed to the angry mob "—and however they try to besiege us next."

Though she spoke with confidence, the protesters exuded such evil, the hairs on the back of Venus' neck rose.

This revolution is about to get vicious.

Chapter 11. Billy Jack Fears Damnation

Billy Jack Burns had such a huge erection here in this fancy, flower-covered gazebo, it was like he had a telephone pole in his tuxedo pants. And it only throbbed bigger and harder when he looked down at them big, juicy breasts all bunched up and pressed together in his bride's white leather dress. He couldn't wait to say "I do" and take his hot little firecracker of a "Wife" back to their newlywed love nest.

But the pulsing noise of the Husbands, Inc. helicopters — which were apparently chasing away the media invaders — sounded like thunderbolts of damnation from heaven.

I know Momma and Daddy, Jesus and God, are all lookin' down on me like I'm the most vile heathen ever to walk the earth... all for the love of money.

He could see Daddy in the pulpit now, jumping up and down, consumed with the Holy Spirit as the entire congregation of Sanctified Baptist Church whooped, hollered and shook their tambourines in agreement.

"And I came here to tell 'ya, my brothers and sisters," Daddy would shout as the organist punctuated his proclamations with ominous chords, *"that in the Bible,*

Timothy Chapter Six, Verse Ten says, 'For the love of money is a root of all kinds of evil. Some people, eager for money, have wandered from the faith and pierced themselves with many griefs.'"

Right now, Billy Jack was eager for money, and here in this sexual utopia run by Madame Roman, he sure had wandered far from his faith back in rural West Virginia.

And I'm about to get pierced by many griefs, after I pierce my bride with this massive boner about a million times over the next 12 months. Lord, help me...

He stared down at Claire Montague. When he'd first met her a few days ago, during their initial interview, his first thought was "sexy Medusa." All those bright red curls, coiling around her shoulders and bouncing when she talked and turned, had brought to mind the Greek mythology character who had snakes for hair and could turn a man to stone with one glance. That had sent a chill down his spine.

But after she'd gotten to talking about how she was a painter and loved art history, especially paintings and sculptures inspired by nature and all the religions of the world, he'd felt a kinship. She was only 24, pretty much abandoned by her party-lovin' parents back in California. Now she was looking for a man who was grounded and religious.

Why she had to bring that other girl named Nikki with her, Billy Jack had no idea. That spiky-haired gal was the best friend, supposedly, and the maid of honor. But she had downright snarled at him instead of saying hello, and she looked like she either wanted to heave up her guts or slice him with a razor tongue. Billy Jack had never seen a maid of honor look so darn mad.

I shouldn't be worried about someone else being mad. Because all of heaven is mad at me right now, here in this pit of sin where I'm sellin' my soul to the devil.

He could just imagine Daddy pointing down at him, like he used to do every Sunday morning to the townsfolk inside the sweltering-hot church. He would aim that accusatory index finger at some poor man or woman, and yell:

"God is fuming mad at you this mornin'! That's right, almighty God is ANGRY, because you're a sinner! You're lettin' the temptation of the devil corrode your mind with lust, defile your body with fornication, and condemn your soul! And I'm here to tell 'ya now, God's gon' punish you with the weeping and gnashing of teeth, and the burning in hellfire forever!"

Too many times, Billy Jack had seen grown folks burst into tears, shaking like they were possessed by a demon, after Daddy got through with them. After he'd whip them into a frenzy of speakin' in tongues, fallin' out with the Holy Spirit, and wailing like it was the end of the world, they'd stumble out into the bright country sunshine, pale as ghosts, gripping their Bibles like their lives depended on it.

Now, a precious baby girl's life did depend on Billy Jack's "work" here at Husbands, Inc. That big check he would take home for little Ellie Anne one year from now would save her life, even if it cost him his own salvation.

Born with a rare lung disease, she needed a lifetime of treatments that, for starters, cost an arm and a leg. Or $150,000 to be exact. So when Billy Jack had heard from a buddy back home that he could make that much money in one year at Husbands, Inc., it sounded like a simple solution. It would take him half a lifetime to earn that much money back in the mining town where he was from. Sure, he'd applied to a slew of jobs in some of the nearby cities, but with just a high school education, good-paying work on this side of the law was near impossible to find.

He loved nothing more than cooking, and he'd hated to leave his job as a cook at Bessie's Country Kitchen. But there, he'd earned only a fraction of what Husbands Inc.

was offering. Plus, how hard could it be to "play house" with a girl who was rich enough to afford this place? From what she'd told him, all he'd have to do was live in a fancy log cabin and fish to his heart's content on the pond right behind it.

She hadn't even mentioned consummating the marriage, but maybe she was just too much of a lady to bring up something that was implied between a man and his wife. And while he had yet to see the house, she'd said it had a big kitchen where he could cook while she was up in her painting studio.

It sounded like heaven, but all the guilt slithering through his 26-year-old body made Billy Jack fear the coming year would be more like hell.

Would Ellie Anne make it another 12 months without the treatments? She was getting all the tender, loving care a two-year-old could ever need, but the family's health insurance just didn't cover what the doctors called "experimental" treatment that could make her healthy.

So here I am, ready to sacrifice my soul to save my baby girl...

He only felt worse, remembering that he'd lied to his family back home. He'd told them he was in Nashville working at a Christian record company, because he didn't want to shame them with the knowledge that he was, at the end of the day, a despicable prostitute.

Still, his plan seemed simple and fool-proof. He would earn the money, take it home for Ellie Anne to start her treatments, then come back for more assignments to pay her future health care costs. That would be his way of repenting for his terrible sin that had brought the child into the world in the first place.

Oh Lord, I am a horrible man...

He couldn't even let his mind wander into the abyss of grief and guilt that had created his beautiful baby.

He glanced down at Claire's pretty chest. Lust flamed

through his body and filled his head with a hundred different ways to become one with his bride. That pouty little mouth, the tight space between her breasts, and hopefully an even tighter place down below, would all help ease his mind — and relieve the throbbing woody in his pants — in just a few hours.

Sex between a husband and wife was not the sin of fornication, from his understanding. In fact, his Daddy was always quoting Corinthians Chapter Seven, Verse Two, from the King James Bible: *"Nevertheless (to avoid) fornication, let every man have his own wife, and let every woman have her own husband."*

Billy Jack knew he was manipulating the Scriptures to justify his wrongdoing. This girl would be his wife on paper, but entering into the marriage with the goal of divorcing a year later — and getting paid for it! — contradicted the sacred vow that men and women made in front of God to "love and to cherish... 'til death do us part."

Daddy's voice thundered through his head: *"The Bible says, if you live according to the flesh, you will die!"*

Billy Jack's dick tingled as he caught Claire casting a lusty look up at him. That girl was just as horny as he was. Soon as they could get that helicopter out of here and get on with the wedding, they could say "I do," eat some cake and go christen the marriage bed. He hoped their house was stocked with food, because the way she was making bedroom eyes at him, they would be spending the next few days in their birthday suits.

Yeah, I'm about to live according to my flesh, alright. I just hope the guilt doesn't kill me, and poor little Ellie Anne can survive a whole year before I finish my dirty deeds here...

Chapter 12. Ceremony Titillates and Terrifies

As Venus hurried out of Sea Castle, 20 minutes late for the ribbon-cutting ceremony for Husbands, Inc. International, she ticked down a mental list of what other problems might erupt. Blaring sirens and chanting protesters out front only cranked up her anxiety — and rage at John.

He had compromised her credibility in the eyes of her 200 guests. She promised them no media, and media showed up. She assured them complete discretion here, but their faces could very well have been captured by TV cameras and broadcast worldwide. That could put their reputations, their businesses — and their lives — at risk.

Damn John! That vindictive bastard is capable of anything. It's time to drop my video A-bomb and shut him up for good. That would top her "to do" list after today's festivities.

"Everything has to be flawless from now on," Venus told Kimberly as they approached the big, white tent with Gus and Mario.

"We're off to a good start," Kimberly said with a wink and a nod as she stopped under the scalloped edge of the tent, which had no walls.

Inside, on stage, 10 sexy cowboys were dancing to sultry music, as the clients and franchisees shrieked and cheered from rows of white chairs. Shirtless in jeans, boots and wide-brimmed hats, the men strut, gyrated their hips and flexed their broad, bare chests in a well-practiced, choreographed performance.

As the women visually devoured the men, Venus felt so lit up inside, she was like a giant sparkler on the Fourth of July. Better yet, she was the fuse on a dynamite stick that was about to blast women around the world into an erotic Independence Day.

"Venus!" a furious woman shouted. "You promised no paparazzi!"

Claire Montague stomped toward Venus in her white leather wedding dress and platform sandals. She looked anything but blissful as her veil blew back over an explosion of red corkscrew curls, which bounced like angry exclamation points around her bare shoulders. Gus and Mario stepped in front of Venus.

"It's okay," Venus told them. As she faced Claire, the men positioned themselves to block the guests under the tent from seeing a potential confrontation. Venus exuded concern: "Claire, did you leave your wedding?"

"Yeah, to tell you how pissed off I am!" Claire's dark green eyes were sharp with anger, dominating her small, pointed nose and little pucker of a mouth set in clear, creamy skin. "If my parents see this on the news, my life will be fucked!"

"Claire, I apologize profusely," Venus said, gently touching the young woman's arms. "You will receive something special to make up for that. And since your parents are so far away, consumed by their work, chances are extremely slim that they would see—"

"Today better be your only fuck-up!" Claire fumed. "Or I'll sue you into next year and go to the media myself to say this place is a fraud!" She stormed away.

"Kimberly," Venus said. "Assign a personal concierge for Claire Montague and her Husband. Make everything extraordinary for her. Anything she wants, she gets."

Kimberly nodded and typed into her iPad. Ear-splitting cheers exploded under the tent as the cowboys did their grand finale — dancing off the stage and into the aisles.

Eden was on stage, behind a red acrylic podium emblazoned with the Husbands, Inc. logo — a silhouette of a muscular man holding a bride in his arms. Under that, it said: HUSBANDS, INC. *OUR BUSINESS IS YOUR PLEASURE.*

"Ladies," Eden said, "here is the CEO and Co-founder of Husbands, Incorporated, Venus Roman!"

Venus dashed up on stage and announced, "Welcome to Husbands, Incorporated, where our business is your pleasure!" The company's sultry, funky theme song boomed from speakers at each corner of the tent as the dancers departed.

"We love you, Venus!" the women shouted as they rose for a standing ovation.

Beside the podium was a blue and green, papîer-maché globe — four feet wide — tied with a red ribbon that said: HUSBANDS, INC. INTERNATIONAL. Holding the globe was a super-muscular man named Joe Hinds, posing on one knee like Atlas in Greek mythology. He outstretched his arms to balance the entire world on his back and shoulders. Three other buff men stood beside the globe; they would pass the planet onto each other's shoulders as Venus spoke.

This moment was exactly as Venus had envisioned: the sun glimmered on the blue lake to her right, and sheer euphoria glowed in the eyes of the women before her as they sat in four sections that extended to the back of the tent. Her security team was nearby, with additional guards stationed around the tent.

Yes, the rest of the day is smooth sailing. But—

Kimberly's expression suggested she was hearing very bad news. She was standing at the side of the tent, closest to the house, talking into her headset. Beside her, Eden turned pale.

Something's wrong...

Venus forced herself to exude excitement as she shouted, "Congratulations, ladies! You're part of the sexiest revolution in world history!"

Two bare-chested men — a suntanned blond and a bald, molasses-brown hunk — offered Venus a crystal goblet of water on a silver tray.

"Thank you, gentlemen," she said, sipping as the men stood at her sides.

"Ladies, now that I *really* have your attention," she said playfully, "I want to address a question that's been all over the media today: the legality of Husbands, Incorporated. This company was started only after intensive research and exhaustive consultations with lawyers."

Venus made eye contact with several women, including Jane Collins, as she said, "I want to assure you that every aspect of your marriage, and your franchise, is 100 percent legal. From the moment you and your clients choose a Husband, until the divorce is finalized one year later in Guam, you can rest assured that we are in complete compliance with the law."

As Venus stepped from behind the podium with the two hunks, she glimpsed Kimberly. She looked shaken, talking with Mario and Gus, whose eyes glinted with something grim as they focused on Venus.

Now I know something is very wrong...

Venus' heart pounded with worry as she ran a fingertip along the muscular contours of the men's arms.

"Ladies, I applaud you," she said, "for having the courage to seek the answer to life's million-dollar question: How do you keep the love alive, after we vow to love and to cherish, 'til death do us part?"

The women were silent, leaning forward as if Venus were about to reveal winning lottery numbers.

"Husbands, Incorporated, is the answer to this question that has vexed writers, philosophers and lovers since the beginning of time. Because too many of us have discovered the tragic reality — that love dies!" Venus exclaimed. "And that monogamy is a myth!"

Blond Adela Larsson from Sweden, sitting in the first row, wiped her teary blue eyes, and offered fresh tissues to Vondra Dixon of Jamaica, whose braids were woven into a crown and cascaded down her back. Both women were

Olympic track stars whose marriages had failed; the more they had excelled on the world's athletic stage, the more their spouses' womanizing had become fodder for celebrity gossip magazines.

"Sadly," Venus continued, "we grew up believing the fairy tale, that we'd find our Prince Charmings and live happily ever after."

LaShawn Hawkins from Brooklyn, New York, nodded, as did Georgetta Lane from Dallas, Texas, beside her. LaShawn had been married to a pro football player; Georgetta's ex-husband owned a company that manufactured athletic shoes and clothes. Moving in those elite circles had united the women years ago, and now, despite their 15-year age difference, they were bonded by the trauma of high-profile divorces.

"You fantasized about your wedding day as little girls," Venus said. "Found your Prince Charming... put on the big white dress... played house, had babies, supported your husband's career.... then realized five, ten or fifteen years into it, that the white picket fence felt like prison bars... and your Prince Charming had turned into a frog!"

As cheers and jeers erupted through the crowd, Venus refused to look at her staff. She just had to trust that whatever new problem was brewing, they would handle it, and she could continue her presentation — uninterrupted — with perfect poise.

"Then you realized," she said, "you were locked in the castle tower with diapers and dishes and laundry, while Prince Charming was gallivanting off to conquer new damsels!"

Groans of sadness and disappointment gusted so strongly from the women, goosebumps raced over Venus' skin.

Thirty-something Lisette Pelletier from Montreal, Canada stood and declared, "I felt tossed out like yesterday's dinner!" In the third row, she wore red eyeglasses and a slick, burgundy hairdo that contrasted against her chalky skin. "My husband, he enjoyed me, but he was always trying a new cuisine, with every variety of woman he could find."

Beside her, British department store heiress Ziggy Wild scowled behind huge white sunglasses that matched her straw hat, lacy camisole and jeans. Her auburn hair hung in two ponytails over her yoga-toned shoulders. Ziggy's recent break-up with a European prince had made global headlines, as had her announcement that she planned to open a Husbands, Inc. International franchise in the United Kingdom.

Near her, Moscow native Tatiana Korbakov raised her hand and spoke with a Russian accent: "I am twenty-five, very busy operating my spa in Beverly Hills. I have found that texting, sexting and Internet hook-ups make it so easy for men to be promiscuous. A man's cell phone provides an online catalog of new females, literally in the palm of his hand."

She tossed her long, copper-streaked, black hair over a shoulder, revealing a curvy body hugged by a mini-dress. Exasperation roiled in Tatiana's light brown eyes and tensed her porcelain complexion. "It's impossible to have a real relationship. It's disgusting!"

Venus shook her head. "Ladies, if this beautiful young woman has problems keeping a man's attention, we're all in trouble."

She chuckled along with the women, but her tone turned somber: "I have to laugh, so I don't cry. When Raye Johnson and I founded Husbands, Inc. eight years ago, I was a divorced mother of college students. Our clients were of similar age. Now, to see you, Tatiana, and my 25-year-old daughter, unable to find quality relationships, just makes my heart ache."

As sadness weighted the air, Venus shouted: "No more suffering! You deserve love!"

The women cheered.

"You deserve to feel desired!" Venus proclaimed. "You deserve the gift of being with a man who treats you like a queen, for 365 days a year!"

As the women shouted in agreement and funky music began to play, Venus kissed the cheeks of the two men who were standing beside her, then sent them strutting down the center aisle. The ladies went wild, reaching out to touch their biceps and outstretched hands.

"My mission," Venus said, "is to provide your Prince Charming, and make marriage the magical fairy tale that we were promised as little girls. Welcome to your happily ever after!"

As the music got louder, Venus glanced to her left, where dozens of bare-chested men in Husbands, Inc. shorts appeared with silver trays, offering champagne and chocolate-covered strawberries to each woman. They also handed out hand fans; each wooden stick handle held large, square photographs of a different Husband.

While the men dispersed through the crowd, eight more security guards appeared. They stood around the stage, and where the center aisle ended in back. Venus' stomach knotted.

This is bad, as if we're in imminent danger. Somebody better clue me in...

Whatever it was, she had to keep the women oblivious to any problems, just as they were now — sipping champagne, nibbling strawberries and ogling Husbands.

"Ladies, we know the grim reality of dead love, but I know a secret that changes everything!" Venus exclaimed. "I discovered this secret after my divorce. When I paid the dentist to clean my teeth, or used a credit card for a pedicure and manicure, or flashed cash for a gourmet meal in a restaurant — I got excellent service."

The women watched the Atlas models shift the Earth from Joe to Leroy Moore's creamed coffee-hued shoulders.

"Meanwhile," Venus said, "dating was a terrible disappointment. After 17 years of marriage, all I wanted was an energetic stud who would work his magic on my love-starved body."

Josephine and her assistant Coco from France, in the front row, raised their champagne glasses and smiled. Several women did the same.

"Unfortunately," Venus said, removing the microphone from the podium, then holding it at the base and letting it fall forward like a limp penis, "things went downhill fast, after the thrill of new sex wore off. I *haaaated* that!"

Laughter exploded from the crowd.

"What I also loathed was the dishonesty, deception and deceit," Venus said. "I despised the lies! Too many men tried to play like I was the only one, even though I would overhear them calling other women when they thought I was out of earshot. Or worse, one guy — who'd said he was single — forgot to remove his wedding ring before he came to see me. I was like, 'You're busted, buddy!'"

Laughter and jeers shot up from the crowd. Ziggy from London wiped a tear. Tatiana from Moscow crossed her arms.

Venus shook her head. "That's when I had an epiphany: I got excellent, honest service when I paid for it. But paying for sex is illegal. Marriage, however, is very legal. The problem is, marriage is forever, and by then, the sex has usually gone cold—"

Tall, sun-bronzed David stepped on stage and offered Venus a glass of champagne. His nutmeg-brown eyes glowed with adoration as he held a chocolate-covered strawberry to her lips. She bit, and the women let out lusty shrieks.

"My secret for success is the world's best aphrodisiac," Venus declared as David ran a fingertip over her cheek, toward her lips. "Better than Viagra or breast implants or oysters or sexy lingerie."

Like many of the women who were silent with anticipation, Ziggy from London perched on the edge of her seat. She removed her sunglasses, watching with eyes wide with curiosity.

"The sharpest arrow in Cupid's arsenal," Venus said, "the most powerful incentive to keep the fantasy alive in a relationship—"

David grasped Venus' hand and kissed it; she let out a sultry moan.

"—is Benjamin Franklin," Venus announced. "Bricks and bricks of hundred dollar bills with Mr. Franklin looking up from the center, pursing those lips as if he knows the shameful secret."

Vondra from Jamaica looked sad. Lisette from Canada nodded in agreement, as did Josephine. Others fanned themselves or gulped champagne.

"It's all about the Benjamins, baby!" declared LaShawn from Brooklyn.

As this idea registered on the women's faces, Venus allowed her gaze to sweep past the security guards around the tent; their numbers had doubled. Her pulse pounded with worry.

"Perhaps this is a disappointing reality," Venus said, "but even more grim is the idea of continuing the rest of your life—" she ran her hand over David's chiseled stomach "—without passion in your heart, or the shiver of pleasure in your body."

"Whew, I like the sound of that!" Georgetta from Dallas howled as others cheered.

Venus smacked David's round, hard butt. "The bottom line here," she said with a sly smile, "is that the monetary incentive for the men is unequivocally the secret to our success at Husbands, Incorporated. And it will be the secret to your success as you take Husbands and open franchises of Husbands, Inc. International in your native countries."

David's huge hand squeezed Venus' ass.

"Oooh," she said with a deep tone, turning to him with mock surprise during this well-rehearsed routine. "I *like* the way you to do that."

Marena Barboza from Venezuela laughed with Chanel-suited Mahi Kobayashi from Tokyo, Japan, whose eyes twinkled as brightly as her diamond necklace. The business executive styled her hair and make-up with Audrey Hepburn flair.

Venus resumed a business-like tone: "You are essentially funding a year-long film, starring yourself, and the perfect man that you cast as the romantic hero. You script the relationship, and exactly what you want the man to do."

Venus kissed David's cheek and waved goodbye. He stepped into the audience, rousing cheers as he strode down the center aisle.

"One more thing," Venus said. "For those of you who've felt frustrated and unsatisfied for years — and it seems to get worse as we get older — you are really in for a treat."

Cheering the loudest was Belle Mandelson, a 65-year-old art gallery owner from Portland, Oregon, who was very fit and amazingly wrinkle-free.

"You know what I'm talking about," Venus said. "That blazing hot feeling between your legs, when you need a big, long hose, surging with a fierce, prolonged blast, to put out the fire."

Venus laughed. "I see those fans fluttering. You're hot! And it's only getting hotter in here. Because you're thinking about all these years, when you suffered in silence, wondering, 'What's a respectable woman to do?'"

Gus and Mario suddenly stood at the front corners of the stage.

What the hell is going on? Do they need to body-block me from an attacker?

127

Venus smiled over her worries. "And let's be real. If you were married and hubby wouldn't handle his duties, a piece of plastic only goes so far."

The women roared with laughter.

"It can get the job done for the moment, but what you really need—"

Mike Rivers strode onto the stage in his *Native American Dream* costume: brown suede pants with fringe on the sides, his long black hair flowing over his buff shoulders, and a turquoise necklace that dangled to the center of his hairless chest.

The ladies screamed; Jane was staring like he was a gargantuan steak and she hadn't eaten in years.

"What you really need," Venus said as she ran a fingertip down Mike's arm, "is a big, hard, healthy man—" her hand passed over the sculpted muscles around his belly button, grazing the top of his pants "—to handle your needs."

Leading a chorus of shrieks was German accounting firm owner Helga Bauer, 33, who wore a pin-striped business suit.

"Not only that," Venus said with a sultry tone, stepping around to inspect Mike, "you need a man who will do you exactly as you love to be done. Does anybody know what I'm talking about?"

The women whistled and cheered.

"If you like it slow and gentle," Venus said, "then he'll be tender and sweet. But if you like it rough—" she grinned at the ladies "—because your fire is burning so very hot after all that neglect—"

Venus motioned with her finger for Jane, whose jaw had dropped, to come on stage "—then here at Husbands, Incorporated, we have the manpower to get the job done, very, very well."

As Jane stepped up, Gus and Mario were standing even closer, and Kimberly had never looked so anxious.

Was the emergency alarm going to blare? Trembling with worry, Venus forced herself to look excited as she greeted Jane at the small stairs on the side of the stage, then escorted her to face Mike. Venus touched each of their arms; Jane's chest rose and fell dramatically as she gazed at Mike.

"I believe I've just made a match," Venus said. "Jane, welcome to heaven on earth!"

Mike scooped Jane into his arms. She squealed. Fast-paced, sexy music blasted. Jane touched his face and stared into his eyes; he stilled her quivering lips by kissing her.

"I love this!" Venus shouted as Mike carried Jane off the stage and down the center aisle. "Ladies, can you think of anything more exciting than what they're about to get into?"

As the women cheered, Eden escorted Josephine onto the stage and handed her a giant pair of scissors. The four male Atlas models stood around the globe, holding it up with small handles around the equator.

"I've asked Josephine DuJardin from France to cut the ribbon to symbolize the global launch of Husbands, Inc. International," Venus said. "Not only is she taking a Husband and opening a franchise in Paris, but Josephine has made an extraordinary, ten-million-dollar donation to the Husbands, Inc. Foundation. That will enable women at every financial level to enjoy a year of pleasure and passion here."

The women stood with thunderous applause as Venus hugged Josephine, who then snipped the red ribbon, which fluttered to the floor.

At the same time, rock music and a dozen *Rock 'n Roll Dream* Husbands danced onto the stage, surrounding Josephine. The super sexy men sported skinny jeans, leather pants, long hair, tattoos, and leather jackets. Several slung electric guitars over their shoulders or had drumsticks in their back pockets. As they did a racy dance routine, every client and franchisee was on her feet, smiling, clapping and dancing.

Another fast-paced song began, and a small army of Husbands — including motorcycle guys, blue-suited businessmen, baseball players, construction workers, hip-hop dudes, sailors, doctors and firemen — streamed onto the stage, posing and dancing.

Standing beside the gorgeous men holding the globe, Venus savored this thrilling moment. She refused to look at Kimberly or her security team. Instead, she focused on her guests, who were getting their first taste of unparalleled decadence. The sexy energy was intoxicating; Venus shivered with a *life-gasm*. This was her wildest dream, coming true for thousands of women and men around the globe.

I don't care why my staff looks so stressed. I am on top of the world. And here to stay. No matter what.

But a short time later, as the program concluded with the men dancing into the audience and twirling women in the aisles, Kimberly stepped close.

"What the hell is going on?" Venus demanded.

"A death threat," Kimberly said, shaking and pale. "A man called. He said he wants to kill you."

Chapter 13. A Woman Scorned Cranks It Up

With her head high and her shoulders squared, Laila Sims walked into the Channel 3 newsroom as if she'd just delivered a flawless report. Even though the news director was storming toward her as if Laila had just cussed out the governor on live television.

The buzz of activity in cubicles around the newsroom came to a standstill as dozens of reporters, writers, producers, anchors and assignment desk staffers froze. All eyes were on Laila.

"Laila!" Beth shouted as a security guard stepped out of Laila's cubicle with a large brown box. "You're being escorted off the property now."

"Why?!" Laila shouted. "For coughing on the air?"

"For knowingly allowing a grave conflict of interest to jeopardize the integrity of this news station," Beth said.

Laila plastered a clueless expression on her face.

"Our viewers aren't stupid!" Beth shouted. "They know you, and they know Mike! And there's no way that was a coincidence!"

Laila shook her head. "What—"

Beth turned to a producer, who aimed a remote control at a television on his desk. Beth barked: "Refresh her memory."

Laila and Mike appeared on the TV screen, under an ornate graphic that said, *Engaged! The Channel 3 Wedding Series.*

Beth crossed her arms. "You may recall, the series that you proposed for you and Mike to use your engagement to help couples shop for the ring, the dress, the venue—"

"Okay, okay," Laila said. "But I didn't know Mike was—"

"Bullshit!" Beth shouted. "Laila you're a lot of things, but stupid is not one of them. You knew damn well—"

"I didn't!"

"—that's why you had a coughing fit. No more, Laila. You'll be very successful in this business when you can learn to be honest and find some ethics."

"You can't fire me!" Laila said.

"The first rule of journalism is objectivity," Beth said. "You can't do an objective report on a story when you have a personal ax to grind. Now if you had come to me and said, 'Beth, Mike is at Husbands, Inc. and I want to do a first-person report about how heartbroken I am,' well, you would've had a green light."

That was only part of Laila's idea that she thought would get her out of trouble. But no way was she going to share any of it with Beth now. She snatched the box from the security guard.

"You'll be hearing from my lawyer," Laila huffed. "You will really regret this, Beth."

"No, I think you will," Beth snapped.

Laila marched out of the newsroom with her mind focused on how to get a double dose of revenge. Mike first, Channel 3 second.

Chapter 14. A Barrage of Fists Among Friends

Ted Pendigree could smell John Barker's deception and fear. They were standing face-to-face in front of John's desk, and John was sweating under Ted's suspicious stare.

"Tell me honestly, John, when's the last time you saw Emma?"

If John had nothing to hide, his forehead wouldn't be beading with perspiration. And he would not be giving off the pungent odor of nervous sweat mixed with deodorant and cologne.

"Teddy," John said with a steady gaze and a slight smile. "I saw her at your family's annual Memorial Day barbecue. Remember? Tia and I had the pleasure of meeting Emma's future in-laws."

Something about John's demeanor made Ted's ears ring with a high-toned pitch that announced:

John's lying. And when Emma walks in here, I'll know if she is, too.

Trusting his instinctive hunches, and acting on them, was the secret to Ted's success in his career, as well as with his friends and family. In fact, for the duration of his and Mary's trip to Asia eight years ago, Ted had been haunted by a bad feeling that Emma was up to something. He just hadn't considered that what was up, could have been John's penis.

Now, Ted balled his fists, casting a glare that made more sweat bead on John's forehead. They'd been best friends for too long for John to think he could evade Ted's radar on this one.

It reminded him of the time in fifth grade when John had lied that he was going to the country club with his father, only to make clandestine plans to play a kissing game with Ted's "girlfriend" in the neighborhood park.

After a nasty confrontation, John had promised to adhere to a policy of truth for the rest of their lives. That had come in handy as they protected each other's secrets from girlfriends, then wives, about their respective one-night stands, brief affairs and long-term mistresses.

We know each other's dirty secrets. Or do we?

"Mr. Barker," the secretary said, hurrying into the office with a stack of pink phone message slips. "I've been holding your calls, but a few are urgent."

Ted studied John as he sat behind his desk, as Agnes gave him the messages. Wearing her usual beehive hairdo and thick black glasses with a slim-fitting skirt and sweater, she chattered about John's schedule for the day.

Ted heard none of it, because his worries were so loud.

John knows everything about my biggest secret: Janice. Every detail, starting from the first tryst.

In fact, John had introduced Ted to the stunning tennis instructor at the annual Mackinac Island conference over the Memorial Day weekend six years ago. After a tennis foursome with the Governor of Michigan and a state senator, Ted became mesmerized by Janice's toned, suntanned body, so beautifully displayed in a snug, white tennis dress.

133

Ted and Janice had consummated their mutual attraction in The Grand Hotel that night, sparking a passionate affair that sizzled during countless "business" trips. Some of the best moments of his life had occurred as they devoured each other with their mouths, and he buried his face in the firm curves of her breasts, then ran his fingers through the hot, creamy swell between her legs... and stared into the erotic need in her eyes...

Now, Ted glared at John, imagining him doing to the same to Emma.

My little girl! If he molested my daughter, I'll kill him.

Yes, a primitive urge to kill consumed Ted's senses. This feeling had first overcome him when their oldest child, Patrick, was born 30 years ago. At the time, Ted was a young lawyer in his father's firm, representing the parents of a little boy whose preschool teacher had sexually abused him.

Ted's status as a new father had overwhelmed him with protectiveness for Patrick. And while he empathized with the parents, he marveled at his client's restraint, when the victim's father admitted:

"Of course I wanted to go kill that motherfucker with my own two hands, but that would only make the problem worse. Neither of our sons would have a father, and my wife wouldn't have a husband, because I'd be in prison."

Ted had won a seven-figure settlement from the preschool, but never believed that he himself could demonstrate the same restraint if anyone ever violated his children. This belief became frighteningly stronger when his daughters were born.

Now, Ted's instinct to protect Emma obliterated any concern about the fact that — if spurred to violence against John — it would be a case of the federal prosecutor assaulting a prominent attorney.

No, this conflict was between a father and a predator. Plain and simple. And if John attempted to weave the kind of web of lies that made him so victorious in court — to perhaps allege that Emma had seduced him and that he was helpless against her teenaged wiles — then Ted would pummel him all the more.

As the secretary left, John glanced up, and winced under Ted's glare. "Teddy, really, Venus is the most conniving, dishonest witch. I appreciate that you will not, for one moment, entertain a single word of her venom."

Ted nodded, then glanced at his watch. He had discreetly texted Emma to come here immediately, and she agreed, as she was already downtown for a deposition that had just ended.

"The reporter will be here soon," John said. "Then we have a few hours before the men arrive for our meeting. We can put our heads together to talk about the indictment, the evidence, the arrest and the destruction of Venus Roman on every level."

Ted only heard those words in relation to John. What if Emma confirmed that something scurrilous had occurred — or was still occurring? And what if Ted were miraculously able to stay level-headed enough to pursue the appropriate legal avenues to prosecute John for—

Emma was 17 when we left for Asia; even consensual sex with someone who has authority over her would constitute statutory rape. She turned 18 while we were gone. That would still constitute lechery punishable by a father's brutal wrath.

Ted reeled at the idea of punishing his best friend for a crime that he had prosecuted countless times for strangers. The irony of it tore at his senses.

We left our daughters with the people we trusted most. This would kill Mary!

If sexual molestation had been occurring in John's home, where was Venus? As much as Ted despised her now, he could not deny that she had been an excellent mother prior to the divorce. In fact, Venus had once run in front of a bus to grab Christina and J.J. The kids had dashed into the street while the two families were vacationing in Washington, D.C. to visit the Smithsonian Museums.

Another time, during a family cruise to the Bahamas when the kids were young teenagers, Venus had confronted a creep who'd been ogling and cat-calling Emma and Marla at the ship's pool.

No, Venus would not have condoned anything scurrilous between her husband and my daughter. Never!

But if she had videotaped proof that statutory rape were occurring, and she did not report it to authorities, then she would be guilty of child neglect because she was responsible for the child at the time.

My child!

As Ted seethed, John flashed a smile that only made him look more nervous.

"Earth to Ted! Williams is stopping by later, to tell us—"

"It's not a good idea," Ted said, "having him come here. Cancel the meeting, show a little discretion. I've never liked that bull-headed brute."

"Teddy, don't be a sissy," John said. "We need the FBI in this. It's a federal investigation. After the indictment, we need to gather evidence to ensure a conviction—"

"Johnny! The last case I had with Frank, he trampled all over the rules to get his way. And that trips up everybody in court; we had to dismiss the case on a technicality, and a vicious thug walked—"

John shook his head. "I have been playing golf with Frank Williams for ten years. I've worked with him on countless cases—"

"He doesn't pass my ethical sniff test," Ted said. "He plays dirty—"

"If that were true," John said, "it would've caught up with him by now."

Ted glared at John. "Sometimes it takes a long time for dirty secrets to come into the light."

John's defiant stare looked like he was trying hard to hide his guilt. "You've seen too many bad spy movies, Teddy. Don't you worry about Frank. I'll handle him."

Shaking his head, Ted glanced at his watch.

"Daddy!" Emma exclaimed, striding into the office. "What in the world is so urgent? Don't you have criminals to prosecute?"

Ted rose, beaming at his daughter's professional appearance. With her hair swept back in a twist, she wore pearl earrings, natural make-up and only clear polish on her short fingernails. Her navy blue suit was tailored but not tight, and her white satin blouse was classy, as were her stylish but not stiletto heels. Not to mention, Ted loved the sparkler that Brian had recently slid onto her finger. His little Emma was making all the right moves; she couldn't possibly have—

"Emma!" John said the way he always did, like an uncle greeting a favorite niece.

Still, Ted could almost see flames shooting between them.

Guilty! The word slammed down on Ted's senses like an iron gavel.

John was trying his damnedest to conceal his lechery. And Emma was attempting to feign coolness, but her eyes couldn't contain the burst of heat that—

No! She's looking at him like women look at me after I've made them orgasm.

Ted's ears rang, heart pounded, and every hair on his body stood on end. His lips curled back, and an animal noise shot between his teeth.

"Daddy!" Emma shrieked. "What's wrong?"

Ted's hands became claws. He lunged at John's neck. His lips felt wet, eyes bulging, as he stared inches into the face and mind that had violated his baby girl.

Ted squeezed his fingers hard around John's neck.

John made choking, gasping noises.

"Daddy!" Emma screamed.

The secretary ran in. "Mr. Pendigree! Stop!"

John's eyes bugged with terror. His face was red.

"I oughta kill you with my bare hands, right now!" Ted growled. "Did you think you could get away with this?"

"Daddy!" Emma stomped a foot. "Get away with *what*?"

Ted stared into John's eyes. He remembered what that young father of a molested child had told him years ago about controlling his rage for his family's sake. Ted spat, "You're not worth throwing away everything I've worked for—"

Ted shoved John into the bookcase. The pole holding the American flag toppled on him, as did several law books.

"Stop!" Agnes shouted. "Stop before someone calls the police! The reporter will be here in a few minutes!"

"Daddy!" Emma cried. "What's going on?"

Ted glared at his daughter. "Tell me what happened with him while we were in Asia."

Shock and confusion spread across Emma's face. "What?"

"During your senior year!" Ted shouted. "Tell me he didn't lay a single finger on you!"

Emma shook her head, still looking confused. But her eyes roiled with guilt and shame. "Daddy, what in the world—"

Ted pursed his lips to stop a million expletives from shooting out at his daughter. In his career, he had built a reputation on not blaming victims of sexual crimes, especially young, pretty girls who flaunted their bodies with flirtatious behavior and provocative clothing.

She's the victim here. He's the criminal.

Ted turned to John, who was standing up. Before Ted could stop himself, he charged at John, ramming him into the law books, which tumbled.

As John grunted, the secretary dashed for the phone.

"I'm calling the police," she said.

"No," Emma said, grabbing her arm. "The media would have a field day."

Agnes helped John up; Emma buried her face in her hands.

Ted's fingers ached. His hair felt tousled. What now? What proof did Ted have to prosecute John for a crime that had occurred eight years ago? Ted seethed. If any proof existed, it was in Venus Roman's possession. The problem was, she was the enemy, not an ally.

If I go against John, would he use what he knows against me? Would he tell Mary about Janice and all the other women? Or worse, would he leak my marital indiscretions to the press, causing a scandal that could jeopardize my plans for Congress?

Panting with rage, Ted took a deep breath, somehow sucking down enough composure to stand up straight and look John squarely in the eyes.

"John Barker, I will consider you innocent until proven guilty. We will proceed as planned. But honestly, if I am presented with evidence that proves your guilt in this matter—" Ted wrung his hands and widened his eyes "—I will sentence you to my own personal rendition of the death penalty."

Chapter 15. Women Witness a Shocking Spat

Under the tent on the grounds of Sea Castle, Venus stood behind the podium, concluding the program. The hundreds of excited faces staring up at her bolstered her resolve to deliver on all the decadent promises she was making for their futures with Husbands, Inc.

"After this, ladies, you'll have a chance to talk one-on-one with the Husbands at the Mix 'n Mingle reception," Venus said. "And—"

She shivered with terror.

What if someone really kills me?

She tilted her chin upward. If a clock were ticking on her life, then she needed to accomplish as much as possible, as quickly as possible.

I'll go down in history as the woman who died while connecting women with dream lovers who revived their passion and pleasured them until dawn. Yes, I will be remembered as the woman who made that happen exponentially, around the world!

That emboldened her to continue: "And ladies, we can get on with the business of your pleasure."

Sudden commotion drew her attention to the side of the tent. Kimberly and several security guards were hurrying out.

Now what? A bomb threat? An anthrax attack? My team better handle it to prevent any disruptions—

"Venus!" a woman yelled. "Vee, girl! Get me a new Husband! Now!"

Venus' heart pounded; Raye sounded furious.

Kimberly looked bewildered, dashing alongside Raye, who was stomping across the grass in stiletto pumps. She took tiny steps, restricted by the slim-fitting mini skirt of her tailored, red business suit. Storming behind her was Husband Dante Wilson, wearing an impeccable blue and white seersucker suit, loafers, a straw hat and sunglasses.

"Vee!" Raye exclaimed. "Strike three, this man is out. Time for a trade! Now!"

Venus plastered a calm, cool expression on her face — but panic exploded inside her. She coolly scanned the audience.

"I knew this was too good to be true," Georgetta snapped.

Tatiana looked cynical. Shock froze Lisette's face. Intrigue sparkled in Vondra's eyes. Marena and LaShawn lit up with excitement.

"Raye, you always have superb timing," Venus said, sounding delighted and extending her arms as Raye marched on stage with Danté; two security guards followed close behind. Venus hugged Raye and shook Danté's hand.

"Ladies, this is Raye Johnson," Venus said. "She is co-founder, co-owner and Chief Financial Officer of Husbands, Incorporated. And she's one of America's top wealth managers. As CEO of Queen Financial Services, Ms. Johnson was just named *Financial Advisor of the Year* today by the country's most distinguished business association."

The audience applauded; Raye bowed graciously, smiling. Then anger glinted in her eyes. "Vee, I need a new Husband. Now!"

Cool and confident, Venus said, "Ladies, client satisfaction is our top priority. So when a problem arises, we fix it immediately."

"The problem is," Raye crossed her arms, glaring up at Danté, then turning to the guests, "sometimes the male ego can't handle a woman who's in control. Loves my Ferrari, my house, my boat — can't stand that it ain't his."

Danté snatched off his designer sunglasses and glared down at her. "Naw, baby girl. You just mad that I got control over this joystick an' I won't let you play—"

Several women shot to their feet and booed as Danté continued: "This drill sergeant is always tellin' me what to wear, what to say, what to do, how to fuck — four, five times a day!"

Venus waved away the security guards that were poised to take his arms. She flashed a mischievous smile and said,

"Danté, I recall you were quite eager to engage Ms. Johnson's rigorous appetite."

He fumed: "Rigorous. Not ridiculous. Pay me and I'm out!"

Venus looked up at him. "Danté, you've had four very successful marriages here prior to this. So I'd be happy to give you a re-assignment."

Danté shook his head. "I'm done. Listen, I did the math. Divide 150-grand by 12 months, that's $12,500 a month, times my three months with Drill Sergeant, that's $37,500. I want a check—"

"Oooh, look at them," Raye cooed as 15 Husbands jogged into the tent and past the stage. Her eyes flamed with approval for former Detroit Lions superstar Buck Briggs, who was the black velvet version of Michelangelo's David. He had already served as an exceptionally good Husband for two very satisfied clients. He would be a superb choice—

"Vee, hook me up," Raye said, pointing to Buck. "Now."

Danté watched her ogle Buck, whose dark eyes sparkled as he smiled, flashing his bright-white teeth at Raye. A star-struck glow radiated from his clean-shaven face, with arched brows and cheeks that rose like small apples as he smiled even bigger.

"Look, she's pickin' her next victim," Danté said, "and that brotha's already lost his mind, just lookin' at her." He put his hands around his mouth like a megaphone. "Yo, dude—"

The security guards took Danté's arms.

"Venus, pay me or I'll sue," he threatened.

Venus shook her head. "And you'll never see a courtroom. Your contract requires you—"

"I earned my dough. I gotta warn these other dudes. Yo—"

The guards led him away.

"Danté, you're fired!" Venus announced.

As he was led from the tent, Danté shouted, "My lawyer's gonna jack all you crazy bitches!"

The audience thundered, "Boo!"

"Ladies," Venus said. "It's fortuitous that you witnessed that. It's a reminder that we're dealing with human beings. This is not women's answer to that movie, *The Stepford Wives*. The Husbands are not robots, and unfortunately, their personal issues can sometimes override the power of the very pleasurable and profitable opportunities that we offer here."

Venus put her arm around Raye. "Now, my beautiful, brilliant friend, how can I restore your wedded bliss?"

Raye pointed to Buck Briggs. "With him."

"Outstanding choice," Venus said. "We'll grant you an annulment, and you'll re-marry by the weekend."

The women cheered. But LaShawn crossed her arms, pouting.

"Ladies," Venus said, "Buck is one of the many retired professional athletes who are now available for you at Husbands, Inc. My motto is 'satisfaction guaranteed,' so I guarantee if he's your type, we will satisfy your dream."

LaShawn smiled and raised two hands in praise.

"Vee, girl, I know I didn't hear you say 'weekend,'" Raye said as she locked eyes with Buck. "I'm taking my Heisman Trophy home today. I'm paying too much to go home alone tonight."

Venus pulled out her cell phone and dialed. "J.J., honey, I need a favor — an immediate annulment of Raye Johnson's marriage with Danté Wilson. Please draw up a new *Corporate Companion* contract for her with Buck Briggs. I need this done within the hour."

"But Mom," J.J. said on the phone, "I'm swamped with paperwork for the global franchise applicants."

Venus nodded. "I know, honey. Now please put your phenomenal brain to work and have the papers ready to sign in one hour. Thank you, J.J."

Buck stepped on stage, gently placing his hands on each side of Raye's waist. He stared down with the tenderness and love of a deeply enamored man. Raye ran a fingertip over his lips; her gaze devoured Buck from the top of his bald head, down his smooth, muscular chest, strong legs and very large running shoes. She cooed, "I can't wait to touchdown on *you.*"

"You can do that today at five," Venus said. She turned to the women. "Looks like another match as close to heaven as we can get on earth. Raye is proof that client satisfaction is our top priority here at Husbands, Incorporated."

Raye laced her arm through Buck's and said, "Ladies, your only regret will be that you didn't come here sooner."

Envy and yearning glowed on the women's faces as Raye and Buck strode out of the tent.

Venus beamed. "Now that you've witnessed matchmaking at its best, please follow me to the gazebo to watch a wedding in progress," she said as a parade of shirtless Husbands filed up the aisles to escort the women. "Then we'll head up to the terrace for our Mix 'n Mingle reception and you can start living your dream."

As the women left the tent, Venus phoned her legal team. Former Husbands had tried to sue before, but always lost. Still, the lawyers needed to prepare an offensive strategy, just in case Danté Wilson decided to play dirty.

A death threat... a disgruntled Husband... what next?

Chapter 16. Wedding Enrages Soul Mate

Nikki DeFiore's whole body shook with rage as the Justice of the Peace finally conducted the wedding, now that those friggin' helicopters were gone.

I shouldn't have agreed to this. I shouldn't have let Claire talk me into One Year of Hell. All the money in the world isn't worth letting that hillbilly punk drool and paw all over my girl.

Their relationship was about love; this charade was about money. And Nikki's heart literally hurt. Good thing she hadn't eaten today; she'd puke all over Country Boy if she had the chance.

It didn't help that Venus Roman and all those women were standing around the gazebo now, probably fantasizing about how they'd pick a guy and get married right here. Nikki glanced at all those horny bitches at the waist-high, flower-covered ledge.

Didn't they know they could be much happier and freer with another chick instead of a dude? Didn't they know how liberated they would feel if they stopped trying so hard to get and keep a fickle, dirty, promiscuous man? Didn't they know how freakin' awesome it was to feel so deeply connected to someone that you felt like if she died, you would instantly stop breathing, too?

The strong scent of tiger lilies was nauseating; Nikki held her bouquet with one hand and pressed her other palm over her queasy stomach. She glanced at Claire, who looked smokin' hot in her veil and sexy dress that lifted up her tits in a way that made them look delicious. But Country Boy was looking like he wanted to slobber all over them.

No, she promised she wouldn't let him touch her. So I have to pretend this is our wedding. It's the only way I won't lose my mind for a whole year of this lie.

145

Country Boy grinned down at Claire; she smiled back. And those women watching let out little sighs over the soft harp music being played by that chick in a flowy dress.

"Do you, Billy Jack Burns, take Claire Montague as your lawfully wedded wife?" the Justice of the Peace asked.

The groom smiled. "I reckon I'd jump off a bridge if I didn't."

Oh, how Nikki wished he would. Then she and Claire could go back to California and live happily ever after. Fuck the inheritance; Claire had money from selling the Malibu house, and they could hawk their paintings for a living.

"Yes," Country Boy said. "Yes, sir, I do."

Claire smiled. Nikki wanted to heave, but Venus Roman was staring at her. And for Claire's sake, Nikki faked a smile. Earlier, Claire had warned her to play along — because all of it was an act.

"Just keep your eyes on the prize — us," Claire had kept saying.

But Nikki wasn't much into delayed gratification, especially if it involved that guy touching her soul mate. She and Claire were made for each other in every way; they'd known it since they were four years old and Mom — a housekeeper at the Montague Mansion — would bring Nikki to work when Grandmom got sick and couldn't babysit.

Little did anyone know, Claire and Nikki would play wedding in Mrs. Montague's dresses, always kissing on the lips and loving it. Now, if Nikki had to watch Claire kiss Country Boy... or think about his slimy dick and straw-colored pubes contaminating the Nirvana between Claire's legs...

Nikki gripped her stomach and clenched her teeth.

"Do you, Claire Montague, take Billy Jack Burns as your lawfully wedded husband?" the Justice of the Peace asked.

Through her veil, Claire looked amused. Her red curls bounced on her bare shoulders as she said, "Yes, I do."

Nikki felt dizzy.

I'm going to puke and faint all at once. No, I can't ruin this for Claire. For us.

The Justice of the Peace said, "You may kiss your bride."

"Wee-hoo!" the groom exclaimed. Animal lust blazed in his eyes as he raised Claire's veil. He leaned close to kiss her; the female spectators cheered.

Nikki's heart pounded. Her knees went weak. And a strong arm around her shoulders kept her from crumpling to the floor.

"You look beautiful, Nikki," Venus Roman said with a knowing stare. Nikki felt stunned by the shock of staring into Ms. Roman's eyes — they were so knowing and powerful, and sparkling with excitement, yet compassion. Something about her, from the delicious scent of her floral perfume to the aura of peaceful energy around her, made Nikki stare back in awe.

This woman is a freakin' queen.

Nikki tried to pinpoint exactly what inspired that thought, but all she could see was the warmth and empathy radiating from the owner of this place that Nikki hated. It was like time stood still, yet only a split second passed.

I wish I were as confident and cool as her...

Before Nikki could blink, Venus removed her arm from Nikki's shoulder, then stood before the newlyweds to say, "Congratulations, Claire and Billy Jack!"

As they smiled at Ms. Roman, waiters entered with champagne for everyone and all those women swarmed around the newlyweds.

"A toast," Venus said, "to Claire and Billy Jack, and a year of wedded bliss."

Everyone cheered.

But Nikki dashed to the rail and puked into the lake.

Chapter 17. Police Presence Hints at Power Play

Indignation prickled through Venus like a million tiny needles as she faced a team of law enforcement authorities in her office. They had just shown up, unannounced, as the Mix 'n Mingle reception was beginning on the terrace outside the French doors.

This is absurd! It has John and Ted written all over it, and I'm going to obliterate them both before this is over. If they want war, they'll get it.

For now, she hated the way these people were invading her space. The air of macho domination that they radiated was the antithesis of female empowerment that she cultivated at Husbands, Inc.

One man in particular — Detroit FBI Director Frank Williams — made her skin crawl. Everything about him exuded a bullish air. He was tall with a thick upper body, and his posture leaned forward, with his wide forehead down, as if he were about to charge and gore any obstacle in his way.

Including his wife, Valerie. Last year, he'd been all over the news for beating her. But she had recanted her story the next day, saying it was all a big misunderstanding, including the photo of her with two black eyes that had aired on every TV station. Now it was a joke for his misogynistic ass to come here under the guise of protecting Venus Roman.

But most incriminating was that Frank had been friends with John since before the divorce. Venus remembered the day about 10 years ago, when Frank's testimony as an FBI agent had helped John win a high profile trial. They'd gone out to celebrate on the golf course and wherever else until three in the morning, and the rest was history.

Since then, Frank had been cited in news reports for either testifying or providing evidence that helped John win in court.

The two were frequently photographed together at high profile events around town, as reported on the society pages of local magazines and newspapers. And on more than one occasion, Venus had seen them at upscale restaurants such as Chateau d'Amour, where they frequented the martini lounge.

Birds of a feather flock together. Or should I say, dogs travel in packs. I don't trust him, or any one of these men.

Now, she maintained perfect poise and a cool mask of confidence as she said, "Gentlemen, your show of force today is overblown and unnecessary."

She stood beside her massive, ornately carved, Brazilian rosewood desk. Its richly oiled, red hue matched the spiral staircase and floor-to-ceiling bookshelves that extended up two stories to a book-lined balcony whose windows overlooked the grounds.

Two cozy velvet chairs up there served as Venus' reading nook; the shelves contained her favorites, including spiritual books, and authors who had inspired her in high school and college: Henry David Thoreau, Zora Neale Hurston, William Shakespeare, Alice Walker, Maya Angelou, Virginia Woolf, Harriet Beecher Stowe, Langston Hughes, Maxine Hong Kingston, Mary Shelley, and many others.

This office was her sanctuary, and she needed to quickly expel these people who were linked to John.

"I've gotten threats before," she said, glancing up at two armed security guards who stood watch at the windows above them, as more guards were also doing in the turrets at each corner of Sea Castle. "That's why I have my own private security force, and four bodyguards around me at all times."

She nodded toward her guards. "They're all former Navy Seals who've worked in the most treacherous circumstances around the globe. I trust them with my children's lives."

The sounds of the party only aggravated Venus more. The sexy music, the sensuous rumble of men and women flirting, talking and laughing, and the clink of silverware on china filled Venus with urgency to convince these intruders to leave, quickly.

"You don't know what you're dealing with here," Frank said with an accusing tone as if she'd done something wrong. His voice was deep and grating, and he had an odd way of breathing as he spoke — like a simultaneous snort and blow. "We need you to know how dangerous these threats are, Venus."

"Please call me 'Ms. Roman,'" she said firmly. "Threats? There's more than one?"

"Considering the riot-like atmosphere in front of your house," he said, "multiple threats should come as no surprise. We've traced the threat that came into your secretary's phone to that group outside, Men for Traditional Marriage. But they're the least of our problems."

Frank's dark eyes were full of aggression as he looked down on her. His bad energy raised the hairs on the back of her neck. Because Frank was simply the bigger, badder embodiment of John's rage — with a gun on his hip, a powerful title in front of his name, and an army of officers to do his dirty work.

In fact, Venus could almost see John's angry, gloating face superimposed on Frank, and every one of these uninvited guests: the police chief and his deputy; the head of the local Homeland Security office and his deputy; the county sheriff and a deputy; and two local uniformed cops.

The lone female FBI agent stood with the men around two leather couches and four high-backed chairs facing the huge fireplace. Closer to Venus were J.J., Kimberly and Husbands, Inc.'s two top lawyers, Yolanda Napoleon and Adam Applebaum.

"Rodriguez," Frank barked at the woman, "give Venus the low-down on what she's up against."

"Ms. Roman," said Agent Rodriguez, "one of the threats was made on the blog of an international terrorist group that has cells in Europe, North Africa and Asia."

Agent Rodriguez radiated professionalism and empathy. She wore a navy blue pantsuit, with her black hair pulled back into a bun; her cosmetic-free complexion was as clear as maple syrup.

Something about her put Venus at ease. Still, her badge said FBI over her name, and that roused suspicion that John and Ted had tapped into their "good ol' boys network" to lead their witch hunt. And if Frank thought he could use a female agent to engender trust from another woman, he was dead wrong.

Agent Rodriguez' wedding ring sparkled as she held up a piece of white paper and said, "I'll read a portion of the threat, which our office translated to English: '*The infidel who has created an evil whoredom to spread across the planet, will fry and burn in Satan's hellfire. She will carry the corpses of the blasphemous prostitutes back into the devil's workshop where she was born.*'"

A chill slithered through Venus.

Agent Rodriguez cast a somber look and said, "The note also says they want to blow up this house, with you and all the women from around the world, and the men you hire, inside."

Venus shook her head. "Go ask any of those protesters out front, and they'll say the same thing."

The Homeland Security director stepped forward. "Venus, these terrorist bloggers, they want to send a message to the world, by using you as an example to set back women's rights."

"It's Ms. Roman," she snapped.

His tone was impatient: "You should also consider the very real chance of attacks on your infrastructure: cutting off your power source, tampering with your water supply, infiltrating your program here. Venus, you should also be wary of anybody unusual who shows up out of the blue and tries to get close to you."

Venus crossed her arms as goosebumps prickled her skin. Where was the line between viable threats and scare tactics?

"Your enemies are out to kill!" Frank declared. "It's no secret. The protesters outside have been all over TV, vowing to hack into your computer system to steal your client lists and go after every single woman who's used your business—"

"We already know that!" Kimberly fumed. "Our cyber-security team is constantly upgrading our system with the best firewalls. Our e-commerce website is impenetrable."

Venus added with a bored tone, "Just as no can penetrate the grounds here."

J.J. stepped forward. "This house was literally built as a fortress. Our high-tech surveillance only makes it more secure."

Venus cast a proud gaze at her son. He'd come to work here straight out of business school, and had implemented several policies and procedures that streamlined the process and boosted profitability. Though he was married to a delightful young woman, he devoted long hours here while she worked her way up the corporate ladder at one of the Big Three automotive companies.

"We can't take any chances, Venus," the Homeland Security director said. "You're one of the most high profile — and hated — women in the world, especially now that you're taking this business to countries that oppose women's rights. We have orders from Washington to protect you—"

Venus crossed her arms. "Well, you can call the President and everybody else. Tell them that I'm fine. We don't need your help."

Agent Rodriguez beamed with admiration toward Venus, until Frank glared at her.

"I refuse to live in fear," Venus declared. "Part of our daily security routine is a sweep of the buildings and the grounds with bomb-sniffing dogs. We do this twice daily during special events, including the one that I'm *missing* right now. Plus, I do not want a single dime of taxpayer dollars spent beyond crowd control—"

The county sheriff stepped close. "Venus, we've got orders—"

"It's Ms. Roman," Venus said. "Now, I appreciate the news flash, gentlemen, and Agent Rodriguez. But I kindly request that you please leave before my guests know you're here."

The police chief turned down the corners of his mouth and shook his head. "We're not all leaving. Our agencies are coordinating a plan to provide you and your complex with 24-hour protection until it's determined that the threats are no longer viable. Which could, quite frankly, last for the duration that you're in business."

Venus closed her eyes. *That will happen when hell freezes over. These officers will be out of here by week's end.*

"That's the cold, hard truth, Venus," said the Homeland Security director. "This is a situation of international scope, considering the women you have here from around the world. It's our responsibility—"

Venus cast a cool, confident look at them. "I have a hot tip for your investigation. Trace the origins of the blog for the so-called terrorist group, and I guarantee it will loop right back here to Detroit. To the law offices of John

Barker, the best friend of U.S. Attorney Ted Pendigree, who's planning to run for Congress."

Her words inspired a lot of shaking heads and crossing arms amongst the visitors.

"Those two are on a mission to destroy me," she said. "In fact, I'm certain that Ted Pendigree will make the destruction of Husbands, Incorporated part of his campaign platform. Men for Traditional Marriage will probably be his biggest supporters."

The Homeland Security director stood with his legs wide apart, like he was standing his ground in *her* office. "Venus, we're mobilizing our officers now. You'll all be better for it."

Venus cast a questioning glance at the Husbands, Inc. lawyers, who stepped forward.

"I think we should go along with this for now," said Yolanda Napoleon, with her usual no-nonsense tone. Her narrow face was as beige-brown and stiff as her starched khaki pantsuit. With her short, black hair gathered at her nape in a plain barrette, her eyes were sharp and assured. "I recommend a 'better safe than sorry' approach for now. Just in case there's any validity to the threats."

Adam Applebaum nodded, shaking his graying brown curls. Wearing a black suit, crisp white shirt and colorful silk tie, he pulled off his tortoise shell glasses to reveal serious dark eyes that contrasted with his jowly cheeks.

"It would be a horrific liability," he said, "if any harm comes to our domestic and international guests or the Husbands who come from across America as well."

Venus exhaled, annoyed, glancing at the law enforcement visitors. "My position is that you handle crowd control out front, but law enforcement personnel inside my home and my business are not, and will not, be needed. Ever."

Frank cast a defiant glare down at her. "I know you're used to callin' the shots around here, but this one's not your decision to make. We got our marching orders from Washington—"

The Homeland Security chief put his hands on his hips. "We didn't come here to ask your permission, Venus. We came to let you know how we're planning to proceed. Now we need an itinerary of all the events for your international visitors."

Venus met his domineering stare with equal confidence. *OK, I'll let them think they're getting their way. But this little war game will end as soon as I drop my video bomb and destroy the man calling the shots: John Barker.*

Kimberly shook her head. "We provided an itinerary to the police chief, months ago, for traffic issues involving our chartered buses for the off-site events. Tonight we're going to the opera downtown, and some of us will be going with Madame Roman to the Fox Theatre to receive her award Sunday evening."

The sheriff said, "We'll provide escorts to each event, with heavy presence at each site, to manage the protesters."

Kimberly nodded. "Our week culminates next Saturday night, when our annual Masquerade at Sea Castle brings an influx of limousines because people from across America fly in to attend the ball."

As Kimberly talked, Venus ticked down a mental list of all that might be necessary to shield herself and the company from the prying eyes of law enforcement. And if this were part of a scheme by John to seize the video she'd mentioned on the phone this morning, then they were wasting their time. They would never find it. They would have to watch it along with John, Ted and the rest of the world — on television!

The police chief pointed to the two officers. "Ms. Roman, Officer Brown and Officer Camry are assigned to your personal protection. They will be with you for twelve-hour shifts. We'll have two other officers replace them here at night."

Venus nodded at them, noticing that the handsome, buff officers wore no wedding rings.

I'm going to persuade them to try a new, more lucrative line of work...

The Homeland Security director said, "Our officers are setting up a command center on the street in front of your property, and we've got a multi-agency team of officers on the perimeter. The Coast Guard and Sheriff's Department are patrolling the water, along with your boats, and we've got choppers—"

"Gus," Venus said, "coordinate in whatever way is necessary for the time being."

He nodded.

"Kimberly, escort our guests to the door," Venus said. "J.J., let's get back to the urgent matter you were handling."

As the visitors trailed past Venus, Agent Rodriguez cast a look that was deliberately hidden from her peers. Her eyes sparkled as if to say, *I got your back* and even, *You go, girl!*

But her allegiance was to a boss linked to John. And for that, no one, not even a woman, could be trusted.

𝒞𝒽𝒶𝓅𝓉𝑒𝓇 18. Publicity Brings Money and Malice

As Raye strode through the second floor offices of Husbands, Inc., she tingled with anticipation to take her new Husband home. After all that stress with Danté, she needed an onslaught of orgasms to relax.

Meanwhile, the sights and sounds of booming business up here were just as much of a turn-on. But where was Eden? They were supposed to meet to talk about new benefactors for the Foundation.

"Yes, we have several packages available," an operator said into her headset. She was one of dozens of employees taking calls and facing computers in cubicles surrounded by glass-walled offices. "If you'll go to our website, Husbands, Inc. dot com, you can see pictures of some of our Husbands and the marriage themes that we offer."

Ringing phones and talking operators charged the air with excitement and urgency that registered in Raye's mind as one big *cha-ching!* All this had begun as an idea shared by her and Venus eight years ago, and now Husbands, Inc. needed 250 employees to run its headquarters.

"Yes, you can finance your Husband with monthly payments on our secure e-commerce website," said a male operator in the next cubicle. "It will provide you with instructions—"

"Raye!" Eden exclaimed, hurrying toward her with an iPad in hand. Her tiny silver Star of David earrings glimmered as her hair bounced.

Raye hugged her. "Girl, it's off the chain up here."

Eden crinkled her nose when she smiled, the same way she did as a girl when they'd giggle about boys. "Yeah, because the Parklawn Princesses rule! We were the coolest girls around, now we're smokin' hot bitches in business!"

They blew air kisses over their fingertips and laughed.

"As you can see," Eden said with a more serious tone, "business has never been better. It's so amazing that online applications have doubled over the past two years. And just this week, we've had a ginormous spike, thanks to the media attention and those lunatics protesting outside."

As phones rang unanswered, Raye said, "Call in more operators. They can't even handle all the calls."

Eden nodded. "Great minds think alike. I already called in the reserves, for the phones, and for processing online applications." Eden pointed to two long rows of computers where people were working.

"We've got round-the-clock shifts," Eden said. "I anticipate this kind of volume for the rest of the week and even after the global orientation."

Two men were in the glass-walled conference room at the center of the office. They were sitting in the white leather chairs, working on computers at the long, glass table. Each wore a black jumpsuit with CYBER LION SECURITY across the back, with the animal jumping up through the letters, looking ferocious with its mighty teeth exposed.

"Eden," Raye said, proud that Momma's Ritzy Diva Designs had created the cyber-security company's distinctive jumpsuits. "Tell me they're upgrading security with all this volume and controversy."

"Absolutely," Eden said. "Can't be too careful. I just talked with your brother; he's on his way, to oversee the installation of new firewalls. Who knew, back when we were kids and little Whittaker would magically fix TVs and clock-radios, someday he'd be running the best cyber security firm in the Midwest?"

Raye laughed. "Momma used to fuss at him something fierce when he'd spread that electronic stuff all over the kitchen table when it was time to eat!"

Eden smiled. "I loved how he made money by fixing stuff for kids in the neighborhood. If it was broken, Whittaker could fix it."

"Yeah," Raye said. "It's hard to believe his company has been keeping Queen Financial Services safe for 20 years."

"All he does is work," Eden said. "We need to hook him up with a hot female!"

"Believe me," Raye said, "I've tried. He's very picky. Maybe if we can find another super serious workaholic, so they can help each other chillax—"

"Well," Eden said, glancing at the busy operators, "before he finds the woman of his dreams, he's got a lot of work to do here. Now that our secret is out, the haters are coming from every direction."

Raye stopped in the middle of the cubicles. "Fortunately, we're also attracting billionaire benefactors. They're flying in for a meeting after the global orientation. So right now, this conference call will allow us to explore a preliminary strategy about their relationship with the company."

Eden nodded.

"At the top of the list," Raye said over the chatter of operators, "we've got an oil heiress in Texas who's eager to contribute. As you know, the designer GiGi Gateau is coming for the grand finale next Sunday. And a hedge fund billionaire in New York who's had three Husbands wants to help other women find their pleasure here in the Promised Land."

Eden laughed. "It's important that we—"

"Call the police!" an operator shrieked. Raye and Eden turned; the woman was ghost-white and trembling. "Oh my God, call the police!"

Eden grabbed the phone from the woman's grip and listened. Her eyes grew huge. "Who is this?"

Raye put her hands on the woman's shaking shoulders and glanced at her nametag. "Theresa, what happened? What'd they say?"

"He... he... he said he was going to kill us. All of us! He had an accent. He said men are going to rise up and put us in our place—"

Raye put her arms around Theresa as Eden listened on the landline and dialed the police on her cell. All around them, operators watched, but continued with their calls, including the routine script that included: "This call may be recorded for quality purposes."

Raye pulled out her phone and dialed Venus.

"Damn, her voicemail is full!" She tried Kimberly, but got her voicemail as well.

Raye waved to all the operators, who stared with wide eyes and shocked expressions.

"Don't miss a beat, ladies and gentlemen," Raye said. "This is to be expected, considering what's going on outside. Nobody said it would be easy to change the world, so let's keep on steppin'."

The operators looked worried, but kept working.

Raye guided Theresa to the lunchroom. "You okay?"

"Relax, girl," Raye said with a soothing tone as she held the operator's trembling hands. "It's probably just some jerk calling from his parents' basement. We'll have the police on him in a heartbeat."

Theresa shook her head, still looking spooked. "He just sounded so evil. It was like, shooting through the phone into my ear. Pure evil."

The terror in Theresa's eyes made Raye shudder.

𝒞𝒽𝒶𝓅𝓉𝑒𝓇 19. Plotting to Protect the Erotic Realm

Venus inhaled deeply as she stepped onto the huge terrace that stretched along the backside of Sea Castle. At her sides were Gus and Mario, while Derek and Decker watched her from the banister. The two cops were observing her from about five feet away.

She had already issued orders to her staff to keep an eye on those two, lest they attempt to snoop around on John's behalf, if they were so inclined.

I don't trust any of them...

Venus' insides burned white-hot with anger that all those people were using their macho authority to impose their rules on her empire. Unfortunately, Eden had just called to alert her of the phone threat that the operator had received upstairs. That would only bolster the law enforcement team's argument that their presence here was needed.

Now if Venus could just escape the watch of Officer Brown and Officer Camry long enough to show the video to Raye, they could strategize a plan to stop them all.

Raye, where are you?

Venus scanned the crowd, thrilled that her guests and the Husbands were oblivious to the death threats and intrusive law enforcement.

I have to keep it that way...

The party was one sensuous flow of male and female bodies mingling in romantic, lustful unison to sexy beats played by a dee-jay. From one end of the terrace to the other, euphoria glowed on women's faces as Husbands talked, laughed and danced with them. Others stood at the edge, looking out at the grounds and the lake.

Uniformed wait staff offered champagne, jumbo shrimp, chocolates and skewers of fresh fruit. All the while, hostesses introduced clients and franchisees to Husbands deemed most compatible with each woman's preferences. Whether in costume or regular clothing, all the Husbands were strutting their most delectable stuff.

"MMmmmmm," Venus moaned, inhaling the scent of perfume and cologne mixing with the sweet aromas wafting from four silver fountains that streamed champagne and chocolate fondue. The pure passion charging the air made Venus envision a red haze in the bright sunshine around the umbrella tables that were crowded with couples.

"Girl, there you are!" Raye said, darting toward her and grabbing two champagne flutes from a waiter's tray. She handed one to Venus. "Vee, I need a drink, bad. I was just upstairs in the offices. One of the operators got a threat. Freaked her out! Eden called the police."

Venus stiffened. "They're already here. Apparently some international terrorist group is blogging about us in a very bad way."

Raye scowled. "She said he had an accent."

Venus stiffened. "I don't care what kind of accent he had, or where he was calling from. I'm certain it will all be traced back to John."

"I'm with you on that, Vee," Raye said, clinking their glasses. "Now let's toast to the two bodacious bitches who are officially taking Husbands, Inc. far beyond our wildest imaginations! Anybody who tries to stop us will get their ass royally kicked."

Venus smiled as they toasted. "Hear, hear! We have the power, baby!"

As they sipped, Raye froze. "Vee, girl, those protesters out there, and threats, this is some serious drama."

"That's why every police agency in town just stopped by," Venus said. "Unannounced—"

"I don't trust them, either," Raye snapped. "All those groups endorsed Ted Pendigree when he ran for Congress the first time, which means John has his dirty little hands all over them now."

Venus leaned toward Raye and said, "I have the perfect ammunition to make them all go away."

"I love that feisty look in your eyes!" Raye exclaimed. "What is it?"

"Something I've been keeping since the divorce. I didn't use it back then, because John's blatantly bad behavior with Tia gave me all the leverage I needed. Plus, my lawyers had warned it could be used against me. But now—"

Raye's eyes widened. "Too much suspense, Vee. What is it?"

"I'll show you as soon as we can sneak away from the prying eyes of those guys," Venus said, nodding toward Officer Brown and Officer Camry. They were standing with Kimberly at the banister as she pointed toward the yacht, the cottages, the pool and the inns. "They're assigned to watch me."

Raye laughed. "Looks like they're 'bout to get recruited by one of these hot mommas." She smiled as Tatiana from Beverly Hills sauntered up to Officer Camry. "These women think the cop uniforms are part of the program!"

"Gotcha!" Venus said playfully as Officer Camry greeted Tatiana. "Watch him sign up so she can take him home."

"Damn," Raye said. "That girl could make a dead man's heart beat."

"Among other things," Venus said. "Look, his partner isn't doing much worse." Tall, curvy Vondra from Jamaica was standing close to Officer Brown.

Near them, Josephine from France was being serenaded by her *Rock Star Dream*.

"Check out our newest benefactor," Venus said. "I anticipate she'll be the first of our guests to open a franchise. Just imagine, Raye, one day we'll be at the grand opening of Husbands, Inc. in France."

Raye beamed. "I don't even have a word for that. Just a sound." She clinked her crystal flute against Venus' glass, smiled, then sipped champagne.

But the sound of John's voice this morning shot through Venus' mind. *Could John and his threats jeopardize our global quest? And what if my plan to use the video to stop him doesn't work?* She tilted her chin higher, refusing to entertain anything but victory.

"I hate that those two cops are watching my every move," Venus said. "In my mind, they're like spies for John. If he can conspire with an Air Force General to let the media invade our air space, then he'll dictate orders to law enforcement guys like Frank Williams, and all of his fraternity brothers in high places."

Raye shook her head. "Neanderthal is in for a rude awakening. As my mother used to say, 'God don't like ugly.'"

Venus scanned the lusty couples. "I have to keep everyone oblivious to the threats and other problems—"

Raye finished the sentence: "—so they can all get buck wild *and* help us build our multinational dynasty."

Adela from Sweden was casting a smoldering look up at a man dressed as a *Latin Lover*, in a slim-fitting, red bullfighter uniform. Mahi from Japan and Marena from Venezuela were slow-dancing with *California Surfers*. Mike Rivers was feeding chocolate to love-struck Jane Collins.

"She will lose her mind under him," Venus said playfully.

"Who wouldn't? She looks familiar," Raye said, as Jane turned her back. "But you're right. Won't know what hit her—"

Venus nodded discreetly toward Claire Montague and Billy Jack Burns as they held a knife to cut a towering white wedding cake on a table near the banister. Nikki watched, guzzling two glasses of champagne.

"They're adorable," Raye said. "Don't give the knife to girlfriend, though. I can see right through that ménage à terror."

Venus shook her head. "I hope Claire and Nikki can find their own bliss after this—"

"Vee, check them out," Raye said, smiling as a Buck Briggs look-alike flexed a bicep for LaShawn from Brooklyn, who beamed like the sun.

"Touch down!" Raye cheered. "A girl after my own heart. Venus, I can't thank you enough for the immediate replacement—"

Venus laughed. "Danté was fine with his first four Wives. He just couldn't handle you!"

"Heisman will," Raye said. "He's doing his paperwork right now. Girl, look at this. All these women have stepped into our paradise, and I bet there's not a dry pair of panties in the place." Raye raised her glass for another toast. "To the revolution!"

As they tapped glasses, Venus added, "And to the two brains making it happen."

Raye sipped. "Vee, think about it. This all started ten years ago when I busted my real husband with one of his skanks on our boat. All these men and women should praise the heavens for my divorce settlement. And yours."

Venus raised her arms and tilted her face to the sky. "Thank you, heavens!"

Raye smiled. "We were just two horny divorcées at the gym, complaining about how hard it was to keep a guy's attention, and bam! The billion dollar idea exploded like all the orgasms we were about to have."

"Ha!" Venus exclaimed. "We were huffing away on stair-climbing machines, and you got right to the point—"

"Sure did," Raye said. "My exact words were, 'I wish I could just rent a dude to fuck me silly whenever I want. No chit-chat, no possessiveness, no drama. Just hours of jack-hammering. Big, hard and long-lasting. That's all I ask.'"

Venus laughed. "But your name for the company, well, we had to tone it down—"

"What?" Raye asked playfully. "You didn't think 1-800-DIAL-A-DICK was a good name for our business?'"

They both laughed so hard, they held their stomachs.

"Sorry to interrupt," Kimberly said, rushing toward them with her iPad. "But this report just started airing, like every 10 minutes." The screen showed John on Wolf News Network.

"Oh thank God I'm not married to him anymore," Venus said as the rage burning in his eyes riled something deep in her soul. "I am just baffled by his rabid hunger for vengeance." She stared at his hateful expression. "That's exactly how he looked in the courthouse after the judge granted our divorce." Venus flashed back to that awful moment:

"You're giving up the best thing you ever could be in life — my wife," John fumed. *"You have no education, no skills, and you're staring down 40. Venus, you will spend the rest of your years wishing you had stayed with me! It's all down hill, and over the hill—"* he let out a nasty laugh *"—for you, from now on!"*

Her laughter echoing off the courthouse hallway walls only made his face turn crimson.

But now it was Venus whose cheeks burned with exasperation as she glared at John on the news. He was in his office, speaking into a WNN microphone:

"We are seeking an indictment against Venus Roman on the grounds that Husbands, Incorporated is a male prostitution ring. It violates a number of state and federal laws—"

"He's pathetic!" Venus declared. "Everything we're doing here is perfectly legal and he knows it. I already talked with the lawyers this morning. They said he has no case and no evidence, but we need to—"

"Strategize our defense," Raye said. "If Neanderthal wants to get in the ring with us, he's about to get T.K.O.'d."

"Adam and Yolanda are still in my office," Venus said. "Let's go see them now."

On the screen, John added, *"The federal prosecutor and I consider this male prostitution ring an assault on the traditional family values that make America great. Venus Roman will soon be trading in her gigolo du jour for a female cellmate—"*

Raye held up her champagne glass. "Not on my watch, baby!"

Venus' heart pounded with urgency to stop them immediately, by leaking her video to the media. But as she and Raye headed inside, those two cops followed.

"Miss Roman, we're right behind you," Officer Brown said as he and his partner entered with Gus and Mario.

"I'm having a private meeting with my lawyers," she said. "Gentlemen, you're welcome to wait outside my office."

"We've got orders to keep you in our sight," Officer Brown said.

"Then your orders are changed," Venus said, bolting into her office, where her attorneys were sitting at the conference table beyond the couches.

"Yolanda, call the Pentagon and the White House if you have to," she ordered, "but get someone to tell these officers that I am entitled to privacy in my office and in my bedroom!"

Chapter 20. A Sinister Strategy Takes Root

If John had a tail, it would be between his legs. Because Ted was standing on the other side of the desk, staring at him like a wolf moving in for the kill. It made John squeeze harder, so all this fear wouldn't make him shit his pants.

If Ted confirms the truth, he'll kill me.

And calling Emma in here! What a bastard. She had left the office in a fluster after Ted had stormed out without so much as a goodbye. Then John had cleaned himself up in time for the Wolf News Network reporter to interview him.

Now Ted was back, with his hair combed and his demeanor calmed. But something sinister glinted in his eyes.

"Johnny, tell me what happened while Mary and I were in Asia!"

John let out a cool chuckle.

Damn Venus! If she does indeed have any video, I will get a warrant to search and seize. Then once I get the video, I'll destroy it, and Ted will never confirm anything!

Ted had that piercing, accusatory stare that had made him a superstar prosecutor. It made John's legs feel wobbly as he came around the desk, casting a pleading expression at his friend.

"Ted, I don't know what just set you off when Emma was here, but this is exactly what Venus wants. The day you choose to entertain her lies over our life-long friendship, fraternity brothers and all, is the day that—"

John's eyes glazed with tears. He buried his face in his hand and exhaled loudly.

Ted's tone was ominous. "Honestly, John, my gut tells me you're lying. And Emma's reaction confirmed that she's hiding something. So here's my warning: Don't ever give me any evidence to prove what Venus is alleging. Understand?"

"You have my absolute word," John said, never looking away from Ted's stare.

He doesn't believe me, but he's going to play along until he can confirm otherwise. Innocent until proven guilty. Ha! There is no proof, and Emma is sworn to secrecy.

The phone buzzed. "Mr. Barker," his secretary said, sounding agitated, "a gentleman from Husbands—"

The office doors burst open. A large black man stepped in. John immediately thought to call the police, but this fellow looked quite dapper in an expensive seersucker suit, leather loafers and a straw boater hat.

"May I help you, sir?" John asked as Ted stood defensively.

Agnes bolted in behind the man. "I'm sorry, Mr. Barker, he—"

"Are you the guy from the billboards and commercials?" the man asked, holding a large envelope.

"You know, where they say, 'Thank you, John Barker,' and you say, 'Attorney John Barker, winning for you?'"

"That would be me," John said.

The man held out his hand. "I'm Danté Wilson. Formerly employed by Husbands, Incorporated."

John and Ted exchanged a curious glance. All the raw emotion of their prior conversation froze inside John; perhaps this fellow would be the perfect distraction.

"Mr. Wilson," John said, "You said, 'formerly employed'?"

"Yeah, I just quit. No I got fired, during my fifth gig as a Husband," Danté said, holding up the envelope. "I got the contract, and all the paperwork in here. What they're doin' ain't right. And I wanna make those crazy nymphomaniac bitches pay—"

Recognition sparked on Danté's face as he stared at Ted. "You're the U.S. Attorney! Now I know I came to the right place!"

"Come on in," John said, motioning for Danté to take one of four wing-backed chairs around the coffee table.

Ted stepped toward him to shake his hand. "Ted Pendigree. Good to meet you."

As they sat down, Agnes said, "I'll get coffee," and headed through a side door.

Ted asked, "Now Mr. Wilson, what exactly is your objective in coming here?"

"I was hoping to use my earnings to go to law school someday," Danté said, "but right now I got the most scandalicious case. Here." He handed the envelope to Ted, who opened it and spread its contents across the coffee table.

"These will prove very convincing for the grand jury." Ted turned to John. "We couldn't have asked for a better key witness."

Danté leaned forward. "Hold up. We need to discuss what's in this for me."

"Work with us, son," John said, "and you got yourself a job right here. We'll make you the next Johnny Cochran."

Danté grinned. "I can work with that."

Ted held up the documents. "Exhibit A, the bogus marriage contract, the flimsy pre-nup, divorce instructions. This is a rock-solid case."

John scanned the materials. "We need to call up that young man, the Wolf News Network reporter who interviewed me today. We got one helluva follow-up story — *The United States of America versus Venus Aphrodite Roman, CEO of Husbands, Incorporated.*"

Danté nodded. "Yeah, that's what I'm talkin' about!"

John smiled as he scanned the documents. "How do I hate thee, Venus? Let me count the ways: prostitution, premeditated divorce—"

Danté said, "And if my wife gets with her next victim before I sign off on a split, we *got* the adulterous bitch."

Ted chuckled as he applied hand sanitizer. "A prosecution for adultery. Now *that* would make some headlines."

As Agnes served coffee, Danté took a sip. "I want yawl to prove this pre-nup is whack, so that rich bitch can pay me alimony. And I want damages for breach of the marriage contract. Yeah! She and Venus Roman are through!"

"Knock, knock," a female voice called.

"Gracious!" Agnes huffed, setting the tray on the coffee table.

"I'm looking for John Barker," the woman said.

John and Ted immediately recognized the Channel 3 reporter; they stood.

"Laila Sims!" John exclaimed. She was even cuter in person than on television, and what a body! "How can I help you?"

"I have a proposal for you." Laila glanced at Danté. "I didn't mean to interrupt, but nobody was—"

"All media interviews go through me," Agnes announced.

"I'm not media anymore," Laila said.

"Yes," Agnes snapped, "I just watched you doing a TV report in a helicopter."

"That was my last report for Channel 3," Laila said. "I got fired because I was so pissed off that my fiancé left me and got hired as a gigolo at Husbands, Incorporated."

"Oh, hell yeah!" Danté shot to his feet. "Girl, you definitely in the right place!"

John maintained a poker face, despite the excitement rattling through his body.

"This is a trick," Agnes warned. "She's probably got undercover cameras. Don't say another word until I confirm her story with Channel 3."

"Good idea." John scanned Laila, who carried only a small handbag.

Danté stepped over to Laila and extended a hand, which she shook. "I'm Danté Wilson. Must be somethin' in the air today. I got fired from being a Husband right about when you got the ax from TV!"

Laila coughed. "Fired? Why?"

"Well, I was just about to tell—"

Agnes returned. "I just called Channel 3. Her story is true." She turned to Laila. "I'll get you some water. And cough drops."

"Thank you," Laila said, turning toward Danté. "Now why were you—"

"Please, join us," John said, offering her a chair.

John almost smiled at Ted, who winked. The revenge gods couldn't have been more generous if John had scripted this impromptu venge-fest himself.

Venus is done!

Chapter 21. Betting Everything on the Dream

Jane couldn't believe how amazing the wedding stylists were making her look here in the Husbands, Inc. salon. Four people, all slim and chic, were fluttering around her like she was a movie star preparing for the red carpet on Oscar night.

"There," the hairdresser said, securing Jane's hair in a clip under the veil. "A little hairspray," she said, spraying profusely, "and you, sweetheart, look like a million bucks!"

The make-up artist came close to her face, examining the black eyeliner and fake lashes. She dusted more powder over foundation that made Jane's skin appear flawless.

"You are officially 'bride-ified,' as we call it," the stylist chirped.

As another person adjusted her form-fitting, white satin dress, Jane stared in the huge mirrors under a chandelier whose sparkly light made her look picture-perfect amidst the salon's elegant, pale pink décor.

I have never felt this pretty. Or terrified!

A handful of other brides were getting glammed up in the same wall-length mirror by teams of stylists and make-up artists. Did those gals also feel this jumpy inside?

"Jane, you look fantastic!" the hairdresser said, stepping back to admire her. "Nervous, but fantastic."

"Oh, no!" Jane panicked. "I have to look cool and confident."

Fear flashed in her fake blue eyes — one more thing to worry about! Fortunately, she could sleep in these contacts, but what if she had to remove them and her Husband saw her real eye color?

The stylist lowered the veil over Jane's face and said, "There. When your Husband lifts this veil to kiss you, I want all worry gone from you. Just take deep breaths and think about the most exciting year of your life."

Impossible! Just a short time ago, she and Mike had completed the paperwork in the office and signed the contract. She had already written the hefty check for $200,000 to purchase her year of pleasure. The first $150,000 was for Mike's payment. The rest was for: administrative fees; training; on-going quality control; medical and psychological tests for both of them; tickets to events, such as the super popular Masquerade at Sea Castle next weekend; and the trip to Guam for the divorce at the end.

Cripe, this is a huge mistake...

Jane's heart pounded. She was surprised that Raye had not called her, but perhaps her financial advisor had been too busy handling eight-figure portfolios to notice Raye's withdrawal. It was so irresponsible to bet all her money on this silly fantasy. In one year's time, she would be homeless, broke and—

Quit it, Jane!

She inhaled deeply, and actually smiled at herself in the mirror. *The financial damage is done. It's time to just roll with it and have a good time.*

All she had to do was step outside the salon, into the waiting arms of her future Husband. He would ride her on a white horse down the beach, into the woods to the teepee where they would exchange vows and spend their wedding night.

"Okay," Jane announced. "I'm ready." Her beauty team cheered as she stepped toward the door. Suddenly it swung open — and almost struck her face.

"Holy cripe!" she shrieked.

Raye Johnson stood in front of her, staring in shock at the near-miss.

Oh please don't recognize me! Jane prayed that the veil disguised her face.

"Jane, don't forget your purse!" the stylist called, dashing over with the tiny satin pouch.

Raye stared at her. "Jane?"

"Jane Collins, pretty as a picture," the stylist announced. "About to get her *Native American Dream*, lucky girl!"

"Jane Collins?" Raye said incredulously, lifting the veil.

A red ball of panic exploded inside Jane. Her heart hammered.

Darn it! Raye's gonna think I'm the most idiotic client ever. But it's my money!

"Girl," Raye pleaded softly, "tell me you got a scholarship from the new Husbands, Inc. Foundation."

Jane looked down.

"Jane? Tell me some long-lost aunt paid for this as a gift."

Jane shook her head.

"You got an inheritance that I don't know about?"

Jane looked up with guilty eyes, wishing she could be as beautiful and confident as Raye for just one day. She braced herself for a tongue-lashing. She'd seen Raye's temper; it wasn't pretty.

"I am in awe," Raye said sweetly. "You look so different! Who knew this hot body was hiding all that time. Brunette to blond, brown to blue eyes, pale face to camera ready. But—"

"Raye, I have to go," Jane said, unable to stop a huge smile. "I'm getting married. I'll come to your office to explain."

Raye looked worried. She opened the door to let Jane pass, and followed her into the hallway.

Oh. My. God. Jane could barely breathe, because Mike "Thunder" Rivers looked so gosh-darn sexy and handsome. With his hair flowing over his bare shoulders, he wore brown suede fringe chaps and a turquoise, choker-style necklace that dangled leather strips and beads down his chest. Boy, this place did a good job of training these men! Because Thunder was gazing at her with an expression like she was a beauty queen *and* like he was wildly in love with her!

"Jane," he said, smiling, "you are breathtaking."

Raye clapped as Jane and Thunder stood side by side. "You two look hot and happy together! Jane, I'm glad I could inspire you." Raye winked. "Let's talk soon. Congratulations!"

When Jane looked up into Thunder's admiring eyes, everything became a blur. Nothing mattered now, except that she was going to love every second of her *Native American Dream.*

Chapter 22. Delivered Into Temptation

The setting sun cast a golden glow over the lush woods as a horse-drawn carriage took Claire Montague and Billy Jack Burns up the dirt road toward their log cabin. A man in a tuxedo was driving, while they sat close on the silver velvet seat, sipping champagne.

"I can't wait to get you in there," Country Boy whispered, "and let the romance begin." His arm around her, and the bulge in his tuxedo pants, made his intentions clear. "One of the prettiest brides I ever seen. Never thought I'd end up on the other end of America with a girl like you."

Claire smiled. "That makes two of us."

For a heterosexual chick, this would be a dream come true. But Claire felt like a vegetarian heading toward a steakhouse; the destination would offer nothing that she was supposed to eat.

Instead, Claire craved a future where she and Nikki could savor the dream-come-true of their own wedding, barefoot on a tropical beach, whether it was legal or not. All that mattered was their commitment in their hearts and souls.

Now, if only Nikki can make it a whole year. But can I? Billy Jack's eyes smoldered down at her, and his hot breath tickled her cheek. His lust made her tingle in a place that would, in 366 days, be tattooed with *Nikki*.

"Can't wait to see the little love nest you picked out, sweetie pie," he said. The carriage rocked slightly, causing his crucifix to shift over his bow tie. He smiled with those lusty eyes again. "Sweetie Pie."

Claire almost laughed. How much of this guy was real, and how much was acting in his role for the *Country Boy* package?

She smiled. "Sweetie pie?"

"That's my name for you, Sweetie Pie." He kissed her forehead.

Another delicious tingle... no! I have to think of Nikki.

Despite her outburst at Venus Roman today, Claire had to admit that she loved the idea of a personal concierge for the whole year to make up for the paparazzi helicopters today. She also had to give some love to Venus for helping her find this property to lease for a year, for an extra 100-grand. Located about 20 miles north of Husbands, Inc., in Bloomfield Hills, it was behind a guarded gate to keep the media out, and the log cabin was a half-mile into the woods from there.

The property's best feature was the secret cottage where Nikki would live, so Claire could sneak away and visit her as often as possible. She'd already established her excuse for time away, telling Country Boy that she'd be taking painting classes at a local university. Plus he planned to go fishing on the pond behind their cabin, and twice a month he had to attend quality control classes that were required of all Husbands.

Now, she could not stop her sexual curiosity from blazing in her eyes as she looked at him.

What if I like being with a guy?

Her stomach cramped. The truth was, she'd been curious for a long time. Back in L.A., when she'd dated all those guys to make her parents believe she was straight, some of them had a certain quality that she liked. Oddly, for all the things she loved about women — being expressive about emotion, becoming very attached quickly, and being super sensitive, sensuous and loyal — she found it refreshing that guys lacked those qualities, either entirely or just less intensely than chicks.

Maybe if Claire tried a penis, and debunked the mystique, she could live happily ever after with Nikki. After all, their sex life was amazing. And nothing made Claire cum better than when they were making love with their purple glass, double-headed dildo... and looking into each other's eyes while scissoring... and letting Nikki work magic with her tongue in Clitsville while fucking Claire with a dildo.

Claire shivered. *Man, I can't wait to sneak away and see her...*

"You cold, Sweetie Pie?"

"Yeah," Claire said. Big mistake. He took off his jacket and put it around her bare shoulders; his male scent wafted up from the fabric. She inhaled deeply and closed her eyes as lust overwhelmed her.

I'm gonna fuck him. I hope I hate it. Haaaaate it!

Her heart pounded as the carriage stopped in front of a magnificent log cabin.

"Glory be to Jesus," Country Boy exclaimed. "Woo-wee! You got me livin' like a country king out here!"

He kissed her forehead again. She shivered, and cast a lusty look up at him.

"Well alright then," he said with a low, sexy groan.

Shit! I picked Country Boy because I thought he'd be the farthest thing from sexy...

He jumped out of the carriage and held her hand as she maneuvered in her body-hugging dress. Her white satin thong felt soaked. That ravenous look in his eyes didn't help, especially when he scooped her in his arms. She laughed; no one had ever carried her like this as an adult.

The carriage driver dashed onto the wide porch and opened the double doors. He glanced around the surrounding woods and smiled. "I'm sure you two will be staying inside for quite awhile," he said, "but there's been a lot of coyote sightings in this area, so be careful if you go out at night."

Billy Jack grinned and made a playful growling sound at Claire. She laughed.

The driver chuckled, then stepped aside as Billy Jack carried Claire up the front walk, up the porch stairs, across the porch and over the threshold. As the doors closed behind them, Claire hated that she desperately wanted him to kiss her.

"Sweetie Pie," he whispered, leaning into her. Her lips parted as if he were Nikki—

Oh God, please forgive me. I didn't know I would feel this way. Please make me hate it. I'll just try it. Then I'll feel repulsed, and I'll say something religious to Country Boy to make him not want me for the next 364 days. Please...

His hot, full lips brushed ever-so-gently against hers. She inhaled his hot, clean breath, clawed her fingers through his hair, and pulled him closer. Their lips locked in a slow, satiny dance that made Claire melt inside. His scent, and his hard body against hers, and his strength holding her up, with her feet dangling in the air, electrified her as if Ni—

No, don't think about her...

Their lips devoured each other as he carried her into the vaulted living room, with its rustic furniture, stone fireplace and open staircase leading to a balcony and the bedrooms. A plush, white polar bear rug and pillows beckoned from the floor in front of the blazing fireplace. He laid her down, then stood over her, undressing quickly. Nikki had seen his slim, muscular body in online photographs when she picked him, but he looked even more buff now. His hairless chest glowed in the firelight with perfect pecs over a tapering waist and firm abs. She hoped he was going to remove the big crucifix shining in the firelight over his solar plexis. He never lost eye contact with her as he removed his socks, pants and—

Oh shit! What's he gonna do with that?

The bulge in his white cotton boxer briefs was the same size as—

He pulled them down; his dick swayed, rock hard, pointing straight ahead. Yeah, it was the same size as her favorite purple dildo. The nest of straw-colored hair at the base of his dick looked like something she wanted to paint. She almost laughed at the idea of painting a penis and male pubes; Nikki would have a fit! He knelt beside her, pulling off her shoes, looking at her dress for an exit point.

"The zipper's in back," Claire said. He rolled her on her stomach. Then he dropped oh-so-soft kisses along her bare shoulders. She quivered.

"Yeah, Sweetie Pie," he whispered. "I see what you like." He slowly unzipped the dress, then peeled it off. His touch was heavenly as he kneaded the flesh of her ass. Claire moaned, arching her back, wishing he would quench her curiosity immediately. He ran a finger over the soaked satin of her thong.

"Oh, yeah," she moaned. "Right there."

Billy Jack turned her over, then pulled down her thong with his teeth.

"Sweet Jesus," he moaned, gazing at Lola. That was the nickname that Nikki—

Claire's heart hammered. *What the fuck am I doing?* She was betraying her true love. Cheating.

The friction of his tongue, in one long lick over her clit, sent a shiver through her; goosebumps erupted across her body, making her nipples harden into two points. He licked her like a pro, and she cried out, clawing his head.

"I'm gonna make you squeal all night long, girl," he groaned. His rhythm was amazing. A super-soft lick, then a firmer one, over and over—

Claire screamed as she convulsed with orgasm. *Oh shit, I can't believe I came that fast! He's almost as good as Nikk—*

Tears filled her eyes.

"Yeah, Sweetie Pie, I got more ways to make you cum so good you cry," he said, kneeling before her with his huge cock pointing just above her throbbing coochie.

Claire couldn't wait another minute to feel him inside her.

"I want it now," she panted. "Now!"

He smiled slightly, with those smoldering eyes, as he leaned down over her. His crucifix felt cold as it rested on her chest, but his dick was hot as it poked her thigh.

"A real man should put all his bride's previous boyfriends to shame on their wedding night," he declared, staring into her eyes. "That's why my dick is hard as an oak tree, ready to go all night long."

Claire stared into his eyes, wondering what he'd think about the fact that she'd never had a boyfriend, and the only thing that had ever been up her pussy was Nikki's tongue and their sex toys.

Actually Bible Boy sounded surprisingly progressive. She had assumed that he would ascribe to society's stance that guys should bang as many chicks as possible, while females should stay chaste until marriage. That totally pandered to the male ego, because a virgin could never compare her husband's dick or endurance to prior lovers. *Maybe he'd be cool enough to handle the truth about me someday...* They kissed ravenously as she writhed beneath him, hoisting up her hips in anticipation of feeling him inside her.

"Billy Jack," she whispered, staring into his eyes. "It's gonna be extra good for you, 'cause you're about to go where no man has gone before."

He smiled. "I've never been married either."

"No, I mean, I'm a virgin."

He stiffened. A crazy expression — anger? — flashed in his eyes.

"Don't worry," Claire said, "you won't hurt me—"

He shot to his feet; his dick swayed above her like her mother's scolding finger whenever she caught Claire and Nikki kissing as girls.

"I saved myself for marriage," Claire said.

"This ain't a real marriage," he said.

"Right, so what's the big deal?" Claire demanded. "Why do you look so crazy-mad? Don't most guys want a virgin bride?"

"Billy Jack Burns ain't most guys," he said, shaking his head. "I'm a Bible Belt boy. My momma and daddy taught me morals." Anguish twisted his face. "Jesus, help me!"

Claire laughed. "Did Jesus tell you it's okay to be a gigolo?"

"Don't mock the Lord," he said, frantically looking around the room. "Where's the phone?"

She stood, pressing her breasts into him, grinding her hips into his thigh. He pulled away.

"I gotta call Madame Roman, get me another assignment—"

"You can't," Claire said, hating that her va-jay-jay was so wet and hungry, while this guy wasn't cooperating. If he didn't act right in a minute, she would call Venus Roman herself. Or, what could the concierge do about this? Kimberly had provided a phone number to call for anything, anytime.

"I got an escape clause in the contract," he said. "Anytime during the first week, if I feel uncomfortable, I can bail."

"I'll tell Madame Roman you're impotent, and you won't get another marriage," Claire said. "So come here and fuck me like a Husband is supposed to do on his wedding night."

Her words hung in the air, echoing in her shocked mind. Maybe complying with his refusal would be a blessing in disguise. Maybe the love angels were trying to spare her from violating her commitment to Nikki by having intercourse with a man. She crossed her arms, glaring at him.

"I'd rather jump off a bridge than take a girl's honor—"

Claire sauntered toward him, pressing her body against him. "I'm your Wife. The Bible says it's okay."

"Where's the phone?"

She glared at him.

"Claire, where's your cell phone?"

"I'll tell you after we make love," she cooed, cupping her breasts up toward him, making her nipples tickle his stomach.

"I ain't goin' to hell for you, Eve, tempting me with them poison apples."

Claire busted out laughing. "I get it! This is part of your Bible Belt act. You have to pretend you don't want me, so it'll be even more exciting when we—"

He grabbed his shirt and ran to the door. A loud chorus of crickets greeted him from the shadows of the woods and silvery glow of moonlight on the dirt road. A bird shrieked. And a coyote howled. "That moon," he said as if he'd seen a ghost. "A moon that big can't be a good sign."

Claire pressed her nude body into his backside as he stared outside. "It's a Super Moon," she said. "It's good luck because the moon is closer to the earth than usual. That's why I chose today as our wedding day."

"Oh Lord, help me."

"Bible boys aren't supposed to be superstitious!" She laughed, sauntering back toward the fireplace. "Would it help if I told you I've been with twenty-five guys? So it's easier to fuck a whore than a virgin—"

"No!" he shouted. "A lady is supposed to save herself for her husband. I can't—"

Claire sprawled in a seductive pose on the rug as the fire warmed her.

"Hey Billy Jack Burns," she said with a mocking tone, "unless you want to run outside and be coyote vittles, you need to mosey on over here and do what your bride is kindly requestin', Country Boy."

Chapter 23. Raye Wrestles With Déjà-vu

Raye loved the way Heisman was digging his fingertips into the flesh of her hips as she rode him into erotic oblivion. He'd already made her cum three times, with a variety of techniques, and she was about to enjoy orgasm number four.

I knew he'd be a perfect match. I just didn't know how perfect...

They'd been fucking for three hours since she'd first brought him home earlier than expected. The wedding ceremony at Husbands, Inc. had been short and sweet in the chapel, which was in a round, stained-glass turret at the southeast corner of the mansion. The paperwork was complete; she was officially divorced from Danté Wilson and married to Washington "Buck" Briggs.

While driving her Ferrari home, he had put both hands on the wheel, and sang her favorite Luther Vandross songs that were digitally loaded into the stereo.

After valet parking here at this luxury high-rise, they'd come straight to the bedroom, without so much as a tour of the palatial penthouse, or even a glimpse at the spectacular views from the balcony off her master suite.

Now, she was right where she wanted to be — impaled on a huge, bionic cock connected to this model of male perfection.

"Damn, baby," he groaned, gazing up at her. "I love how you're workin' it. You got so much energy!"

"Oh, hell yeah," she moaned as lightening bolts of pleasure shot up from between her legs and ignited every cell in her body. His eyes glowed with adoration as he watched her tremble.

She ground to a halt, staring down at this fine ass man on her white Egyptian cotton sheets and pillows. Soft light glowed through the floor-to-ceiling, white sheers – which covered the glass wall overlooking the river and downtown skyline.

I am one lucky bitch. Raye smiled, gazing at the light sheen of sweat that made Buck glow from the top of his sexy, bald head, down all six-feet, four-inches of him.

With a sultry voice she said, "Score another one for you, Heisman."

"Goin' for the gold, baby. I made it to the romance Olympics with you; I gotta represent."

"I get the gold," Raye teased, running her fingertips over the baby-smooth mounds of his pecs. "I'll give you silver."

He smiled. "Who you talkin' to? I earned my Super

Bowl ring by mastering the game."

Raye raised his left hand and kissed his diamond-studded wedding band. "You've already got the ring, thanks to Venus working some marriage magic for us. But you need to play hard for another 364 days to get your signing bonus."

Heisman put his hands on her waist and pulled her upper body down against his. He kissed her passionately. "Play like this?"

Raye smiled. "Yeah, play like you think you can win against this queen of hearts."

He cupped her face in his hands, casting a potent look from his big, dark eyes as he whispered, "I always win."

Raye laughed. "Heisman, you're here so I can always win the love game. I get what I want. You get what you want—"

"But if the fantasy starts to feel real," he said with a serious tone, "let's roll with it—"

Raye's smile withered.

Oh no, not this shit. Here it comes...

It was too early in the marriage to set him straight, like she had to do with every Husband. They always tried to use all that stuff about "feelings" and "love" in a sorry attempt to lure her into a "real" marriage and thus acquire ownership of her wealth — and her heart.

Never.

Buck's face lit up. He spoke tenderly: "What if I found my home turf and want to stay and play—"

"Then you've stumbled onto some AstroTurf," Raye snapped. "It's just an illusion that the grass is real or greener—"

"What if it's true love?"

"Out of bounds!" She made a hand gesture like a referee. "This game ends with a trip to Guam, so you can be off to score elsewhere—"

He grasped one of her thighs in each of his giant hands.

"Raye, baby, don't you want your man to say, 'I love you'?"

Raye made a sound imitating the buzzer announcing the end of a quarter during a basketball game. "Say 'I love you,' and you lose. I never say it. And I always win."

He sat up, so that she was straddling him, and they were staring face to face. He cupped her jaw in his palms. "What if I'm 'the one,' your soul mate, and you picked me out of a line of men because I'm destined to make you believe in love again?"

Raye playfully tapped his chest and said, "Then you are trippin'!"

He didn't laugh. "I'm serious. I know we're supposed to stick to the contract, but—"

"Then let's do that," she ordered. "Our contract says nothing about love, destiny, soul mates or any of that nonsense."

His dick went limp inside her. His eyebrows drew together as sadness filled his eyes.

Raye crossed her arms, exhaling loudly. She was starting to feel déjà-vu. Did she need to reveal that his predecessor was gone because he had refused to follow the rules? Maybe. But something about the look on Heisman's face made her feel soft inside.

"Raye, I've admired you from afar for years. I read about you in magazines. Some of the biggest names in the NFL told me personally, before I ever knew about Husbands, Inc., you're the best money manager they ever met. And every time I heard your name, I felt a connection." His face glowed with affection. "So when I saw you today, lookin' at me like *that*, I was like, this is my lucky day. Your brains, your beauty, your accomplishments are unreal."

Raye smiled.

"By the way, congratulations on your award today."

"Thank you."

"So just indulge me one thing," he said. "Obviously you have your reasons for doing this, but does it mean you've given up on real love?"

"Heisman—"

"My name is Buck."

She cast a solemn look into his eyes. "This is the first and last time we'll discuss this. In the past, I've been played like last year's March Madness. Never again."

Heisman shook his head. "No, baby, I been burned, but I still believe—"

She crossed her arms. "Look, Buck. I wrote the textbook for 'How to Beat Playerology 101.' Men are schooled to win over the girl by shoveling up every line in the book about true love. Make it feel like a fairytale until she hands over her heart. Score the winning point, then sprint off to win another love game, while girl number one and her broken heart live terribly ever after. Alone."

Sadness roiled in his eyes. "Raye, you should still stay open to finding the perfect—"

She slid off his soft cock. "Do you stay open to the depression, drinking binges and bankruptcy after your injury gave you the boot from the NFL?"

Something hard, and hurt, flashed in his eyes. "We're not supposed to talk about real life."

"Then don't talk about real love," Raye said. "It makes your dick limp, and I don't like that. At all."

Chapter 24. Scoring a Touchdown for Life

Buck Briggs' whole body surged with determination to make Raye change her mind. He hated that she had gone from orgasmic to icy in a matter of minutes. Now she was just sitting there on the bed beside him.

I have to make her fall in love with me.

He'd been enamored with Raye Johnson for years; now he needed to use his powers of persuasion to transform that tiny glimmer of possibility in her eyes, into a state of mind that would inspire her to say, "I love you, Buck Briggs."

First, he had to convince her to deactivate the Fort Knox-caliber security system around her emotions, and grant him access into the steel vault where she protected her heart. The only way to crack the code was to calibrate the best combination of sex, romance and special moments to prove that he was her perfect mate — forever.

Then we can have a real marriage.

So now was the ultimate kick-off, when Buck would give her what she seemed to love most: obedience to her desires, in and out of bed — along with better sex than she'd ever imagined. Determination shot into his cock; it bumped her thigh. She smiled.

"Yeah, baby," she moaned. "That's what I'm talkin' about."

Buck laid her on her back, then grasped the backs of her legs above the knees. He pressed them toward the bed, making a giant "W" of her body. With her Brazilian-waxed pussy spread wide open — giving maximum exposure to his powers of persuasion — he admired this erotic end zone.

Competing against Raye's steely willpower to capture her mind, body and soul had just become his life's ultimate goal, with the Husbands, Inc. "marriage" as his playing field. And since Raye's playbook would rate him as a winner if he scored too many orgasmic touchdowns for her to count, then he was about to become her MVP.

Buck stared into her eyes, which roiled with hunger for sex and control that equaled his desire for love and stability. The truth was, he was tired of being a husband-for-hire, but he needed the money, and he had no skills that would earn this much cash in a year. Prior to Husbands, Inc., he'd lost his house, his cars and his self-respect in a haze of booze and blunts. He'd had too many women to count, and couldn't remember most of their names.

The first two gigs here had helped him pay off his many debts, and he'd finally started saving. But what the hell would he do after this?

I refuse to be a stud for life.

He was 37, and he ached for the kind of love his parents and his brother had, with someone who would stick by him, no matter what. Someone who doted on him because she loved him for *him* — not for his NFL career or his Super Bowl fame or his looks. Someone like his brother's wife, who nursed Lincoln through his kidney transplant operation.

With his huge cock hovering over her, Buck bent down to kiss Raye's mouth, letting his lips express that this was her last bout with a contractual, detached, loveless arrangement.

Because Buck Briggs will have her saying "I love you" before the week is through.

His every thought, and a superhuman urge to win her heart, flooded his cock to become bigger and harder than ever before. As it hovered, pointing at Raye's bald exposure, it was like a thick underline on the silent promises he was projecting into her eyes. He touched the tip to her creamy wet flesh, then—

Ram!

"Oh, hell yeah, baby," Raye gasped.

Then, as if hammering a million nails to secure something in place forever, Buck pounded relentlessly. He knew his plan was working as he watched the euphoria sweeping across Raye's face — eyes glowing with shock, lips parted.

"Oh shit," she panted, "what... are you... doing... to me?"

Thanks to his natural stamina, and the on-going fitness training at Husbands, Inc., with weight lifting and cardio, he could go like this all night. But they were going to the opera with Madame Roman, so Buck was going to make love to Raye now, then continue after they returned.

"What—" she gasped.

"Baby, I'm not gonna talk about it. I'm just gonna do it. And you'll be screaming those three words—"

"Yeah," Raye whispered — her eyes still sharp as she trembled with pleasure. "I. Always. Win."

Chapter 25. Sins of the Past Haunt Here and Now

Billy Jack stepped outside, onto the porch. His heart raced, and he was breathing just as fast. The moon cast an eerie glow on the dark woods around the house. He was used to all the sounds of nature, but tonight they seemed to mock him.

Oh Lord, what have I gotten myself into? I didn't think this through. I was blinded by desperation to help the family. Couldn't see that I was steppin' from one sinful mess into a much bigger one.

All for the love of money. No, the need of money.

Money that was in very short supply back in West Virginia. Money that would make things right for poor little Ellie Anne. Now God was inflicting His wrath.

Oh Lord, I just hear the word 'virgin' and lose my mind.

Because his sinful fornication with Suzie Mae had violated his own brother's marriage bed, and now a sweet little child was suffering the brunt of it.

Why couldn't I resist Suzie Mae's temptress trickery? Why did I betray my brother by spoiling his virgin bride? Lord, please don't let Zach ever find out!

Zachariah had been away in the Middle East, serving in the U.S. Army, while Suzie Mae had stayed home, working in the town's grocery store. They were engaged, and she was saving herself for Zach, because they planned to marry after his first deployment.

Maybe Suzie Mae had found Billy Jack comforting while Zach was gone. After all, they looked like twins, even though Zach was two years older. But as soon as Zach had left, Suzie Mae was all over Billy Jack, teasing him with kisses and sweet treats in the dark. Even when Suzie Mae would get all hot and beg for it, Billy Jack would remind her that she had pledged her virginity to Zach. Then Billy Jack would take himself a cold shower and pray for strength to stay away from her.

But a week before Zach returned, Suzie Mae had laid on some seductive moves that made Billy Jack iron-hard — all night and clear into the next day.

Now, despite the cool night air on his face, his cheeks burned with shame, just as they had when he and Suzie Mae and their families had greeted Zach at the airport.

As planned, Zach and Suzie Mae married the following week, and made love for the first time on their wedding night. Suzie Mae later confessed to Billy Jack that she had pretended that it hurt, so Zach would believe she had saved herself for him. She even cut her finger on purpose to stain the sheets with blood as proof that she was giving her maidenhead to Zachariah Burns.

Nine months later, when Ellie Anne was born, it seemed obvious that Zach was her daddy.

But Suzie Mae and I know. And God knows.

The truth was prophesized in Suzie Mae's dream — of holding a baby girl — during those 24 hours that Billy Jack had spent in bed with her.

"I'm gon' make you a daddy 'fore this is through," she *whispered when they woke up and made love again.*

"No, you and Zach gon' get married and that's that," Billy Jack said. *"Like this never happened."*

Oh, but it had. And it had plunged Billy Jack into the

lake of fire. Weeping and gnashing of teeth didn't begin to describe how he felt, watching that baby struggle to breathe in the incubator with all those tubes. Then, seeing Ellie Anne suffer for the past two years had hurt him more than any torture he could imagine.

"God's laughing at me now," Billy Jack whispered as a coyote howled in the distance and the wind *whooshed* eerily through the trees. "Stupid Billy Jack! Tryin' to fix one sin with another one!"

But oh Lord, not another virgin!

His head filled with Daddy shouting at the top of his lungs from the pulpit:

"And I say the Devil! The Devil will cast his net to trap a good man in a pit of sin! The Devil will do it! And God is watching. God seeeeeeeeeeees! I came here to tell yawl this mornin', God sees it all! And when a man gets snared up by the Devil, he'll get a double whammy of fire and brimstone! Because God will be ANGRY! God is angry at you—" his father pointed at a woman in the front pew. *"And you!"* He pointed to a man at the back. *"And you!"* He pointed at Billy Jack.

"God is furious, outraged!" Daddy shouted, jumping up and down. "Angry! Angry at any man, woman or child who DARES to step into the Devil's workshop!"

That particular sermon had been especially frightening because Billy Jack was 15, and he'd just lost his virginity to a fast-as-greased-lightening girl in town named Francine. He'd climaxed just as fast as her reputation, and was terrified that she'd get pregnant or that his father would find out and whup him into the next county.

Seven or eight years later, Billy Jack sure had stepped into the devil's workshop, right between Suzie Mae's legs. Now he'd plopped himself into a whole 'nother one here.

Lord, please help me make this right...

"Billy Jack!" Claire called seductively from inside. Her threat replayed in his mind. If she told Madame Roman that he was impotent and he couldn't get another assignment, then he'd fail to earn the money to help Ellie Anne.

He wished he could stop projecting all the negativity from his past onto his new "Wife."

Since I'm already going to Hell, maybe I should just relax and enjoy it...

A horrible feeling wrenched up from his gut. He had the sensation like when he was a boy, and he was in deep trouble, and Momma was gon' whup his tail for sneaking cookies or breaking her favorite vase in the front room.

He looked down at himself. He was a full-grown man. If the only way to help his baby daughter was to "work" here at Husbands, Inc., then he would do so with gusto.

But not with a virgin. I won't be cursed again. Tomorrow, I'll get me a new assignment.

Now he just had to fend off that temptress long enough to get out of here in the morning.

Chapter 26. Old-Fashioned Love in Wi-Fi World?

As the limousine whizzed toward downtown, Venus was stiff with tension on the plush back seat. Worries whipped through her mind like a tornado, stirring up worst-case scenarios.

Death threats... protesters... the media... Danté's outburst... John's hunger for destruction... invasive police protection...

This roaring anxiety deafened her to the excited chatter between her parents and her daughter, and the romantic whispers of Raye and Buck in a distant corner.

Venus wished she had not watched tonight's "breaking news" about the death threats, because every reporter except Sasha Maxwell had a way of putting a doomsday spin on everything. As did FBI Director Frank Williams, who was interviewed repeatedly in the mobile command trailer parked near Husbands, Inc.

Venus let out an exasperated sigh, hating that the sensationalist reports had put worry in the minds of clients, franchisees, Husbands and her family.

Tonight will be a grand distraction. And this week will culminate in victory for me, and the women of the world, no matter what comes at us. End of story.

Right now, 200 clients and franchise owners — along with as many Husbands — were riding behind the limo in charter buses en route to the Detroit Opera House. Venus was treating everyone to her favorite love story, *The Phantom of the Opera*. After the show, she was hosting a gala reception for her guests with the cast.

Meanwhile, a small army of law enforcement cars and motorcycles was escorting their caravan. This outing defied the police chief's recommendation that she cancel it because of protests and death threats.

Our enemies will neither control us nor confine us.

A thunderous rumble outside the limo reminded Venus that the female bikers were also escorting them to show support. Those fanatical demonstrators were now disgracing TV screens all over town with their rants about taxpayer dollars being used to guard the "gigolos and whoremongers" with police protection.

Meanwhile, here in the limo, Mario was driving, while Gus sat on the other end of the back seat with Venus, and the two cops were in a squad car behind them.

Venus shifted; all the stress was setting off a hot throb of lust between her legs. And nothing tamed tension like a good penis-pummeling.

Maybe I should take a Husband — to pleasure me every night. Plus, a marriage would show the franchisees that I practice what I preach.

But it was equally important to focus all of her energy and attention on making the global launch as perfect as possible.

Tomorrow, the clients would meet with hostesses about their selections. At the same time, the franchise owners would have the first of several meetings with international law experts about operating Husbands, Incorporated in their countries.

"Buck, you are too much!" Raye said with a sexy laugh. Her orgasmic glow left no doubt that Buck Briggs was a star player in the bedroom. He was whispering in Raye's ear as she crossed her long legs and dangled a stiletto at the tips of her red-polished toenails. They were comparing how much bigger his hands were than hers. Though his were twice as large, Raye would always have the upper hand in that relationship.

"So Grandma and Grandpa, when I walked out on stage," Christina said, "the director clapped, and this unbelievably gorgeous guy came out. I almost fainted!"

Venus' 25-year-old daughter perched on the edge of the seat that ran the length of the limo; her bare legs stretched toward the opposite side, where Venus' parents sat close, captivated by Christina's story about her latest audition in New York City.

Christina's face flashed with wide-eyed exuberance that accentuated her resemblance to John. She tossed her sand-hued ponytail and grabbed her phone from the seat.

"But I'm so in love with Peter," she gushed, "it's like I don't even care how gorgeous another guy is. Peter sends me the sweetest texts all the time. When I get back, he's taking me to meet his parents on their yacht in Palm Beach."

Venus' mother, Lillian, clasped her hands. "I hear wedding bells. We'll take you both to dinner when we visit New York next month."

Venus' father, Isaac, nodded. "So we can meet this young man who's putting the sparkle in your eyes."

Venus' heart ached for Christina to find the kind of love that her parents continued to enjoy. Now 70 years old, they were holding hands, and even looked alike.

Dad's combed-back, silver-black waves framed a sun-weathered face that testified to their years of walking, cycling and golfing. Mom wore her butterscotch-hued hair in a modern bouffant: brushed back, slightly teased on top for volume, then swooping forward in two curls just below her ears. The deep contentment and *joie de vivre* dancing in their blue eyes, and the quickness of their mouths to smile, magnified their resemblance.

Dad's silk tie and dark suit complimented Mom's magenta dress with braided gold trim. They wore diamond wedding bands that they had exchanged during a recent ceremony to renew their vows on their fiftieth wedding anniversary; a new emerald-cut solitaire set in diamond baguettes glistened on Mom's finger.

"All my girlfriends are jealous that I found such a great guy," Christina said, glancing down at her phone, which she gripped under her sparkly pink-painted fingernails. "I mean, the whole dating scene in Manhattan is nuts! You go out and these masses of drop-dead gorgeous girls are just mobbing every bar and club."

Christina lifted her phone. "And guys have like, a million girls at their fingertips at all hours."

Venus' father shook his head. "This world of instant everything is robbing the next generation of an important virtue. Patience. Delayed gratification."

"Oh forget about it, Grandpa!" Christina groaned. "If one girl isn't available, a guy has only one thing to say: Next!"

"J.J. was just telling me," Venus' mother said, "how technology is killing courtship. I wish he were here instead of working so much. Anyway, he showed me an article about how young people don't know how to go on a formal date, or communicate face-to-face." She imitated texting. "It's all with the thumbs."

Christina nodded. "Unfortunately, the next hook-up is as easy as ordering lunch online. Only it's free."

Venus chuckled. "Testosterone fortified by wi-fi! That does not bode well for fidelity. And if he's rich, handsome or athletic, his moral corruption may worsen exponentially."

"For guys," Christina lamented, "the selection of women is like a candy store that's always getting huge shipments of new treats. They could just binge all day and night and never eat the same candy twice."

Venus' father shook his head. "My child, you will find a man who likes only one confection: you. I hope Peter knows, he's found the best."

"Yes, dear," Venus' mother added. "Never settle for anything less."

Christina beamed. But Venus winced inwardly. She had met Peter a few weeks ago in New York. Handsome, well-mannered and dedicated to using his Ivy League education on Wall Street, he was a very good catch. But when Venus had warned her daughter that this guy had "Casanova" stamped across his forehead, Christina had retorted: *"Mom, don't impose your cynicism on my life!"*

So now, Venus didn't dare ask her daughter where Peter was on this Friday night while Christina was home for the Husbands, Inc. International launch. Or how many other women he was stringing along.

"Mom, I'm not going to *buy* a husband," Christina snapped, glancing at Raye and Buck. Turning to her grandparents, who were holding hands, she smiled. "I want real love."

Venus' mother said, "You have to close your eyes and *feel* a person to know if they're right for you."

Her father nodded.

"That feeling," her mother said, "means everything, because when you meet the right man, you'll—"

Mom and Dad finished the sentence in unison: "Feel it in your heart and soul."

Christina's eyes glazed with tears.

"You're so silly," Raye said softly as Buck whispered in her ear, then grinned.

Christina glanced at her phone. "Eyes open, eyes closed, Peter is like *all* I can feel. I just know he'll give me a ring before I turn 26. Mom, get ready for a *real* wedding. I want someone to love me for the old-fashioned reasons."

"I hope you find that," Venus said, unable to stop profound sadness from bursting out of the place deep in her heart where she normally suppressed her true feelings about romantic love. Now she feared that soul-stabbing truth might whack the giddy glow off Christina's face and cast her daughter into the despondent gloom that had inspired thousands of women to walk through the doors of Husbands, Incorporated.

"I think it's disgusting to pay a man to pretend to love you," Christina said. "I mean, Mom, I know Dad turned into a total moron, but the world still has good, respectable men who don't get corrupted by—"

Ching! The sound from her phone made Christina glow like a light bulb. "It's a text from Peter!" But as she read it, she scowled. Slumped. Slammed the phone to the seat. Crossed her arms.

"Christina, honey, what's wrong?" Venus asked.

"He broke up with me!"

Venus fought the urge to grab Christina's phone to call Peter and—

"Oh hell no!" Raye said, looking up. "Girl, give me that phone."

Venus' father looked perplexed. "How could he break up with you?"

"By text, Grandpa!" Christina cried, picking up the phone. She slid next to Venus, reading the blue dialogue bubbles on the screen: *"Chrissie: Sorry 2 tell u. I'm not ready to lock down in a relationship. Hope u understand. I guess I'm breaking up with u. It was fun."*

Christina sobbed into Venus' shoulder.

"Better to weed out the jerks early on," Venus said softly as she stroked her daughter's head, which smelled like coconut shampoo.

"Oh hell no," Raye said. "Give me that phone. That boy just messed with the wrong—"

"No!" Christina cried, gripping her phone.

Venus held her close. "Christina, remember, you're writing the script of your life. You can create a triumphant scene, or you can let the villain sit in your director's chair and cast you as the victim. You have *all* the power."

Her father slid beside Christina and took her hand. "Somewhere there's a better man out there who's wishing on the moon right now—"

"The moon!" Christina exclaimed, sitting up with mussed hair and black smudges around her eyes. "No wonder! Mom, roll down the window, there's a Super Moon—"

"What's a Super Moon?" Venus pushed the button to lower the tinted window. A huge, orange disk glowed over the city skyline. "Good heavens! I've never seen—"

"It's good luck for you, Mom," Christina said as she leaned next to Venus to stare at the moon. "Anything you begin under the Super Moon is extra magical."

"Good luck? Magical?" Venus echoed, awed at the enormous moon. "Mom, Dad, take a look—"

"We'll wait until we arrive," her father said. "Delayed gratification is a virtue."

"I haven't learned that one yet," Raye announced as she and Buck stood in the sunroof. "Vee, look at this moon! No wonder today is so crazy!"

199

Venus laughed. "Christina says it's good luck, so I'm going with that."

Because if I ever needed magic, I need it now.

Chapter 27. Wedding Night Distress

Claire lay naked on the plush rug, in front of the fireplace, as Billy Jack slept on the couch. He was under a southwestern style blanket, wearing only his crucifix. So much for his stubborn refusal to sleep.

She and Nikki always stayed up late painting, partying or making love, so Claire had easily outlasted him. That had enabled her to call Nikki to reassure her that no, she had not fucked Country Boy.

Yet.

This ridiculous charade made Claire hate her parents even more. If they weren't such assholes about her inheritance, she wouldn't be in this log cabin in the Great Lakes State, wanting something that used to repulse her.

This was also strike two for Venus Roman. The world media — as Claire had read on the news feeds on her phone — was already going crazy about death threats against her. And if Country Boy remained uncooperative, the media would love to run the juicy headline: HIGH-PAID HUSBANDS, INC. GROOM REFUSES TO MAKE LOVE ON WEDDING NIGHT.

Claire thought about calling the concierge and saying, *"Um, my Husband won't fuck me. Can you send someone over who will?"*

But she wanted this guy. She liked that he was such a simpleton, whereas some of those Husbands looked like the world-class slicksters back in L.A. Country Boy looked adorable in his sleep. His bare chest was rising and falling, while the blanket covered him from the waist down.

Oh, shit. It looked like a pole was raising the blanket

200

over his crotch. Claire smiled.

"Oh, Suzie Mae," Country Boy whispered with his eyes closed. "Sue—"

He reached under the blanket to touch himself. Claire walked over and slowly pulled up the blanket. The room was so warm from the fireplace, he wouldn't feel a chill. Though he was asleep, he was stroking his schlong. It stood straight up; her coochie throbbed at the sight of it. She ran her fingertip along its length and circled the tip of the head around the hole, which was wet with a few drops of clear liquid.

"Oh, Suzie Mae," he groaned.

Claire quickly, gingerly, straddled him on the couch. She faced his feet, in case he woke up; maybe a glimpse of a bare back would make him think she was the chick in his dream. Claire aimed her hips over his dick, and with a quick tilt—

"Ohhhhh shiiiiiiit!" she whispered.

His body jolted under her, as her ass glided over his groin, back and forth, creating the most luscious friction—

Oh no, I hate that I love it.

It was different than a dildo because it was hot. She could almost feel a chemical reaction between his skin and her juices. Like a delicious burn.

"Suuuuuuuuzzzzzzzeeeee....."

She glanced back; his eyes were closed. She pressed her fingertips into the place where his tongue had so expertly danced earlier. Then she somehow got a rhythm, a grind, like sexy dancing, with her hips making a slow circle over his pelvis.

I loooooooooove this...

Her temperature shot up. Her head swirled.

This could get addictive.

Suddenly his fingertips on her back made her gasp. Was he awake? What if he came before she did? Would it make a mess? She'd seen his test results and knew he was clean, but—

Claire rubbed herself faster, thrust harder. She wanted to cum on him, before he woke up or squirted his stuff. Would it get soft after that?

Almost instantly, Claire shivered with orgasm. It was long, intense, and amazing. Very different than—

No, I can't even think her name right now.

Billy Jack began to tremble beneath her. His fingers grasped up her back. And she felt a hot gush inside her pulsating coochie.

"Oh Suzie Mae," he groaned.

Claire smiled. All she had to do was climb off, cover him with the blanket, and he'd never know.

"Lord forgive me!" he shouted.

She jolted up and spun around, making his wet schlong flop out as the gooey swell between her legs smeared on his bare stomach.

"Get off me!" he shouted.

"You loved it!" Claire teased, as the salty-sweet scent of sex filled the air.

"You tricked me!" he accused.

Claire laughed. "You tricked yourself. In the big city, you'd be *called* a trick. So quit the moral hissy fit. 'Cause you'd definitely jump off a bridge if you met the real me!"

Chapter 28. Super Moon Delivers a Star

As Venus stepped out of the limousine near a private entrance to the Detroit Opera House, a thunderous chorus of shouting men assaulted her ears. It was the protesters on the other side of the building, where they were restrained by police barricades.

Are the people who want to kill me among them? Did John hire Men for Traditional Marriage to harass me?

Maybe I can show the video to Raye in the morning...

Officers Brown and Camry stood near her, as did Gus and Mario, while Derek and Decker were already inside the building, doing a "walk-through" to check their route and seats.

"Vee, let's make a wish," Raye said, grabbing her hand as they stood behind velvet ropes and security guards. Her family was exiting the limousine, while the guests and Husbands were disembarking from charter buses in a high-fenced parking lot.

"Now," Raye insisted, "like when we were little. Look up."

"This feels silly," Venus said, following Raye's example by gazing up at the huge moon.

"Girl, you know it works," Raye said. "Remember how it made Greg Stryker ask you to the senior prom, and I snared—"

Buck appeared at her side. Raye smiled and said, "Well, I got my wish, too."

"Okay," Venus said. "I wish, starting right now, I have the best year *ever*. In ways that are so grand and opulent, I have to see and feel it to believe it."

Raye kissed her cheek, then smiled at the moon. "Make that a double, Mr. Man in the Moon. I want the same thing!"

Buck smiled. "You two are a trip!" Then he gazed at Raye. "I'm your super man in the moon, because your wish is my command, baby."

"That is so corny," Raye said as they laughed.

Venus smiled, then noticed Christina was also staring up at the moon — and crying.

"I wished for an awesome guy to sweep me off my feet," Christina sobbed into Venus' shoulder.

"Chrissie," Venus cooed, "gloom only attracts more gloom. Let's get swept away by the Phantom tonight."

Christina rolled her eyes. "It won't cheer me up to watch a girl who has two guys madly in love with her, when I can't even keep one!"

Raye put her arm around Christina. "Put a positive picture in your mind, focus only on that, and believe it will happen in three-D." She glanced at Buck, then smiled. "That's my secret. And your Mom's. Works every time. So don't let that knucklehead get you down."

Venus' heart ached as Christina sulked.

What good am I, if I can't help my own daughter?

"Pretty soon," Raye said, as the women and Husbands approached to greet Venus before heading into the theatre, "you'll look as happy as all these women."

Venus reveled in the euphoria glowing on the women's faces.

"Madame Roman," said Josephine DuJardin as she walked with her *Rock 'n Roll Dream*. *"Vous etes un beau cadeau pour toutes les femmes dans le monde.* That means, 'You are a beautiful gift for all the women in the world.' Merci. You and your entourage must come to France as my guests to celebrate."

"Thank you, Josephine! We'll be honored to join you." Venus tingled from head to toe as they exchanged cheek kisses.

When the last of the guests had entered the building, Venus and her group stepped inside, police officers in tow.

"Mr. Roman," Buck said, striding beside Venus' father. "I want to hear how you and this lovely lady are so happy, after a half century."

"Destiny," Dad said, his face lighting up. "Let me tell you all about it."

In the gilded lobby, happy couples streamed into the theatre, arm-in-arm.

I wish I had brought an escort. In fact, Venus yearned for a man to wrap his arms around her, to distract her from her worries.

"Hurry up, Mom," Christina said, standing near the crowded staircase, where ushers were examining tickets to guide people to their seats. "It's about to start."

Flanked by her security detail, Venus was looking down, pulling the tickets from her rhinestone-studded purse.

"We have Box A," she said, handing the tickets to an usher as her parents, Christina, Raye and Buck watched. Venus looked up at the usher — and froze.

Good heavens! He is exquisite.

Her gaze shot down to his left hand as he took the tickets. No wedding ring. This man would make a perfect Husband for a very lucky lady—

The Classic California Surfer package. No, we'll create a new one: Tarzan.

His hair, falling in wavy tumbles over his shoulders, was like a lion's mane around his smooth, clean-shaven face. Venus stared up into his large, honey-hued eyes that were framed by perfectly arched, brown brows. His Roman warrior nose was in perfect proportion to his wide jaw and chiseled cheeks. His full lips looked as succulent as fresh raspberries. Tiny silver hoop earrings adorned each ear. His thick neck suggested athletic brawn, and a muscular build filled out the black velvet tuxedo jacket over a stiff, open-collared white shirt and black slacks. His butter-soft, black leather loafers suggested a preference for simplicity, comfort and luxury.

Most importantly, his eyes blazed at her. His unblinking stare radiated disbelief, awe and captivation. His lips parted; he looked like his breath was caught in his throat. Like he wanted to speak, but was stunned into stillness and silence.

Exactly as I feel. Oh... my... God...

Electricity crackled from her head to her toes. Goosebumps danced over her skin. An odd sensation fluttered inside her chest, like a huge flower was suddenly blooming.

A tone, like her ears were ringing, muted the chatter around them. Everything seemed to fade to gray in contrast to this Technicolor masterpiece of male perfection. But he was far more than gorgeous—

"Earth to Mom!" Christina called as people bustled past them up the stairs. "Let's go!" She quipped something to Raye about how, "Mom is always recruiting those meatheads everywhere, even on the sidewalk in New York!"

Raye retorted with a snippy, "Watch your mouth, girl. Those handsome hunks let Moms pay for you to live in the Big Apple and go to auditions without having to wait tables."

Venus could not look away as this man's gaze devoured her. She closed her eyes. But she still saw his face. And she *felt* him. Her entire being was saturated with a deep knowing: *He's mine. Forever.*

Venus opened her eyes and laughed. He was awestruck, studying her; the tiny spokes and textures of his irises were spinning like a kaleidoscope of gold, topaz, bronze and copper, creating a new, marvelous vision for her to behold with each second as he gazed with almost supernatural intensity.

A delightful chill tickled her skin, yet she suddenly felt hot. And she saw flashes of gold. It was subtle, almost subliminal, but it was there, in her periphery, around him. *Around us.*

"Venus Roman," he said, holding their tickets in hands that were as beautiful as the best creations of sculptor Auguste Rodin. His voice was deep and smooth.

"The tickets?" she asked with a sensuous tone.

His visual affection lingered on her until he realized he was still holding the tickets. "Oh, I confess," he said with a sexy laugh. "I'm a little star struck—"

"Blame it on the Super Moon," she said playfully, trying to ignore that she was trembling inside as if she were cold, or feverish, or scared. Or all of the above.

"Actually," she said coolly, "I couldn't tell up from down right now, either. Crazy day." She glanced up at her parents, who were smiling at her. Raye and Buck watched with amusement.

"Mom!" Christina called impatiently, crossing her arms. "Do your recruiting later!"

The guy smiled, flashing large, white teeth. Tiny lines around his eyes suggested years of fun in the sun, rather than age. He offered his left arm.

"Madame Roman," he said, "it would be my honor to escort you and your group to Box A."

Venus smiled. Protruding from his outer jacket pocket was a magazine folded vertically so that only the upper left quarter of its cover was showing. As a result, Venus' left eye peeked out from the cover of *Time* magazine. Also in his pocket, obscuring her nose on the magazine, was a worn paperback copy of Henry David Thoreau's *Civil Disobedience*.

A nametag over his left breast said Rex.

"Yes, Rex, you may," she said, linking her arm in his as the security crew encircled them.

"Ladies and gentlemen," Rex said to her group, "please follow me to the best seats in the house."

As he led Venus up the first step, Raye whispered with a smile: "Cupid's doing some serious sharp-shooting tonight. I have *never* seen you respond to a man with *that* look on your face."

"I always have the power," Venus whispered back. She cast a lusty gaze at Rex, then a serious one at Raye. "Always."

While walking with Rex to the balcony box seat closest to the stage, she glanced down at her guests and Husbands in the first few rows of main floor seats. Many were looking up, smiling and watching her with this magnificent man.

She shivered, overwhelmed with the feeling that their individual energy was fusing into a force field that made the air sparkle around them. She felt like some invisible part of herself had plugged into him and was jolting her with a new sensation, a power, that she had never felt. And the way the corner of his mouth kept trying to raise up in a smile, and his eyes glimmered as he glanced at her, made it clear that he was plugged in and sparking like a live wire as well.

Good heavens, what in the world is happening?

Her parents and daughter took their seats, as did Raye and Buck. The security crew observed as Venus stood near the velvet drapes at the back of the balcony. Gus was almost touching her left shoulder, as he focused on Rex.

Meanwhile, her gut told her that this handsome young usher was 100-percent benevolent. Glancing at the book in Rex's pocket, she pressed the back of her hand to her forehead.

"Thank you," she said melodramatically, "for helping me escape my quiet desperation, frittering away my life with the details of what to wear to the opera."

His eyes blazed. "A beautiful woman who knows Thoreau."

She cast a seductive look at him. "I've done my share of transcendental meditation."

Rex let out a sexy groan, fell to his knee, and took her hand. "Please, marry me now," he said, gazing up at her.

Venus laughed. "In my business, sweetheart, I'm the one who does the asking."

"This isn't business," Rex said with a dead-serious expression. Though Gus was watching him closely, Rex kept his gaze fixed on Venus. He pulled out the magazine and tapped her face on the cover.

"Anyway, I'm afraid, my lady, that you're a fraud. The diamonds, the box seats... you represent the money-hungry materialism that Thoreau blamed for corrupting the human—"

Venus pulled her hand from his and said with playful haughtiness, "Give me decadence, or give me death."

He shook his head. "Your decadence is sounding the death knell for real romance and true love—"

She rolled her eyes. "Romance is already dead. And true love is a lie."

He stepped close enough to kiss her.

"Hey, buddy," Gus said, blocking him.

"It's okay," Venus said, inhaling Rex's unique scent. It was really fresh, like handmade, herbal soap from an expensive specialty store, mixed with a natural, masculine musk. Venus inhaled discreetly, over and over, filling her lungs with *him*.

His voice was as deep as a groan: "The fire in your eyes—"

"—could burn you," she said seductively.

"No," he insisted. "The fire in your eyes sent me soaring, with my heart roaring; I floated high as the sky, with a feeling that money can't buy."

"Good heavens," Venus sighed. She masked her fluttery feelings with a cool, confident expression as his eyes promised something she couldn't even acknowledge or imagine. They roused an overwhelming sense that she had known him forever. For a split second, she envisioned her spirit dancing with his, because they were finally reunited, and it would be safe and unfathomably joyous to surrender to his love.

But those ideas so profoundly contradicted her beliefs, her business, her life's mission, and her global quest, that they were like sparks falling on a glacier. Gone in an instant.

The house lights flickered, then dimmed. As Venus turned to take her seat, her father handed a gold box of Godiva chocolates to her mother and said, "No opera is complete without your truffles, my love." Her mother beamed, then kissed him on the cheek.

Venus was about to sit down when Rex's breath tickled her ear as he whispered, "Love for a lifetime. That's not for sale, either."

Venus glanced at Raye and Buck, who were whispering and giggling like newlyweds.

"Looks pretty damn good to me," Venus declared. "You should try it. In fact, you could earn a helluva lot more as a Husband than you do as an usher."

He bristled. "I'm not for sale."

"Everyone has a price, sweetheart," she said, settling into her chair. Gus remained standing, staring at Rex. She pulled a business card from her purse and handed it to him. "Really, you'd be perfect."

Guys like him made ideal Husbands. The combination of youth, good looks, physical fitness and an interesting personality — plus the harsh reality of a low-paying job — usually inspired great enthusiasm for such an opportunity. However, that motivation was lacking in rich guys who didn't need the money and were spoiled by a steady stream of gorgeous, young, money-hungry women.

But this guy would make a perfect Husband.

Venus stared up as his eyes roiled with a million emotions. He took the card, knelt beside her, and declared close to her ear, "I'm going to be your husband. The real kind. Forever."

Venus tossed back her head and laughed softly. "Husband for hire, maybe. For one year."

"True love lasts for eternity," he said.

She froze. Something deep in her soul still ached to believe that fantasy.

"Mom!" Christina whispered. "The show's about to start."

A glimpse at Christina reminded Venus of the Casanova in New York who had just digitally dumped her. Not that Rex, a reader of Thoreau, would be so cold and heartless, but he was indeed a handsome young man who likely had a bevy of beauties competing for his attention.

Despite the wisdom in his eyes, conviction in his heart and apparent maturity of his mind, he was probably a decade younger than Venus. No way would a 30-something man honestly devote *all* of his attention to one woman for any length of time — unless he was being paid to do so.

The theatre darkened. She saw nothing. But she felt hot breath on her ear, smelled his essence, and heard his determination: "You'll see me again, Venus Roman. And you'll let me love you as you've never been loved before."

Venus shivered. With the rustle of clothing and a cool *whoosh* of air, he was gone. She inhaled his lingering scent; her tongue twitched to taste him.

Hot waves of arousal rippled through her. And that odd sensation in her chest again brought to mind the image of a huge, blooming flower. Venus pressed her hand over her heart. It was pounding, and all she could see in her mind's eye was that enchanting man named Rex.

Chapter 29. Morning-After Misgivings

Jane Collins nestled her nude body into her *Native American Dream*, as he slept behind her inside their wedding teepee on the wooded grounds of Husbands, Inc.

The yellow glow of daylight tempted her to raise her eyelids and face the first full day of what would be the most amazing year of her life.

She just wanted to lay here and savor every sensation: his breath against the side of her neck; his large hand fanned over her bare stomach; the hot length of his body behind her; the softness of the fur blankets enveloping them; and the earthy scents, the chirping birds.

Oh, and memories of last night — what unbelievable lovemaking! Jane could have cried tears of joy — and sobbed that she was almost 35 years old and had not even known that such pleasure was possible.

She wanted to run to Venus Roman and bow in gratitude for allowing a regular girl like herself to feel even a minute of what this man had done on their wedding night.

Pamela, I hope you're watching, because here I am. Jane sighed with pleasure, which elicited a soft moan from her Husband.

Oh, cripe! Her eyes flew open. Hot pangs of panic shot through her.

He's gonna wake up and smell my morning breath. My hair must look like a rat's nest, and I bet my make-up is smeared like raccoon eyes—

Quit it, Jane! She had to relax. The beams of sunlight shooting down from the top of the teepee were so beautiful. His turquoise necklace lay on the fur blanket, just inches from her fingers; she touched it, as if to confirm that this were real.

If only this teepee had a bathroom where she could avoid being too real by brushing her teeth and freshening up.

His soft groan vibrated through her. He ran his hand over her stomach and up to her breasts, which he stroked softly, while something lower down hardened against her backside. He gyrated slightly, then kissed her neck. "May I?" he whispered, gently pressing himself between her legs.

How would he do that while they were lying on their sides? What if he turned her over and tried to kiss her? Back during her two marriages, morning sex had been nonexistent, except during the honeymoons; Jane had always had a chance to hop up, go to the bathroom and make herself presentable.

Now, being with this intimidatingly gorgeous man who had probably bedded the prettiest girls, she was terrified that he would find her repulsive.

Quit it, Jane! I'm the one paying for this; I should enjoy every expensive second.

She pressed her backside into him, and let out a soft, "Mmmmmmmmmm."

In an instant, the fantasy became real once again. All those lonely nights when she'd read about the Indian warrior who took his bride, and showed her pleasures like she'd never known—

That's me, right now.

Jane closed her eyes as he thrust and thrust. He gently turned her on her back, raised her knees, and pressed the bottoms of her feet into his chest.

"Oh my gosh," she whispered, staring in awe at him. "You're so beautiful."

"You are, Jane," he said, penetrating her in a way that made her gasp. He leaned down to kiss her; she wanted to turn away, but if he wasn't concerned about his mouth, she'd try not to worry about hers. He tasted as clean as last night; she prayed that she did as well. For a long time, as he continued to make love to her, her mind whirled:

Are my fake eyelashes still on?

I'd love to take out these contacts.

Did my deodorant wear off? Do I stink?

Is anything jiggling?

Could laying on my hair during sex pull out the extensions?

Is he looking at me like that because he's being paid to do so, or would he think I was hot if we met elsewhere?

Last night, he'd demonstrated that he aimed to pleasure her to orgasm several times. Now a puzzled look in his eyes revealed he was trying hard to accomplish that same goal.

"Did you climax?" he asked.

Panic seeped through her. She closed her eyes and moaned; he continued thrusting. If only she could get up, find a mirror, a toothbrush and a shower. Then she'd be happy to slip back into his arms and relax enough to fully enjoy him, as she had last night.

But now, sadly, as Jane had become well-practiced during the unsatisfying sex of her prior marriages, she cried out and forced her body to tremble. As she faked it, she fought the urge to cry for feeling too hideous to enjoy herself.

She just wished this interlude were over, so he would stop looking at her like he really loved her. Boy, Venus Roman sure trained these men well. Meanwhile, Jane made a mental note to always wake up with him in a place where she could dash to the bathroom to primp while he was still sleeping.

So much for the authentic Native American experience. Those squaws were so naturally beautiful, they didn't have to worry—

He closed his eyes and began to shudder. Thank goodness he was finally having an orgasm so they could leave and go get cleaned up. Jane wanted to sob with relief and despair all at once.

No! Not in front of him!

She smiled up at him; he smiled back.

"Oh, geez," she sighed. "I know I'm a mess. Ratty hair, raccoon eyes and all."

"You look pretty," he said. "Natural."

She laughed nervously. "You're supposed to say that, even when the beauty shop magic wears off."

"I speak the truth," he said, slowly kissing the backs of her hands, then gazing at her in a way that made her melt inside.

Wow, what a good actor! His profile said he had worked briefly in film, and obviously the training at Husbands, Inc. was all about pretending to be a woman's fantasy man. So he could say he spoke the truth all day long, but none of this was the truth.

Jane shook her head. "I'm just a plain Jane, trying to play glam-girl. You're the one with the exotic looks to die for."

An odd expression glinted in his eyes, almost like she'd hurt his feelings. "The real me—" he stopped himself. "I'm exotic for you, Jane."

"What were you going to say about the real you?" she asked.

He laid beside her, covered them with the fur blanket, and reached for his necklace. His hair tickled across her chest; he gazed down at her tenderly.

"The real me," he said, "is what I learned in my tribe. We honor humility. Surrender of self, for the greater good of the people."

Jane gazed into his dark eyes, wishing she had just an ounce of his confidence. "Your tribe. Sounds so exotic—"

He almost winced. "Inner beauty is eternal and all-powerful, as we say in our culture."

Jane shook her head. "That's really nice, but outer beauty sure will take you places. Lack of it? Keeps you stuck, stuck, stuck. Ask me, or any other plain Jane—"

He ran a fingertip from her temple, over her cheek, to her lips. The tenderness glowing in his eyes baffled Jane; how could he possibly look so loving when she probably looked so awful right now?

"Find your inner beauty, Jane," he said with a compassionate gaze. "It will change the way you look—"

Jane's face burned with embarrassment. There, he said it; she needed to change her look. "Hey, that's easy for you to say, since you're like the perfect man, straight out of a romance novel."

His eyebrows drew together as he stared down at her. Her stomach burned with hunger and all the self-loathing that she had to keep buried from his sight.

"What, Thunder? You look like you can't take a compliment. I wish someone *would* call me exotic. Just once. You don't know what it's like, going through life as the invisible brunette—" Jane caught a peripheral glimpse of her extensions; she laughed cynically. "Well, blond for now. But the real me—"

Sadness — no, it was pity — flashed in his eyes. "As you think, so you are," he said.

"Listen," Jane snapped, "I can call myself a goddess all day long, but if folks even bother to take one look at me, their eyes flit to the nearest bubbly blond in a heartbeat."

He gently grasped her face, resting her jaw in his palms and staring into her eyes. "Say, 'I love Jane.'"

A bad feeling crawled over her skin like a burning rash; a nervous giggle shot from her mouth to stop emotion from putting an ugly look on her face. "No, *you're* supposed to say that!"

He did not smile or laugh. He just kept staring into her eyes. "Jane, you have to say it first, to yourself, before you can believe me or anyone else saying it."

Jane closed her eyes to shut him out and to hide the hot gush of sadness that rose up from her heart. Or was it her soul? Wherever it came from, it made her want to burst into tears.

I've never said, 'I love Jane.' Ever. Should I?

In fact, she couldn't remember her parents ever saying they loved her. Even her ex-husbands had only said it a few times.

The truth is, I don't love Jane... never have.

So she certainly wasn't ready to start declaring that now, especially without looking in the mirror to see just how wrecked she looked after sex in a teepee in the woods.

Thunder brushed his lips over her closed mouth. He was so gentle and warm. And amazingly, he felt so real, so authentic. She opened her eyes and gazed up into his. Man, was he good-looking!

"Say, 'I love Jane,'" he ordered with a tender tone. "If I can say it, you can say it."

"That would sound conceited," Jane whispered over a hot lump of sadness in her throat.

"No, it would sound beautiful. And beauty begins here—" he placed one of her palms over her heart, and the other on her head, which felt like a matted mess. "You have to love yourself before you can believe that anyone else can love you."

Jane really didn't need this gorgeous hunk to lecture her about inner beauty. He had no idea what it was like—

"As a child," he said softly, with a sad glint in his eyes, "I was teased for not being like the other kids at school."

Jane's heart ached at the thought.

"But my grandfather would say, 'Thunder, the most beautiful thing about you is invisible: your spirit. Let that shine, and soon everyone will want to be your friend.'"

Jane wanted to feel something profound, but that just didn't make sense. His spirit? Yeah, that sounded nice, but she knew first-hand, mean kids weren't trying to get all deep and spiritual—

"You may not understand yet," he said, as if reading her mind, "but my grandfather said my spirit is called Peace Warrior, and that I must always work to make peace in the world. Only *after* I made peace inside myself."

Jane tried to absorb what he was saying. But she wasn't spending all this money for a philosophy lesson.

"May I share something about my past?" he asked.

"Of course."

"I was engaged once," he said, "before coming to Husbands, Inc."

"Was," Jane said playfully.

"My fiancée was beautiful and successful," he said, "but she was so caught up in her appearance, her weight, her clothes. It didn't help that her job put her in the public eye."

"So what's wrong with that?" Jane asked. "Us women have to look a certain way to keep your attention. Especially a man like you. My gosh, I can't imagine, in a real relationship, how intimidating it must be for the girl, knowing so many other women who want you—"

Sadness flickered over his face, but he quickly cast a loving gaze that he must have learned at the Husbands Academy.

"I apologize for getting off script here," he said. "Just trying to make a point. My ex, she couldn't enjoy herself because she was always worried about looks. And since you're making a big investment in our year together, Jane, I just want you to enjoy it to the fullest."

Something happy fluttered in her stomach. She loved his honesty and good intentions. Yeah, she had a plan to stop torturing herself about all the exterior beauty stuff. In the Peace Corps, she'd be in some hot, sweaty corner of the world with no mirrors or magazines or movies to constantly remind her of how she was "supposed" to look. Plus she'd be so busy helping the villagers with farming or plumbing or schooling, that her appearance wouldn't matter. As for now, however—

How was she going to stand up naked in front of him in the bright light of day? Would her thighs look enormous? Would her belly jiggle? Oh cripe, what about her butt?

I should have lost five or ten more pounds before coming here—

"Jane," her Husband said with a tender gaze, "I think you will enjoy being with me more if you enjoy being with yourself first."

Her cheeks burned with embarrassment and confusion. Could he actually see how uncomfortable she was?

"Listen, thanks for all your Indian wisdom," she snapped. "But you make it sound like I hate myself—"

As soon as the words shot out of her mouth, they seemed to turn around and stab her in the heart.

Actually that's true. I do hate myself. Nothing about me is good enough. Not my looks, not my life, not my personality. Never has been, never will be. That's why I have to pay to be with a gorgeous man.

Sadness consumed her. Darn it, if she started to cry, she'd have a puffy, red face on top of the black eyes, morning breath and matted hair. She had to quit having a pity party.

"Before the year is over," Thunder said gently, "you will be saying, 'I love Jane,' and you'll mean it. That's the gift I will give you for this marriage, lovely Jane. It's something I learned from my ancestors, and it's within the realm of my role as your *Native American Dream.*"

The loving expression on his face blurred as tears filled her eyes.

This is the most embarrassing moment ever! He can't even focus on the romance because I'm such a basket case...

Chapter 30. Undercover and Overjoyed

Laila Sims couldn't believe she was staring into the eyes of the woman she planned to destroy.

"It's an honor and a pleasure to meet you," Laila said as she shook Venus Roman's hand. They were standing in the sun-splashed, brick-paved courtyard between the eight ivy-covered cottages that housed the Husbands Academy.

This long-awaited moment roused a wicked cough in Laila's chest; she swallowed hard to force it down.

I will not blow my cover! I will not!

Over Venus' shoulder, Eden was leading about 20 women into the courtyard, which was centered by a circular fountain. From its tile basin rose a 10-foot, white marble Venus de Milo statue. Sunshine sparkled in water spraying up from a half-dozen smaller figures of male and female warriors who gazed up lovingly at her.

"Goddess of Love, Beauty and Sexuality," a woman said, reading a green-tarnished, copper sign on the fountain.

"That's me," Venus said with amusement, still shaking Laila's hand under the watchful eyes of bodyguards and cops. "My parents had no idea when they named me Venus Aphrodite, that I would become a professional matchmaker."

Laila focused with laser beam intensity on her enemy. Ha! The bitch had no clue that she was greeting an undercover reporter with a hidden camera, a broken heart and a hunger for vengeance.

Laila made sure the lens inside her small handbag, which was securely slug over her shoulder, was aiming straight at Venus Roman. This would capture the Pariah of Love in action as no one had dared to do before. It would also collect evidence here to show that this whole operation was immoral, outrageous and hopefully, illegal.

All while making me the hottest reporter in America. Any job in any city at any salary — and any man — will be mine for the choosing!

As soon as she gathered enough video and information to begin her TV news exposé, Laila planned to contact news directors and producers at TV stations and networks across the country, letting them know that she would soon be available as a "special projects" reporter with the most scandalous story in America.

Among them: her former boss at her first journalism job at the tiny local news station in Bay City, Michigan. Over the past seven years, Laila had kept in touch with Sally Miller, whose star had shot through the media galaxy to make her the special projects producer at Meteor Multimedia Network. Now Sally topped Laila's wish list of future bosses. After all, the "M" in MMN was for Meteor. As in "meteoric rise," which would soon describe Laila Sims, for having the guts to go undercover in this scandalous lair of sex and seduction.

"Welcome to Husbands, Incorporated," Venus said with a silky-smooth, deep voice. Her eyes seemed to dance with delight while casting a piercing, probing stare right through Laila's head. "We're excited for you to choose a Husband and let the fantasy begin."

Laila grinned, sucking down air to calm her jittery throat and lungs. So far, everything was going even better than planned. First, she had succeeded at becoming a late add for this weekend's orientation. The registration process had included a complete psychological and physical evaluation — including a gynecological exam and blood test for HIV and other sexually transmitted diseases. While that had seemed invasive, Laila found comfort in the fact that this company took aggressive steps to reduce the risks involved in intimate relationships.

She had also learned that an extensive background check was conducted for every female client and every man who applied to become a Husband. Anyone with a criminal record, psychological problems or contagious health condition was disqualified.

That boosted Laila's confidence about her goal to choose a Husband today. Earlier, Eden had announced that if at any time during the tour or the official Marriage Mixer and dinner dance this evening, the women could identify men who interested them. Now, Laila's luck had just spiked when Venus Roman had suddenly walked up to introduce herself, as she was doing for each client.

"I can't even tell you," Laila said, "how excited I am to be here. It's a dream come true."

Venus consumed Laila in an intense stare that raised the hairs on the back of her neck.

This bitch has x-ray vision. I better be extra careful...
That cough burst out, and Venus kept staring.

Shit! Does she recognize me?
Laila prayed that Venus was fooled by the disguise: big glasses, a shoulder-length black wig, heavy make-up and a fake registration profile. Registered as Mitzi Glass, her application described her as a former restaurant owner from the resort town of Saugatuck on Lake Michigan.

"Mitzi," Venus said, "I sense that you're on a mission here."

Laila coughed again. That motherfucker John Barker had told her that she'd passed the background check, and that her identity would not be compromised by the credit card, driver's license or Social Security number that he used to create her phony profile.

When her journalistic side couldn't resist questioning him about why he had such quick access to counterfeit credentials, he had offered a devious response about "the legitimate need for undercover work in complex legal cases." He had glowered a look at her like, *How dare you question me!* Under normal circumstances, that would have prompted her to interrogate him on camera. But now they were standing on the same proverbial side of the microphone, and he was footing the bill. That was all that mattered right now.

"Yes, I'm definitely on a mission," Laila said, refusing to allow another cough to shoot up from her scratchy throat. "A man mission."

Venus smiled. Did she believe the lie? Or was she going to play along with Laila's charade?

But how could she know the truth about me? No, she can't. Stop being paranoid!

"You've been hurt," Venus said. "It's written all over your face. A broken heart—"

"Me and every other woman around us," Laila said coolly, wishing she had a bottle of water to soothe her throat. "That's why we're here."

Venus put her arm around Laila, who suddenly felt relaxed, even giddy. Venus smelled like lush flowers, and her touch was soothing, almost therapeutic.

Laila stiffened with anger; how could she feel such a good vibe from the woman she wanted to annihilate?

"Well," Venus glanced down at Laila's nametag, "Mitzi Glass, we are going to take extra special care of you here at Husbands, Incorporated. I promise that your experience will far exceed even your wildest expectations."

Before Laila could smile, or speak, Venus winked, and like a silk scarf fluttering in the breeze, she slipped away, into a semi-circle of women who were waiting to shake her hand.

What the hell!? Laila's mind spun in a million directions. It seemed like Venus knew exactly what Laila was scheming. But how could she?

She can't! So stop worrying about it and get to work. Laila looked around. Many of the women were peeking into the cottages to watch the men in their classes. Maybe Mike was among the students.

Laila glanced down at her hoisted-up, enhanced chest. She loved how the U-shaped cut of her orange sheath dress exposed the luscious, golden brown mounds of her new D-cups. If Mike saw her now, he definitely would not recognize her from the neck down. Oh, how Laila looked forward to the moment when he would see what he was missing — *after* she had successfully executed her undercover sting operation.

"Mitzi, from Saugatuck," a woman said, reading the nametag and extending a hand. "I'm Julie from Chicago. My ex-husband and I used to sail to your town. Then I realized why he loved it so much. He's gay!"

Laila smiled, shaking Julie's hand and laughing along with this woman who had pin-straight, brown hair, pampered skin and a very country club air about her.

"Believe me," Julie said, "I've more than made up for it. I'm here for my third Husband. You?"

"First time," Laila said.

"Well, welcome to the best year of your life!" Julie said. "Will you be taking your Husband back to Saugatuck?"

"No, I'm actually going to lease one of the Husbands, Inc. properties. I love that concept."

Julie nodded; her diamond-covered hoop earrings sparkled. "I just tried that. It definitely enhances the fantasy when you experience your man in a new venue. So, Mitzi, which Husband package would put the biggest smile on your face?"

Laila shrugged playfully. "I don't know yet."

"I'm going for the basic *Boy Toy* this time," Julie said, unaware that she was speaking directly into Laila's hidden camera. "I went wild with the *Latin Lover* the first time around. Then I had a *Baseball Player.*"

"How were they?"

"If nothing else," Julie said, her eyes lighting up, "these men are trained to do some things in the bedroom that will make your toes curl."

Laila smiled. "Oooh, I like the sound of that."

"I hope you don't have to work," Julie said.

"No, I sold my restaurant," Laila said. "I'm taking a year just to enjoy life."

"Good, because you won't want to get out of bed!" Julie's nipples suddenly made themselves known under her tailored, taupe linen dress. Goosebumps rose on the suntanned skin of her toned arms and chest, where a diamond heart pendant hung on a gold chain.

"What do you do for a living?" Laila asked.

"Spend my alimony on a new Husband every year," Julie said with a matter-of-fact tone. "We never had kids because we never had sex. I'm only twenty-eight, so I still have plenty of time to find a real husband and be a mom. I figure I'll get this out of my system first."

"Did you go to college, or have a career?" Laila asked.

"I worked in my parents' company for a few years. I have a trust fund—" Julie smiled. "Geez, why am I telling you my life story? What about *you*, Mitzi? How exciting to own a restaurant!"

A bell chimed. All the women became silent and turned to Eden, who was holding a tiny silver bell as she said, "Ladies, Madame Roman will lead this part of the tour."

"Thank you, Eden," Venus said. "Ladies, we've reached what you might call the secret laboratory, where the perfect Husbands are created for you."

Venus pivoted slightly, holding up her arms toward the single-story, white brick cottages. Each had French doors and matching windows with flower boxes overflowing with green vines and purple bougainvillea.

"You'll notice that each cottage has a sign indicating what skill is taught inside," Venus said, standing near a white shingle with ACTING STUDIO carved in metallic gold block letters. "Our instructors have decades of experience in their areas of expertise, so we can guarantee a blissful marriage experience for you."

So many feelings overwhelmed Laila as she stared into Venus' eyes. They were full of fire for life, love and lust. While Venus was much older than Laila, she was more stunning than any young woman. She radiated power and confidence and purpose, announcing to the world that she loved her life so much, she was beaming like the sun.

Holy crap, that's what Mike was always talking about!

Rage shot through Laila; she forced herself to convey an excited expression. She hated that Mike had wasted so much of their time together by lecturing her about "inner joy" and "self-love" and all that garbage. Why couldn't he understand that she worked on television, so she had to be skinny, coiffed and picture-perfect at all times — *on the outside!*

As for their relationship, didn't he know that chicks who "let themselves go" found themselves alone and lonely in a heartbeat? Legions of hot bitches were always waiting in the wings to seduce a gorgeous guy like him away from the woman who loved him. She hated that Mike could talk all that shit as a guy. The standards were different, and he knew it, partly because it seemed like the good-looking guys far outnumbered the pretty women. They had their pick of the chicks anytime, anywhere.

I haaaaaaate that! And this place only fuels the fire by robbing the dating scene of all these gorgeous men!

Laila coughed, vowing to channel her outrage into her exposé. She couldn't wait to see her reports on global television about how Husbands, Inc. was nothing but a perverse, relationship-busting prostitution ring.

"Ladies," Venus said, "here at the Husbands Academy, the men undergo rigorous training. As you know, you write the script for your perfect marriage. You are essentially the filmmaker, creating the ultimate romantic fantasy—"

Julie nudged Laila's arm and whispered, "I heard she screws every guy before she lets him be a Husband. Sort of like taste-testing for quality control." Julie giggled. "I don't believe that. Not enough hours in the day—"

Laila smiled, never looking away from Venus. Yes, she exuded sex, but in a classy, sensuous manner. No way did she look like she'd had sex with the thousands of men of Husbands, Inc.

But had she fucked Mike? The thought made Laila's throat spasm; she massaged it. Something about Venus' aura, however, calmed her. How could Venus be so alluring in a way that seemed to have nothing to do with her physical features? She had a unique luminescence that made it downright enchanting to stare at her.

"Have you ever seen someone with such charisma?" Julie whispered. "I swear, if I were a dude, I'd do her in a heartbeat."

Laila looked into Julie's eyes. "Sounds like you've got a girl crush."

Julie shrugged playfully. "Guilty."

"I think that makes two of us," Laila smiled. Yet she reeled inwardly with rage that she wanted to hug Venus, not hate her. All she wanted to do was stand next to that woman and hope her mysterious X-factor would rub off. *I would own the world!*

"As luck would have it," Venus said, "the men who are training for the *Boy Toy* package are about to complete their class."

The Acting Studio doors opened and a dozen men streamed outside. Julie moaned as several women offered expressions of approval that were anything but ladylike.

"Holy fucking cow!" Laila said within range of her secret microphone and Julie. "It's like central casting for the hottest hunks in America!"

"Oh my gosh, listen to your potty mouth!" Julie exclaimed. "I love it!"

Laila turned to make sure the camera captured the women's facial expressions as well as the sexy men's incredible handsomeness. They wore blue jeans that hugged in all the right places, along with white cotton t-shirts that showed off their broad shoulders, smooth skin and tapered waists.

"I want that one," Julie said, pointing toward a chestnut-haired, brown-eyed guy with dimples. "I've learned to use my panties as my 'man meter.' If I look at one and feel instant wetness with that telltale tingle, then I know I've found my guy."

"I like your method," Laila said, smiling but refusing to admit that she, too, felt a hot, wet throb between her legs. She had always been a relationship type girl, meaning she couldn't have casual sex with a guy. She needed an emotional connection and a commitment that he was with her and her only. That was partly why the whole concept of Husbands, Inc., was so objectionable. How could these women spend a year fucking a stranger?

"I have found heaven on earth," a woman moaned behind her. "I want to slurp them down whole, one after another."

Laila smiled, then frowned.

Wait, I'm supposed to feel furious. This is the place, and Venus is the woman, that robbed me of my fiancé. This hell is sucking good men away from good women like me, stealing our chances to marry the men we love!

Laila wanted to shout at the men about the broken hearts they'd left behind when they came here. All for money. What pathetic, fucking losers! Couldn't they get a real job? Didn't they know prostitution was abhorrent?

She coughed really hard. Hell no! She would not have another coughing fit. That had ruined her career at Channel 3.

But it put me on a path to something bigger and better...

Thanks to another angry "ex" who was her new partner in crime, John Barker, she had everything she needed to obliterate their common enemy. What perfect timing, walking in on John, the prosecutor and Danté Wilson, so they could conceive the conspiracy of the century. Together, they would reduce this place to a smoking pile of rubble. Now Laila was free to pick a Husband, live in a Husbands, Inc. house, and prepare her exposé that would help nail the prosecution of Venus Roman.

As the hunks-for-hire walked away amidst whistles and sighs from all these desperate, horny bitches who had to pay for a man, Laila and her secret camera watched the Madame describe how this whorehouse operated.

"Step closer, please," Venus said as Eden opened the double doors to another cottage, revealing a male instructor standing before two-dozen men in a large room.

Laila scanned their faces. No, Mike was not among them. Since she had seen him the other day during her live report, did that mean he'd already undergone this training? If so, for which package? Laila's whole body ached as she imagined him fucking his new bride in her wedding dress.

"This is Pierre," Venus said as the tall, bald instructor stepped outside. "He worked as an acting coach in Hollywood for thirty years before joining us."

Pierre nodded. "Right now I'm training Husbands for the *Hip Hop Star* package. When they're hired here, they select one to three roles that are a good fit for their physique, personality, past experience and interests. You're welcome to observe."

Pierre stepped back inside, where he demonstrated how to walk. "You want swag, but don't look like you're trying too hard," Pierre said as they men nodded. "You must radiate confidence — *machismo* — in a way that is sexy, not intimidating."

Laila captured it all on camera as she seethed inside. Mike, with his failed attempt at acting, probably loved this. So much for his endless chatter about self-love and authenticity. This was all fake! What a hypocrite!

Suddenly a new stream of men filed into the courtyard, surrounding Venus. Two guys in pinstriped suits stood at her sides.

"Now I know some of you ladies are wondering how anyone can play a role, around the clock, for a full year," Venus said. "But we spend a good portion of our lives pretending. Pretending!" she exclaimed, looking straight at Laila. "We do it everyday. We construct beautiful masks to hide our ugly human frailties. If you think about it, our masks come in all forms. Wearing certain hairstyles or clothing. Altering our bodies with surgery to look sexy or younger. Laughing when we want to cry. Smiling when we want to scream."

"Damn, she's describing me," a woman sighed as others uttered sad sounds of agreement.

But Laila barely heard them because her heart was pounding so loudly in her ears. She hated that Venus Roman was right. Laila had always felt that she had to be perfect, for as long as she could remember. Her mother, the former beauty queen who loathed that her little Laila had loved climbing trees and playing football with the neighborhood boys, had indoctrinated her with a female code of conduct:

"Girls don't play in the dirt. Girls don't cuss. Girls look pretty and behave like a lady at all times. And when girls grow up, they shave and wear make-up and pretty clothes and perfume. A lady doesn't have sex; she saves herself for her husband. You have to look your best, my little Laila, or your husband will leave you like Daddy left us because I got old."

Laila balled her fists. She trembled with anger that her mother had inflicted her shallow philosophies and fucked-up broken heart onto Laila:

"Men will love you because you have the exotic beauty of my Irish heritage and your father's Brazilian blood," her mother would say, refusing to allow Laila to cut her waist-length hair. Chopping it off was the first thing Laila had done at age 18 after leaving Detroit to study on a journalism scholarship at Northwestern University in Chicago.

"Always say you're Brazilian and Irish," her mother said, *"never 'mixed' or 'mulatto' or anything ordinary like that. And certainly not 'black' or 'African American.'"*

Laila always argued that the labels didn't matter because she knew that someday, people would value her as an excellent journalist, regardless of her complexion or heritage. She also thought it was a joke to call herself Brazilian or Irish because she knew nothing of either culture. Neither did her parents, who were the most sliced-white-bread-eating, uncultured, TV-watching folks she knew.

Their greatest talent was to weave delusions of grandeur. They had finished high school before embarking on empty, superficial, go-with-the-flow-to-nowhere lives. Mom had never even made it to the Miss Michigan pageant. And Dad's so-called career as a model seemed to get him more work waiting tables than posing for cameras.

If Laila had not asked her mother to stay in her apartment and use her car while she was on this undercover assignment, Mom would still be staying with a girlfriend and taking the bus around town to modeling auditions that only depressed her because she was now pegged as "middle aged." Meanwhile, her father called every few weeks to say hello and provide updates on auditions for modeling jobs and commercials in Florida.

Neither of them had changed one bit, still languishing in the "starving artist" lifestyle. As a child, Laila would have literally gone hungry if they hadn't lived with Dad's brother, who owned a family-style restaurant and whose wife was always cooking healthy, wholesome meals.

But high school was hell. Dad disappeared, later sending a letter to Laila apologizing that he "had" to move to Florida "for work." Meanwhile, Mom's resulting emotional breakdown landed them in a tiny apartment, living off welfare and Laila's earnings as a clerk at her after-school job at the local video store.

One consistent theme was her parents' perpetuation of the fantasy of Brazilian heritage. Her father had grown up in Detroit's Brewster-Douglas Housing Projects, claiming that his straight black hair had come from his long-deceased grandmother, allegedly a celebrated samba dancer in Rio de Janeiro.

The only trace of this legacy that Laila had detected within herself was her lifelong passion for Latin dancing. Her parents had taken her to lessons for as long as she could remember, mostly because they loved to see her in the frilly costumes in recitals and pictures.

Laila had also loved watching movies with people doing the sensuous, synchronized movements of the Cha-Cha, the Rumba, the Samba and the Tango. In college, she'd seen *The Last Tango in Paris* with Marlon Brando and Maria Schneider, but the 1972 movie's theme of a relationship based on sex seemed outlandish.

And here I am now, at Husbands, Inc., pursuing just that.

This was even more ironic because Mom had always fixated on Laila finding a rich husband whom she would marry in a huge, opulent wedding. So when Mike talked about becoming a famous Hollywood actor, Mom had stars in her eyes, and absolutely loved him. Needless to say, after Mike broke off the engagement, Mom had spent a whole week in bed, literally sick. She never understood that Laila wanted to provide for herself, and that whatever a man brought to the proverbial marriage table would simply be extra icing on her already delicious cake.

Of course coming here had only sent her mother into another devastated tailspin: *"No man will marry you for real after that!"* Her mother had yelled through the phone when Laila called to let her know where she'd be, secretly, for the coming weeks or months. *"I don't care if it's for your career! That place wrecked you at Channel 3. Your reputation is ruined! Dirty!"*

Now, Laila shook her head to expel Mom's angry words. Why was her mother so desperate for Laila to have a "real" husband, when marriage had brought her such heartache?

"It's a losing battle," Venus said, wrenching Laila from her thoughts. "Pretending in real life only fills you with more emptiness that you try to escape with more pretending. But here, thankfully, we've solved the problem!"

Venus beamed. "We're *honest* about pretending! Everybody knows why they're here, what they're doing, and how they'll be richly rewarded for it."

"Amen to that!" a woman exclaimed.

"Follow me," Venus said, stepping to the next cottage, whose sign said PLEASURE. "How many of you have ever dated or married a man who had the table manners of a farm animal?"

Laila laughed; Julie, still at her side, laughed louder.

"Or who became lax about personal hygiene?" Venus asked. "Worse yet, have any of you dated or married a man who didn't know that we like orgasms, too? Or perhaps he just didn't have the skills or equipment to make it happen?"

A woman with a southern accent announced in a low tone, "My ex-husband still doesn't know what a clitoris does, or where to find it. That's why I emphasize 'ex' before I say 'husband'."

Eden opened the doors to the cottage, revealing two-dozen men sitting at long tables around a male instructor and a life-sized, rubber mannequin of a female torso. Its legs were spread to showcase its graphically detailed, anatomical correctness.

"Direct stimulation of the clitoris with the fingertips or tongue," the instructor said, demonstrating with his hand on the mannequin, "with a repetitive circular or back-and-forth motion, is the best way to make a woman orgasm."

Laila loved that her camera was capturing that. Or maybe she was just excited that she would be a beneficiary of such instruction during her stint here. Not that Mike had ever been lacking in the lovemaking department, but how could anyone say it was a bad thing that Venus' empire was teaching men how to pleasure women?

Laila stiffened. *Hey wait, whose side am I on?*

She almost laughed out loud. It was hard to be objective when talking about orgasms. Especially while looking at more gorgeous men in one spot than she'd ever seen.

Eden closed the doors and said, "Each man receives a complete medical exam to ensure he is HIV negative and free of disease, both sexually transmitted or otherwise. His genitals are physically inspected, and his blood and other fluids are analyzed. He also undergoes physical and mental evaluations to make sure he is mentally and physically fit for the rigors of being your Husband for 365 days."

At the next cottage, marked HYGIENE, an instructor was telling the group, "Unless your Wife specifically requests otherwise, you must keep your breath and body odor-free at all times. After every bowel movement, you must either shower, use a bidet or cleanse yourself with a soapy washcloth, to prevent odor."

That elicited more than a few cheers from the women, and Laila caught it all on camera.

Next, at the ETIQUETTE cottage, an instructor stood before dozens of Husbands sitting at elaborately set dinner tables.

"Spoon your soup away from you, toward the outer edge of the bowl," the instructor said. "Do not slurp. Always chew quietly, with your mouth closed, unless your Wife requests otherwise. Noisily expelling air from your body in any fashion is completely unacceptable—"

Laila giggled as the women around her high-fived her and Julie.

"Hallelujah!" said the woman with the southern accent. She unknowingly faced Laila's camera and declared, "Venus Roman for President!"

"Queen of the world!" another woman shouted.

"You're a prophet!" someone else yelled.

The women applauded.

Venus pressed her palms together, as if praying, and bowed. "Thank you, ladies! Your excitement and satisfaction mean everything to me! Everything!"

The energy of the moment was so powerful, Laila quivered with gooseflesh. She had never considered the euphoria that so many women would feel in this environment. If all of them had experienced heartbreaking loss at some point in their lives, and now Venus Roman was making up for that a million times over, how could that be bad?

"Excuse me," Julie said, "I'm going to find my *Boy Toy*. I'm sure I'll see you around, or at the Masquerade Ball. Good luck, Mitzi!"

Laila definitely wanted to interview Julie for her exposé. "Hey, Julie, can I have your number? Maybe we can go out to lunch sometime, or go on a double date with our new Husbands."

"I'd love that!" Julie handed her a thick white business card that simply said in dark blue script, "Julie Wellington" with her phone number. Then she strode away.

Suddenly all the cottage doors opened. Men of every size, build and complexion poured out, filling the courtyard with *Cowboys, Businessmen, Bikers, Rockers, Hip Hop Dudes, Latin Bullfighters, Fire Fighters, Surgeons, Football Players* and more.

The women clapped and shrieked with delight. Venus and Eden watched in amusement.

And Laila wanted to scream obscenities at these money-hungry, heartless gigolos. She scanned them, searching for Mike. Looking into his eyes would blow her cover, because he would surely recognize her behind the glasses and wig. Worse, one look into his deceitful face would set her off! All the humiliation and sadness and disappointment of losing him — and her job! — not to

235

mention watching her mother suffer through her loss, would ignite her like 110 pounds of C4 explosive.

A coughing fit threatened to burst up her throat. She breathed deeply to calm herself. Because losing it right here in front of Venus Roman would leave Laila with nothing but a supremely fucked up life. She would have no man, no job, and no undercover plan to wreak vengeance.

The courtyard felt claustrophobic as men and women crowded around the fountain. Laila rubbed her throat as a low, hot rumble charged the air; it was the combination of the deep bass of so many playboys, pierced by a cacophony of female shrieks and laughter.

Lust electrified the air so potently that Laila was getting a "contact high" — her nipples hardened against her lace bra, and a hot, wet swell between her legs reminded her how long it had been since Mike had worked his magic down there.

The idea of having great sex as part of her "assignment" here sparked a tingle behind her belly button. But she doubted that she could really enjoy sex with a stranger. That seemed so sleazy. However, she'd have to go along with the program long enough to capture secret, sexy video of daily life with her Husband.

She scanned the men for a potential mate. She needed a good communicator, who would tell her (and her hidden camera) what inspired him to become a husband-for-hire, and what he thought about it on a mental, physical, moral and spiritual level.

The men were gorgeous, but so far none stood out. Laila slowly turned 360 degrees to allow her camera to capture everything: the lust-swept gazes on the women's faces... the charming chatter of the men... the triumphant glow around Venus Roman...

Bingo, baby! This report is gonna stun the world!

As she watched a *Cowboy* flirt with a woman, Laila thought of old western movies with scenes in a whorehouse. This felt like the wild, wild west, with gender role reversal and an agreement to spend a year together, rather than just an hour or a night.

"You are too beautiful to be alone," said a deep voice behind her. The Spanish accent and baritone rasp were so sexy, it roused gooseflesh from Laila's toes to the top of her head.

Holy shit...

She was almost afraid to turn around, because if the man were half as handsome as his voice was seductive, then she was in big, big trouble.

"I sense that you are pondering what has brought you here," he said, standing so close behind her that his hot breath tickled her ear.

Laila inhaled his scent. It was so delicious, she closed her eyes to savor it. If it came from a bottle, it would be called *Pure Man*. Because it was clean, yet musky and spicy, and unlike anything she'd ever inhaled.

His fingertip touched her cheek; it made her feel like a dynamite stick was sparking inside her. Heat flickered over her skin; her face felt hot. And her mind filled with the sudden image of being taken by him in a torrid tryst of animal lust. She imagined herself on her back, him between her legs, pinning her knees back against the bed to penetrate her, and pummel her with a long, thick—

No! I don't even know him! I haven't even seen him!

Laila hoped he was ugly. She didn't even *want* to meet a man who could ignite her so feverishly with his voice, his scent, his breath on her ear and his finger on her cheek. If he were an exquisite lover on top of all that—

"You are wanting to open your eyes and behold this man who has set you on fire with a single touch," he whispered so closely that his hot lip touched her ear.

Laila shivered.

"You cannot find any words to say because you are overwhelmed with thoughts that perhaps are not ladylike," he whispered with that luscious Spanish accent. "And perhaps feelings that are so intense that they are frightening you—"

My camera... Oh my God, I have to get this on camera! But it was facing forward, and he was behind her. Plus, though it was top-of-the-line, she did not know if the microphone would pick up the audio of his voice over the noise around them. She had to turn around so he could speak directly into the mike.

Oh, but she didn't want to move. The length of his body behind her and above her — she could sense that he was at least a foot taller — radiated heat and magnetism that seemed to pull her backside toward him. The split-second thought of pressing her flesh against this man who could only be delectable sent yet another shiver through every cell in her body.

Holy shit, I can't do this. If this guy spoke another word or touched her with his whole hand or actually looked into her eyes, she would lose her mind. She tried to summon detachment. That was a tool she used during TV reports to stop herself from feeling emotions that might interfere with her ability to tell the story, especially when covering tragedies.

But she couldn't find it. This guy's heat had obliterated her ability to emotionally detach. She was defenseless. It didn't make sense. All these other men were simply one-dimensional eye candy. Laila had thought that would make it easy to execute this undercover sting operation. She never anticipated meeting someone who would arouse such overwhelming feelings.

And I haven't even looked at him! This guy is a professional seductor. I need to get the hell away from him. I'll tell him to leave me alone.

But before Laila could spin around and say, *"Thanks, but no thanks,"* the man took one step that was as graceful as a dancer, and he was in front of her.

I am so supremely fucked right now...

He had the same swarthy, Latin look as Mike — clean-shaven bronze skin, a prominent nose, a wide jaw with sculpted cheekbones, a broad forehead and large, dark eyes fringed by thick, black lashes. All framed by straight, black hair pulled back in a ponytail. She couldn't see if it was as long as Mike's.

This man's eyes smoldered down at her as if he'd known her forever and had been born to love her.

No! This isn't how it's supposed to happen here! It's supposed to feel shallow and superficial!

"I was drawn to your essence," he said. "I felt you before I saw you."

Any other day, Laila would have laughed in his face. But the air felt on fire with his magnetism, and it was engulfing her like she was a helpless little duckling in a tidal wave. She only wanted to hear more sensuous declarations.

Her gaze trailed down to his lips. They were thick and shaped like a perfect pink bow on a present.

If this man kisses me, I will be lost... Lost!

Her face felt hot. Sweat dampened her push-up bra. Arousal soaked her lace panties.

His lips drew together and he blew down on her cheeks. He raised his classroom binder and fanned her. The motion only sent the salty-sweet scent of lust from the couples around them, and his amazing *Pure Man* aroma, in great gusts into her face. With his other hand, he removed her glasses.

"I need to look into your eyes," he said. Delight and surprise flickered across his face as he stared at her. "*Mi amor*, I am going to replace the heartache in your eyes with joy and pleasure."

How arrogant! This man didn't know her or what she'd been through. And why did he think that she would pick him? His face beamed that she would, while the rest of him came into focus.

He wore a red and black bullfighter costume that was form-fitting, from his broad shoulders to his tapered waist to his long, strong legs. A red satin cape swooshed slightly behind him as he fanned her, and the black satin ribbon around his neck must have been connected to a hat hanging on his back.

"Yes, I have a hat," he said, "and my hair is long."

Laila gasped. That was the second time he'd spoken in response to her thoughts. He turned around, revealing a ponytail hanging halfway down his back, under a black hat.

"Where's your crystal ball?" she asked with a hard tone as he faced her. "Because you're clearly a mind reader—"

"No, I can sense the desires of your heart," he said. He folded her glasses and put them in his pocket. Then he set his binder on the ground. He placed both hands gently on her jaw; his fingertips tickled her skin as lightly as feathers. Then he lowered his face toward hers. She would have smacked any other man for attempting this. But now she felt a magnetic pull from her lips to his, from her body to his, and a kiss couldn't happen soon enough.

"I feel that flames of desire are burning between us," he whispered, "and we must allow them to consume us in the heat of passion as we have never known."

Laila wanted to laugh because he talked like he was reciting dialogue from some hokey romance novel. But it sounded so good. After all, this place was about fantasy. It didn't have to sound real.

Real sucked. Real broke your heart. Real left you angry and alone. This guy, and his super suave *Latin Lover* routine, felt too good to let go.

As he lowered his lips to hers, Laila closed her eyes. He kissed her. *Whoosh!* Her entire being flamed in a flash of yellow-orange-red heat.

I am so fucked. Literally and figuratively.

As a firestorm of lust consumed her senses, her mind spun with panic. *What if I love being with him so much that I want to spend the entire year here? What if I love this experience, and can't go through with my exposé?*

John seems like such a mean-spirited woman-hater. Would he kill me? Could I be prosecuted for this?

The man's lips – *holy shit, I don't even know his name* – his lips plied hers with a hunger that felt like he would devour her entire body until she convulsed with countless orgasms and begged for mercy. As his strong hands touched her back and he pulled her into his delicious scent and intoxicating heat, his tongue flickered between her lips, sideways, in a way that promised unbelievable pleasure elsewhere.

Laila lost track of time and space. *Where the hell am I? What's going on?* Her eyes fluttered open; all these people around them…

She closed her eyes, then realized that she had just glimpsed Venus Roman, standing nearby, watching her with a knowing smile.

Chapter 31. Ted Vows to Stop Run-Away Train

As he walked toward the stone steps of the federal courthouse with John Barker and their star witness Danté Wilson, Ted Pendigree felt like he was stepping onto a run-away train that would crash and burn in a very bad place.

While Ted had mapped out a precisely legal route and legitimate final destination for the case against Venus Roman and Husbands, Inc. in court, John had invited a cast of questionable characters on board. And each one carried his own itinerary for stops in shady places that were too close to the wrong side of the law to pass Ted's impeccable ethical inspections.

These included Detroit FBI Director Frank Williams and his cyber expert Rippstyx, as well as shipping magnate Gregor Nikolai. John had spoken with them by phone en route — after insisting that Ted ride here with him. Now John expected Ted to meet with these men for a "strategy session" after court today.

"After we get the grand jury to issue an indictment," John said, "that will open the door for the FBI to raid Husbands, Inc. and get us all the evidence we need to send Venus to prison for the rest of her life. May she rot in bull dyke hell!"

Ted stopped in his tracks. "Danté, please excuse us a moment."

"No problem," Danté said. "I need to make some calls before we go inside, anyway." He turned his back and pressed his phone to his ear.

Ted leaned close to John. "Tell me honestly, are you behind the death threats? You, or your so-called friends? I will not be associated with illegal behavior!"

John snarled with indignation. The lust for vengeance in his eyes was the same as the lust for sex that John had shown during so many wild nights out — at local restaurant bars, the country club, and legal conferences — when both of them had, in wilder days, enjoyed too many female conquests to count.

I've cleaned up my act. No more one-night stands or multiple mistresses. Just one, safe, discreet lover. Or so I thought. Based on her behavior lately, Janice would not be on board for Ted's catapult to Congress. It was just too risky.

But as Ted had become more cautious, John had gotten exponentially more flagrant. Now, Ted couldn't shake images of John on top of Emma.

"John, you're so rabid for Venus' blood that it's blinding your judgment," Ted accused. "You're associating with people who are too far in the shadows for

242

my comfort level. Now you either get them out of this, or I'll pull the emergency brake on everything. This whole endeavor needs to be concise, controlled and completely clean in terms of legality and ethics."

John's expression of feigned confusion only piqued Ted's anger.

"It hurts me," John whimpered, "that you're questioning my professionalism."

"Save the theatrics for your juries," Ted snapped. "This is my final case as prosecutor, and I demand excellence and squeaky-clean morality at every turn."

John huffed. "Let me remind you that Frank Williams is the head of the Detroit offices of the Federal Bureau of Investigation. That is not 'in the shadows' as you call it."

Ted pursed his lips, inches from John's face. "Let me remind *you*, John, that Frank would be in prison for spousal abuse right now if his wife had not suddenly withdrawn her case! And Nikolai? He's a gangster and pimp of international scope!"

John let out a low growl. "Teddy, I don't like your holier-than-thou attitude. Gregor Nikolai is the reason Joe Reynolds is a judge today. You can't deny that our highly respected fraternity brother has been instrumental in our rise in the legal field."

Ted wanted to throw up his hands in frustration at John's skewed reasoning. "That does not obligate me to lower my ethical standards!"

Sadness washed over John's face. "Teddy, I would think that during my time of extraordinary duress, you of all people, would be on my side. But this condescending verbal assault—"

Ted felt dirty, like he needed a long, hot shower. He turned his back on John and stomped up the stairs.

"Ted, wait!" John caught up.

"Johnny, I'm going to go in there to announce that we will not proceed with our request for an indictment. You lack the mental clarity to responsibly tackle something that could have catastrophic consequences if not tightly controlled—"

John stepped in front of Ted and said, "I've already announced this on the news. Teddy, you pull the plug right now, and you better believe I will take dear, devoted Mary on a trip down memory lane that will make you regret this!"

Ted froze.

"The Hamptons last summer," John said. "You told Mary it was a fraternity gathering, when really you were in that beach house alone with Janice for four days."

"No, you wouldn't!" Ted spat.

"Monterrey, two years ago," John said as if ticking down a well-rehearsed evidence list for a jury in a no-brainer trial. "Conference for U.S. Attorneys? Maybe. Romantic bed and breakfast retreat with a beautiful tennis instructor? Definitely."

Ted's chest ached; he was trembling. Of course he'd seen John's vindictive streak in action over the years. Among his most notable acts were: tipping off another lawyer's wife about his infidelities, after the guy "stole" a woman that John was fucking; blacklisting a court reporter amongst their attorney friends, because the woman had rejected John's advances; and blocking a doctor's application at the country club, because the man had provided damning testimony that made John lose a high profile case.

But John had never had a reason to wreak his boundless vengeance on Ted.

If he molested my daughter, he certainly would have no qualms about destroying my marriage or my quest for Congress.

Ted's insides felt shredded, bloody, raw.

John narrowed his eyes at him and said in a low, sinister tone: "And Ted, whatever you think happened between me and Emma, which was absolutely nothing, you have no proof. As for what's been happening with you and Janice, I have plenty of proof. Now turn around, go through that courthouse door, and let's do this."

Chapter 32. A Weapon of Digital Destruction

Raye's high-heeled sandals clinked across the marble floor as she followed the butler through the two-story foyer of Sea Castle. Jonas had white hair, combed against his head in waves that framed a face as smooth and dark as a coffee bean; his eyes shined with the wisdom of his eight decades on Earth.

"Raye, you look just like your Momma right now," he chuckled. "You got that look in your eye, like you're fit to be tied. Somebody better look out!"

Raye smiled. Back when she was very small and lived with her mother in one of Detroit's poorest neighborhoods, Jonas was their neighbor. He'd worked as a doorman at one of the fancy hotels downtown Detroit and attended their church, where they had continued to attend even after moving to Oak Park. He'd even served as an usher during Momma's funeral there.

"Yeah, John Barker better look out," Raye warned playfully. "My new Husband and I spoiled our breakfast in bed this morning by watching TV. He and the extremely ungrateful Danté Wilson were spewing malicious vitriol all over the airwaves. It's time for us to muzzle those—"

Raye almost said "motherfuckers," but she respected her elders, so she said, "scoundrels."

Jonas nodded. "The Scripture says, 'No weapon formed against me shall prosper.' Like when that no-good heffer tried to sue your Momma about some nonsense—"

Raye stiffened. "She accused Momma of stealing a dress design—"

"Right, and I reminded Mamie like I'm tellin' you. And what'd the judge do? Dropped that case like a hot brick!"

Raye smiled as Jonas winked.

"Hello Ms. Johnson," said two police officers guarding the door. "She's expecting you."

Derek and Decker ushered her inside, where Neanderthal was still ranting on news reports on the big TV over the fireplace.

"Vee, we need to push the mute button on him for good," Raye said.

"We will," Venus said. Her face was taut as she sat at her desk. Kimberly stood beside her, holding her computer tablet as stress crinkled her forehead.

"Kim-Kim," Raye said, "you need to take advantage of your surroundings and let one of these gentlemen help you relax. I promise, you'll feel like a new person."

It was baffling how such a vibrant, attractive woman could be around hunks like Gus and Mario – who were standing behind Venus by the French doors – and all the Husbands here, and not partake of the pleasure.

Kimberly pursed her red Betty Boop lips and shook her head. "I don't want the distraction. I'm holding out for the real deal."

"Well in the meantime," Raye warned, "all work and no play makes Kim-Kim very uptight."

Kimberly rolled her eyes as Raye turned to Venus and said, "Unlike the goddess of love here, who attracted another young suitor at the opera last night."

Venus smiled.

"Damn, Vee, you went from stressed-out to lit up like a star!" Raye glanced at Kimberly. "Kim-Kim, this man was not only tantalizing, but Mr. Literary had some serious X-factor going on. X, sex, Rex—"

Raye and Venus simultaneously blew kisses into the air, then shared a smile.

"Parklawn Princesses in the house!" Raye exclaimed.

"Kimberly," Venus said, "I had the kind of lightening bolt moment that you're waiting for. It was unprecedented. Definitely worth the wait."

Raye froze. Buck was claiming to have feelings like that, but she didn't trust him for a minute. She suspected that he wanted to score huge financial prizes in the game of love, by buttering her up about "real" marriage. Never. She shook her head, but couldn't stop herself from marveling at the look she'd never seen on Venus' face.

"Girl, you better come back to your senses," Raye warned. "We don't play like that."

A somber expression washed over Venus' face, but it did not extinguish the fire in her eyes. "Like I said last night, I always have the power. So do you."

"That's what I'm talkin' about," Raye said.

Kimberly turned off the TV and said, "Venus, all the costumes are set out in the ballroom for the couples to choose for the Masquerade Ball. We need to go over the menu—"

Venus nodded. "Thank you, Kimberly. Can you give me about twenty minutes with Raye?"

"I'll check on the breakfast," Kimberly said, slinking past Mario's beefy chest as he opened the door to the terrace and she slipped outside.

Excited chatter, classical music and the scent of coffee and maple syrup burst inside as Raye glimpsed the sunny terrace. It bustled with wait staff as franchisees enjoyed omelets, French toast and fruit at umbrella tables.

"Damn, all this security," Raye said as Mario closed the door. "I almost fell over when I saw that trailer with the Homeland Security logo. And the squad car at the front door."

"It's only temporary," Venus said, pulling the blinds closed and locking the office door. "Because we're about to annihilate Enemy Number One—"

"How?"

Venus pushed a button to close the drapes. The room darkened as she said, "Gus, Mario, allow no one to enter." They nodded.

Venus pulled a laptop computer and a DVD from her desk drawer.

"This is our weapon of digital destruction," Venus said, inserting the DVD, which appeared on the screen as an icon called JOHNVIDEO.

"Oh Vee, tell me you have a sex tape!" Raye exclaimed. "Is he with a stripper? Another man?"

Venus shook her head. "No, I never told you about this, but when I decided to divorce John, I wanted leverage for court. Proof that he was cheating on me. So I hid a video camera in his briefcase."

As Venus clicked on the DVD, it opened to reveal a file that was also called JOHNVIDEO. She pushed "play" and said, "You'll see, he put the briefcase on the dresser facing the bed."

"I can't wait!" Raye watched as the screen showed an empty bed in a luxurious hotel room. A girl's voice said:

"My dad would have a coronary—"

"Sweet young thing," a man said. "Your daddy asked me to take care of you while he and your mom are in Asia. I'm simply honoring his request."

"Whaaattt?!?!?" Raye's eyes grew wide. "That's Neanderthal's voice! And she sounds like jail bait!"

The video showed John, nude with an erection, standing beside the bed.

"Come here, Emma," he said. A big-busted teenaged girl in a school uniform — short plaid skirt, white knee socks, white blouse and blue sweater — appeared beside him.

Raye's mouth dropped open. "Emma Pendigree!"

"You know what I like," Emma said, stripping naked to expose womanly C-cups and a shaved hoochie.

"Your daddy doesn't need to know what a horny little bitch he's got for a daughter," John said as he laid Emma on the bed. He spread her legs and dove face-first into her crotch. Then he raised his head, and smiled devilishly with glistening lips. "I'm gonna fuck you 'til you can't walk across this room, little girl."

Emma playfully smacked his head, pushed him back between her legs and ordered, "Eat like your life depends on it."

Raye made a retching sound. "My egg white omelet and oatmeal will not look nice on your hard wood floor."

Then she grinned. "Vee, they might've used cannons back when this place was built, but we're about to fight back digital-style!"

Venus beamed. They blew air kisses.

"How old was Emma?" Raye asked. "He could get prosecuted for statutory rape."

Venus shook her head. "This happened right after that Valentine's Day from hell. John said he had a business trip, but I knew better, so I planted some hidden cameras."

Raye made another retching sound as the video showed John having intercourse with the girl. She remembered the big birthday party that Venus and John had hosted at the country club for Emma's eighteenth birthday while her parents were away.

"Ted is gonna kick his ass all the way back to China," Raye said, watching their bodies move in rhythm. "They look like this is nothing new."

Venus crossed her arms. "I'm stunned by his hypocrisy. Making bogus claims against *us* for prostitution, when he's the child molester, betraying his best friend's trust. It's beyond despicable on every level."

Raye snatched her phone from her purse. "Indictment

my ass. It's time to obliterate Neanderthal with the click of a mouse."

As they watched with disgust, Raye said, "Vee, let's have my brother anonymously upload this onto the Internet, it'll go viral, and the most popular lawyer in town will be exposed as a perverted pedophile. He'll be ruined under a tsunami of Internet outrage!"

Raye's stomach flipped with excitement. Her thumb pressed a single key to speed-dial Whittaker.

"When Ted sees this," Raye said as her brother's number rang, "he'll be John's judge, jury and executioner. Then he'll go to prison—"

"Exactly," Venus said. "But Raye, wait—"

"Hey Queen Raye!" Whittaker exclaimed through the phone. Raye smiled at his loving tone as he said her childhood nickname. But Venus looked so stressed, Raye mouthed, "What?"

"Hang up," Vee said. "Let's talk about how to proceed."

Raye shook her head. "Whittaker, let me call you in a minute."

"Okay," he said. "I'm actually on my way back to Sea Castle to check on the new firewalls."

"Fabulous," Raye said. "I'm here. See you in a few." She hung up and glared at Venus. "You are *not* gonna punk out on me, girl. You just showed me this for a reason, so—"

Venus crossed her arms. "I was thinking of releasing the video with more of a mainstream media approach. Like with Sasha Maxwell at MMN."

Raye grimaced as the video showed John's bare butt moving up and down between Emma's legs. "It's so graphic! What if her producers play it safe, and don't air it right away, because they have to get lawyers involved?''

Venus shook her head. "I feel strongly that Sasha Maxwell would do whatever she can to help us. Fast."

"Neanderthal is so sneaky," Raye exclaimed, "he might know someone at MMN who could—"

"No, his contacts are at Wolf Network—"

"Vee, we don't have a second to waste!" Raye trembled with urgency. "Haven't you watched the news? John's coming after us like a pit bull!"

Venus nodded. "That's why I want Sasha to expose this on her program. The Goddess Show is bold, yet since it's on MMN, it's sanctioned by a respected news organization, so no one can claim the video is fake—"

"I say her *and* Whittaker, for a double-whammy," Raye said.

"I want to keep Whittaker's hands clean," Venus said. "And I think Sasha will help us in a way we just haven't thought of. I'm so impressed with her, I've granted her exclusive rights to interview me Sunday night at the awards ceremony, and to emcee the Masquerade Ball."

"Cool, she's definitely a kindred sister," Raye said, scrolling through her phone contacts. "I still have her producer's number. They invited me on her show tomorrow, to talk about being *Financial Advisor of the Year*. Here's the number—"

"Raye, wait," Venus said.

"Now what?" Raye snapped.

"Yolanda and Adam are coming so I can show them," Venus said.

Raye stomped her right foot. "Vee, those candy-asses will say, 'Don't do it.' And we can't waste a minute!"

Venus shook her head. "Thirty minutes won't hurt us. But since my lawyers warned me about using it during the divorce—"

"This is different!" Raye's pulse pounded with anger. "What? Are you worried about Christina and J.J. seeing this? What good will you be to them if John gets his way and sends you to prison?"

Venus exhaled loudly. "Of course I'm worried about

the kids. But I need to make certain that there's no legal risk for me—"

"There's a HUGE risk," Raye snapped, "if your lawyers try to play it safe, as usual, and veto the idea altogether. Meanwhile, Neanderthal, Ted and whoever else are ganging up against us!"

Venus looked pale. She closed her eyes.

"Vee! We're the bold bitches who built Husbands, Incorporated! We need to act now to save it, by striking back bigger and bolder. We can make John sit down and shut the fuck up!"

Raye glanced at the disgusting video.

I should get a copy and just handle this myself. I'll call Whittaker and Sasha. Then we can just move past this little bump in the road and win this battle.

But Venus looked determined as she said, "They'll be here any minute."

Raye fumed. "Vee, we've got clients to serve and Husbands to hire! Think of all the miserable women out there — around the world! — waiting for us to show them the better way."

Venus tapped a key that made the time flash over the center of the screen, which was still showing John's bare behind.

"Yeah, time is up for his ass," Raye said.

"Raye," Venus said, "since we have so much at stake, the lawyers need to tell me the best strategy, so it can't backfire on us—"

"Doesn't matter," Raye said, "because the damage would be done to John and Ted instantly." She glanced down; her phone displayed the number for Sasha's producer.

"Yeah, Daddy, I like that," Emma moaned.

Neanderthal responded with a grunt.

"Gross," Raye said. "Vee, how many back-up copies do you have?"

252

"Two. On flash drives in my bedroom vault."

"When's the last time you looked at them?"

"It's been years," Venus said.

"We should make sure they're still good," Raye said, "and make more back-up copies. Can't be too careful."

Gus announced, "Venus, the lawyers are here."

Raye stiffened. "Vee, I don't give a damn what they say. This video is our only trump card. Playing it to beat Neanderthal guarantees that we win."

As the lawyers entered, Venus pushed keys on the laptop. "Eject," she said. "I'll show the video on the big TV screen for them. Ugh, why isn't the eject function working?"

Raye's heart pounded. "Vee, maybe Kimberly should do it—"

Beep! The computer hummed.

Raye gasped. "What the hell does that mean?"

Venus turned pale. A red message flashed across the screen: DISK ERASED.

"No!" Venus shouted. She clicked on the disk.

Red letters announced: DISK BLANK.

"Oh hell no!" Raye snapped. "Vee, go get the flash drives. They better still work, or we are jacked!"

Chapter 33. From the Fryin' Pan into the Fire

I'm trapped.

Billy Jack stared at the fishing pole that he was holding over the large pond behind the log cabin.

Our house of sin.

From the outside looking in, he was living on Easy Street. Yeah, Easy Street paved with gold.

Here he was, shacked up with his "Wife" for a year, and all he had to do was fuck, fish and cook, then get paid what would be a king's ransom back home.

"But I jumped feet first into Satan's lake of fire," he said out loud as a bird screeched above him.

He just couldn't believe that Madame Roman was showing no mercy on his situation. This morning when Claire had let him use her cell phone, the CEO had laughed when he confessed that his personal morals prevented him from having sex with a virgin.

Rather than sympathize, she'd said the problem with the paparazzi helicopters that interrupted the wedding had obligated her to take extra special care of Claire.

"Billy Jack," Madame Roman said, "if you perform as Claire's Husband above and beyond what she expects of you, then I will personally add a $25,000 bonus to your payment at the end of the marriage. It's imperative that Claire's experience here is nothing short of extraordinary."

It was like that lady didn't even care that he was having a problem. All that mattered was making Claire happy. The women at this place, they were ruthless.

Lord help us... The world would be mighty scary if women were in charge.

Actually women *were* in charge. All his life, he'd watched Daddy try to keep Momma happy by working himself darn near to death down at the mill while he built up the church enough to quit his day job. Momma had rewarded him by keeping good, hot food on the table, with a steady supply of his favorite peach cobbler.

And if the sounds coming from their bedroom were any indication, she was keeping things hot in there, too. In fact, Momma seemed to have magic powers over Daddy, with just a look in her eye or the way she touched him or changed the tone of her voice. The bottom line was, Momma always got her way.

Now, a hot wave of shame rippled through him. *I'm so glad Momma and Daddy aren't here to see what I got myself into ... even though it's even worse 'cause they can see everything from heaven.*

Daddy was right, and he'd said it many times in his sermons: starting with Adam, all men were cursed to fall prey to a woman's wiles. If Suzie Mae hadn't had so much power over Billy Jack's mind and body, he would have resisted her temptation to climb into bed and break number seven of The Ten Commandments. Though he hadn't consulted with a minister about it, Billy Jack was certain that her engagement to Zach had made their sexual relations count as adultery.

Still, it wasn't fair, how much power the women had over the male species. They were so pretty and they smelled so good. They didn't hardly have to do anything but cast one of them sultry looks a guy's way, and shove their bosoms up—

Billy Jack's dick turned rock-hard, right here on the fishing dock. It drove him crazy to remember how Suzie Mae had the prettiest nipples in the middle of all that round, creamy skin—

"Lord, help me," he sighed as two green dragonflies whizzed past.

He had prayed for help this morning, but apparently the Lord was busy, because Billy Jack Burns did not get delivered from temptation. After dreaming of Suzie Mae all night, and indulging his lust by blowing his jism up into his new "Wife," he woke up this morning to find his cock taunting him something terrible. And there was that Medusa-haired Jezebel, standing there with her pretty titties pointing right at him, and that tight little puss—

He shook his head, trying to stop the memory of last night and this morning. Lucifer's lust had overwhelmed him, and he'd taken to thrusting like all his anger and regret

255

and worry and fear had become jet fuel inside his veins, and he suddenly had super human stamina.

Can't believe I fucked her for four hours straight. And the little bitch loved it! Sweetie Pie, my ass. She's as fast as greased lightening.

He had to praise God that he could escape to this fishing spot. His behavior this morning had shown Claire that he obviously no longer had a problem with making love to her. No wonder she had let him use the phone and showed him where the land line was. He probably sounded so confused, saying he couldn't fuck a virgin when he'd just spent all morning drilling into her like he would strike oil.

Actually, he *had* struck it a little richer. Now that Madame Roman had promised him another 25-grand – which could only help Ellie Anne — he felt like the devil had given him a free pass to be as heathen as he wanted to be. But what had Claire meant about him hating to meet the "real" her?

He sure didn't like that she was treating him like a prisoner when it came to using the phone. Thank God she'd been kind enough to allow him to also call home.

"Unka Bill!" Ellie Anne cooed. Her sweet little voice melted his heart. He made goofy noises and she giggled, but she started to wheeze, and had to go take her breathing treatment.

Then and now, Billy Jack's heart ached.

I wish I could take the pain for her.

His mind fast-forwarded 12 long months to the day when he would receive those checks. Lord, why didn't Zach's medical benefits cover his baby's treatments? Why was the world set up with the "haves" and the "have-nots"? Why couldn't everybody get the medical help they needed, especially a baby girl who hadn't done nothin' to nobody to deserve all that suffering?

Suzie Mae and Zach were on a long waiting list at a special hospital foundation that gave money to poor children who needed expensive, life-saving medical care. Meanwhile, Ellie Anne wheezed, coughed and just laid there sometimes, staring off into nowhere. The rare lung disorder made her so susceptible to infections, she'd taken ill with pneumonia last Christmas and almost died.

God please help my baby survive 363 more days until I can get them this money...

He prayed that he wouldn't need to sell himself to the devil for a second or third time.

He stared blankly at the pond. It was so smooth around his line, it looked like glass. Madame Roman said it was stocked with all kinds of fish, and it would make his day to catch some. He'd promised Claire that he would whip up his grandmomma's secret batter recipe, so he could fry her some fish in that gourmet kitchen.

That's how I feel. Like a fish. Caught and thrown in the fire. By my own sorry hand.

Chapter 34. A Bride's Erotic Interlude #2

Claire hurried up on the porch of Nikki's cabin, which was nestled in the woods on a path that was just a five-minute walk from the log cabin.

"Nikki, Boo, I'm here!" Claire rang the doorbell as her heart pounded with excitement to see and touch her beloved. Every inch of her ached to hold her close, look in her eyes, and hear her voice.

So glad I snuck away from Country Boy. He was fishing on their pond, after promising that he'd cook his catch for dinner, and that it would be the best fish she'd ever had.

She thought he would cum on himself when he first saw their kitchen's stainless steel, restaurant-grade stove, the double refrigerator and the expansive island. *"Thank you, Jesus, for deliverin' me into my dream kitchen,"* he said, *running his fingertips over the granite countertops and red knobs on the stove. "I'm gon' piddle around in here all day long."*

If he really could cook, that would be an extra bonus, because Claire couldn't find her way around a stove to save her life. Back in L.A., she and Nikki either ate out, got take-out, or threw together easy salads. As for now, she just hoped that Nikki couldn't see, taste or smell that she'd been fucking Billy Jack all morning.

She'd kill me...

"Nikki!"

The door swung open.

"Oh hell, yeah," Claire moaned. "You look delicious."

Nikki's eyes sparkled with excitement and love. She was wearing faded denim Daisy Duke shorts that showed off her creamy thighs, a swath of her toned stomach and the starburst of diamonds in her pierced belly button. Her tiny white cotton tank top pushed up her tits and caused enough friction to make her nipples point right through.

Claire was sure she would explode with the noxious mix of lust, love and guilt churning inside her.

Fuck! How can I leave my sexy Nikk-Nikk here in the woods while I'm off fucking Country Boy for a whole year – all for money?

But without money, we'd be screwed.

Like I've been all morning. Claire's coochie was still hot, wet and swollen from all that incredible hetero sex. Afterwards, she had soaked in the bathtub for a long time, hoping all of his stuff had come out of Lola. She'd washed her hair, scrubbed her skin, brushed her teeth and gargled over and over to make sure every trace of him was gone.

Then she'd spent an hour painting, to let her body cool down before heading over here.

But how could she do this for 12 more months? What if she loved his dick so much, she wanted it all the time? Would the novelty wear off? Could she lose her appetite for him altogether?

Now, as she devoured Nikk-Nikk with her eyes, a lifetime of emotion coursed through her. She was closer to Nikki than anyone in the whole world. As a child, when her parents left her in the care of nannies in the Bel Air mansion while they traveled the world, it was Nikki who'd spend the night and snuggle close while she slept. Claire had convinced her parents to pay for Nikki to attend private school with her. They'd learned to drive together. Laughed, cried and shared their deepest secrets and dreams.

So why the hell would I jeopardize that by fucking Billy Jack?

Yeah, he made her cum all over the bed, but it was just physical. Claire's twisted state of mind reminded her of hetero chicks who just wanted to "try" lesbian sex. No relationship, no emotional intimacy, just slurping on other females to satisfy their curiosity. Nikki and Claire had too many friends who'd gotten snared into those dead-end hook-ups. They always felt used and frustrated, especially if the straight chick acted like she was questioning whether she were gay. It wasn't fair, but Claire couldn't blame a chick for wanting to explore, just like she was doing with her Husband right now.

Besides, her relationship with Nikki was crystal clear. The deep emotion that Claire felt, just standing here with Nikki, reminded her that the physical pleasure they shared saturated down to her soul.

Maybe I can have them both at the same time.

If she could convince Nikki to try a threesome, then Country Boy would love it so much, they could "come out" to him and Nikki could hang out — maybe even sleep —

with them in the log cabin. Then, when this was all over, they would never have a dude again.

Now, Nikki's eyes blazed as she stepped close. Claire inhaled her soft perfume as their parted lips brushed lightly. Nikki's tongue slipped into Claire's open mouth, and that set off fireworks.

Nikki led her upstairs to her white bed draped with mosquito netting. It contrasted with the lacquered pine of the walls and bedposts made of tree trunks. On the fluffy comforter laid their favorite double-headed dildo, which was like two penises fused at the bases, to pleasure them simultaneously. Candles glowed inside the stone fireplace as sensuous music and a sultry female singer created an über-sexy vibe.

Claire ran her hands down Nikki's shorts, over the soft curves of her exposed ass. She nuzzled her face between those scrumptious breasts that she had missed so much for the past 24 hours. At no time or place did Claire feel happier or safer than when her head was in Nikki's chest. The warmth, the soft scent, the satiny skin, the round curves and the sound of her heartbeat all combined to create Nirvana.

For a minute, Claire didn't even need to make love. She just wanted to stay right there.

But Nikki took Claire's hands and pushed them to the front button of her shorts, guiding her to unzip as they looked into each other's eyes and kissed. Claire ran her palm along the snug crotch of the shorts, eliciting a moan from Nikki.

"I'm so fuckin' hot right now," Nikki said, guiding Claire's hands to pull down her shorts. Then Nikki yanked off her t-shirt, and Claire pressed her face between her breasts, cupping them with her hands, allowing her hungry mouth to taste a flavor she had missed amidst all the male tastes and textures of Country Boy.

No, don't think about him now...

Claire smiled. It was time for the windshield wiper treatment, Nikki's favorite. She laid her down on the bed, then spread her legs to reveal the glistening, pink jellyfish framed by bald plumpness. Claire leaned close to inhale the sweet, clean scent. She ran her fingertips up and down the lips, marveling as if she were seeing Nikki for the first time. She poked a finger inside the hot creaminess, then spread the wetness across both lips and over her clit.

"I need you so bad right now," Nikki whispered, with a love-swept gaze. "Show me how much you missed me."

Claire stuck out her tongue, then lowered it to the highest spot on Nikki's clit. She began the windshield wiper motion over the ripe cherry, licking back and forth, softly at first, then with increasing pressure. Just when Nikki would moan the loudest, Claire would lighten the pressure, only to gradually increase it, over and over. At the same time, she stuck three fingers into her pussy — Nola — stroking her g-spot.

It didn't take long for Nikki to scream and quake from head to toe.

Claire laid beside her, held her and pressed long, lingering kisses all over Nikki's face and neck. She laced her fingers with the hands she had been holding for as long as she could remember, and she whispered into her ear, over and over, "I love you, Nikki Boo. I'm yours forever, Nikk-Nikk."

*   *   *   *   *   *   *   *

Nikki was still trembling when she buried her face in Claire's chest. She just wanted to lay there, listening to Claire's heartbeat. But she also wanted to make Claire shiver, *if* she found no trace of that nasty man contaminating her beloved. Nikki rubbed her face down Claire's stomach, then made her tongue do circles around her belly button, and down to Claire's bald mound.

"Lola's ready to play," Nikki said with a sultry tone that made Claire smile. "And Nola wants to kiss Lola later," Nikki said, envisioning how they would press their pussies together, look into each other's eyes, breathe each other's breath, and scissor their way into the best orgasms ever.

"Hell yeah," Claire moaned.

For now, Nikki's mouth watered as she stared at Claire's blooming clit. She craved to wrap her lips around it. But she had to smell it first. Then she'd know if he'd been there. Nikki nibbled the soft skin of Claire's groin that would be tattooed with their names in interlocking script as soon as this was over. Yeah, that was the deal: get married, wear wedding rings and have matching tattoos in that spot that no one else would ever see.

The thought of their wedding day made Nikki smile now, as she nestled her cheek against Claire's inner thigh. She almost didn't want to go all the way down on her right now.

What if he was there, and I smell his disgusting cum... or worse, taste it...

Just the thought of man-cum inside Lola made her want to puke all over the place.

Claire's lips and clit looked so swollen; she always got that way when she was eating Nikki out, because it was such a turn-on. The past 24 hours, since they'd made love in the downtown Butterfield Hotel before the wedding, felt like a million years.

Now, Nikki loved how Claire's hands combed through her hair as her head descended ever lower. She glanced up and smiled as she ran a hot palm over Claire's luscious thigh. Then her fingertip stroked upward from the bottom of her slit, gently brushing over her clit.

"Yeah, baby," Claire whispered. "I missed you so much."

She's clean. She has to be.

Nikki laid on her stomach between Claire's legs. She stared at the center of her universe, then leaned close and inhaled. Oh how she loved the salty-sweet scent of Claire's hairless pussy. Her lips parted, she stuck out her tongue, and—

She froze.

I just don't want to know. If Claire had fucked him all night and loved every second of it, Nikki preferred the bliss of ignorance. She glanced up at Claire, whose face glowed with anticipation and a little confusion.

"Is money more important than me?" Nikki asked.

Claire twisted her face, then whispered sweetly, "No, you're more important than money. That's why I want to get it so you can have a perfect life, forever, with me." Claire stroked the top of Nikki's head.

Nikki gently rubbed her forehead... her cheeks... her nose... her chin... in the hot, wet softness between Claire's legs. Round and round, back and forth, she deliberately grazed Claire's clit in a way that made her squirm and moan.

Then she stuck her tongue inside Lola, and with one big licking motion, trailed the tip of her tongue in soft, tiny strokes across her clit.

"Ooohhh," Claire moaned.

Nikki grabbed their favorite purple glass dildo and slid it into Claire's pussy. Then Nikki knelt over the other end as Claire sat up. Facing each other, they stared into each other's eyes, and kissed passionately as they gyrated on each end of the dildo.

At the same time, each touched the other's clit in soft circular motions, and soon, they were both shuddering with orgasm, simultaneously kissing with the head-swirling passion of their love, moaning and shaking in the beautiful way they had been doing for so long.

Panting, they became still. Nikki slid back, off the dildo. She pulled it from Claire's pussy.

And there on the end was a curly, straw-colored hair. His hair. Inside Claire.

"Holy fucking shit!" Nikki shrieked. Her already pounding heart hammered harder. She gasped for air.

Claire, who was laying back with a serene expression, sat up. "What?"

"You fucked him!"

Nikki threw the dildo toward the fireplace. It hit the brick and shattered. Purple shards showered onto the floor. Then Nikki ran to the bathroom and heaved up her heart and soul.

Chapter 35. Playing the Role of a Lifetime

When the limousine came to a stop, Mike stiffened with apprehension as he glanced out the window at the upscale condominiums. The ultra modern dwellings looked as uncomfortable as Jane appeared with herself.

"Thunder, we're here," Jane squealed, squeezing his hand. "Our love nest for a year. You're gonna love it!"

Mike kissed her cheek, relieved that she was so much happier than this morning in the teepee.

Man, this chick is like Laila on steroids. Everything I wanted to get away from in Laila, I have to deal with — times ten! — with my "Wife" for 364 more days. If this doesn't hone my acting skills for Hollywood, nothing will...

Mike wanted to do such an extraordinary job as a Husband that he could bank the money from this marriage, and go at it one more time. Then with 300 G's socked away, he could head out to L.A., go to auditions and become a movie star.

His second stab at fame and fortune wouldn't be like the first time, when he'd gone to Cali with nothing but a dream and a couple of Benjamins in his pocket. Waiting tables hadn't paid the rent, and he'd known it was time to get out of dodge when he even *considered* being "gay for pay." Multiple offers of 10-grand per night with rich producer dudes who proposed "long-term arrangements" could have had him livin' large. But taking dicks up his ass was *not* going to be Mike's path to stardom.

This, however, was just fine. For now, it was the best acting job he could get, and all he had to do was live for free, follow the Husbands, Inc. rules, and fuck his Wife.

The problem, unfortunately, was Jane's very bad acting job, trying to play an impossible role when she needed to learn that her authentic self was the true star.

"Welcome home," the limousine driver said, opening the door.

Despite the hot sunshine wafting into the car, Mike almost shivered at the sight of all that gray cement. The detached condo was a two-story rectangle with a sharp-peaked roof. The top level had floor-to-ceiling windows, and the angle under the roof was a series of triangular glass pieces fitted together like a prism. Its backside, like its identical neighbors, had expansive decks overlooking the marina where sailboats and pleasure cruisers bobbed in private boat wells.

Mike, now wearing blue jeans, a ponytail, his turquoise necklace and a leather vest, stepped out of the limo. He held Jane's hand as she carefully maneuvered in her tight mini skirt, snug halter-top and high heels.

As required by his contract, Mike lifted her into his arms to carry her over the threshold. He followed the limo driver up a cement, plank-like walk toward the gray double doors. The other homes lining the drive seemed to have more life — colorful flowers, flags, and bicycles. To the left, a couple came outside, jogging toward the street and waving. To the right, a convertible red Corvette gleamed in the driveway.

Mike nuzzled his face into Jane's chest, getting a nose full of too much perfume. She giggled. If she could afford to spend two hundred grand on this fantasy, then buying one of these expensive numbers must have been no big deal for her, either.

"Thunder, kiss me," Jane said, her unnaturally blue eyes gazing up at him. He'd never seen someone transform so dramatically from quiet and almost bummed out to giddy and peppy, just by taking a shower and changing clothes back at Husbands, Inc.

Mike pressed his lips to hers; she moaned and gripped the back of his neck, writhing in his arms.

The limo driver swung open the front doors and Mike carried Jane inside. The house had masculine energy, with the lingering scent of men's cologne. Jane was clearly leasing this place as part of the deal.

"I chose this condo because it's like stepping onto the pages of *Architectural Digest*," Jane said. "I think it's sophisticated and sleek."

"You have excellent taste, Jane," Mike said.

The driver set their suitcases on the cement platform that was the entrance hall, then closed the doors. A quick glance at the modern design filled Mike with dread; this place looked as uncomfortable as Jane did in her sky-high heels, tight clothes and high maintenance beauty routine. How could he transform both her and their home into a better fit?

"Just you and me," Jane said, slipping down to stand. She wrapped her arms around his waist and pressed her cheek into his chest. He kissed the top of her head, but felt something lumpy; last night while making love, he'd felt that she had hair extensions sewn into her natural hair. He'd also seen a hint of brown at the roots. So far, her hair, eye color and fingernails were fake; at least her breasts were real.

"C'mon, let me show you around, then we can make love," Jane said.

Mike ran his hand over her ass and cast down a smoldering stare that made her gasp. He pressed her hand to his crotch, where the big rod inside his jeans let her know he was ready to rock. If this girl was nothing else, she had a nice, tight pussy and perky tits. She was responsive when she let herself go, and Mike planned to bring that out of her even more.

I have to unleash her inner freak, or I'll go nuts!

He'd known right away that he couldn't get roughneck with her last night like he had with Venus. But he couldn't keep his raw dog needs all bottled up for a full year. So he had a solution: transform Jane into one super nasty, freaky bitch. Maybe that would boost her confidence and show her how to love herself from the inside out.

This wasn't in the contract, and it would take a lot of work. So if they could just stay in bed for the duration of the marriage, and only come out for food—

"Can we eat in bed today?" he asked.

Jane giggled. "Wow, you read my mind. They're delivering a gourmet lunch for us in two hours. It's a gift from my financial advisor. Then we have to go pick our costumes for Masquerade at Sea Castle."

"What do you wanna be?" he asked as she led him down three steps into the living room.

"Your squaw," she said, giddy. "I've always dreamed about that—"

"Then we'll make it come true, Jane."

"Yay!" she said, pointing up. "Check out the openness." The living room ceiling was the roof, peaked with glass walls. A metal-railed balcony was just above them. Jane pulled him across gray carpeting that was the only thing soft about this place.

But plodding over the plushness in her high heels only accentuated her ridiculous walk; she took long, languid steps, like a runway model. Sexy? No. Wobbly? Yes. As she strutted through the living room, she lost her balance and grabbed the back of a low, sharp-angled gray couch.

Embarrassment pinched her face as Mike strode close and took her hand.

"Isn't the fireplace romantic?" she said, pointing to the floor-to-ceiling mantle of clear glass bricks around a metal-spiked sculpture where no fire could burn.

It looked like an igloo. Mike hugged Jane's backside; hot lust shot through him. As he spun her around and pressed his open lips to hers, her nipples pressed into his chest.

"Hurry, let me show you the rest so we can get frisky," she said with a giggle.

Mike chuckled. For someone who was trying to be sexy, she sounded ridiculous.

Jane pulled him by the hand through the large, open space that flowed into the kitchen and dining area.

"Thunder, don't you love this place? We're going to be so happy here." She scratched the top of her head, pressed a finger to her eyelid, then nervously looked at her reflection in a mirror on the wall. Her face was stiff, but disapproval flashed in her eyes.

Mike had the feeling that he had committed himself to a walking, talking psychology experiment. That had been his major during the two years he'd spent at Wayne State University; it was fascinating to study human beings, to understand what made them so damn wacky.

What would this chick be like if she relaxed and acted normal?

She pulled him onto another cement surface that held an acrylic dining room table. Over it hung a ball of swords shooting every direction, with lights glowing at its core. The kitchen was stainless steel everything – cabinets, counters, appliances. Not a single dot of color caught his eye.

"Look at the stairs," she said, pointing to an acrylic staircase beside the wall of windows overlooking the marina. The sunshine was so bright, the stairs were almost invisible.

"Wow," he said, hating the idea of walking up those steps every day. "Life ain't no crystal stair."

She cast an odd look at him, then smiled. "Langston Hughes. That poem was my friend Pamela's favorite. I'm surprised you—"

"In my tribe, we celebrate all cultures," Mike said, "and literature is one of the best mirrors into the soul of a people."

"I'm like the biggest fan of romance novels with Indian—"

Jane stopped, flashing that same worried expression as last night when he'd explained why he wasn't wearing a feathered headdress with his *Native American Dream* costume. Prior to coming to Husbands, Inc., he'd seen news reports about a fashion show that had come under fire because the models wore Native American headdresses. It was disrespectful for non-Natives to wear them just for the fun or fashion of it, because headdresses were sacred, with deep symbolic meaning.

As someone who'd been disrespected with names like spick, wetback, Speedy Gonzales and Poncho Villa, he was the last guy who wanted to diss another persecuted culture.

"Thunder, just tell me if I ever say anything politically incorrect, okay?" Jane said. "There's no ethnic flavor in my generic white blend—"

He smiled. "Jane, don't put yourself or your heritage down. We're all unique and special. By the way, I appreciate your sensitivity."

Jane flashed an awkward smile. "Let's go upstairs."

Mike gingerly followed her up the stairs, staring at her ass to avoid looking down through the clear planks beneath his feet or the window and water to his right. Her black miniskirt was so short, he could see the bottoms of her butt cheeks and the sling of her black thong. His dick throbbed.

In the master suite, which was as sleek and gray as the rest of the house, Jane's high heels tapped the stone-tiled floor surrounding a platform bed that faced the water. She cast a lusty gaze at him, then held up her index finger as if to say, "Come here."

Something about it made him think she'd seen that in a movie, and this was her first time doing it with a man.

"Jane, there are no curtains," he said, glancing at the wall of windows overlooking the marina and houses across the water. "My culture values the privacy between a man and a woman as we perform a sacred act."

"I love that!" she shrieked, reaching for a control panel near the gray suede headboard. "Now, let me remember how this thing works." She pushed several buttons, causing beeps and chirps. A panel on the wall opened to reveal a TV. The bed vibrated, and soft jazz played from hidden speakers.

"Cripe, which button is it?" Jane whispered. Finally, a low hum accompanied curtains sliding out of metal poles at the corners of the windows; in a flash, gray drapes covered the windows.

"Now I can make love to you, Jane," Mike said, unbuckling his jeans as she watched hungrily. She held his gaze as she pulled off her top and ran her hands over her black lace, push-up bra. Then she pulled off her skirt to reveal a matching thong.

As she laid back, her skin was smooth and suntanned, but her hip bones protruded and her stomach looked painfully thin. Suddenly she flipped over onto her knees, sticking her ass up for him.

"Yeah, baby," he groaned. "I like that."

Jane giggled, then moved her ass in uneven circles.

Does this girl ever eat? Laila lives on lettuce, but at least her ribs and spine don't stick out. This chick could use some meat on her bones, especially her ass and those stick legs. Can't be too rough or she'll break...

Still, Mike just couldn't complain about getting paid to fuck for a year. Plus he didn't have to invest time into getting to know the girl. He could just get right to it.

Now naked, his dick was a hot rod. He pulled her thong to reveal her glistening slit. He ran his fingers over it, then reached around to her tits as his dick slid inside—

"Ooohhhh, you are the best lover." She giggled. "I can't believe I'm talking like that."

Mike thrust just hard enough to watch goosebumps dance up her back. Fucking her was so different than Venus. This chick was stiff and unsure of herself, like she wasn't used to having sex, much less enjoying it. In contrast, Venus was always so comfortable, confident and uninhibited about unleashing the sex goddess that she hid beneath her classy image.

Being with Venus had opened the door to a whole new side of himself. First, based on her multi-orgasmic reactions and desire to see him four times a week for the past month, the training at Husbands, Inc. Academy had catapulted him from the *top* of the charts, to *off* the charts. Second, she had shown him that it was okay to go roughneck on a "lady," which he had not done for a good 10 years.

The problem was, when he was in an official relationship with a girlfriend, he just could not get as nasty as he wanted to be. No, he saved that for the toss-away chicks. Those were the freaky girls he kept around for sex; likewise, they expected nothing in return except a good time. They never accused him of disrespecting them, and they never demanded all the romantic bullshit that had nothing to do with sex: foot rubs, flowers and candlelit dinners.

Those chicks just wanted to fuck, and that was all Mike wanted from them. Simple and straightforward, that saved all the time and energy for smokin' hot sex.

Meanwhile, a real relationship was far more complicated. After falling head over heels in love with his very first girlfriend in high school, he got an extremely rude awakening in the bedroom. She was a virgin, so he was gentle during their first time. Then, as she warmed up and began to enjoy sex, he'd tried to throw down with the moves that made him king amongst the 'round-the-way girls in the neighborhood. But no, his girlfriend just wasn't havin' it. He should have known that a studious, church-going young lady wouldn't appreciate the same things as the hoes.

"Don't treat me like a tramp!" she sobbed. "Treat me like a lady!" That meant slow and gentle "lovemaking" after the mushy-gushy confessions of love, massages, chocolates, dinner dates and all the other stuff that she demanded "in exchange" for "intimacy." It was as draining and dull as a full-time job, and the sex wasn't even as exciting.

So why keep a girlfriend at all? He loved her companionship and affection. But he still needed to satisfy his need for the wild, freaky stuff. So he kept getting it – in secret and with condoms – from his casual chicks on the side. He didn't like that he had to do that, but if the girlfriend wouldn't fulfill the fantasy, then he needed two or three girls who would.

As a result, Mike had learned to never mix his two sex personalities on a woman he loved. The hot, rockin' raunchy stuff was for casual hook-ups, while he played the lovemaking gentleman with his girlfriend.

Now, he half-smiled at the irony.

It's funny how we play roles in real life, too...

But now that he was in the fantasy world of Husbands, Inc., where Venus had shown him that the ultimate lady could appreciate his rougher side, could he somehow merge the two with Jane? He had to. Since his motivation was to get paid — and an extramarital affair would jeopardize that — then having a hoe or three on the side was not an option. *I have to stay monogamous. So Jane has to be my Wife and my slutty bitch.*

Now, he fucked her extra good from behind, reaching around to touch her clit and make her explode with orgasm.

But then she looked back at him and demanded, "Thunder, do you think I'm sexy?"

He smiled. "Of course I do, Jane."

"No, really," she said. "If we weren't in this situation where you're supposed to flatter me, would you think I'm hot? Would you want to be in bed with me?"

Mike forced his face to cast a loving stare at her. They had taught him that in the Husbands Academy — how to fake an expression that projects the opposite of what you're feeling. If he could speak his mind right now, he would say, *"I prefer women who are natural and comfortable with themselves, who radiate beauty from the inside out, and who feel free to be as nasty as they wanna be in bed."*

But he wouldn't collect the big check at the end of this gig by speaking his mind.

"Jane, you're stunning," he said with a smoldering look in his eyes. He caressed her ass, then turned her onto her back and leaned over her, never pulling his dick out of her body. "You're a beautiful and desirable woman."

She looked up at him with eyes full of doubt. "Are my boobs big enough?" She pulled up her bra, then cupped them in her hands.

"Perfect," he said. "Natural."

"Do you think I'm fat?" she asked, running her hands over her thighs.

"Perfect," he said, lying again. If he could get her to eat more than the fruit she'd nibbled at breakfast today, and pack a few curves onto these bones, she'd be amazed at how much better the sex would be.

"I don't want you to see me without make-up," she said. "I feel like I have to be the perfect, hot girl for you."

He thrust gently, to keep the momentum going. Hopefully she would shut up and let him work his magic. "Jane, you chose me as your Husband, so I'll be everything you want me to be. This year is about what *you* want, not what *I* want."

She crossed her arms. "Oh, you just want the money."

His dick was going limp. Would that set her off even more? He had learned long ago to never entertain a woman's lose-lose questions or comments; no matter what response he gave, she'd be upset. He'd been here too many times with Laila and other women.

"I know what I signed up for," he said, "and that includes the fantasy of being a newlywed with a fun, sexy Wife. You should just relax—"

"No, no, society says a woman has to look a certain way to be sexy." She shook her head, then pressed her acrylic fingernails to the outer edges of her fake eyelashes, as if they were coming loose. "And I want to be that for you."

"Just be yourself and you'll be amazed—"

"Myself? Ha! That would bore you to tears."

Mike's heart ached for her. Through the plastic blue hue over her eyes, he peered into the soul of a woman who was lost. Sadly, she mirrored the person he once was. So long ago, as a teenager, he'd fantasized about being a blond-haired, blue-eyed guy who always had it easy. Guys like that at school always got the girls, the awards, the praise from teachers.

Whereas he had the Greek-Italian-Mexican-Native American look that was overlooked and viewed as oddball, even in the hood where he grew up. Back then, he saw his looks as a fast pass to nowhere but the bottom rungs of society, because he didn't see any businessmen or movie stars or politicians or even news anchors who looked like him.

Thank God he had discovered acting at that one-day workshop at his school when he was 16. An African American actor named Sammy Laine, who had won an Oscar, was traveling the country, hosting workshops at urban schools to encourage demoralized guys like Mike to get into theatre, television and film.

"A million possibilities are bursting inside you right now," Sammy said. "It's your job to carry them around in the best character you can be, and let them out in all their glory when the time is right."

Now, Mike's heart ached as he gazed down at Jane. Somehow, he would become her Sammy, and help her be the best character she could be, every day.

But it'll take a miracle. Because this girl is her own worst enemy.

Chapter 36. Time to Play the Trump Card?

"Hallelujah!" Raye shouted as the repulsive sex tape played for the lawyers. It was the only viable copy, playing from the flash drive in Venus' laptop here in her office. The second flash drive that Venus had retrieved from the safe in her bedroom was blank.

"Oh thank heavens," Venus sighed. "I was afraid all hope was lost."

The lawyers crossed their arms, watching the video in a way that let Raye know, they would not endorse her defensive attack.

"Vee, we need to make copies right now," Raye said, pulling out her phone. "Then we can call the media—"

"No, we can't play dirty," Adam Applebaum snapped, shaking his curly head. "This video was obtained without John's knowledge, and he could prosecute you, Venus."

Yolanda Napoleon nodded toward the French doors leading outside. "You've got all these powerful women from around the world here. We have to keep your image sparkling clean. Above reproach!"

Raye felt like her head would explode with frustration. "This is an emergency! Kill or be killed!"

"Raye is right," Venus said. "John didn't earn his pit bull reputation by playing nice. He goes for the throat, clamps down and doesn't stop shaking until he's killed his prey."

Adam, wearing khaki pants and a green polo shirt, adjusted his tortoise-shell eyeglasses. "I recommend a private meeting with John. Let him know you have this, negotiate a deal where he rescinds his threat of an indictment, and promise that this sex tape will disappear."

Raye stomped her foot. "That is the most punk-ass way to play a trump card! We need to blindside him. Blast him out of the game!"

Venus rose from her desk chair. "Adam, Yolanda, your unwavering commitment to doing things right, is the reason you've helped this company grow and thrive since the beginning. But you're used to dealing with people who play by the rules. John doesn't."

"Judges do," Adam said. "Look, there's a joke that a prosecutor can get an indictment against a ham sandwich if he wants to. You, the defendant, and your lawyers don't even have to be present. It's a behind-closed-doors process that quite frankly can smack of unfairness, because an arrest warrant can result."

"Oh hell no!" Raye snapped. "So Venus could get arrested in front of all these rich, powerful women?"

Venus turned pale. "That would be catastrophic!"

"We have to fight fire with fire!" Raye insisted.

"We do," Venus said.

"No," Adam said. "John and Ted are fighting with smoke and mirrors, not fire. They have no case. Their indictment is groundless and we'll prove it in court."

Venus crossed her arms. "I have neither the time, nor the desire, to go to court. Not for the humiliation of being arrested, and not to indulge my ex-husband's tantrum."

Yolanda added, "Venus, it really could work to your advantage, in the court of public opinion. Any proceedings would remove all doubt about the legality of Husbands, Incorporated."

Raye tapped her foot. Her thoughts fast-forwarded to getting a copy of this video and emailing it to Whittaker and Sasha before the lawyers could blink.

This bomb is as good as dropped on John Barker.

But Venus still looked pensive. "What's the risk? If you allow them to rake me over the coals in front of a male judge who may be sympathetic to John, Ted and men in general?"

"That is a possibility," Adam said, "but the legal facts are black and white. They have no case, so it would be rash and reckless to stoop to their level by putting this video out—"

"This meeting is over," Venus said, motioning for Gus to let them out. "Yolanda, Adam, let's agree to disagree on this."

Raye snatched up her phone. She already had the number for Sasha's assistant on the screen. She pushed "call," and cast a defiant glare at the two milquetoast lawyers.

An energetic, young voice answered: "The Goddess Show, this is Pepper."

"Hey Pepper, Raye Johnson, we spoke last week."

"Of course, we're excited to have you on the show tomorrow."

"Thank you," Raye said as the lawyers left. "Venus Roman and I have some video to share with Ms. Maxwell. Can we come to the studio in about 30 minutes?"

"She actually has a block of time open," Pepper said. "We'll see you then."

Raye hung up, shaking with urgency as she stepped close to Venus at the computer. "Vee, let's make copies now."

Venus glanced at the flash drive, which was protruding from the side of the computer. She closed the video file, then started to use the cursor to drag the JOHNVIDEO icon onto the desktop.

"Raye, I have some blank flash drives on that shelf," Venus said, pointing to a tray between books. "Can you please get them? I can make copies now—"

"Sure." Raye turned toward the shelf, grabbing the package of three flash drives.

"Venus!" Kimberly shrieked, bursting into the office. "Our website is down, and the whole network went dark. I think we've been hacked—"

"Oh shit!" Raye exclaimed.

Venus turned to the computer. The screen turned blue, and everything, including the JOHNVIDEO icon, disappeared.

Chapter 37. The Dream Becomes a Nightmare

After so much great sex, Jane's ears were ringing, and her legs were trembling, as they stepped into the garage. She teetered on her high heels, so Thunder steadied her while she pushed a button on the wall. As the garage door rose, sunshine illuminated her boss' silver Porsche.

"This house is a far cry from the teepee," Jane said, gazing up at Thunder, "but this car has got some horsepower for you!"

He smiled. "I'm honored to chauffeur you anywhere you want to go." He kissed her forehead as they checked out the car.

It was quite an upgrade from the 10-year-old compact car she'd sold to help finance this whole deal. And the house, wow, she had forgotten so much since that quick tour with her boss a month ago.

I should've come over and gotten comfortable, and introduced myself to the neighbors.

While the super modern furniture and décor wasn't her style, she loved the far-away fantasy of the condo. Even though it wasn't nearly as comfortable as the cozy, country-style furniture that she'd sold with her own house. Since her boss had just left town a few days ago, she'd stayed in a hotel and had her clothes delivered here this morning. That would bolster the illusion that she either owned this house, or had leased it as part of her wedding package.

Cripe... I hope I can get away with this. If my boss finds out I'm harboring a Husband here, I will be up a very stinky creek.

Ever since those media helicopters had shown up yesterday, she'd been worried about someone taking their picture and putting it on social media. Or that she and Thunder would get bum-rushed by all the TV cameras outside Husbands, Inc., and somehow her colleagues — or worse, her boss — would see her, clear on the other side of the world. She shook her head, praying that Madame Roman's no-media policy meant that Jane and Thunder would never be exposed in the newspaper, in a magazine or on TV.

This morning, she'd watched news reports that included video shot from those helicopters; though too close for comfort, she considered it a lucky omen that only the back

279

of her newly blond head — and not her face — had appeared on global television.

"Thunder, you get to drive my car all year," she said, handing him the key as she stepped to the passenger side of the convertible.

She felt giddy about being in a Porsche, but she had to play it cool, so he'd think it was hers. Truth was, her boss had stood here and handed her the key with no instructions other than getting gas, oil changes and regular washings.

"Sea Castle, here we come," Thunder said, sliding into the driver's seat.

"If they don't have costumes for an Indian warrior and his squaw," Jane said, getting in, "I want to be Barbie and Ken. Those were my favorite dolls as a girl."

Thunder chuckled as the car roared. "Jane, you seem more relaxed since we ate those massive ham and cheese sandwiches and fudge brownies. Meals delivered to the door? I could get used to that!"

Jane ran her hand along the thick muscles of his bare arm. "I was starving! But I'm more relaxed by what you did with your tongue and your you-know-what." She giggled.

"My what?" he said playfully, backing out and pushing a button to close the garage door. He stopped in the driveway and looked at her with a big smile. "My what, Jane?"

"You know," she said nervously.

"Say, 'dick' or 'cock.'"

Jane's face burned with embarrassment.

He touched her cheek. "I guarantee you'll enjoy making love even more when you can express yourself in a certain way."

"That just sounds so crude." Jane giggled again because she loved this. All that lingo she read about in women's magazines... what if she could really talk like that? She looked into his eyes and summoned courage from deep down. "OK. Dick."

Mike grinned, and she laughed, leaning back on the black leather headrest. The stunning blueness of the sky made her pause.

Wow, this is my life! Sitting in a Porsche with my gorgeous Husband, laughing. Thank you, Pamela, for pushing me to do this...

Jane couldn't remember ever feeling so excited in one moment about so many things at once.

"Cock!" she blurted.

As they laughed together, Thunder revved the engine. In the bright sunshine, his handsome profile made her gasp.

Oh my God, I get him all to myself for a whole year! I am loving this!

Another revving engine caught their attention. It was in the next driveway. That red Corvette. And inside sat a platinum blond, tanned woman with gold sunglasses and pink-glossed lips.

"Oh my God," Jane said, horrified. "Barbie is our next door neighbor."

Thunder looked perplexed. "Is she new to the neighborhood?"

Before Jane could think, *No, I am*, her mind fast-forwarded. She had next week off for their "honeymoon," but then she'd have to return to work, leaving Thunder here all alone, all day, with *that* next door.

Oh my gosh, I wish I had purchased ManGuard Service.

That was something Madame Roman offered as extra protection against a man going astray, even under contract as a Husband, to engage in sex with other women or even men. Some women, Madame Roman had explained at the orientation, had been burned so badly by cheating men in the past, that they could not proceed in any relationship without the added assurance of fidelity, especially when paying such huge sums for their year of wedded bliss.

But another 25-grand for ManGuard to monitor her Husband around the clock was out of the question for Jane. The money she would earn at her job would be just enough to cover the expenses as agreed upon with her boss: utilities, food, gas and minor upkeep. Any extra cash would go toward entertainment, like going out to dinner and the movies with Thunder.

Granted, he did have to spend time at the quality control meetings and working out, but he would have a lot of time here at the house by himself.

Barbie turned off the motor and stepped out of the car. Her straight hair hung to the middle of her back, and her short dress revealed super-fit legs. As Thunder backed the car out of the driveway, the neighbor removed her sunglasses and stared at them.

Jane gasped. Her heart pounded.

Oh no, he's gonna screw her! All day, every day, while I'm at work...

As Thunder drove away, he took Jane's hand and kissed it. The breeze blew his long hair back over the bucket seat, and he slipped on black sunglasses. He looked like an absolute dream.

And this is about to become a nightmare...

Chapter 38. Husbands, Inc. is Under Attack

This could ruin us!

Venus felt dizzy as she learned the magnitude of the attack on the Husbands, Inc. computer network. She and her team were standing in the glass-walled conference room in the second floor offices, facing Cyber Lion Security CEO Whittaker Johnson.

"Preliminarily, it looks like the hackers used malware to collect data and wipe out your system," he said, sitting at the glass conference table, facing her laptop computer.

Whittaker exhaled, running a large hand over his close-cropped, black beard and hair as he glanced at Venus, Raye, Gus and Kimberly. Large, silver-framed glasses magnified Whittaker's almond-shaped eyes, which appeared wise beyond his 33 years. The worry tensing his cinnamon-hued complexion, oval face and full lips mirrored his sister, who stood beside him.

"Neanderthal is behind this," Raye spat. "It's got his special brand of evil all over it."

"Evil intentions, indeed," Whittaker said, "to orchestrate an attack like this. After they pillaged the network of names, email and street addresses, credit and debit card numbers, PINs, expiration dates and even social security numbers—"

"No!" Venus cried. The room seemed to spin as she envisioned an angry mob of clients, franchisees and Husbands storming toward her. "We have the most intimate data a person could provide."

The background check system and the application process required everything from blood work to psychological exams to financial information and social security numbers. And for all the men and women whose applications had been rejected over the years — for extremely embarrassing reasons such as infectious diseases, criminal records and mental illness — their information could now be exposed as well.

"This absolutely *cannot* happen!" Venus cried.

Whittaker shook his head. "Unfortunately, after stealing personal data, the worm would then destroy everything in its path, including your video."

Venus felt so dizzy, she dropped into one of the white leather chairs around the table. She hated feeling overwhelmed by this excruciating powerlessness to block her enemies from destroying her and the global mission of Husbands, Inc.

"Oh my God," Venus gasped, her chest rising and falling in panicky gasps. "They can't stop us! They can't!"

"You okay, Vee?" Raye stroked Venus' shoulder and gazed down tenderly.

Clicking on a keyboard punctuated the silence as Kimberly began typing on an attachment to her computer tablet.

"The good news is," Whittaker said, watching her, "this is the worst case scenario. My team may discover that it's not as cataclysmic as what I just described."

Whittaker glanced past the glass walls, where Derek and Decker were observing 12 men and women working on computers at the operators' stations. Like Whittaker, they wore black jumpsuits with the Cyber Lion Security logo on the back.

"My team's diagnostic is assessing the damage," he said. "Then we'll know exactly what we're working with."

"In the meantime," Gus said, "we need a pro-active plan to protect ourselves and our clients, and to implement the best damage control."

Kimberly kept typing and did not look up as she announced, "I'm composing a mass text and email for all past and present clients, franchisees and Husbands. They need to contact their financial institutions to monitor for any unusual activity."

She pointed to a flash drive. "Thank goodness I've kept all important data on this, and I can use my personal email."

"Good," Gus said. "Stress that this warning is merely precautionary. Use words like proactive, protective and preventative, and emphasize that we'll provide more information as soon as our investigative team assesses the extent of the damage."

"This is a nightmare," Venus groaned as Kimberly continued to type. "I don't want to alarm our clients unnecessarily. But we have to keep them informed before they hear something in the media."

"Or they'll be even more pissed," Raye said. "Meanwhile we need our damage control to include a powerful PR strategy to counteract the inevitable media storm."

Venus' head spun. She tried to breathe deeply to calm herself, but it felt more like hyperventilating. Suddenly, she envisioned the handsome usher at the opera, and a comforting sensation consumed her like a warm embrace.

"Have you reported this to the authorities yet?" Whittaker asked.

"Oh my God, no," Venus gasped, glancing at the distant office door, which was closed. The two police officers stood in the hallway, because she'd prohibited them from entering and eavesdropping. "That would give the FBI free reign to come snooping around up here."

"I understand your concern," Whittaker said, "but gathering evidence is the only way to prosecute—"

"Never!" Raye snapped. "That's exactly what John wants. On the news, he kept saying, 'federal indictment.' That means federal law enforcement — the FBI — would be in charge of getting evidence for him. Never! I'd bet a million dollars they're all in bed together on this. Getting off on their power trippin' orgy of harassment. Persecution!"

Venus tried to shake horrific images of Frank Williams prowling around here on John's behalf.

"No," she said, "we will not report this to them. If the media somehow gets wind of it—"

"They already have," Kimberly said, glancing down at a TV news report on her computer tablet.

Venus straightened her spine and stared at Whittaker with laser-beam focus. "Right now, our only hope is for

Whittaker Johnson to make cyber magic happen. Tell us they didn't steal our clients' personal information, then retrieve, restore, resuscitate the video—"

Whittaker chuckled, making a tiny pinch gesture with his fingers. "Like Momma used to say, sometimes all you need is the faith of a tiny mustard seed to do the impossible."

"That's what I'm talking about!" Raye exclaimed. "Parklawn Princesses in the house!"

Raye blew a kiss, while Venus mustered a smile.

"I am so confused!" Kimberly exclaimed. "What video?"

"It's a sex tape," Raye snapped. "Of Neanderthal and a girl."

"Gross," Kimberly said.

"Very," Raye added. "And if it lands in the right place on the Internet and goes viral, then somebody—" she glanced up at the ceiling "—was working some divine intervention to do us a huge favor. But if they stole it—"

"Even if John got it, he'd destroy it," Venus said. "We still need it to use it. Whittaker, how long will all this take?"

"Could be an hour," he said. "Could be a week, but I better get to work."

Kimberly still looked confused.

Raye said, "Venus was copying a file called JOHNVIDEO from the flash drive onto the desktop when the cyber thugs zapped our system."

Venus nodded. "Kimberly, I'll show you when Whittaker makes a miracle happen for us."

Whittaker flashed a pessimistic expression. "Yeah, when I find a diamond in the black hole of cyberspace. My team's top priority is to restore the system to process your online registrations. We'll also install a new security system."

Raye glanced at Kimberly's flash drive. "Vee, are you sure you don't have any other back-up copies of the video?"

Venus closed her eyes and exhaled with frustration. "No." She stood on wobbly legs. "I'll pay you to work around the clock. We'll feed you, and you can sleep in one of the guest suites here."

Whittaker nodded. "Good thing I don't have a social life or a hot date. It's Saturday night." He glanced at Kimberly, then back at Venus. "I'll do my best, but I can't promise—"

"Just do it, Whittaker," Venus said.

Minutes later, with her security team in tow, Venus strode toward the Orientation tent as Kimberly updated her on the day's activities. A vicious undercurrent of worry tugged at her every thought, especially when Kimberly pointed to her computer tablet.

"The media says Men for Traditional Marriage is taking credit for hacking our network," Kimberly said somberly. "They've already started picketing the homes of clients with marriages in progress. In four states so far."

"We have to stop them!" Venus said, pausing near the tent. "Call Agent Rodriguez and ask what's our recourse."

As Kimberly dialed, Venus peeked into the tent, where the international guests were sitting at tables. They were taking notes by hand and on computers during a presentation about security precautions for international franchises.

Zahra was at the podium, moderating the panel of four men and women, who sat at a dais on the stage.

"Ladies," Zahra said, "now that our experts have provided an overview, you will have individual consultations this afternoon about security dangers and precautions pertaining to the cultural, religious and legal systems in your countries."

Zahra thanked the experts, who stepped off the stage.

"Next," Zahra said as Raye took a seat at a front table, "our International Coordinator, Myles Albertson, will explain how a Husbands, Inc. Liaison will be assigned to each of you, for the first year of your operations, to help streamline the launch of your franchises. Each Liaison has undergone intensive training to understand the laws and cultural practices in the country where they will be assigned. Myles?"

Wearing a beige, skinny-cut suit, brown loafers and a crisp white shirt and tie, Myles walked with so much pep in his step that his brown, wavy, side-parted hair bounced as he approached the podium.

Both Venus and Raye had dated him at the Academy, until he fell head over heels in love with Eden at Venus' Sweet Sixteen party. The same thing happened when he met Zahra at Raye's party a month later, so the Parklawn Princesses officially declared Myles a playboy. Now, he embraced his status as the consummate bachelor because he had more fun than any man they knew outside the walls of Husbands, Inc.

"Good morning," Myles said, standing behind the podium. "When I studied at the London School of Economics, I met people from around the globe who shared a common vision for education and achievement. Now, being here with you today, I'm thrilled to help you embark on a common vision for bringing the passion and innovation of Husbands, Inc. International to your native lands."

Myles raised a hand toward Venus, who wished he hadn't. Too many women looked stressed, and she did not want the attention right now.

"Madame Roman," he said, bowing. "Thank you for gracing us with your presence."

"Good morning," Venus said, smiling and waving at him and the women. "I'm delighted to see all of you here." She hated that Ziggy Wild's worried expression mirrored the same anxiety on many women's faces as they turned toward her.

A horrible, jittery sensation overwhelmed Venus. The cyber attack had the potential to put them, and every client across America, in jeopardy.

And if the international clients felt Husbands, Inc. was being persecuted here in "the land of the free, home of the brave," would that dissuade them from attempting such a revolutionary endeavor in their homelands?

Every woman here had at her fingertips a portal to the media: cell phones, computer tablets and laptop computers. If they hadn't seen the news yet, they would soon. Plus, Kimberly had disseminated her text alert about the hacking and security breach.

Venus shivered with panic; it was so numbing, she grasped the tent pole. She closed her eyes, breathed deeply, and summoned strength from deep within.

I will not be defeated. I will not!

"Now," Myles said, "it's important to consider the moral codes in your countries, which can sometimes be more influential than the laws and customs—"

Oh my God.

Marena from Venezuela, Orianna from Nigeria, and Lisette from Canada were sitting together, focused on Myles. They were all radiating confidence and excitement that they were embarking on a rock-solid business venture.

They haven't heard the news yet. These women trust me, but in a flash, they could hate me—

"Madame Roman," said Mahi of Japan, who had left her seat and walked over. "I am very concerned about the stability of your company in the wake of this cyber-attack." She glanced at her phone, which showed a news report and Kimberly's text that began with "URGENT!"

Mahi sharpened her gaze at Venus. "I need assurance that this crisis is being managed and contained. Otherwise, I will withdraw my investment—"

"I assure you, Mahi," Venus said with perfect poise and confidence as several women watched, "the situation is being handled with the utmost expertise as we speak. It will be resolved and our system will be stronger as a result."

The woman shook her head. "My advisors warned this would be a high-risk venture from the start, due to its controversial nature."

"Please," Venus said, "proceed with complete confidence that you will receive everything that I promised."

As Mahi nodded, Venus was tempted to go on stage and make an impromptu announcement that the cyber-attack was being resolved, but her instincts said it would be better to address that during the luncheon in a short while. So she cast an assuring smile at the women and stepped away with Kimberly.

"What did Agent Rodriguez at the FBI say?" Venus asked. "If Men for Traditional Marriage is taking credit for the attack, I want them prosecuted now, and thrown *under* the jail for theft, trespassing, harassment and anything else."

"Voicemail," Kimberly said. "I'll keep trying."

"Hacking is a federal crime, right?" Venus asked. "If so, we have to navigate around Ted Pendigree."

"Yolanda and Adam are in your office," Kimberly said, "to answer your questions."

Venus' entire body ached with tension. And it could only be soothed under the relentless jack-hammering of a strong, tireless man. David could do a superb job of that before the luncheon, but her mind's eye was focused on Rex. In fact, he had been her final, delicious thought before sleep last night, and the first image to enchant her mind upon waking this morning.

His eyes promised so much love — good heavens, no man has ever made me feel like that with one look!

Venus shivered. She ached for the intriguing stranger to touch her, hold her, make love to her. Yet oddly, the depth of feelings that he roused within her, promised that he had so much more to offer than his body. For that, she almost didn't want to indulge her physical desires with him just yet.

This is a first...

Kimberly took another call, then said, "Venus, the caterers have everything ready for the luncheon. And couples have started arriving to select their costumes in the ballroom."

Dread was shadowing Venus' usual excitement about Husbands, Inc.'s biggest annual event: Masquerade at Sea Castle. She and Raye had hosted the costume ball since their first year in business. Now people from across America flew in to partake of the dining, dancing and decadent romance. This year, with her 100 international guests, it would be bigger and better than ever.

Unless we fail to stop John and his cohorts from doing even more damage...

Anxiety accelerated Venus' steps up the flower-lined path to the house.

Hurrying alongside her, Kimberly asked, "By the way, will you be wearing your usual mermaid costume?"

Venus exhaled, wondering how all these problems would affect the gala. "Good heavens, Homeland Security will probably send a small army to patrol our party."

Kimberly nodded toward the Husbands who were sunbathing by the pool. "What about your escort? Who will be your King Neptune? I need to get his measurements for the costume."

"No," Venus said. "I want something different this year." She envisioned Rex beside her at the party. "Like Tarzan. Fur boots, suede loin cloth—"

"I saw that in the catalog," Kimberly said as they entered the central hallway. "But I need a size so I can custom-order it. Oh, and what about an escort for the awards ceremony tomorrow evening?"

Again, the Thoreau-loving heart-throb came to mind. She was intrigued that he seemed to have the intellect to engage her brain, and the brawn to delight her body.

Rex would make one hot Husband. My Husband... I want him. I want to touch him; I want him to touch me.

As they traversed the foyer, she had the urge to bite him, and feel his teeth on her neck, his fingertips clawing her flesh, his dick pounding her into erotic oblivion.

"Kimberly, please call the Opera House and invite a young usher to join our luncheon today."

She nodded. "Do you know his name?"

"Rex. I didn't get his last—"

Kimberly smiled. "Actually, he called while you were with Raye, and again while we were with Whittaker. I was just about to tell you—"

"If I've ever needed a delicious distraction, it's today," Venus said. "What'd he say?"

"He wants to stop by and become your Husband," Kimberly said. "I told him that he's welcome to apply to become *a* Husband—"

Venus laughed. "Excellent. Please call and invite him to lunch at noon."

"The lunch is at 12:30."

"I know. Send him out to the yacht first."

𝒞𝒽𝒶𝓅𝓉𝑒𝓇 39. Plotting an Offensive Strategy

Sitting at a table under the Orientation tent, Raye watched Myles Albertson wow the women as he talked about operating Husbands, Inc. International in their countries.

But she wasn't hearing him over her brainstorm that was thundering and crackling with ideas to trounce their enemies.

Since Neanderthal is captain of the team, we need to tackle him first. Then they'll all go down... So... what evidence could Raye and Venus gather to expose John's dark side? What other offenses had that unscrupulous, unethical bastard committed over the years? *Let's see...* Men like him were motivated by sex, money and power. Yes, money...

Suddenly Raye remembered what another financial professional had told her years ago: that John Barker had made millions on an insider trading deal that had never been exposed because everyone who knew about it was intimidated by his vindictive reputation.

That's it!

Raye shot up from her seat, darted onto a path leading toward the beach, and called her friend, Abe Sandstein, a financial advisor who had left Detroit a few years ago.

"To what do I owe the privilege of a call from The Queen?" he asked over the honking horns, sirens and screeching buses of Manhattan. "Haven't seen you since the conference out in San Diego."

"Ha, look who's talking!" Raye exclaimed, walking along a cobbled path lined with hedges exploding with pink roses. "You're the media's new 'it guy' for all things Wall Street. The Dow is up? Talk to Abe. That new tech IPO? Let's find out what Abe Sandstein thinks!"

They shared a laugh as Raye passed couples walking arm-in-arm.

"Thankin' my lucky stars every minute," Abe said. "Life is good. So what's up, oh great Queen? If you're calling to recruit me to be a hot Husband at your house of pleasure, sorry, I just got married and became a dad—"

"Congratulations, you sound happy," Raye said, inhaling the scent of roses. "Actually, a lot of forces are coming against Husbands, Inc. right now, led by your favorite lawyer."

"Don't tell me, Detroit's answer to Machiavelli," Abe said. "The one whose commercials say, 'Thank you, John Barker,' even though a lot of folks want to say, 'Fuck you, John Barker.'"

Raye laughed. "I love how you don't mince words. So Abe, I need ammunition, and when you were here, you said John was involved in an insider trading deal—"

"Huh! That guy should be in prison right now."

"Well he's barked up the wrong tree this time," Raye said, approaching the beach, where two women were shrieking with amusement as they played volleyball with a pair of *Boy Toys*. Their excitement bolstered Raye's determination to defend this paradise.

"Hey," Abe said, "my wife is calling. Can you hold a minute?"

"Sure." Over the rose hedges, Raye watched a tall man with a lion's mane of golden brown hair bolting across the grounds with Kimberly; she was on the phone while he focused straight ahead at the yacht, where Venus was standing at the bow, staring at the lake and sky.

"Oooh, it's Mr. Literary, and he's on a mission," Raye whispered as a green hummingbird suddenly hovered in front of her. "Score one for Vee."

Mr. Literary's elegant, flowing gait resembled Venus' unique way of walking — like the silvery, liquid shimmer of mercury. Wearing jeans and a white shirt, he took long steps, with perfect posture. He looked athletic and strong, determined and dignified. With all that, Rex exuded indescribable sex appeal.

Damn, when he and Vee get together, the whole world will see shooting stars.

Raye smiled, excited for Venus to get some of the same kind of lovin' from Mr. Literary as Buck was giving her. This morning, he had promised:

"Raye, baby, I'll be right here when you get back. After I feed you lunch, I'll give you an eight-course desert. The eight represents infinity, because you won't be able to count all the times I take you to kingdom cum..."

Now, Raye's nipples hardened with anticipation of spending the rest of the day, until tonight's dinner-dance, in bed getting Bucked. Hopefully, Mr. Literary would sweeten the bitterness bombarding Venus.

A flurry of color around the gazebo drew Raye's attention. Festive Latin music played as four Flamenco dancers flounced ahead of a bride in a sexy, form-fitting dress and high heels, as a *Latin Lover* groom awaited inside.

Raye smiled. That wasn't just any *Latin Lover*. That was Ricardo Lucio.

And I know who the bride is, too. Ha! That girl is in for way more than she bargained for.

"I'm back," Abe said, "ready to help you bring down a very bad guy. I trust that if you'll use your utmost discretion to protect both of us—"

"Abe, I promise, you'll have a new nickname for me: Stealth."

"I like that," he said. "If I can help you get that guy off the streets, I'm at your service. Let me call you from home, so I can direct you to the evidence you need."

Raye smiled.

Neanderthal is going down!

Chapter 40. Passion and Promises Fail to Persuade

Vacuous. Hedonistic. Sad.

Rex pondered those words as he traversed the grounds of Husbands, Inc. with Kimberly, who was taking nonstop phone calls about wedding cakes, flowers and now, a Tarzan costume.

"The deluxe version," she chirped. "Yes, genuine suede and authentic fur boots. But I'll have to call later with the sizes."

Rex surveyed clusters of men and women by the pool, on the beach and in a Latin-style wedding party near the gazebo.

This is so wrong...

These people were all bypassing the succulent tastes and textures of life's most decadent feast — falling in love. They were cheating themselves by indulging in dessert as the main course.

Dessert alone is poor nourishment, and it doesn't even taste as sweet if you skip the spice and substance of the entrée.

Now it was his heart that skipped a beat as he gazed across the rolling lawn, past the dock, to the front of the sleek white yacht. Venus stood on the foredeck, her hair and suit illuminated so brightly by the sun that an aura glowed around her. Under the close watch of security guards, she was staring at the water through black sunglasses.

As a few fluffy white clouds dotted the sky, the sun sparkled on the light chop of waves as if God had sprinkled a million diamonds over Lake St. Clair.

"There she is," Kimberly mouthed, still on the phone as they strode quickly.

Rex fought the urge to grin. He had never felt so electrified. In fact, just before their first encounter last night at the opera, he had felt an odd sensation, like a blue-white web of electricity crackling over his body. Then, during that magic moment when he first looked into her eyes, elation had flowed through him, rousing a shiver that cast a golden glow over today, tomorrow and forever.

With her and only her. She's mine. I'm hers. From now on, everything is about 'we' and 'us.'

If Rex had been searching for his ultimate life purpose, he had found it yesterday in an enchanted, new dimension as they stared, mesmerized, into each other's eyes for the first time.

Now I have to do everything in my power to stay there with her, forever.

That's why, as soon as Kimberly had called him today, he had hopped onto his motorcycle and zoomed here. Thankfully, his black helmet and its dark glass shield had hidden his face from all those TV cameras in the media horde out front. Too many people, especially vengeful ex-girlfriends, were still watching for a chance to strike back at him for abandoning them as he had ascended into his spiritual awakening and virtuous lifestyle.

Coming here contradicted his principles of keeping a pure heart, mind and spirit. He had given up living through the flesh long ago, and was therefore no longer controlled by his physical appetites for food, booze and sex. Yet superficial pleasure was the premise of Husbands, Inc., for people who'd apparently given up on real love.

I'm here to show Venus that there's more...

"No," Kimberly snapped on yet another call. "Tell the clients they cannot take photos of the costumes. Warn them that violating the 'no photo' policy could result in immediate expulsion."

Rex inhaled deeply to deflect Kimberly's high-strung vibe. *Man, my yoga and meditation class would do her a world of good.* He still felt light and floaty from teaching this morning.

"Daily meditation," Rex told a dozen men and women, "enables you to open your spiritual energy channels to receive love, healing, prosperity, peace and joy."

As the students lay on yoga mats in the studio in a downtown loft, Rex said, "Now imagine you're floating up a golden beam of light, which takes you to an ethereal place where your spirit is free to thrive in perfect health, love and happiness. Focus on that. Release all the negativity of the physical world, and let it elevate you to a magical place where you will be shown that anything is possible."

Along with his students, Rex closed his eyes. He envisioned Venus in a stream of vivid scenarios in which he was helping her cultivate romance and love around the globe.

Now, his heart leaped with excitement — and angst. Because last night, he had witnessed her split-second ability to switch from love-swept to ice-cold, looking at him like another piece of meat to hawk at this man market.

"Hit it hard!" shouted a woman playing volleyball on the beach with muscular men and bikini-clad women.

A man lunged for the ball, then volleyed it over the net, taunting, "How 'ya like me now?"

A very fit woman on the other side leaped up to slam it to the sand.

"That much!" she shouted triumphantly.

Rex bristled. *It's wrong to create a world where romance is a sport, and every game is fixed. The woman wins the relationship she wants; the man bags a cash prize. Both lose out on discovering the ultimate gift of real love.*

Rex strode faster toward the yacht; Kimberly sped up. In her flouncy green blouse, sparkly headband and leggings, she reminded him of a fairy in the bedtime storybooks he used to read to his little brother and sister.

Now, how could Rex ensure a happy ending with Venus? How could he help her expand her business to provide real matchmaking with the goal of marriages that were truly *'til death do us part*? This question had haunted him ever since he'd first heard of Venus Roman and Husbands, Inc. — just 24 hours ago.

Yesterday he'd stopped at his favorite Middle Eastern restaurant for the vegetarian lunch special: lentil soup, stuffed grape leaves, hummus, tabouleh, babaganoush and falafel. As he'd sat at an outdoor umbrella table amidst the lush herb and vegetable garden, Venus had stared up from the cover of *Time* magazine under the headline MESSIAH OR PARIAH?

With one glimpse, Rex was stunned with déjà-vu, as if he had known her forever. Since his spiritual awakening at the ashram in India, Rex believed that nothing was a coincidence, and that every experience, no matter how mundane or monumental, was an integral part of one's divine journey. Therefore, he was certain that Fate had deliberately arranged for someone to leave that magazine on the table, so he could devour every word with his delicious lunch.

After that, at home, he'd read and watched countless online interviews with Venus Roman. And though he rarely turned on his television, he'd tuned in to local and national news reports about threats on her life.

While overwhelmed with the desire to protect her, his heart ached that her work was making such a tragic statement about love and marriage. Yet he empathized deeply; his own family and relationships had prodded him to take drastic measures to protect himself from deceit and disappointment.

But I can't tell her the truth yet. She would not have invited me here today if she knew who I really am...

His heart gonged with panic as he approached the yacht.

The one thing she hates most, she said in every interview, is dishonesty. And here I am, being exactly that on the most fundamental level. As soon as I win her love, though, I'll tell her everything.

After all, he had very good reasons for presenting this identity to the world. Rex discerned divine affirmation for this belief as he glimpsed two swans swimming in unison near the beach.

"Rex, I'll leave you here," Kimberly said, waving at hulking guards on the yacht, and two police officers at the staircase leading to the upper deck. "They'll escort you to her, and to the luncheon."

"Thank you," Rex said, awed that he was about to see Venus Roman. Yesterday, before his shift at the Opera House, he'd meditated on whether he would ever meet her. While breathing deeply and sitting with his legs crossed in the silence of his carriage house, his inner voice that always spoke loudly and clearly had answered:

"Love her like you have never loved, and she will do the same for you."

Then he saw a vision: He and Venus were on a yacht, surrounded by friends, family members and turquoise water. They were facing each other, reciting vows before an officiant. Rex slipped a wedding band – with four rows of diamonds – onto her finger. It was an old-fashioned ceremony — no prenuptial agreement, no payment, and no scripted behavior.

"Because when love is true," his inner voice said, "you don't need written instructions. Your heart tells you what to do or say, and your heart is never wrong."

The meditation had concluded with a dazzling flash of colors — from red-orange-yellow to green-blue-purple to gold — that made him feel feverishly hot. Hours later, heat consumed him again, during the surreal moment when Venus appeared at the Opera House, and they looked into each other's eyes, stunned and speechless.

Now, as he stepped onto the dock, his footsteps on the wooden planks echoed his pounding heart.

She's going to laugh at me again, and tell me how much she loathes the impossible fantasy of real love.

The two dark-suited guards who'd accompanied Venus to the opera last night now led him to the fore deck.

"I knew you'd come," Venus said, turning around, removing her sunglasses, and consuming him with smoldering eyes.

His knees threatened to buckle, so he took a deep, calming breath of fresh lake air. Rex stared at her in utter wonderment. She was like a perfect diamond; all the facets — her eyes, her lips, her aura — were sparkling so brightly, he wanted to stop and bask in her light.

"You'll be honored to know," Venus said with a sultry tone, "that you've inspired an entirely new Husband theme: *Tarzan*. The hair, the muscles, the perfect face—"

Rex bristled. "That's not why I'm here."

"Of course it is," she said, framed by the vast blue water and sky. "You want to be a Husband."

"Yes, *your* Husband," he declared. "Not a Husband for hire."

"There's no other kind in my world," she said, glancing at the bodyguards, who were watching about 10 feet away. As were more guards on a speedboat anchored nearby, while law enforcement vessels zipped back and forth across the lake.

"Rex," she said, "do you have a last name?"

"Lancaster."

"Rex Lancaster." Her eyes were an enigma, blazing with power that paralyzed him, yet burning with something else that made his heart ache.

"You have sad eyes," he said tenderly.

She tossed her head back and laughed heartily toward the sky. A sudden, cool breeze off the water suggested that the universe was affirming her disagreement.

"Venus, the fire in your eyes blazes so hot because your heart is aching for more than what you're getting. It's yearning for someone to nurture and pleasure your heart, soul and body all at once. Right now you're only getting one of three—"

"So what are you, a psychologist?" she snapped. "Now that's one Husband theme we won't be providing here. You can keep the gloomy — and erroneous — analysis to yourself, sweetheart."

"The Goddess of Love is hiding behind a mask of indifference toward love," Rex said. "And you've built an empire on heartache and longing. But deep down, there's nothing you want more than what your parents have—"

"Every woman wants what my parents have!" Indignation glinted in her eyes. "But it's like a four leaf clover, a blue moon, a red diamond. Extremely rare, impossible for most."

"Not impossible," Rex said, stepping close enough to inhale her. "Venus, you and I are connected in a whole different dimension. Don't deny that you feel it."

If her eyes were daggers, they would have sliced through him. "Rex, what I *feel*, is that I'm looking at an extraordinarily handsome young man who's very intelligent, and quite cocky—"

He smiled. "Then tell me what you saw when you closed your eyes last night—"

Venus instantly glowed with joy, as if her entire being were blooming like an enormous rose.

Overwhelmed with delight and relief, he let out a sultry, "Yeah."

Regret tensed her face; she turned, glancing at a screeching seagull that splashed down on the water, snatched a fish, then soared toward the sky.

She laughed. "Mother Nature is so brilliant. Did you see that? The symbolism is divine."

Rex pointed near the beach, where those two swans formed the shape of a heart as their necks curved and their beaks touched.

"We can learn a lot from the synchronized beauty of nature," Rex said, as she observed the swans and gasped. He smiled. "Gotcha."

The heat in her blue eyes frosted over. Her tone was icy: "I'm too busy to take a Husband—"

"Good," Rex shot back, "because I don't endorse that you're brokering marriages for desperate women and cash-hungry men."

She stepped past him, waving to her guards, who immediately approached. "Rex, this meeting is over," she announced. "Your moral opposition to our mission disqualifies you from applying."

"Mr. Lancaster," said the big, platinum-haired guard. "This way."

Rex turned his back on the man, so he could face Venus, but she pivoted toward the lake.

"Venus," Rex said with a pleading stare at the back of her head. "Let me show you how to take your mission far and beyond what you have now."

She was still and silent.

"Mr. Lancaster, let's go," the guard ordered.

But Rex did not budge.

𝒞𝒽𝒶𝓅𝓉𝑒𝓇 41. A Heartbreaking Surprise

Claire pounded so hard on the door to Nikki's cottage that the skin scraped off her knuckles.

"Nikki! We have to talk! Open the door!"

Claire's entire body burned with worry. She hadn't eaten since the pubic-hair-on-the-dildo incident. Nikki had become hysterical and ordered her to leave, but Claire had gotten halfway to the log cabin, and turned around. Now, she was determined to make Nikki come to terms with the reality of their situation.

"Nikki! I know you're in there!"

A melancholy love song by their favorite female performer blared through the screen in the open kitchen window.

I should break in... and make her listen to me.

Claire stood on the deck, staring into the blur of green and brown woods all around. She pulled her cell phone from her pocket, dialed her parents and merged the calls.

"Hello my little angel," Mom said with the same super mellow voice that usually meant she'd just smoked a joint. But now that she was in the convent, she was probably just high on religion or whatever all those women did together.

"Hey Princess!" Dad said. His voice was gravelly from drinking, smoking and screaming rock 'n roll songs for three decades.

"Mom, Dad," Claire said, plunking into a deck chair, "can you come visit me now? I really want you to meet my Husband."

The line was silent.

"Hello?!" Claire spat. "Anybody there?"

"The Order is preparing for an ordination ceremony," her mother said.

"I got shows in Tokyo, Singapore and Sydney," her father added. "That's why we picked your birthday, when me and your mom can both take time off."

"But that's six months away!" Claire protested.

"Us coming to meet him won't get you your inheritance any sooner, dear," her mother said.

"I hope that ain't your motive," Dad said.

"No, no," Claire insisted. "I'm just excited for you to meet my Husband. He's the opposite of all the guys in L.A."

Her dad snickered. "Must be. Any cat who can convince my Princess to leave California and move to God-awful Dee-troit—"

"Dear Lord, Dale, watch your language!"

Her father laughed. "For Christ sakes, woman, don't lay that holier-than-thou bullshit on me."

"You guys!" Claire shouted.

"Dale," her mother said. "I'm praying that you repent for your life of sin. You'll see, there's a better way—"

"Mom, my Husband is really into the Bible. You'll love him."

"Lovely," Mom cooed.

But her father laughed. Claire cringed.

"The Bible?" her father roared. "When's the last time you put down your paint brush to read the Good Book, girl?"

"He reads it to me while I paint," Claire said. Actually, Billy Jack had recited from Genesis after walking into her studio — in an upstairs bedroom —as she painted a lush nature scene before leaving for Nikki's. He had insisted it was the Garden of Eden.

"Mom, Dad," Claire said, "I really need you both to come and meet him."

"Your birthday is still six months away," Mom said. "We'll come then and give you what you want."

Claire plunked down on the step, feeling like an abandoned five-year-old all over again. "Why do I have to wait half a year to see my parents?"

"Unless you and your new dude can fly to Asia and Australia to see me," her father said, "this is my life. God only knows where your mother is holed up—"

"The convent is in Argentina," her mother said. "You know that!"

Claire rolled her eyes. Her voice trembled with pain and frustration: "Mom, Dad, thanks for always being there for me. I'll see you on my birthday."

She hung up and shoved the phone into her pocket.

"This sucks!" she shouted, then banged on the door. "Nikki, let me in!"

Claire pulled a deck chair up to the kitchen window. She pushed in the screen and climbed inside.

"Nikki!" Claire sighed, glimpsing her on the couch. Nikki's pale, sullen face lit up for a moment as Claire strode to her and sat down. "Nikk-Nikk, I'm so sorry!"

Claire held Nikki's trembling shoulders as Nikki sobbed, "I can't do this! It's disgusting!"

"I'm trying to think of a way to bail," Claire said. She had an idea — a bluff — that she hoped would make Nikki see things more clearly, so she'd finally resign herself to staying here and riding it out for a whole year, if necessary.

"Let's just go!" Nikki shouted.

"No, I have to wait six months to get my—"

"I don't give a fuck about your money!" Nikki screamed.

"I know," Claire said as sadness consumed her like fire. "That's why I came to tell you something." She kissed Nikki's forehead as the words bunched up in her throat.

Hope filled Nikki's bloodshot eyes as she stared back at Claire.

"A choice," Claire said through trembling lips. She dreaded hearing herself say the words she was thinking, but hopefully her bluff would work.

"Nikk, your first choice is, stay here and deal with this for half a year. My parents come, I get the money, I tell Country Boy he can stay in the house for the rest of the time and get paid as if I were there. But we leave. Get our paint studio on the beach, in the city, whatever. And we live happily ever after."

"Or?" Nikki demanded.

A million bad thoughts splattered through Claire's mind. *Don't say it!* her inner voice was screaming. *If Nikki calls your bluff, you're fucked!*

But no, Claire didn't believe Nikki would.

She's got nothing and no one without me.

Nikki ran a hand through her spiky hair. "Claire, what's my second choice?"

Hot waves of sadness threatened to scorch Claire from the inside out. "I can free you from the torment of my parents' bigoted, manipulative plot."

Nikki almost smiled. "Cool, but how?"

Claire shook her head. "No, it's not cool. Since you don't support my right to get my inheritance by any means necessary, we have a fundamental disagreement. It's really a deal breaker. So Nikk, you can just go."

Nikki turned sickly pale. "Go? Then see you after you're done with this?"

"No," Claire said. "If you can't support my decision to go through with this to appease my parents, then I can't support you once it's over."

Nikki squeezed her eyes, then focused on Claire.

"You don't think money matters in life," Claire said, certain that this would make Nikki realize that her only option was to stay. "I know that money *does* matter, so call me a materialistic bitch or a ruthless money whore. I don't care. That money is rightfully mine, and since my parents are incredible assholes, this is what I have to do to get it."

Nikki's brows drew together as she stared at Claire for a long moment. Claire's stomach cramped; her heart ached. Any minute, Nikki would say, *"Okay. I see your point. I'll stay and get through this somehow."*

But an odd expression – one that Claire had never seen – flashed across Nikki's face.

"Okay," Nikki whispered. "I'll go." She stood and walked out the door.

Now Nikki is the one who's bluffing. Her cell phone was on the coffee table, and she hadn't even taken a bag.

Claire leaned back on the couch, confident that within five minutes, Nikki would walk right back in here, and they'd be reunited for the duration of this insane scheme.

307

Chapter 42. A Desperate Plea: "Marry Me"

Rex's heart pounded with anxiety as the security guards stepped toward him. But he stood his ground, plaintively staring at the back of Venus' head. She was facing the lake while standing at the rail on the yacht behind Sea Castle.

"Venus," Rex pleaded, "if you can honestly tell me that you haven't imagined us together, then I'll leave now and never come back."

A seagull screeched overhead, and the guards hulked at his sides.

"Time to go, Mr. Lancaster," the dark-haired guard said.

Venus glanced back over her shoulder. "No, come here, Rex."

Rex stepped to her side, while the guards remained close.

"Venus," Rex felt like his heart was wide-open, pouring love through his gaze as he stared down into her eyes. "When you marry me as a real husband, the old-fashioned kind, I'll be your biggest selling point. Ever."

She looked doubtful. "And just what would that selling point be?"

"That true love really does happen—"

"No, I just don't see how," Venus said with a shrug. Sadness glinted in her eyes; she looked toward the swans, which were floating gracefully side-by-side.

"Here's how," Rex said, taking her hand. "If Venus Roman, the world's most outspoken opponent of traditional marriage, can find true love, then hope is not lost for the masses—"

Venus snatched back her hand. "Why do you think you can walk in here and convince me that you're different than any other man—"

"Because I am." Rex wanted to confide that he'd been celibate for a whole year. But she would laugh. He hadn't even told his closest male friends, because it defied the norm in a world where sex saturated music, movies, magazines and the mainstream mentality that goaded men to feast on an endless buffet of females, from puberty to senility.

At the same time, society brainwashed many women to measure their value with sex appeal, so they eagerly served themselves up as consumable fodder in an attempt to lure men's attention and affection.

Rex knew this because extremely desirable women offered him the "all you can eat" special every day. But since breaking up with a girlfriend last year, he refused to squander himself on casual or dead-end relationships.

"Venus, I've studied all the religions of the world, and I live by golden nuggets of wisdom from each," Rex said, relieved that the guards had stepped back. "One comes from the Bible, Matthew Chapter Seven, Verse Six. It sums up my philosophy about relationships."

She looked curious.

"It says, *'Do not give dogs what is sacred; do not throw your pearls to pigs. If you do, they may trample them under their feet, and turn and tear you to pieces.'*"

Venus clapped. "That is *exactly* why every woman here is protecting herself behind a legal agreement. I think I'll add that Scriptural endorsement to my repertoire. Thank you, Rex."

He bristled, then declared, "I'm going to spend my life convincing you that I'm different."

"Marriages here last only one year," Venus said. "Because I'm different, too. I'm gloriously detached from the wretched yearning for true love, and that has been the most liberating experience of my life."

"Ah, detached," Rex challenged. "That implies that the yearning is still within you—"

"Wrong!" Venus snapped. "I like everything in black and white, as spelled out in our contracts. My master script doesn't venture into the murky gray area where fickle emotions rule, and heartache is guaranteed."

Rex inhaled her scent — soft and sweet like gardenias. "Let me be the man who shows you the most colorful, real-life fantasy—"

Venus laughed. "Oh, Rex Lancaster, you're good!"

Sadness swept through him. "Stop looking at me like I'm one of your money-hungry studs!"

"That's how I look at men," Venus said. Her tone was hard, but tenderness softened her gaze.

He took her hands in his; they were so soft and delicate, he resisted the urge to press them to his lips.

"Venus, I have a confession," he said. "All night, I stared up into the blackness of my bedroom, thinking: *'If I can't hold her in my arms while we sleep, then I don't want to sleep at all.'* So I didn't. My entire essence ached to be next to you, just holding your hand."

He looked down; her hands were so small in his, and her diamond ring sparkled. Her eyes shimmered just as intensely.

"And if I could hold you while you sleep, just to comfort you, and make you feel safe—" he glanced at the bodyguards "—that would be as close to heaven as a man could get."

For now. Making love with her would be the ultimate gift — best cherished on their wedding night.

She pulled her hands from his and crossed her arms. "I don't need comfort—"

"Your eyes say you do," he said.

She closed them.

"Venus," he pleaded, "when I turned 35 this year, I prayed that I would be alone until Fate brought me someone of equal or higher caliber than myself. She was delivered on the wings of my prayers last night."

"Rex," Venus said, glancing at the water. "You know that saying about all the fish in the sea?"

"Of course."

"Then tell me, with all the beautiful women in the world, why would you choose one who's philosophically out of reach and nine years older than you?"

As he reveled in the wisdom in her eyes, he said, "Love is timeless."

"Ovaries aren't," she quipped. "A man your age usually wants babies at some point—"

"Not me," he said. I helped raise my brother and two sisters. Our parents always left us with babysitters, so I did my best to give them affection and love while—"

Rex closed his eyes, remembering the little ones' despair and Sheila's tailspin into teen pregnancy, a troubled marriage and now a miserable existence at age 33.

Venus studied his face. "There's a lot going on in there."

"Yeah," he said. But revealing the drama of his past would be better saved for a future disclosure about his family. "Venus, I've dated, I've traveled, I've met women from around the world, and—"

She looked bored.

"And the fire in a woman's eyes has never ignited me like yours has," he said. "You have this supernatural potency—"

She smiled slightly, as if amused.

"It reminds me of how my mother's eyes used to twinkle at my dad," he said softly. "And when she looked at me, she had this look of awe, like, *'Look at this little miracle that we created for the world. Our baby boy is going to do something that makes people happy.'*"

Venus crossed her arms. "And you're doing that by ushering people to their seats at the opera?"

Her piercing tone made him pause. "I teach yoga and meditation. I help people tap into their spiritual power to find inner peace and improve their lives."

"That's noble," she said flatly.

"Venus, you're already harnessing your power. So let me love you, and your life will go from remarkable to immeasurably astonishing."

She scowled. "There you go with the psychology again. What makes you think I don't already have an *amazing* life?"

"Your eyes tell me everything," he said. "You ache for real love. I'm the one in a billion who can provide what you deserve."

She crossed her arms. "You've obviously never been married, because you're naïve to the dreadful reality—"

"I once vowed to *never* marry," Rex insisted. "As a kid, I hated that my dad was a flagrant womanizer. He killed my mother's joy—"

Venus lit up, as if he had switched from speaking a foreign language back to English.

"Yes!" she exclaimed. "Because men are hard-wired to crave variety. You love the excitement of the chase, the triumph of conquering, the thrill of adding one more to your roster, before strutting off to find the next—"

"Venus!" he pleaded, holding her hands. "Don't condemn me for the sins of my gender. The mindless consumption of females, just for the sport of it, is horribly empty. Miserable."

A collage of beautiful faces and bodies danced in his mind, but their greedy motives and schemes made him envision a grotesque swirl stamped GOLD-DIGGING EX-GIRLFRIENDS.

Topping the list was Nellie. His first girlfriend had the face and body of a centerfold, but her manipulative mind was pure poison. Over the years, she had called, emailed and even shown up unexpectedly, using temptress trickery to lure him back.

Now, staring at Venus, Rex wanted nothing and no one but the pure soul that roused within him the most euphoric, passionate, urgent desire to spend the rest of his life helping her promote authentic love.

Venus shook her head. "It's so easy to say what you're saying. But the inevitable truth plays out down the road, when, unfortunately, actions speak louder than the most eloquent words."

"No, no," he said, squeezing her hands. "I want you to see, how luscious it can be, when you feel free; to live and love with a divinely matched mate, brought together by God and Fate—"

She glowed with intrigue as he continued: "—fused as one in mind, body and soul, laughing and loving 'til we grow old; then floating up into eternity, not as you, not as me, but as us, as we, for all of heaven to see; and make others believe, that this kind of love, they, too, can achieve."

Venus' eyes welled with tears; he wiped a single droplet rolling down her cheek. At the same time, a speedboat roared past. As its wake splashed and gently rocked the yacht, they stared into each other's eyes with unblinking curiosity.

"Rex, your poetic talent is impressive," she said. "But I don't indulge the fantasy of real love anymore—"

"That's what you tell yourself," Rex accused. "You said in all those interviews, when you were a girl in your parents' bridal shop, you believed in love—"

"Believed!" she insisted. "Emphasis on the 'E-D' at the end."

"You can believe again," Rex said. "You deserve someone who'll love you out of the purity of his soul, not because he has dollar signs in his eyes."

Rex lifted her hand and examined her ring. "You wear a heart on your ring finger, and diamonds are forever. But what does it mean?"

Venus tilted her hand, making the diamond sparkle in the sunshine. "It means I'm married to the business of romance. And I love it. Now if you'd like to apply to become a Husband—"

"*Your* Husband, Venus. For life. It's my mission to replace the sadness in your eyes with joy."

Venus' shoulder twitched, as if she were cold. But she blushed, and her gaze softened.

Rex, still holding her left hand, dropped to one knee. He gazed up at her shocked face.

"Venus Roman, I promise to spend the rest of my life proving that real love can be better than a million marriages with your Husbands-for-hire put together."

Tears glistened in her eyes as she stared down at him.

"With me," he pledged, "you would not surrender your power. Our synergy would enhance your power — and magnify it, multiply it, amplify it — because your mission would be fueled by two souls, two hearts, two minds—"

As she wiped her eyes with her right fingertips, Rex held her left hand and said, "Venus Aphrodite Roman, please marry me."

She pulled him up, close. "You are superb."

Rex was sure that she was imagining their magnificent future together.

"I'm stunned," she said. "This is a first."

He raised her hand to his chest. Over the thin white cotton of his shirt, he pressed her palm to his pounding heart.

She smiled and whispered, "Bravo!" Her eyes hardened, and her tone became business-like: "All that time at the opera, you've gleaned some excellent theatrical skills. Forget Tarzan. I see *The True Love Package.* Or *The Real Romeo. The Passionate Poet!*"

"No!" Rex protested. "I am not a package, or a theme, or a performance ordered on a website. I'm a man!"

"Yes, an exquisite man." Venus pulled a phone from her pocket and dialed. "Eden," she said, "I'm sending Rex Lancaster up to apply. Please expedite his application so he can partake of this weekend's festivities."

Rex shook his head. "No, Venus! This is not what—"

"Gentlemen," Venus said, calling her guards, "please escort Mr. Lancaster up to the house for processing."

As she stepped toward him, Rex breathed deeply to diffuse the anger sparking through his every cell.

Patience. Have patience. Time and circumstance will melt the ice around her heart...

He trusted that. But as the guards stood close, he loathed being dismissed as if he were one of the masses of men in her risqué realm.

"Venus, I'll go through the process if it means I can become your Husband."

"*A* Husband," she snapped.

He cast a determined look down at her and vowed, "At your side, you'll be unable to hide; that you know in your soul, you cannot control; the enchanting fascination, of love that defies your wildest imagination."

Her lips parted with wonder. He continued:

"I am the face that will erase, every trace of sadness from your eyes; and fill them with enchantment for the rest of our lives."

She gasped. Her eyes glazed. And she turned toward the water. But not before he saw her shudder again.

Chapter 43. A Toast to Honor Among Thieves?

John Barker found it prophetic that he was meeting with Ted Pendigree, Frank Williams and his cyber expert, Rippstyx, on Gregor Nikolai's yacht. They were sailing on the international waterway between the United States and Canada as the sun blazed on the sleek, black vessel.

"Gentlemen," John said, facing the men on the aft deck. They sat around him in a circular, leather booth that was built into the shiny teakwood floor and walls. "Before we get off this boat, we will have sealed Venus Roman's proverbial coffin, to stop her from taking her debauchery worldwide."

Ted, who was applying hand sanitizer again as he sat across from John, was so enraged, his lower lip was trembling. Even though things had gone well in court, and Ted had done exactly what they'd discussed to convince the grand jury to indict Venus, he was still trying to weasel out of the deal.

All the way here, in John's car, Ted had whined about his "misgivings" and "apprehension" about going forward. He needed to just shut up and cooperate, and John had everything he needed to make him do that. Then, once John retrieved the alleged video from Venus, Ted would have no ammunition to strike back.

"Hey Rippstyx," John said, "you sure you didn't pillage any video from the whorehouse's network?"

"Like I said, bro," Rippstyx answered, "all I found was the two-minute promotional video on their website, and a bunch of testimonials from women and men. That's it."

John seethed, not looking away from Rippstyx, whose appearance offered no hint that he was the military-trained cyber genius who had hacked the Husbands, Inc. network.

Thin, olive-skinned and around 30, he wore silver dog tags over a DETROIT t-shirt that exposed the red, green and blue vines and flowers tattooed down his arms and up his neck. Two silver rings held open nickel-sized holes in his earlobes; his short, dark beard extended into his buzz cut.

Rippstyx's voice was oddly goofy and gruff all at once: "Sorry, bro, I know you hate her, but she ain't stupid. Wouldn't leave the goods sittin' around where somebody like me could snatch it."

Ted cast appalled looks at Rippstyx and exclaimed, "That is criminal! I am obligated—"

"To shut the fuck up," John ordered.

Frank's nostrils flared as he huffed at Ted: "Always knew you were a candy-ass. But don't worry your little squeaky-clean brain cells, Mr. Prosecutor. You do your thing; we'll do ours."

"That's why I *am* worried," Ted said, glancing down at his phone in his hand. "The media is all over this story."

"Yeah, bro, and Men for Traditional Marriage is taking responsibility, just like they will for tonight's big surprise." Rippstyx pointed at Ted's hand sanitizer on the table. "All our hands are as clean as yours on this."

Ted's cheeks reddened with anger.

"Let's get down to business," John said as the boat hummed beneath them and the wind struck his face. He had never felt so much hostility toward his best friend. But Ted's fists had provoked within John a beastly anger and guilt. And now, in some twisted way that John refused to psycho-analyze, he was hurling it all back at Ted.

"Gentlemen," John said. "We're doing historic, monumental work. Together, we'll stop the rampant spread of immoral debauchery that men and women are buying and selling under the guise of the most holy, sacred institution. Marriage."

Frank laughed. "In other words, we're gonna put them horny bitches in their place!"

As John chuckled, Frank high-fived Rippstyx.

"Over here," Nikolai told four bikini-clad "waitresses" as they appeared with trays of sushi and cold beer.

Tall and thick, Nikolai wore a dark business suit with his salt-and-pepper hair slicked back from an always tanned, pampered face. The sun glimmered off his clunky gold watch, bracelets and necklace.

"I'm delighted you could join me in this most appropriate venue for our discussion," Nikolai said, as John ogled huge jugs on the brunette chick. "You have my full support in this venture."

Ted's anger was apparently blinding him to the prime tits and ass surrounding them. He was becoming such a boring, goodie-two-shoes in anticipation of his bid for Congress.

"Gentlemen," Ted said, "truthfully, I need to tell you that I should recuse myself from this case, as should Judge Reynolds, due to our past history with the defendant when she was your wife and our friend, John. Judicial objectivity is impossible—"

Frank let out a bark-like, "Huh!" He glared at Ted like he wanted to punch him. "Now that's some more spineless, cop-out shit, if I ever heard it. You seem to have lost the balls that made you who you are, Mr. Prosecutor. I suggest you find 'em in a hurry, and proceed full speed ahead like we plan to do."

Ted, framed by the Ambassador Bridge stretching high across the river behind him, shook his head. "Honestly, it's not my call. I could proceed all I want, but if the Judicial Tenure Commission decides—"

Frank roared with laughter. "We'll just make sure they don't decide anything that goes against what we want."

A speedboat whizzed past, its noise underscoring Frank's words and forcing the men into silence.

All the while, John's dick was rock hard as he watched the Asian waitress bend her sweet little behind over the table to serve each man a tiny plate of wasabi and sliced ginger. Another girl, whose black thong showcased the red lips tattooed on her ass, gave everybody a mini bowl of soy sauce.

Ted looked at the sushi like he wanted to vomit; ever since childhood, he'd hated fish and spicy food.

"Teddy, this boat has left the dock, so to speak," John said. "Once we slap Venus with that indictment, it's up to you to lead the prosecution. You can't wimp out on us. That would be disastrous for your Congressional campaign."

As the men helped themselves to the salmon-covered and crab-stuffed rolls of rice, nori and vegetables, Ted cast a disturbed look at Rippstyx.

"In all honesty, gentlemen," Ted said, "I'm extremely concerned that this could backfire on all of us in a very bad way."

John's eyes watered with the spicy shock of the green horseradish paste as his taste buds delighted in the salty soy sauce and the soft, chewy textures of rice and fish. At the same time, he eyed the girls, who were pouring bottled water for each man. If only he had their ripe melons and tuna tacos in his mouth right now—

That will come later, as promised by Nikolai.

John cast a sly smile at his friend, whom he had met years ago when the Russian-born billionaire first came to Detroit. Their friendship, sealed over cigars and investment deals at the country club, had earned John entrée into an international party scene where sexy girls took center stage.

Ted had always shied away from Nikolai's flashy lifestyle, and now he looked horrified by the nearly nude girls.

"Teddy," John said with a hard tone, "don't even think about calling in a replacement. This case will win you every right-wing vote out there, and you'll be a shoe-in, come election day."

As the yacht entered the channel between tree-covered Belle Isle and waterfront homes in Windsor, Frank glared at Ted. "I'll tell you what. I'm not likin' this mamby pamby attitude on the part of our good prosecutor. So let's resolve this right now."

Ted turned a shade whiter as he stared back at Frank and said, "Honestly, I need assurance that this endeavor will remain entirely above board. I have some left-wing critics who will hang us all out to dry if—"

"If what?" Frank bellowed. "I'm the goddamned director of the Detroit FBI. I resent your insinuation that I would do anything *but* remain above board."

Frank glared at Ted like he wanted to toss him into the river.

"Gentlemen," Ted said nervously, "we need to examine the consequences of our actions if things don't go the way we hope."

Rippstyx, despite a mouth full of food, laughed. "I've never met you, bro, but I read about how you nailed drug dealers, mobsters, rapists and killers. But Ted Pendigree the legend, and *you*, seem like two different people."

Ted looked shaky. "To tell the truth, I became legendary by demanding the utmost integrity in every case that I touch."

Frank sloshed another piece of sushi through a brown-green puddle of soy sauce and wasabi on his plate. "Good, then we all got the same code of conduct. Johnny, take the floor." Frank popped the dripping ball into his mouth. "Damn, this is good." He nodded at Nikolai. "Thank you, my friend."

"You are very welcome," Nikolai said, checking his gold cell phone, which was on the table.

The brunette handed John a napkin to wipe his fingers; Ted hadn't even sipped his water.

"This battle plan calls for an all-out assault on every level," John said. "That includes: the grounds of

Husbands, Inc.; the financial front; all their employees; the gigolos; every one of the foreign bitches who are there; and all the clients she already has across the country."

Rippstyx nodded. "Tall order, bro. What about biological warfare?"

Frank let out a sinister chuckle. "Yeah, send in some AIDS-infected rascals, to spray up them horny bitches—"

"Or a dude with genital warts," Rippstyx said. "Herpes, gonorrhea. That'll have everybody burnin', drippin', and droppin' dead."

As the men howled with laughter, John said, "That would be very bad for her business. I like the way you think."

Rippstyx nodded as he smeared wasabi on his sushi. "Turns my stomach to think about young dudes humpin' those old, crusty cows."

"Hey, I saw some hot young things in there," Frank said. "They oughta be in regular relationships, so the man in charge can enjoy what they got."

John scowled. "Yeah, but there's just as many old hags with saggy tits, cottage cheese asses, and faces that look like bunched up paper bags."

"If there's one thing I hate," Frank snorted, "it's an old, dry pussy."

Rippstyx chugged beer. "You ever thought about plantin' a couple dudes in there to spy—"

John's mouth burned from the horseradish as he thought about Laila working on his exposé. Ted wouldn't have the balls to mention it, so it would remain classified. No need to share it with these men, who might have their own ideas about how it should play out.

I'm the general of this war; they're just my foot soldiers, helping me win.

Laila shared their lowly rank. And if that little tart didn't hold up her end of the deal, she would be as burnt as Venus Roman when all was said and done.

"I like that idea," John said. "Planting some guys on the inside—"

"The thing is," Frank said, ogling the blond chick's tits that were barely covered by tiny squares of black fabric over her nipples. "We're about to strike so hard and fast, we don't have time to get something like that up and running. Don't need it."

Frank turned to Ted and barked, "Eat, drink, be merry, my friend. You only live once."

Ted fumed. "I need to get home as soon as possible." He held up his cell phone and glanced at the time. "I have a lot of work—"

Frank reached for more food. "Relax! Our fine friend Mr. Nikolai is rollin' out the red carpet for us to enjoy the good life for the afternoon. We work hard. We deserve it."

The blond perched on the back of the booth and massaged Ted's shoulders.

Frank chuckled. "She'll help you relieve some stress, Mr. Prosecutor."

Ted slid away from the woman's reach and glared at John. "Honestly, I need to get back."

"Let's talk business," John said. "You'll be back home to sweet little Mary in no time."

John looked around the table. "First, that awards ceremony is at the Fox Theatre tomorrow night. We need to coordinate with our partners to make sure Venus gets slapped with her rude awakening at just the wrong time."

Ted turned to Nikolai. "Gregor, can you please have your captain take me back to the dock?"

Frank made a loud breathing sound and glowered at Ted. "I gotta say that's rude, Mr. Prosecutor. Sit tight."

Frank pointed toward the huge blue expanse of Lake St. Clair ahead, and the Michigan shore to the left. "Nikolai promised us a cruise past the Motor City's most notorious whorehouse."

Ted winced.

"Then we're gonna sail into the wild blue yonder," Frank said, nodding at the girls, "for a pleasure cruise."

Ted bolted toward the rail, dialing his phone and standing with his back to the men.

"Ted!" John shouted. "Come back here!"

"John, this is bullshit!" Frank said. "I don't know what kinda stick he's got up his ass, but he's got a job to do for us."

John stood. "I'll whip him into shape." He approached Ted, who was on the phone.

"I'm sorry," Ted was saying. "I don't know what time I'll be back. I'll call as soon as I know." He hung up and scowled at John. "I was supposed to take Mary to her sorority's barbecue this afternoon."

"She's been fine plenty of times while you were out to play with Janice," John accused. "Teddy, I meant what I said. Since your accusations have hurt me so much, you owe me this. You owe every man in the world, the performance of a lifetime in court, to stop Venus from unleashing her anarchy in male-female relationships."

"You are sick," Ted groaned as if he were in physical pain.

"Teddy, men's dominance is at stake. If Venus takes this around the world, she will do irreparable harm to unborn millions of boys and men—"

"Stop!" Ted looked gaunt and weak. For a moment, the pain of their broken friendship gnawed at John so fiercely, he couldn't breathe.

But I have to do this to cover my own ass. And bring Venus down.

Plus, no other prosecutor could work with them the way that John wanted. A good lawyer could prove that Venus was in fact operating on the right side of the law. Then John would have no case. And bringing her down on the legal front was the most absolute strategy to shut her down and get her locked up.

The roar of a police boat drew John's attention to a yacht docked behind a mansion, whose sprawling grounds were bustling with men and women.

"There it is," John said, pointing to Sea Castle. "The prostitution palace that Congressman Pendigree shut down."

Together, they scanned the scene.

"There she is," John said, pointing to a blond woman on the upper balcony. "I hate that bitch so much I can taste it."

Ted scowled. "Honestly? Your hatred has put you on a kamikaze flight that could take us all down—"

"Hatred?" John accused. "You assaulted me yesterday! In my office, with witnesses! You're damn lucky the Wolf TV reporter didn't show up early and get it all on tape! Talk about a kamikaze flight!"

Ted's face tensed with pain. "You defiled my daughter. Now you want to devastate my wife. Mary would die if she found out about Janice—"

John shook his head. "An eye for an eye. If you don't help stop Venus' all-out war on marriage and men's power, then I'll destroy you." He took Ted by the elbow and turned toward the table. "So let's get back to work."

Chapter 44. Sincere Seducer or Sinister Saboteur?

On the terrace outside her master suite at Sea Castle, Venus watched a speedboat race across the lake. Its fishtail-shaped wake rocked a smaller boat, putting it in jeopardy of taking on water and going under.

Two more speedboats barreled past, making the small vessel bob helplessly, trapped in the churning waters.

That's how I feel. Venus retreated inside the white-draped cabana, about 20 feet back from the balustrade where Gus and Mario stood watch amidst potted, orange-blooming hibiscus trees.

As she gazed out at the lake, her heart was thrumming with anticipation to learn more about the most exquisite pleasure cruiser ever to sail into her midst. But was Rex Lancaster showing up now to sweep her into a passionate paradise? Or to suck her into dangerous depths?

"Venus!" Eden entered, computer tablet in hand. "Wow, meeting up here feels like an escape from all the insanity. Speaking of—" a gloomy look washed over her freckled face "— Kimberly just got an update from the FBI about the death threats and she wants to tell you—"

"Eden, I have one rule for this meeting." Venus sat on a plush rattan couch near chairs and a sunbathing mattress. "We discuss only the business of my pleasure. All the bad stuff will still be there in 15 minutes, so let's just indulge this."

"Indulge, indeed," Eden said, as her tablet showed video of Rex jogging by the lake at sunrise. "Rex Lancaster is either a precious gem or a very convincing counterfeit."

"Or both." Venus glanced at police boats roaring back and forth on the lake. The noise allowed her to hear only nerve-wracking snippets of Gus' phone conversation:

"John Barker... FBI... threats."

"Venus," Eden said, "Rex was *beyond* perturbed about the interview, background check and physical exam. He kept saying, 'I'm only doing this so she'll say yes.' I reiterated that *he* wouldn't be the one asking, because the women here have the power—"

"Yes," Venus said. "We have the power." Hence, those two police officers, despite their insistence, now remained in the hallway outside her master suite. Neither they, nor their law enforcement colleagues, would ever set foot in the sacred space of her bedroom. Or onto the second floor, for that matter.

"Rex is in perfect health," Eden said, clicking to a screen showing the results of his blood work and physical. "Vegetarian. Doesn't drink, doesn't smoke. Doesn't even date, according to my sources and his phone records. He calls his sister, a housewife, a brother and sister, and about a half dozen people across the globe."

Venus shook her head. "It's hard to believe he doesn't date."

She glanced down at the yacht, where Husbands and women were drinking champagne in the Jacuzzi on the upper deck.

"Well, as we always say," Eden added, "there's a big difference between dating and fucking. Maybe he's not taking anyone out to dinner, but he could be taking someone to bed."

"Who?"

"As far as we can tell," Eden said incredulously, "no one. Phone records, emails, and preliminary interviews prove he's kind of a loner."

"Bizarre," Venus said.

"A global loner," Eden said as the screen showed the pages of his passport. "It's got more stamps than the U.S. Post Office. But this guy is anything but jet-set. He's traveled every continent on a shoestring budget. Back-packing, staying at hostels, even doing chores in exchange for room and board on farms in Europe and South America."

Photos showed a younger Rex hiking a mountain trail beside a Peruvian man and a donkey, then standing in front of the ancient Incan ruins of Machu Picchu.

"A free spirit?" Venus asked. "A spy? Or a con man on the lam?"

Eden nodded. "Gus had his international people confirm what my sources in D.C. said: this guy's profile is as clean as a monk's. In fact, he spent two years in India, studying meditation."

Video showed Rex outside a flower-covered temple; he was bald, wearing an orange cloth draped over one shoulder and secured with a rope at his waist. Another video clip featured him in a hip café, wearing jeans and a leather jacket on a stage, reciting spoken word poetry.

"He's perfect, and his timing is suspect," Venus said, imagining John picking Rex out of a crowd — maybe even at the Opera House — and proposing a wicked scheme. "Make sure he's not connected to that nouveau riche country club mafia that cavorts with John."

Eden nodded. "So far, I've found nothing to confirm any connection—"

"Those guys are notorious for having spoiled kids with roguish intentions," Venus said. "Gregor Nikolai's son is in jail right now for bilking wealthy widows out of millions."

Eden nodded. "Check, on all of the above. This guy's so perfect, I wondered if John paid him to beguile you, as a ploy to annihilate us."

Venus groaned. "I hate that our cynicism has reached new lows."

"I know," Eden said, "but I've seen John in action too many times—"

"Eden, that's it!" Venus exclaimed. "It's time to expose all the ghastly skeletons in John Barker's closet."

Eden clicked to another screen on her iPad. "You know better than anyone, I've been stewing about that for years. But my attorney warned that John was such a master at covering his tracks, I'd do better to just move on."

Venus flashed back about ten years, when Eden was office manager in John's law firm. She'd worked for him since graduating from Michigan State University, but suddenly left for a new management position at a large corporation. She thrived there, and it was only after Venus' divorce that Eden divulged her real motive for leaving John Sebastian Barker & Associates: the firm's unethical tactics for obtaining evidence to win trials. That included hiring people to spy, break into homes and offices, and commit bribery.

"Ugh," Eden said. "I was so afraid I could be implicated as a willing accomplice, even though I didn't know it." She shook her head. "That was the worst time of my life. Then getting divorced—"

Venus put her arm around Eden and said, "All that prepared you to become Business Manager here at the coolest company in the world."

Eden smiled.

"And I think," Venus said, "the stars have aligned to finally ease your mind. Make a list of anyone who might be willing to come forward and talk about John's dirty deeds."

"Done," Eden said. "I knew it would come to light someday."

"Right," Venus said, as two jet skis whizzed across the lake.

"Meanwhile, what I learned from working with John," Eden said, "is that if it *feels* wrong, then it *is* wrong. If it feels right, well, that's why the Parklawn Princesses are running things around here."

Venus blew a kiss. "You got that right!"

"Now, back to Rex," Eden said, holding up the tablet. It showed a gated, Beaux Arts style mansion whose long driveway led to a six-car garage with a residential space above it.

"He lives in this carriage house behind the Butterfield Mansion," Eden said, pointing to a staircase that led to a balcony, a door and a dozen windows. "He's been there for 15 years. Last year his income was $22,000."

"Does he rent?"

"One of my sources said he occupies the carriage house in exchange for walking the dogs and overseeing the car collection. Nobody lives in that mansion except the servants—"

"So sad," Venus said, remembering news reports when Mr. and Mrs. Butterfield were killed years ago.

Eden frowned. "All the money in the world, and their private jet crashed—"

"Near Singapore, right?"

"Yeah, they were building a hotel there," Eden said. "Now a distant nephew is running the company—"

"Good heavens," Venus sighed as the screen showed Rex on a chrome-and-black motorcycle, wearing a black leather jacket, jeans and boots.

Eden smiled. "His vehicle of choice. A souped-up Harley—"

"Oooh, I want to ride," Venus cooed. "Make a note that he'd be good for the *Biker Package.*"

Eden chuckled. "This guy thinks he can create his own theme: *The Venus Roman Deluxe.*"

"Does his psychological exam show any evidence of obsessive behavior?"

"Zero," Eden said. "He's as emotionally well-balanced as they come." Eden clicked to a picture of a Jeep. "His winter vehicle. He's worked at the Opera House for about six years." Her tablet showed him in a yoga studio, instructing a class. "And he's a yogi and teaches meditation."

"Ex-wives, kids, parents?"

"None of the above." Eden clicked to video showing Rex on a sailboat with a young man and woman. "His brother and sister own a sailing club about twenty miles north of here, on the lake."

Eden wrinkled her nose. "Said his parents are deceased, and that checked out, but—"

"You don't look convinced."

"I got a super sincere vibe from him the whole time," Eden said, "until I asked about his mother and father. He looked really sad. I think he's omitting something big."

"Or something gross," Venus said.

Eden crinkled her nose. "Yeah, like maybe he's John's long-lost, illegitimate son."

"Now *that's* sardonic!" Venus said.

"But possible," Eden said. "John was a 22-year-old law student when Rex was born—"

"There's zero resemblance," Venus said. "Plus, John makes my skin crawl; this guy makes me tingle."

"Yeah," Eden said. "I officially noted that Rex Lancaster's X-factor is off the charts."

Venus glanced down at the couples playing volleyball on the beach; long, lithe Orianna from Nigeria was among them, squealing and jumping all over the powdery sand in a skimpy silver bikini that showcased her shapely breasts, flat stomach and athletic legs and butt.

Watching from the path was a hostess leading a tour group of 20 young, attractive women. They reminded Venus of her daughter's lament about throngs of beautiful women in Manhattan creating a "kid in a candy store" playground for men.

"Eden, put ManGuard on Rex for a day or two. We're not the only ones admiring his sex appeal."

"Speaking of," Eden said, "he didn't set off my gaydar, but it takes one to know one. So I had Antonio chat him up, and our dear Creative Director says Rex is a certified, card-carrying heterosexual."

"I got that feeling as well," Venus said. "Your overall rating?"

"A 95. He may get 100 when we clear up the question marks about the parents."

Venus nodded. "I think there's more. Last night he was wearing shoes that suggested financial means far beyond his paltry annual income."

Eden shook her head. "Maybe he likes rich older women who take care of him—"

"If so," Venus said, "then he's campaigning hard to get this one on lock-down for life. No chance." She smiled. "Now, best things last. His physique?"

Eden beamed. "Extraordinary. His measurements meet your exact specifications. I'd say you struck gold."

Venus smiled. "Good work, Eden. Have Kimberly call him back here so I can tell him myself that he'll be my next Husband. *If* you and ManGuard find nothing suspicious."

Eden shot to her feet. "This could be the magic bullet we need right now."

"The magic distraction," Venus sighed.

"Exactly," Eden said. "For you and for the franchisees. We'll send them home with visions of a love-swept CEO and the most fantabulous wedding they've ever seen."

"As opposed to protesters, cyber-hackers, death threats and John ranting on the news," Venus said.

"Positive press, baby," Eden exclaimed. "The Parklawn Princesses will rock the spotlight once again."

Commotion near the yacht drew Venus' attention. Red and blue lights flashed on two police boats surrounding a 30-foot Chris Craft full of men. They were chanting, "Gigolos go home!" and holding placards that said, CLOSE THE HOUSE OF SIN and VENUS ROMAN IS THE ANTICHRIST.

"You are all under arrest for trespassing," an officer announced through a megaphone as a Coast Guard boat circled them.

"Oi vey," Eden exclaimed. "Lunatics by land, and now by sea."

Venus let out a disturbed laugh. "The antichrist? Now *that* is creative." She felt jittery with a new sense of urgency. "Let's have my wedding on Friday, and Rex will be my Husband at the Masquerade Ball Saturday night."

"Perfect," Eden said, taking notes on her iPad as Venus watched the police board the protesters' boat.

"Set up a meeting with Antonio," Venus said. "I want to hear his most decadent ideas for the wedding décor, food, and cake—"

"The media will jump all over this," Eden said. "Romantic opulence in the midst of a storm—"

"Call Sasha Maxwell," Venus said. "Give her exclusive access to cover the wedding for *The Goddess Show* on Meteor Multimedia Network."

Eden blew a kiss. "I just have one word: hot!"

Venus scanned the grounds below. A horse-drawn carriage was carrying Mitzi Glass and Rico Lucio from their wedding in the gazebo up to the terrace for cake and champagne. Hostesses were leading clusters of women on tours. And two *Native American Dream* couples were galloping on horseback near the beach.

"Venus Roman, go to hell!" shouted a man on yet another boat of protesters. "Venus Roman, go to hell!"

She turned to Eden and spoke with a triumphant tone: "This marriage will show the whole world that Husbands, Inc. will always reign supreme, no matter who or what is coming against us."

Chapter 45. Love in the Lap of Luxury

As Raye stepped off the elevator into her penthouse, she vowed to leave her worries at the door.

For the next six hours, she would savor the thrill of Buck transforming into her personal Mark Antony. The ensuing passion would surely leave her speaking Greek, as Cleopatra once had.

Sultry jazz soothed her mind and muscles as it pulsed through the foyer — a 20-foot, gold marble octagon lit by Egyptian-style sconces. Occupying the wall facing the elevator were two life-sized, black panther statues that appeared to prowl toward each other, their eyes glistening with faux emeralds.

Above them hung a gilt-framed portrait of the legendary Queen of the Nile, and between them was a gold table displaying a crystal vase with two-dozen red roses.

"Where would you like this, Ms. Johnson?" the doorman asked as he exited the elevator with a large garment bag.

"In my Husband's dressing room," she said, glancing down at her initials scrolled in black marble at the center of the floor.

"Sure," he said, striding into the tall, marble-columned archway that led to the master suite and guest rooms. Bright sunlight glowed from another archway leading to the living room and library, and a delicious scent wafted from the third archway, which led to the dining room, kitchen and media room.

"I'll have your car ready at eight," the doorman promised, returning to the elevator.

"Thank you," Raye said, slipping out of her high heels as the gold doors closed.

"Baby," Buck exclaimed, striding out from the living room, wearing a black satin robe and velvet slippers monogrammed in gold.

"Ooh, I love coming home to you," Raye sighed, melting into his arms, loving that he was nude and aroused under the thin fabric. His gaze smoldered down at her like he would rather be with her than with anyone in the world.

"Mmmmm," she moaned, inhaling deeply. "You smell even more delicious than whatever Quinn cheffed up for lunch."

"I hope you didn't eat yet—"

"No, I was planning the annihilation of Neanderthal," Raye said. "I am ravenous."

Buck pressed his hot mouth to hers, kissing her so passionately, she felt dizzy. Then he ran his hands up and down her back. "I missed you," he whispered, staring into her eyes.

"Mmmmm," she purred, inviting his luscious lips to devour hers once again.

He led her by the hand into the gray marble kitchen, where her uniformed chef stood at the sizzling, gourmet stove.

"Ah, Ms. Johnson," Quinn said, placing two silver skewers of cubed swordfish over beds of mixed greens, sliced avocado, grape tomatoes and grilled asparagus.

"The swordfish," he said, "marinated in my special Caribbean jerk seasonings. And I made your favorite champagne vinaigrette. For dessert—" he pointed to crystal bowls of raspberries and blackberries "—delicious on the lips, harmless to the hips."

"That's why I love you, Quinn," Raye said.

The chef grinned, but Buck flinched.

"Quinn," Raye said, "we'll eat in the bedroom."

Minutes later, after the chef had arranged their lunch on a table beside the glass doors leading to the balcony, Buck stood by the bed and kissed her ravenously. He let his robe fall open, aiming his huge erection at her.

"Oooh, I can't wait to get all of that," she purred. "Wait here, I want to show you something. A highlight of the year."

He beamed as she dashed toward the hallway leading to their his-and-hers bathrooms and dressing rooms.

She couldn't stop herself from grinning as she slipped into her custom-made, gold dress, along with 14-karat jewelry for her forehead, neck, fingers and upper arms. Then she slipped into gold sandals that laced up her calves. After refreshing her black eyeliner and red lipstick, she sauntered into the bedroom.

"Meet Cleopatra, Queen of Egypt," Raye said, posing in a sexy way, with her hand on one of the four marble columns around the king-sized bed.

Raye expected Buck to respond like her previous Husbands: with a superhuman hard-on to turbo-fuck for hours, fueled by excitement to escort one of the greatest queens in world history to Masquerade at Sea Castle next Saturday night.

But Buck's lips poked out, and his woody went limp.

Raye was so stunned, she just stood there, alternating incredulous looks between his disapproving face and his droopy dick.

"Go in your dressing room," Raye said. "I brought you a surprise. Put it on." He stared at her like he didn't understand. She spoke to him like he was as stupid as he was acting: "A costume. To match mine."

Without a word, he walked past her, and returned a few minutes later. Not as Mark Antony, but as a football player.

"No," Raye said. "I had a costume made for you. I just brought it home today."

"I always wear my Detroit Lions uniform to the Masquerade Ball," Buck said, turning to show number 22 and BRIGGS across the back of the blue jersey. The shiny silver tights made his ass look luscious.

"I always dress as Cleopatra, and my Husband is always her greatest lover, Mark Antony."

Buck stepped close, putting his hands on her waist. "Baby, this year is different. I'm more than your lover—"

"You'll be less than my Husband, too, if you don't play by my rules," Raye snapped.

His expression announced that he was stunned — and hurt. "Baby," he said with pleading eyes. "Great minds think alike. I actually had a costume made for *you*."

"Foul on 22!" she snapped. "We need a quick time-out to review the rules—"

"No, baby, I know your rules, but this simple request would mean so much to me." Buck reminded her of the R&B songs from the 1950s and 1960s that Momma always played. Raye and Whittaker called them *"please, baby, baby, baby, please!"* music because the male singer was always begging the woman to love him, forgive him, marry him...

"Buck," she said, "your proposal is arrogant—"

"Raye, baby," he implored. "My ultimate fantasy is for the woman of my dreams — you! — to dress like a cheerleader. My own personal cheerleader."

Raye expected him to crack up and admit, *"Just joking. Of course I'll wear the costume you got for me."* But he was serious.

She crossed her arms. "Buck, I've dressed as Cleopatra every Halloween since kindergarten, and at every Masquerade at Sea Castle for eight years. Venus and I went from having a few dozen couples in the ballroom at Chateau d'Amour, to one thousand guests this year."

Raye resented that she was explaining something that was not open for debate.

"And Venus just told me, Sasha Maxwell will be broadcasting live from the party for an hour on global TV. I have to look more fabulous than ever—"

"Baby, you will! You got the body to rock my costume." He stepped to an armoire and pulled out a skimpy red cheerleader skirt, a belly-revealing tank top, pom-poms and little white sneakers.

"You'll be the envy of every woman there," Buck said.

"You have clearly lost your mind, and forgotten where you are, and who you're with," Raye said, feeling déjà-vu because she'd just said something similar to Danté yesterday. "So kindly snap back into the man I brought home *last night,* and dress as I requested."

He looked hurt. "Baby, this is really important to me."

She crossed her arms, glancing down to admire the way the golden serpent arm bracelet highlighted the curve between her bicep and deltoid muscles.

"Buck, it's not an option. I am Cleopatra. You play the supporting role accordingly."

He shook his head. "What's wrong with changing your game, if it means you can have even more fun?"

Raye shook her head. "As I said last night, this topic is not open for debate. Besides, you couldn't have chosen a worse costume for Raye Johnson, CEO of Queen Financial Services and co-founder of Husbands, Incorporated."

Buck looked confused. "Why?"

"Cheerleaders stand on the sidelines and cheer on the men," Raye said angrily. "If they get paid at all, it's pitiful compared to the millions the male athletes are making."

"What's that got to do with you looking sexy as hell for me as a cheerleader?" Buck snapped.

"The symbolism," Raye answered. "I will not portray myself in a subservient role—"

"Baby, I wasn't trying to make you go off on a feminist tirade. It's just a costume."

"No, but you were trying to intercept me with a master power play," Raye accused. "So here's a quick recap: I am the star of this game. You are my one-man team for one season, so I call the plays—" she glared at the cheerleader costume "—*and* I choose the uniforms. Period."

Buck closed his eyes hard, pursed his lips, and slinked away. When she heard his dressing room door close, she stood in the floor-to-ceiling mirror, adjusting her jewelry and sandals. Five minutes passed. Ten minutes. Twenty minutes.

"Buck, what's taking so long?"

No response.

She marched down the hall and knocked on his door. "Buck?"

Silence. Heart pounding with worry, she opened the door. He was sitting, still in his football uniform, in the chair facing the mirror, with bloodshot eyes.

Raye fumed: "I know star quarterback Buck Briggs is not in here cryin' like a baby, like my little brother did when Momma wouldn't let him wear the Halloween costume he wanted!"

"I can't do this," he said, casting a pathetic look up at her. "My father made me feel like a piece of meat who wasn't worthy of his love unless I scored touchdowns. Now you—"

"You signed up for this!" Raye shouted. "Nobody is forcing you to stay at Husbands, Inc.!"

He stared at her long and hard. "Baby, you look so beautiful."

She stormed to the brass rack holding the garment bag. She unzipped it and pulled out the exquisite leather vest adorned with gold, as well as a satin cape and tunic that would hang mid-thigh.

Buck glared at the costume. "You treat me like a bitch, now you want me to wear a *dress?*"

"Marlon Brando and Richard Burton both dressed like this in the Cleopatra films!" Raye snapped. "Look, I even got you a sword and a ring. You can wear your football uniform to the Halloween party in October. What's your problem?"

Buck scowled. "Baby, I just need a sign that you have feelings for me beyond sex. I mean, you can say 'I love you' to the dude who makes your food, but you can't say 'I love you' to the man who's lovin' you in and out of the bed?"

Raye crossed her arms and exhaled loudly. "Buck, in about five hours, we're going to the dinner-dance. All I want to do between now and then is enjoy you as my Husband, so you need to—"

He rose slowly. Despite her heels, he towered over her, and his shoulder pads made his shoulders look gargantuan. Not to mention, those snug silver pants were outlining an anaconda over one of his muscular thighs.

"Baby, let me make love to you," he whispered with eyes so full of emotion that her breath caught in her throat. He kissed her; she felt like she was melting into a puddle of butter at his feet.

"Put on the cheerleader costume, and I'll show you—" he yanked down his pants and wrapped her fingers around his enormous erection "—how I respond when you play out my fantasies."

Raye just couldn't argue with that huge dick in her hand.

"Okay," she said, "but just because I put on the costume now, doesn't mean I'll wear it to the Masquerade Ball."

Buck smiled. "I promise," he whispered, cupping her jaw in his giant palms. "You won't regret this."

But Raye had a very bad feeling that yes, yes she would indeed regret this.

Chapter 46. Masquerading to Maintain Control

The sexy vibe electrifying the vast ballroom made Venus shiver, but she was so wired with worry, she felt nauseous.

Standing on the stage built in a turret at the front of the mansion, she grasped one of the gilded thrones for balance. Its red velvet seat beckoned for her to sink in and enjoy this extravagant annual ritual before Masquerade at Sea Castle.

"This is bloody fabulous!" shrieked Ziggy Wild from London, as she and several women watched David and four Husbands model gladiator costumes. A three-way mirror behind the men created multiple images of their flexing muscles.

"Work it, baby," cheered LaShawn from Brooklyn, while Lisette from Canada grooved to the throbbing bass beat of piped-in music. Vondra of Jamaica was holding a man's hand over her head and twirling in a princess dress.

David made eye contact with Venus and grinned. His pecs bounced simultaneously, then one at a time, eliciting lusty cheers from the women.

Similar scenes were playing out hundreds of times from here to the other end of the ballroom, where two-story windows showcased a spectacular view of the lake.

Sunshine beaming on huge crystal chandeliers cast tiny rainbows over the couples. They were perusing racks bursting with costumes, and trying them on in Moroccan-style tents of jewel-toned satin.

The couples' chatter and laughter echoed off the vaulted ceiling that Venus and Raye had restored to its original grandeur with ornately carved, gilded coves framing pastel-hued paintings of Greco-Roman gods and goddesses.

The sight, sound and excitement of romance in the ballroom was so overwhelming, Venus closed her eyes and swayed to the sexy music. Her mind's eye flashed back over sexy vignettes she had enjoyed with Husbands, but the elation of just *meeting* Rex had already upstaged every memory. She envisioned making love with him, and her head swirled with a feeling that they would revel in unimaginable euphoria.

Indulging in the delights of a man like him would be my best medicine right now. Or would it poison me?

How could Rex have known the deepest petitions of her heart? He'd spoken of things that she would never admit, much less act on. And the accuracy of his ability to "read" her — by simply looking into her eyes — was freakish.

Maybe Rex is psychic, and John hired him to use that skill against me.

After all, two of the best Husbands here were extremely gifted at employing their natural, telepathic abilities to seduce clients with unimaginable romance and pleasure.

Or perhaps Rex could truly "feel" her. For as long as she could remember, her parents had been able to know what the other was thinking. Whether it was as simple as craving ice cream, or as important as desiring to buy a new house, her mother and father somehow received information from each other's brains without speaking.

During her marriage to John, Venus had hoped in vain for such a connection.

Oh my God, what if John succeeds at indicting me, prosecuting me and getting me thrown in prison?

What if I lose everything?

What if Rex is a fraud with malicious intentions?

What if someone really tries to kill me? And what if that someone is Rex?

Venus felt dizzy, hating that her cynicism was plunging lower by the minute. In the context of her problems, however, the potential for catastrophe seemed infinite.

Gus and Mario were nearby, along with the two cops. She looked past them, toward the huge ballroom doors leading into the foyer. Kimberly would come flitting in here any minute to announce Rex's arrival, and hopefully provide an update about Whittaker and the video.

What's taking her so long?

The doorways bustled with couples streaming in and out, carrying puffy garment bags containing costumes. But Kimberly was not among them. Frustrated, Venus descended five steps from the stage onto the ballroom floor.

It's time to meet, greet and defeat this worry in my mind. Oh heavens, I'm starting to rhyme like Rex...

Grim-faced Orianna from Nigeria emerged from behind a costume rack, as Venus' security team stood nearby.

"Madame Roman," said Orianna, who wore a bejeweled empress costume. "I have received your messages about the cyber attack and security breaches. Now I am being named in media reports in my country that

341

are putting my family in danger, and my businesses in jeopardy."

The angst in Orianna's eyes made Venus' stomach cramp. She held her guest's hands and assured, "Orianna, as you heard during the presentation this afternoon about security, this would probably occur anyway, when you launch the company. That's why, I'm considering all of this as a blessing in disguise. It forces us to fortify our security plans and procedures, to identify any vulnerabilities and eliminate them immediately."

Orianna looked surprised. She drew her perfectly arched brows together.

"Our experts are working around the clock," Venus said. "We'll share our new knowledge with you before you leave, and we'll convey it through the Liaisons once you return to your countries."

Orianna shook her head. "Your positive thinking is admirable, but I am plagued by serious apprehension. The degree of opposition that you are experiencing here in the United States is a warning to foreign investors that our countries may be even more vicious in their disapproval."

Venus nodded. "That's why tomorrow's seminar with public relations experts will teach you innovative ways to control the company's image."

"I plan to attend," Orianna said, "but I am still feeling quite reluctant about this undertaking."

Venus smiled. "It's my mission to fill you with complete confidence before you leave here."

As Orianna walked away, Venus glanced up at her favorite painting on the ceiling: an Amazonesque woman warrior shooting an arrow at a menacing, three-headed beast.

"Bullseye," Venus declared aloud, surrounded by her security team as she stepped into the maze of costume racks, hostesses, men and women.

"I really dig this cowgirl costume," Claire Montague told Billy Jack Burns, as she posed in a red hat and held up a skimpy denim skirt.

"Then I'm your cowboy, Sweetie Pie." He carried the male version of the costume into a dressing room.

Venus approached Claire, who looked pale and gaunt. Her cascading curls accentuated her bloodshot eyes.

"She'll be back," Venus whispered.

"You talk like you're God," Claire snapped. "You're not. Your security people can't even find her!"

"Just keep believing," Venus said, "and things could work out better than you hoped."

Claire turned away and whistled as Billy Jack appeared, dressed as a cowboy. He smiled, then raised a hand toward elaborate Cinderella and Prince Charming costumes on mannequins. "Hey Sweetie Pie, what about these?"

"Or these?" Claire pointed to mannequins displaying a glittery witch costume and a red devil suit.

"Good Lord," Billy Jack exclaimed. "That might be the best one for us."

Nearby, a familiar male voice said, "That's hot!" It was Mike Rivers, watching Jane Collins pose in a French maid's costume with fish net stockings and a breast-hoisting bustier.

"Beautiful," Venus said, clapping as she approached them.

Mike grinned, while Jane gushed, "Madame Roman, I can't thank you enough! These have been the best twenty-four hours of my life."

Venus clasped Jane's hands and vowed, "Twelve months from now, you'll say this was the best *year* of your life."

Jane cast a love-swept stare at Mike. "I have no doubt. Say, do you have costumes for Ken and Barbie?"

Venus nodded toward a hostess. "She can help you—"

"Excuse me," Kimberly said, appearing from behind a woman in feathery angel wings. "Venus, your visitor is here."

Minutes later, Venus sauntered across the foyer floor, over the Sea Castle mosaic. Jonas opened the double doors to the Moroccan Lounge, located beside her office.

"Madame Roman," the butler said as Gus motioned for the two cops to stay in the hallway, "right over there."

Venus stepped into the plush chamber — a textural extravaganza of rich, jewel-toned velvet and silk drapes, low couches and metal lanterns, all under a ceiling tented with magenta satin. Candles on low tables filled the air with scents of vanilla and jasmine, while belly-dancing music aroused a sensuous mood.

Venus followed the sunlight beaming in from doors leading to the private terrace. There, Rex sat on an emerald silk mattress inside the Chinese wedding bed, which was a walled-in canopy of ornately carved wood.

Venus felt dizzy as he looked up into her eyes, then stood to gaze down at her. The electricity crackling between them could have set fire to the very air, and it certainly sparked a blaze between her legs. Tiny flames of lust danced up and down her body.

"I was summoned," Rex said with a playful smile. "A black SUV with dark windows showed up at my door and whisked me to see the Goddess of Love, through a wicked moat of media and law enforcement. I hope that means I've captured your heart."

"It means you are the most refreshing, intriguing man I've met in a very long time," Venus said. "You defy convention. Not only are you physically beautiful, but your brain and the *je ne sais quoi* energy about you are magnificent."

He touched his fingertips to her cheek and gazed into her eyes.

"Rex," Venus said firmly, "I want you to be my Husband. We can get married on Friday."

He shook his head. "You're not going to parade me around and toss me out in a year. The union of you and me—" he leaned closer, his lips almost brushing hers "—is too extraordinary to treat as some cold, heartless business deal."

Despite her pounding heart, Venus whispered coolly: "Sweetheart, you're missing the point of what I do."

He stepped back. "You can't even hear or see what I'm here to offer. Because your heart is frozen in an iceberg of cynicism."

Venus stared back at him, hating that he was absolutely right.

"I want to spend my life melting the ice," Rex whispered. "It's my divine duty, to celebrate your beauty; delight your mind, with love of the rarest kind—"

Venus savored hearing him, smelling him, staring at him, feeling the sensuous vibe as he continued:

"—and nurture your spirit, please don't fear it; I'm here for you, for us, all you have to do is trust."

The tenderness in his eyes made her feel so hot, she wanted to remove her suit jacket.

"Venus, I want to free you to feel life's most beautiful gift. Love."

His hand cupped the side of her face. She closed her eyes, feeling as if she were swaddled in warm velvet.

Oh my God, this is beyond amazing. But what if he's putting on a Husband act — to somehow pre-empt me? Knock me off my game, as Raye would say, to conquer me? Or worse...

A stinging wave of panic submerged her entire being.

No! Absolutely never. It was not an option to even tiptoe out of the security of her guarded world where relationships were controlled by legal clauses printed in black ink on crisp white contracts. Period. She would not risk plummeting into the gray area where people outside Husbands, Inc. languished in the despair of dishonesty and dead love.

Suddenly she flashed back to that horrible moment, shortly after the Valentine's Day banquet, when she was doing laundry and found lipstick — the same color as Tia had worn — on John's underwear. When she confronted him, he looked into her eyes and lied, point-blank: *"You must have dropped your own lipstick in the hamper. Don't be paranoid, Venus!"*

She wasn't. Not then, and not when she'd found salacious emails from his stable of tramps, or hotel receipts. One in particular documented a three-hour, afternoon stay. She confronted John, who rambled about helping his fraternity brother, who'd lost his wallet and needed lodging while in town.

John's flimsy alibis were not all that exposed his lies. Instead, he was busted by the *feeling* that his entire demeanor provoked within Venus. When John lied, she *knew* because her skin tightened over her whole body, while a panicky, dizzying sensation spun through her. All this alerted her — with absolute certainty — that he was trying to trick her.

Now, standing here with Rex, she loved that she and Raye had created a world where women did not have to tolerate such trickery.

No man will ever get the opportunity to inflict his lies on me, ever again.

And though this gorgeous Romeo was presenting a very convincing argument for her to believe the ultimate lie — true love — it sounded too good to be true. That made it easy to stick to her master script.

Still, her heart fluttered as she said, "Rex, the offer stands for twenty-four hours. I'm getting married on Friday, and I'd like for you to be the one who joins me.

But if you decline—" her breath caught in her chest "—
please let Eden know by five o'clock tomorrow."

Then she turned and stepped away.

Chapter 47. The Claws Come Out

In the Sea Castle ballroom, Mike Rivers held up a black
leather Catwoman costume and said, "Jane, you would look
hot in this."

She smiled, pointing to a Batman suit on the rack. "I
think I would faint if you dressed up as Batman. He's like
my favorite superhero."

Mike put his arm around her as they explored endless
racks bulging with shiny alien costumes, sequins of every
color and poufs of fabric that reminded him of Cinderella.

Just like Jane...

Unless he was making her laugh or cum, Jane's face
was stuck in a constant worried expression. It gave Mike
the feeling that she was afraid that the enchanted carriage
that had brought her here would turn into a pumpkin at any
minute. Her glass slippers would come off, and she'd be
back in rags, crying and mopping the floor in some awful
place.

"Barbie and Ken!" exclaimed a hostess, dashing toward
them with a mod men's costume and a hot pink jumpsuit
and giant yellow wig. "These will look great on you two.
Come this way. Try them on."

Jane squealed with excitement. Mike took her hand and
they followed the hostess to a purple satin tent.

"Oooh, look," Jane said, running her hand over a huge
round, blue velvet stool with gold fringe. Ten people were
sitting on it, trying on boots and shoes or watching their
partners model costumes.

"This way," the hostess said, leading them toward the tent's entrance. A flash of blond hair and suntanned skin caught Mike's eye.

Mother fuck me! Who's that?

He stopped, because Jane and the hostess did, while several hippies, robots and pirates streamed out of the tent.

The blond wore black leather — platform boots, skin-tight pants, a rhinestone belt buckle that said ROCKER CHICK and a bustier that pushed up perfect tits. Mike's mouth watered.

My dick is ready to rock her.

Her straight hair around her bare shoulders framed big blue eyes, a perfect little nose and lips that looked made for him to suck on all day and night.

Why the hell didn't Venus match me up with this girl?

A *Rock 'n Roll Dream* guy followed her. It was Tim from Greenwich, Connecticut; Mike had met that tall, dark-haired rich boy during training.

Lucky motherfucker...

Tim was good-looking, but he lacked natural swagger, due to his pampered, boarding school upbringing. As a result, the rocker chick was eyeing Mike like she wanted to sample some Detroit-style swag.

Mike smiled; she responded with a piercing look that said, *I know you want me, but not now.* That shifted Mike from craving to fiending for the most succulent forbidden fruit he'd ever seen.

One taste could cost me 150-grand! But this girl is so unbelievable, maybe it would be worth it...

Because Jane's eyes reminded him of Laila's TV cameras: they caught every detail, to report to viewers later. When a woman had that look in her eyes, the psycho female receiver in her mind was storing the information to broadcast back in a bad way, usually with accusations of him scheming to fuck whomever he'd allegedly been ogling.

Yet Mike was so sure that he'd mastered the art of staring without getting caught, he put his arm around Jane as they navigated the crowded space.

"Coco," Jane squealed. "I love your costume!"

"Hey, dude!" Tim exclaimed, with a macho hand grasp. "How's it goin'?"

"Lovin' the life," Mike said, smiling at Jane.

"Coco," Jane said triumphantly, "this is my Husband, Thunder."

Coco held out her hand; Mike grasped her soft, delicate fingers.

"Je suis enchantée de faire votre connaissance," she said.

Mike felt dizzy. *Holy shit! If I fucked her, would she whisper in French?*

Jane looked even more horrified than when she saw the bottle-blond neighbor with the red Corvette. So rather than respond, Mike continued to stare at Coco. That only made Jane glare at the side of his face, then at Coco, and back to Mike.

"Hey, babe," Tim said. "We gotta go."

Coco looked toward the costume racks. "There's Josephine and Blake. Bye-bye, Jane and Mike."

Mike forced himself to release Coco's grasp. Then she pulled Tim toward an older woman and a young rocker.

Mike didn't dare look at Jane. *I'm gonna have hell to pay.*

A petite chick with wild red curls blew past him, pulling a guy who declared with a southern accent, "Sweetie Pie, you gon' lure me into the devil's lair."

Then the hostess said, "Thunder and Jane, we can go in." Mike walked behind Jane, whose blond hair was teased up slightly on top, to cover the sewn-in extensions. A choking cloud of perfume followed her. The French maid costume suited her well because she was trying so hard to play a role by looking a certain way.

Coco, on the other hand, appeared comfortable with herself, and all natural. Tits, hair color, eye color. Was she even wearing make-up?

"Here you go," the hostess said, leading them into a room with blue satin walls, a low velvet cushion and a giant mirror. She hung the costumes on a rack. "I'll be back in a few minutes to see if you need different sizes." As soon as the hostess pulled a tasseled rope off a hook to release a panel of fabric over the door, Jane spun and glared up at him.

"I know you want to fuck her *and* our neighbor!" she accused, tears streaming down her cheeks. "I came here to have a dream guy all to myself for a year, no worries—"

Mike pulled her close and looked into her eyes. "Jane, stop. I'm with you and only you for another 363 days—"

"And counting!" she cried. "I'm sorry you didn't get the luck of the draw with a girl like Coco."

So am I...

"No, Jane, I'm supposed to be with you for a lot of reasons," Mike said. "Venus Roman has been matching couples for a long time. She knows what she's doing—"

"I wish a man would look at me like you looked at Coco, just once in my life, and really mean it."

The longing in Jane's voice scraped up goosebumps across Mike's body.

Jane turned her back, wiping her eyes, then examining the outfits. "So Thunder, let's take our pretending to another level by putting on costumes. Here." She held out the Ken doll outfit.

He took it, but his mind's eye was replaying every second with Coco. How could she look so pure and pretty, yet insanely seductive and sexy? How could he get hooked up with her as his next Wife? Was she one of the international franchise owners? Would he have to move to France? How could he get close to her – without Jane or Tim around – to find out more? Could he ask Venus?

"Earth to Thunder!" Jane shouted. "You're so blown away by that *femme fatale* that now I'm just plain invisible. Didn't they teach you acting tricks to use when you realize you hate your Wife?"

Her face was so twisted with anger and pain that Mike just stared back in disbelief.

Motherfuck me! This is gonna be the Year from Hell.

Chapter 48. Temptress Taints the Scene

Rex bolted out of the black SUV, dashed up the steps to the carriage house and strode over the balcony. His hands were trembling as he turned the key in his front door. Inside, he dashed to the big, velvet pillows on the floor in his living room, and sat down.

He needed to meditate to calm the chaos in his mind: *Yes... No... Marry her now under any terms. Wait, convince her to do it my way... Don't let her go... Don't compromise your principles...*

Rex closed his eyes and rested his wrists on his knees, pinching his thumbs and forefingers to form circles. He breathed deeply.

Calm immediately began to pour through him like warm, golden light that would amplify his inner voice to provide clear, accurate guidance.

The question right now: *How can I reconcile submitting to the role of a contractual Husband, when I so vehemently disagree with the concept?*

His rational mind demanded answers, while his heart had already decided: *I want Venus Roman forever, under any label or arrangement. She is my one and only.*

No other woman would do. Age, beauty, prestige, wealth — none of these mattered. Rex breathed deeply, and his inner voice ordered: *Tell her the truth about yourself.*

His heart banged with worry. She would hate him for not being honest from the beginning.

Tell her...

He filled his lungs with more deep, cleansing breaths that sharpened his mental clarity and connection to Spirit.

She will love you more. Trouble ahead will help you prove yourself. Stay the course...

What trouble? Legal challenges? Venus' resistance to true love? Threats on her life?

Footsteps on the stairs and balcony preceded a knock on the door. If anyone from the main house needed to speak with him, they would call first. Had the media followed him here?

Slowly, he opened his eyes as annoyance prickled through him. Breathing deeply to shift back into the physical world, he stood up, feeling light-headed.

The peephole framed someone in a white painter's jumpsuit and cap. It was a woman, with her hair up, doing a bad job of disguising herself.

Damn. Nellie can only be up to no good.

And if some unscrupulous photographer were lurking in the bushes, media images of Nellie at his door would look incriminating at best, scandalous at worst, and disastrous in Venus' eyes.

Rex had read about ManGuard, a surveillance program for Husbands, Inc. clients who wanted 24-hour assurance that their spouses were faithful. It certainly seemed feasible that such a service would monitor any man that the CEO would consider for her Husband.

Rex flung open the door and glared at her. "Leave!"

Nellie's mischievous smile probably worked manipulative magic on other men, as would the significant cleavage exposed by the slightly unzipped jumpsuit.

"That's no way to greet your first love," Nellie teased with a seductive stare. She pulled off the hat, releasing brown tresses that cascaded over her shoulders and down her back.

"You're trespassing," Rex said, struck by alcohol breath and cigarette smoke wafting from her hair and clothes. "Leave now, or I'll call the police."

"You're forgetting that I know who you really are," Nellie threatened. "I just saw you on TV, riding your motorcycle through the gates of Husbands, Inc."

Rex shook his head. Who else had recognized him behind his face-shielding helmet?

"I'd recognize you on your bike anywhere," Nellie said, "after all the good times I had riding you." She let out a tipsy giggle. "I mean, riding *with* you."

Rex glanced at Butterfield Mansion about 50 yards away. Perhaps he could call the butler and have the staff escort her off the property.

"Nellie, did you drive drunk? How did you get past the front gates? And where's your car?"

"Took a cab," she said with a sultry stare. "I'm spending the night."

"No, you're leaving. Now!"

She unzipped the uniform, exposed her bare shoulders, and let the jumpsuit fall around her feet. She wore only red panties.

"Cover up!" Rex shouted. "Security cameras are everywhere!"

He pointed to the mansion, whose high-tech security system monitored this expansive property.

Nellie laughed, then turned around — showing her face for the cameras and anyone who might be watching.

Rex reached out with both arms, turned her around and pulled her inside. He grabbed the white jumpsuit from the balcony, looked around, then went inside and slammed the door.

"Put it on and leave!" he ordered, shoving the clothes toward her. "I'll call you a cab."

She pulled the jumpsuit from his hand, tossed it on the floor, and pressed her breasts into his chest. He stepped back, grabbing the phone from his pocket. "I'm calling the police."

She laughed harder. "That would look mighty bad on your job application at Husbands, Inc. You must be bored. Or broke. Why fuck those old hags, when you have me—"

Rex bit down to stop himself from shouting a very uncharacteristic mouthful of expletives. "Nellie, unless you want to get arrested—"

She yanked off her panties; he didn't even look down to see whatever was tattooed on her thighs.

"Get out of my house!" he shouted. "Now!"

She plopped on his meditation pillows, spread her legs and cupped her breasts in each hand, pointing her nipples at him. "You know you want me," she taunted.

Rex's thumb poised over the "9" on the phone pad. If he dialed 911 and the police came to Butterfield Mansion, the media would follow. And that could stir up a hornet's nest of questions and revelations about information that he needed to confess to Venus, before she heard the truth anywhere else.

Rex felt sick at the sight of Nellie's toxic energy contaminating the purity of his meditation space. Those pillows were going straight into the trash.

The panicked urgency to oust Nellie triggered the epiphany that he had hoped to hear in meditation: *marry Venus as soon as possible. Go to her now and tell her your answer is yes.*

Nellie laid back, spreading her legs wider to reveal the tattoo inside her thigh. He'd been with her when she got it in high school. It said PROPERTY OF over his name, with an arrow pointing to her vagina.

"You don't have the balls to call the cops," Nellie sneered. "Because I'll tell them your secret, and I bet you didn't put *that* on your application at Husbands, Inc."

Rex trembled with alarm. He had no idea how to make Nellie leave, short of physically tossing her out. And knowing her, she would twist that around to call it assault.

God help me...

Chapter 49. Pleasure Numbs the Pain

The purple walls of this tented dressing room felt a million miles from reality, but that still wasn't far enough for Claire to escape the guilt and grief of sending Nikki away.

She fucked up. I fucked up. My parents fucked up everything for both of us.

"Try this on," Claire said, handing Billy Jack a devil costume.

He looked horrified, grasping that big crucifix around his neck.

"It's just a costume!" Claire said, over sexy music and the chatter of excited couples in dressing rooms separated only by fabric panels that hung to the carpeted floor.

Billy Jack took the costume and slunk toward a velvet bench. Meanwhile, Claire slipped into a black leather bikini that barely concealed her tits or ass, along with a garter belt, fishnet stockings, and high-heeled boots. She applied a leather mask that covered the top half of her face, and extended well beyond her temples with silver-sequined points. She left the sheer black cape and whip on the hanger, and checked herself out in the mirror.

Yeah, I like that. Her ass looked so juicy, she wished she could bend around and bite it herself. Her coochie throbbed. She was so turned on from checking out all the tantalizing women amidst the costume racks. In fact, she had almost approached one in particular, who looked like Nikki.

But she resisted, because suddenly an idea for a painting came to mind: two giant hands, splashing buckets of black paint over her life, with a red heart drowning in the goop.

I'll call it, "Life Without Nikki."

Letting her leave was the stupidest thing she'd ever done.

I didn't think she'd actually go! Or stay away.

Claire had run outside, screaming for Nikki and looking for her, just minutes after she'd left the cottage. But Nikki could have run any direction through the woods, and Claire couldn't find her. So she called the Husbands, Inc. Concierge, begging for help. Venus Roman herself had gotten on the phone to tell Claire that her security people were looking for Nikki.

"But without a cell phone or credit cards to trace," Venus warned, *"it will be difficult to locate her once she leaves the vicinity of the log cabin and cottage."*

That had become more apparent with every passing minute, because they had so far failed to find Nikki. Making matters worse, the police had told Claire that she couldn't file a missing person report until 24 hours had passed.

Anything could happen between now and tomorrow! My Nikk-Nikk is out in the world with no phone, nowhere to go, and only as much money as she had in her pocket. If any.

Now trembling with rage at herself and at the world, Claire unclipped the dominatrix whip from the hanger. The leather-covered stick topped with a tassel made a sinister *whoosh* as it sliced the air.

"Hey Sweetie Pie," Billy Jack said, staring through a red feathered- and sequined mask that covered his eyes, nose and cheeks. Red horns sprouted from the top of his head, and he wore a long, red satin cape, whose pointed collar extended up around his ears. Under it was a red satin vest and ruffled black lace tie, and black pants. Apparently he'd tucked the crucifix inside the shirt; this was the first time she'd seen him without it.

"Lord, save my soul," Billy Jack groaned as he scanned her costume, then himself in the mirror.

"Come here," Claire ordered, cracking the whip.

"What kinda costume you got on?" he asked.

"Devil's Helper," Claire said.

"Heck yeah, now you gotta help the devil with this!" Billy Jack grabbed a huge bulge in his pants. He stepped toward her with hungry eyes.

All Claire wanted was to escape into the oblivion of sex, where she wouldn't think about Nikki sleeping in an abandoned house... starving... or getting raped or killed...

If I ever see her again, I'll make this all up to her in a ridiculously over-the-top way...

"Get on your knees," Claire ordered.

Billy Jack just stood there, looking confused.

She cracked the whip. "On your knees!"

He did as told. She put her backside in his face.

"Bite my ass," she ordered, watching in the mirror. He bared his teeth and obeyed with an enthusiastic growl.

"Finger fuck me," she said.

As he did, she moaned with pleasure.

"Oooh, I love that," a female murmured in an adjacent fitting room. The chick laughed, then an impression of her ass pressed through the satin wall, like she'd lost her balance.

"Too much champagne for you," a guy said playfully, apparently helping her up because her butt imprint disappeared.

Billy Jack looked worried.

"Fuck me," Claire instructed.

The laughter got louder. The wall suddenly fluttered toward Claire and Billy Jack, and a woman tumbled under it. She landed at their feet, nude and spread-eagled. Her big tits bounced, and her pussy glistened – red and ripe.

"Good Lord a'mighty!" Billy Jack exclaimed. He stepped back from Claire and stared wild-eyed at the chick.

"Oops," the girl giggled. Her huge pink wig hung to her waist, and half her face was obscured by an aqua blue mask adorned with tiny seashells. This mermaid was clearly missing her seashell bra and tail.

"Bailey?" her guy called from the other side of the fabric panel. "Where'd you go?"

Bailey ignored him; through her mask, she stared up at Claire.

Claire's mouth watered as she visually devoured the girl. All she wanted to do was kneel down and stick her face into all those folds of hot, silky sweetness between her legs. But that would fry Billy Jack's mind — and taint his ability to play a convincing role for her parents.

"You've been very bad," Claire said, stepping over the woman and tracing her lips with the tip of the whip.

"I know I've been bad," the chick said.

Claire ran the whip's tassel tip over Bailey's nipples, which instantly hardened.

"You're supposed to be trying on costumes," Claire accused. She traced Bailey's wet pussy with the whip tip. "But you've been fucking."

"Bailey?" the guy called.

"Your Husband is callin' you," Billy Jack said, looking confused. "Girl, you better cover up."

Suddenly the wall rose. A hot guy in a pirate costume — from the waist up — stepped in. Wearing no pants, he had an impressive erection, which glistened like he'd just pulled out of a very juicy slit.

"Bad mermaid," he teased, standing over Bailey in buckled brown leather boots. "You're supposed to pleasure the pirate."

Without so much as a look at Claire or Billy Jack, the pirate knelt down, slid his dick inside Bailey, and banged away.

"Fuck me," Claire ordered Billy Jack. She bent over the velvet bench; he got behind her.

"This devil sure has been lured into a nasty netherworld," Billy Jack groaned, pulling Claire's bikini crotch to the side and whipping out his dick. "And you're about to feel the heat."

Claire smiled as he slammed inside her, all while she watched Bailey's tits jiggle as the guy screwed her.

"I can't remember Halloween ever bein' this fun," Billy Jack said, watching Claire, himself and the other couple in the mirror. "But you sure bring out the devil in this country boy, Sweetie Pie."

Billy Jack then proceeded to hammer Claire into a place where her mind went blank, her emotions went numb, and she felt nothing but one orgasm after another.

Chapter 50. When It Rains, It Pours

Venus hurried up the stairs to the Husbands, Inc. offices, into the conference room, where somber-faced Whittaker was hunched over her laptop computer.

"Any progress?" she asked, with Kimberly and her security team in tow.

Whittaker kept typing without looking up. "Let's consider no news as good news for now. So far, your video is still lost in cyberspace."

Venus closed her eyes as worry whipped through her. She glanced out at the CyberLion technicians working on computers amidst the phone operators, who were processing applications by hand on paper forms.

"What about my clients' information, and the network?" Venus asked. "When will it be back up?"

Whittaker exhaled, leaning back in the chair. "You had the best firewalls, but hackers stay one step ahead. Whoever got you was no beginner, either. I'd bet big money it was some disgruntled CIA or government-type guy who's irked by your operation here."

Frank Williams came to mind; Venus shook her head.

"Then again," Whittaker said, with a lingering look at Kimberly, "teen hackers are little rebels without a cause. Why spray-paint graffiti in alleys or pull girls' pigtails when you can make international headlines by jamming up a computer network? If they can do it to the Pentagon, they can do it to you, Venus."

She grasped the back of her neck to massage her clenched muscles.

Kimberly's phone rang and she answered: "Agent Rodriguez, I called you because—" Kimberly scowled. "No, we're handling that ourselves. We don't need—"

She was shaking her head, listening. "That's really not necessary," Kimberly insisted. "Our technicians are taking care of it." She rolled her eyes. "OK. I will."

Kimberly hung up and exhaled. "She says the FBI is obligated to investigate because a crime was committed. It's not our call, she said, and they're sending a cyber team here now."

"No!" Venus shouted. "They will not come snooping through our computers!"

Whittaker shook his head. "Unfortunately, you have to. Plus, the hackers have already absconded with your information. And who knows, maybe the feds can help track down the culprits and it would work to your advantage."

"I don't trust them," Venus said.

"That's understandable," Whittaker said, "but I've seen them do some impressive cyber-sleuthing—"

Venus' mind spun in a million directions to craft a plan to protect Husbands, Inc. Meanwhile, as anger prickled through her, she craved the euphoric escape of sex.

I'm going to get some as soon as possible. After I take care of business...

And though she could have her pick of Husbands, Rex's face, and a feeling of overwhelming comfort, dominated her mind. She ached for him. Not for sex, but for a hug. Yes, a lose-yourself-in-his-arms kind of hug. She would inhale him, savor his warmth, press her ear to his chest, listen to his heartbeat, and allow his tender vibe to wrap around her like velvet.

"Sorry to interrupt." Eden darted in, looking somber.

"Oh heavens, what now?" Venus groaned.

"Not good," Eden said, raising her computer tablet. "I need to show you in private."

Venus turned to Whittaker. "Not a word about the video to the FBI."

He nodded. "I'll obey the law, but I volunteer nothing." He emanated honesty as he held her gaze for a long moment.

"I'm trusting you to make a miracle happen," Venus said.

"So am I," Kimberly added with a peculiar look that roused a semi-smile from Whittaker.

Venus, Kimberly, Gus and Mario followed Eden into a small office, where they closed the door and watched Manguard on Eden's tablet. The video showed someone in a white painter's jumpsuit and hat, going up the staircase that led to the balcony entrance of Rex's carriage house at Butterfield Mansion.

"We're getting an ID on her now," Gus said. "She arrived by taxi."

The time at the bottom of the screen said today's date, just 20 minutes after Venus had left him in the Moroccan Lounge. On the screen:

Rex opened the door. Anger tensed his face. The visitor pulled off the hat, releasing brown hair that fell down her back. Then the jumpsuit slid down her bare shoulders, and she stepped out of it, wearing only red panties!

Venus' heart pounded; disappointment stole her breath. "He looks like he knows her."

"And he's pissed!" Eden said as Rex talked angrily and pointed past the woman. "Obviously he can't see our camera hidden in a light pole."

"No audio?" Venus asked.

"It's too far," Gus said.

The woman turned, laughing. She was gorgeous: red-glossed lips, clear skin, big eyes, and impressive tits.

Venus felt sick, imagining him hoisting her up against the wall inside the door and banging away.

I bet his money-shunning pauper schpiel is an act, too — just reverse psychology to weasel his way into my world...

On the screen: *Rex turned the temptress around and pulled her inside. He snatched up the white jumpsuit, looked around, went in and slammed the door.*

"Maybe he's really mad and will make her get dressed and leave," Eden said. "Or—"

"He's putting on an act because he knows we're watching him." Venus trembled with disgust, because Rex had insisted that he was different and wanted her and only her.

Not that I believed him. But why lie? That had just downgraded him into the vast morass of garden-variety men. And really, what man could resist fucking that sexy chick?

She couldn't believe that Mr. Virtuous was apparently illustrating a truth that she despised: even men in casual dating relationships refused to be honest about wanting — and having — multiple sex partners. While dating after her divorce, Venus had wished that men would just say, *"Look, I really like you, but I like other women, too. You do your thing; I'll do mine, and we'll have a great time when we're together. Cool?"*

That would remove deceit and suspicion from relationships, when neither person was seeking marriage. But Venus had not met a single man who had the courage to admit this, except for David, who became her first Husband.

Now, since Husbands, Inc. removed the need for such deception and dishonesty, why did Rex feel compelled to lie? Didn't he know that his vehement vow about being so disciplined and principled would only backfire when the truth was revealed?

I could never trust him. Not even as a Husband bound by Venus' standard contract and "script" that had graced her with six successful marriages here.

As for number seven — by week's end — a succulent selection of Husbands awaited her perusal. Or, David would be excellent and easy, with satisfaction guaranteed. Because Rex had just become too complicated. He incited too many emotions. Too many questions. Too many risks.

"Venus, this could indicate all kinds of trouble," Eden warned, replaying the video. "He could be deceiving you in a big way. Or she could be a run-of-the-mill skank on the prowl. Or maybe someone hired her to smear him."

Eden glanced toward the closed door. "Those cops could be reporting information that trickles down to John."

So many bad emotions collided inside Venus that she didn't know up from down. She had the sudden urge to pummel the punching bag in the gym downstairs. Better yet, getting jack-hammered under a tantalizing stud would be the best remedy she knew: exactly what Rex was possibly doing right now.

"Unless he snuck her out a back door," Eden said, "she's still there."

Venus' imagination taunted her with images of Rex's large, elegant hands — the ones that had grasped hers and touched her face so gently — roughly grasping the vixen's bare thighs, lifting her up, and ramming his dick inside her for a quick thrill. Those big tits would bounce in his face, and the tongue that had spun such poetic declarations of love just a short time ago, would lick and flick all over that chick's nipples...

I guess he's casting his pearl on swine. Proverbially, anyway, because that woman is no swine...

Venus quivered with anger — and arousal. She envisioned a bionic male torso behind her, pounding away her troubles as she knelt in gratitude at the zenith of Husbands, Incorporated — her bed.

She leaned close to Kimberly and said, "Please go down to the ballroom, find David, and have him come to my room immediately."

Chapter 51. Laila Gets Wedding Night Shocker

As the white limousine pulled into the circular driveway of a Spanish-style villa, Laila glanced at her new Husband and coughed.

Holy shit, I'm married to a guy I just met today!

She forced herself to breathe deeply to stop a wicked coughing fit that was brewing in her chest. But it clawed the back of her throat as she gazed up at the house where she would live for the next year — with a complete stranger.

Eden Greenfield had recommended this Husbands, Inc. residence to enhance the *Latin Lover* wedding theme, and John Barker had gladly paid an additional $50,000 to lease it.

But now, the reality of going in there, and having sex with this high-paid Don Juan, felt scandalous and scary.

I don't care how pretty the house is, or how gorgeous and sexy Ricardo Lucio is, if that's even his real name. He could be a complete lunatic!

Laila massaged her throat. She couldn't wait to share these thoughts and feelings in her exposé that would put Husbands, Inc. out of business and wreak revenge on Mike.

"Welcome home," the limo driver said as he opened the door. Rico stepped out, then scooped Laila into his arms. A Husbands, Inc. photographer who'd been waiting at the house, snapped pictures; Laila smiled. Looking at pictures of her wedding day was something she'd dreamed about her whole life.

I just didn't know I'd marry a stranger, or that I'd be motivated by hate, not love...

She wore a short, sleeveless, white lace dress whose corset hoisted up her breasts, cinched her waist and accentuated the curves of her hips and ass.

With parted lips and smoldering eyes, Rico stared down at her as if she were the soul mate that he had searched the world for a lifetime to find.

"*Te quiero, mi amor,*" he whispered, brushing his hot mouth ever-so-sensuously over hers.

Hot flames of lust shot through her.

This feels so wrong! Everything he says and does is suspect, because he's being paid like an actor in a performance. Marriage is supposed to feel real...

A pang of reality, however, struck her hard. Because her parents' marriage, and its bad ending that devastated her mother, was heartbreakingly real. Laila tried to think of a married couple she knew who was truly happy—

"You are the most enchanting bride," Rico said. "A man could not be more fortunate."

He kissed her again, and it felt so good, she responded with a moan and a hot, creamy throb between her legs.

His beautiful, dark eyes sparkled at her with such intensity that Laila had to remind herself that he didn't really love her, even though his demeanor constantly declared that he did. At some point, she would ask him — on camera — why he did not pursue a career as a film actor.

Little did he know, he was being filmed right now. Nestled inside the red silk rose behind her right ear, her hidden camera had recorded the audio and video of the wedding ceremony in the gazebo, as well as his passionate kisses in the limo, and now the proverbial step across the threshold.

"*Bienvenido al paraiso, amor mio*," he said, which meant, "Welcome to paradise, my love."

As sexy Spanish guitar music played on a sound system throughout the house, Laila felt hypnotized by the passion burning in his eyes. The décor of the home — rich reds, plush velvets and black wrought iron accents — blurred in the periphery as she stared at him.

"I've never seen a man look so gorgeous in a tux," Laila confessed. Tall, slim and muscular, his bronze skin and ponytail against the white tux resembled her dead dream of Mike as her groom.

No! I can't think of him! But why did I pick a Husband who looks just like the man I hate?

Because it would remind her why she was here: to destroy the place that stole her fiancé.

Maybe Laila would see Mike tonight, at the dinner-dance at Sea Castle. Laila and Rico were planning to attend, to indulge their mutual passion for Latin dancing.

The limo driver closed the front door behind them, then departed with the photographer.

"My last name," Rico said, as he carried her through the entrance hall, "means 'light' in Latin. So I am going to illuminate something inside you that is magical and new."

As they ascended the staircase to the master bedroom, he kissed her so passionately that she was dizzy with arousal. Her only thought became the desire for him to wrap those beautiful lips around the soft, swollen throb between her legs, until she shivered all over the huge, red velvet-covered canopy bed.

Mike had always been so gentle, holding back for some mysterious reason, despite her insistence that it was okay to be rougher. Right now, she wanted this sexy matador to fuck her ferociously.

"I sense that you are ready to leave the lady at the door," he said, setting her on her feet.

Staring into her eyes, he yanked off his jacket and tossed it to the floor. He did the same with his bowtie. Then he put her hands on the front of his shirt, placed his hands over hers, and pulled. The buttons popped off; the shirt ripped open.

"Oooh, I love that," Laila cooed, running her palms over the smooth bronze muscles of his pecs. His skin was unbelievably soft, smooth and hot.

"You are wanting to allow your true animal passion to take you to places you have never been," he said, locking his gaze on hers.

She peeled his shirt off, revealing smooth, sculpted shoulders. Overwhelmed with an unfamiliar feeling — holy shit, it was pure, wild abandon — she dove at his deltoid with an open mouth, kissing, then sucking, then biting —

"*Ay, mi amor!*" he groaned. She stroked the huge bulge in his pants, which he quickly unfastened and pulled off. Wearing only black silk boxers, he spun her around to loosen her corset strings. With a pull and a zip, her dress fell open and slid down around her white satin stiletto sandals.

His fingertips trailed the lace-covered contours of her breasts. Laila tremored as he ran a fingertip down the center of her stomach, past her bellybutton, to the white vee of lace between her legs. He fell to his knees, then grasped her thong with his teeth as his hands cupped her ass.

At the same time, she pulled the black satin ribbon in his hair, releasing his ponytail into a silky cape over the rippling muscles of his back.

His fingertips raked down the flesh of her hips and legs as he removed her thong.

Her dress and panties fell to the floor as he laid her on her back, across the bed. As he grasped her ankles and kissed them, a beam of sunlight shot into the room, dancing on her bare stomach. Her wedding day primping in the Husbands, Inc. salon had left just a strip of hair leading down to what was now a juicy raspberry, throbbing for his touch. Oh, if he would just wrap his lips around it and suck like it was his only sustenance—

"Yes, beautiful bride," he said. "Welcome to our sensuous fantasy where I will make love to you until you are crying for me to stop."

He raised her knees, and he knelt at the side of the bed, where he placed his face just above the hot, wet slick between her legs. He inhaled, closing his eyes like he was praying. "Never have I seen anyone so succulent."

Laila tilted her hips up in anticipation of his mouth devouring her down there.

I can't believe I just met this man and he's got me spread-eagled with his face in my hoochie... and I'm excited about it!

Had adhering to society's strict code of conduct for "good girls," deprived her of enjoying sex to the max? Was it a lie that the best sex happened in a real, loving, committed relationship? What if she liked sex with this stranger more than she had with her real fiancé?

If so, and she'd been missing out on all the fun, then she was about to become one furious bitch.

"You are my Wife now," he groaned, "so I'm going to pleasure you in ways you have never imagined possible."

Laila smiled. "I'm gonna start calling you 'the telepathic lover.' You know what I want before I even say—"

The tip of his tongue touched her clit.

"Holy shit," she moaned, closing her eyes.

A lick followed. Then his lips slid down around it, and he made a sucking motion, alternated by a tongue stroke that made flames dance through her whole body.

"That's puuuuurrrrrrfect." In a flash of white-hot heat, she convulsed and shrieked and clawed the back of his head. "Holy, holy shit," she whispered in shock. She had never come that fast. Ever. She opened her eyes to behold a huge, hard dick pointing straight at her.

In one graceful motion, he pushed her to the center of the bed, and slid inside her.

"Aaaahhhh," she cried as the perfect friction roused tingles through her whole body. He stared into her eyes as he began thrusting, which created a sensation that she had only felt during orgasms with Mike. Goosebumps danced across every inch of her skin, from her scalp to her toes.

As he pumped ferociously, she ran her hands down the sides of his back, to the curve of his waist, to his hips and over the hard, round mounds of his ass.

"Oh my God, I loooooooove that," she cried. Her rock-hard nipples were poking up into his pecs, and his body felt like a turbo-charged piston that would never stop. It was the perfect pace, the perfect stroke, the perfect fit.

Tears stung Laila's eyes. She squeezed them shut.

Oh thank you God, thank you universe, thank you Venus Roman! If I had married Mike, I never would have experienced this. I can't believe it...

"My love, I knew you would be an exact fit," he groaned. "Made for each other."

No, she wanted to say, *you're being paid to perform a duty, just like a plumber or a roofer or a dentist.*

"We have many soul mates," he groaned. Despite his pace, he was not out of breath or even sweating. "We can meet in so many circumstances, even those that seem unnatural."

"Then this is supernatural," Laila panted. Because this dude was reading her mind and fucking her like she'd never known possible.

Holy cow, what if I get addicted to this shit? I could lose my mind. Why would I ever want anyone else if this guy can do me this good?

Panic exploded inside her almost as intensely as that orgasm she'd just had. How could she do an exposé to make Husbands, Inc. look bad, when it was making her feel so good?

I still can... because this feeling can't possibly last for 12 months...

Still, Laila wanted to change her report to encourage other women to try out a bunch of men until they found a dude with skills like this in bed.

Her report... shit! The red rose was still in her hair! The camera was recording all of this. No! She had intended to take it out, turn it off. She did not want to deal with the legal issues involved in videotaping sex with someone who was unaware that a camera was capturing them. Plus, the reports would be provocative enough, without nudity or sex.

I'm a journalist, not a porn queen...

But before she could remove the camera, Rico leaned up and back. He was on his knees, still thrusting, while she was on her back. He pulled her hands between her legs. He pressed the fingertips of her right hand onto her swollen clit, and guided her to make a circular rubbing motion.

Laila looked at him like he was crazy to think she would touch herself like that in front of him. But damn, it felt so good as he kept thrusting. The double stimulation sent intense shivers up and down her legs, over her breasts and into a psychedelic swirl in her head.

"Yes, my love." He smiled. "I am here to show you new ways to enjoy life's gift of carnal pleasure."

Rico's hips maintained that ferocious pumping rhythm that roused goosebumps all over. She began to shiver.

"Oh shit, I'm gonna cum again," she whispered in shock.

Adoration glowed in his eyes. "You may orgasm as many times as you can imagine, my love. I have infinite passion to please you for as long as time will allow."

Laila cast an intoxicated smile up at him. Somewhere in her mind it registered that this was her job and that they never had to leave the house for 364 more days, if she could milk the assignment for that long. How could she keep John and his rabid hunger for Venus Roman's blood at bay long enough to enjoy every second of this *Latin Lover*?

Laila rubbed away her worries as Rico simultaneously mashed them to a pulp.

"Oh my God," Laila cried, as tremors rippled through her body. "Oh my God!"

His face beamed with joy. "Yes, my love. *Si, mi amor.* It is all for you."

Laila was almost afraid to let go, but it felt so incredible—

Like a volcanic eruption, a red-gold shimmer flashed behind her closed eyelids. Tremendous heat blasted between her legs, where her flesh pulsed around Rico's rock-hard shaft and her fingers continued to swirl her entire being into earth-shattering convulsions.

Sounds that Laila had never heard shot through her lips. They were primal screams, cries of pleasure that completely bypassed her brain and erupted from her very core.

And Rico kept pumping.

She pulled her fingers away, but he put them back. "Do not stop, my love. Keep going."

She resumed, and the orgasm continued for what seemed like minutes. Then he kept pumping away for a long time.

Laila just laid there, shaking, moaning and loving every second of it. She couldn't believe that he hadn't orgasmed yet. Mike would have been done long ago. She ran her hands over the sheen of sweat on his back, then gripped his rock-hard ass as he pumped up and down.

If every man could fuck like this, women would get nothing done in life. They would want to stay in bed all the time. As a reporter, when Laila had covered stories about women going crazy over a man, and even going to jail for it, she had never understood it. Now she did.

A shiver shot through her; this time it was more of an epiphany than pleasure. She suddenly felt ecstatic that Mike had left her.

If I had stayed with him, I would have never known that sex could be this good. And the irony is, I thought he was the best ever!

"Turn over, my love," Rico whispered, pulling back and lifting her hips to raise her onto her knees. He caressed her ass and moaned in approval. His hot lips trailed soft kisses over each cheek. Then he angled her body so that her butt was sticking up in the air. He pressed his hands to the back of her waist, and plunged inside her.

"Oh yeah," she groaned, as a whole new set of shivers rippled through her. He took her right hand and placed her fingertips between her legs, helping her get started with a circular motion that made her head swirl.

"I will make you lose count of how many times you orgasm tonight," he promised. "Lay your cheek on the bed and enjoy."

Laila did as told, and soon, she was having another long, powerful orgasm.

Did all the men at Husbands, Inc. learn how to fuck like this? Or was this guy just extra gifted? Was every woman at Husbands, Inc. enjoying this kind of pleasure? Was Julie getting blasted by her *Boy Toy*? And had Mike learned how to fuck this way at the Husbands Academy?

If Laila weren't so pumped with endorphins, she may have felt a pang of anger that someone else was enjoying extraordinary sex with her former man. But she felt nothing — except thrilled that she was in bed with Rico, and that she could stay here for as long as she wanted.

Oh shit, no I can't. John is paying for this. And he's gonna want some dirt, fast.

Without John's money, Laila could never afford this. And without the money, there would be no marriage – or sex with Rico.

Laila's body tremored with orgasm and panic all at once.

I am so supremely fucked right now.

𝒞𝒽𝒶𝓅𝓉𝑒𝓇 52. Going Buck Wild for a Cheerleader

Buck couldn't remember ever feeling this happy — or turned on. But the sight of Raye Johnson sashaying into the bedroom in that red cheerleader costume made his dick as hard as a goal post.

"Damn, baby, this is the sexiest thing I have ever seen in my life!" he exclaimed over the deep bass beat of hip hop music that had started playing before she strutted out of her dressing room. "The woman I love is rockin' that little skimpy outfit hotter than a teenager."

Raye posed in a way that showcased the defined muscles of her smooth, flat stomach. Her legs looked long and toned under the pleated skirt, and that little top made her titties say *bam!*

"Girl, I could give you a tongue bath right now," he groaned, sitting on the edge of the bed to watch in awe. "Wait, what about the pigtails? The costume comes with red ribbons."

"Don't push your luck." Raye popped her ass toward him. The skirt flew up, exposing a juicy curve of booty, red lace panties and her bare thighs. Then, with a flash of shiny red fingernails, she looked back over her shoulder at him — and smacked her ass.

"Work it, baby." Buck grinned.

She thinks she can beat me at my own game, by whipping me into submission to dress like all her other Husbands. But in a minute, she won't know what hit her.

Buck's dick throbbed as if every drop of blood in his body was surging into it. He was definitely playing in an all-new ball game. It was better than he'd ever imagined, and he was sure he would win the ultimate prize: Raye Johnson as his real-life wife.

She is my dream woman, wrapped into one beautiful, brilliant, sexy package.

Buck Briggs had fucked some of the most gorgeous women in the world, with the ultimate tryst occurring at the five-star Hotel de Paris in Monaco. A European prince who loved football had invited Buck and his team for a weekend there to celebrate their Super Bowl victory. After a 10-course meal that included the best steak and seafood he'd ever tasted, Buck and his teammates were surrounded by what looked like contestants at the Miss Universe pageant.

Even better: the women were there to pleasure the players in opulent suites. Buck laid it on a shapely, French-speaking girl from Fiji, who embodied the very definition of an exotic fantasy.

But right now, as Raye Johnson swayed to the sexy beat, she stood head and shoulders above even that experience. Because this seductive side of her personality was icing on the cake of traits that he loved about her — intelligence, fierce independence and invincible strength. The problem was, those same characteristics were blocking him from winning her heart.

So I'll keep using my power of persuasion on her body. He glanced down at his God-given prize that many women had described as "addictive." Then he cast a promising look up at Raye.

"Come here," he groaned, reaching out, grasping her thighs in each hand, pulling her close. He reached between her legs and grabbed a handful of pussy. Her panties were hot and damp. He slid his middle finger under the elastic.

"Damn, baby, you're on fire already."

Her nipples poked two points in her red top, which she wore without a bra. Buck slid his finger around what felt like a warm, cream-filled, butter-soft pastry.

"Tell me how much you want this cock," he said, making tiny circles on the tip of her clit.

"Oooh," Raye moaned, closing her eyes, tilting her head back and running her hands over her body.

"Tell me!" he demanded.

She glanced down at him with a lusty but domineering smile.

"You gotta say some magic words if you want to see my tricks," Buck threatened.

She let out a devilish laugh, then pressed his face into the juicy mounds of her cleavage.

"I love your body language, baby," Buck said, "but you gotta tell me somethin' good—"

She yanked his hand out of her crotch, raised his cream-covered middle finger to her face, inhaled it with an orgasmic expression, then flicked her tongue up and down it.

"Day-yum," Buck whimpered, staring up at her in awe. He almost forgot his challenge: "Speak to me! Tell me how bad you're cravin' this long, strong cock."

She spun around, bent over, and popped her ass in his face. His breath caught in his throat as he stared at the sling of red satin under two round, juicylicious cheeks, above two perfect thighs.

Buck's heart was pounding so hard, he was sure it would crack a rib. It was like his heartbeat was coming from his dick, pulsing through his body. Because he couldn't think straight. In fact, he wondered how long he could last if he started fuckin' her from such an overwhelmingly aroused state.

If I cum too quick, she will be pissed! And that won't help me accomplish my mission of trouncing her plan for the costumes.

Raye was circling her hips in a mesmerizing way. He couldn't look away from the bull's eye between her legs.

"I don't hear you talking," he warned. "I told you—"

She reached around, yanked the crotch of her panties to the side, backed up, and shoved her pussy against his mouth. He grasped her thighs, pulled her closer, and slurped up and down, like she was a triple scoop of praline pecan ice cream.

"Oh hell yeah," Raye groaned, grinding her hips to the beat of the music. "Suck like you never tasted anything so good."

Buck froze. *I told her to tell me how much she wanted me ... now she's telling me what to do. Hell naw!*

He gently pushed her thighs away. But she put her hands on the floor and kicked back both legs in a circular motion around him. Then suddenly the tops of her thighs were on his shoulders. With her inner thighs against his cheeks, she crossed her knees behind his neck, which thrust his face back into her crotch.

Damn! She got me in a pussy headlock!

He wanted to ask her when she'd learned the kind of acrobatic moves that real cheerleaders did. But the salty-sweet scent and taste of her cream, and the shock of this position, just made his dick throb harder.

So he licked. Sucked. And in no time, she was convulsing all over his head and shoulders. As the damp heat blazed from her pulsating flesh, he smiled, loving that he'd pleased her so well.

But hating that he'd just lost round one.

Chapter 53. Boat Ride Gets Nasty

As the bikini-clad girls began to dance, John Barker concluded the meeting. It was nearing sunset as the yacht sliced across Lake St. Clair, with the shores of Michigan and Canada in the far distance.

"Now that we've plotted the demise of Venus Roman," John said, "let's go after the whores who've come to America to inflict depravity in their own countries."

Frank, Rippstyx and Nikolai raised their shot glasses and chugged whiskey, while Ted picked nonexistent dirt from under his fingernails.

As Nikolai checked email messages on his phone, he said, "My associates are reporting that our social media campaigns have been especially virulent for the women in France, Sweden, Jamaica, Japan and Venezuela."

Ted looked sick to his stomach; John focused on Nikolai.

"And slandering the Russian woman has been especially amusing for them," Nikolai added, "because now that she has spas in Moscow and Los Angeles, she is a snob toward Russian men."

"Put that bitch in her place!" Frank declared.

"Double whammy," John said, watching the women grind against each other as sexy music played. "Wreck her in Moscow, wreck her in L.A. Make all those bitches hate Venus for draggin' them into her nightmare."

Ted looked ill. "Honestly? Slander is illegal! I will have no part of it."

Frank play-punched Ted's arm. "Loosen up, my friend." He nodded toward the girls, who were caressing the blond's bare tits. "Enjoy the entertainment."

"My men are oceans away from you, Mr. Pendigree," Nikolai said. "I can assure you, your hands will stay clean, and your name is never known. This is my endeavor. An ode to my wife who found her young equestrian trainer more appealing than her husband."

"Bro, that's rough!" Rippstyx said, pouring more whiskey for everyone and raising his glass. "Let's have one for you! Havin' all these hoes is the best revenge."

Nikolai chuckled as he made eye contact with the brunette, who blew him a kiss and removed her bikini top. She unleashed perfect jugs, then squatted to muff dive on the Asian chick.

John's dick was hard as steel. He couldn't wait to bend one or all of these bitches over the railing and bang to his heart's content. He'd think of Venus with every stroke, and Tia, sitting at home on her fat ass, probably making love to a pint of chocolate ice cream.

"Gentlemen," John said, "we'll follow up tomorrow night, after Venus' big surprise."

The Asian chick sauntered up to John, massaging his shoulders, then straddling his lap and removing her top. Her D-cups were enormous in proportion to her petite body; John buried his face in them while cupping her ass as she gyrated over his crotch. Damn, he could blow a wad right now, but he would wait—

As the blond approached Ted, he shot up from his seat and darted to the railing, fingering his cell phone.

Meanwhile, Frank was making himself at home between the legs of another chick, who was straddling him. Rippstyx had a lap full of ass as a girl shimmied her tits in his face.

In no time, John was bending this pretty young thing over the railing and shoving his shaft inside. With his pants around his ankles, he thrust like he was king of the world.

Nearby, Rippstyx whipped out a surprisingly big schlong and pummeled away, doing the girl in missionary position on a lounge chair. Nikolai was doing the same, as a hoe bounced on his lap.

But Ted was still at the railing, staring out at the water. All stress and no fun was making Ted a very despicable prick.

"Yeah, Daddy, fuck me like that," cooed the young beauty, turning around to cast a seductive look at John.

Man, this is the life.

He would have to talk to Nikolai about celebrating like this, with three or four times as many chicks, after the obliteration of Venus and Husbands, Inc.

That thought, and the tight little twat around his dick, made John tremble with orgasm. He stared up at the orange sky, feeling all-powerful.

But when he lowered his head, he glimpsed a flash of something metal. It was Ted's phone — either taking a picture or shooting video.

Oh hell no! Soon as we get back to the dock, that bastard and his phone are gonna take an unexpected swim, so we can get back to the business of bringing Venus down.

Chapter 54. Heartache Causes Carnal Chaos

Venus flung off her suit jacket, kicked off her shoes and sunk into the plush chaise lounge in her cream-colored master suite. She couldn't wait for David to come swashbuckling in here to provide an erotic reprieve before the dinner-dance.

Sex with him was so stupefyingly superb, it would push her "reset" button to banish Rex from her mind for good.

"I'll be back in ninety minutes to take you downstairs," Kimberly said, perched on a nearby chair. The noise of protesters in a news report playing on her tablet disturbed the peace of Venus' sanctuary.

"House of whores, close your doors!" the men yelled. "Prosecution for prostitution!"

"The louder they shout," Venus said, "the bigger, better and stronger we'll be." She glanced down at her phone in her hand, eager for a positive report from Whittaker.

"The media is like, sounding our death knell about an indictment," Kimberly said as a "special report" on Channel 3 analyzed the death threats and cyber attack.

"Turn that off!" Venus snapped.

Kimberly silenced the news. "They're broadcasting so many lies. And it's super negative—"

Venus tuned out, gazing at the opalescent tiles framing the metal swirls of the fireplace grill. Gold-orange beams of evening sunshine shot in through a window, illuminating firewood on the grate.

My enemies think they can burn me... but they'll get incinerated in the end. While I continue to provide fantasies to women around the world... including myself. Without Rex.

Venus tuned back into Kimberly's chatter: "—but I keep checking with Yolanda and Adam, and they're convinced the indictment is just John trying to huff and puff and blow our house down."

"Over my dead body." Venus shifted, causing her thong to tantalize the throbbing swell between her legs.

Deep voices boomed in the hallway. The doors swung open; the two police officers, along with Derek and Decker, flanked the entryway. David appeared between them.

"I'm here to take care of the goddess," David announced with a hungry look in his nutmeg brown eyes. His huge muscles bulged from under the dark leather and metal of his costume as he strode toward her. A long, sheathed sword hung at his right hip and his yellow hair was bright against his sun-bronzed skin.

"Venus, baby, what's wrong?" Worry radiated from the clean-shaven planes of his broad face as he knelt, kissing her hand. "I almost didn't recognize you."

"What?" Venus cast a questioning look at Kimberly, who was standing, ready to leave.

Kimberly had a pained expression. "You do look different."

"Pale. Stressed," David said. "Like I've never seen—"

Venus sat up straight. "That's unacceptable." She smiled. "Better?"

Neither looked convinced.

"I know how to get you back to normal," David promised with a sexy chuckle. "Can I shower first?"

"Of course," Venus said. He kissed her hand, then strode into the master bathroom and closed the door.

"Kimberly, do I look that bad?" Venus asked.

"Oh no," Kimberly said, looking panicked as she looked down at her tablet. "The nightmare has begun. Look." She held her tablet for Venus to watch video of protesters in front of a New York City townhouse, as a reporter said:

"Couples linked to Husbands, Incorporated coming under siege in 15 states right now—" video showed picketers in front of the offices of Marena Barboza in

Caracas, Venezuela "—while a social media campaign in countries around the world is blasting women who plan to open franchises of the controversial company—"

"Gus!" Venus called. He dashed in through double doors leading to the terrace, where Mario remained. "Why can't the CIA or Interpol or someone stop these lunatics from sabotaging our international guests?"

Gus glanced at the report on Kimberly's device and shook his head. "My global network is honing in on Men for Traditional Marriage guys in the Florida Keys, and a Russian blogger in Istanbul. He was apparently convicted of harassing Josephine DuJardin's assistant—"

"Coco Versailles," Venus said. "I know. Her blessing of beauty has been a real curse—"

"This same guy," Gus said, "is linked to Gregor Nikolai—"

"I knew it!" Venus exclaimed.

"Oh no, that's GiGi's house!" Kimberly pointed to the news report, showing picketers at an oceanfront mansion in Newport Beach, California. Their faces contorted with rage while they held signs that said: END THE MAN SALE and A GIGOLO LIVES HERE.

Then it showed protesters blocking a black Bentley with dark windows as it exited through the driveway's electronic gates.

"Local police arresting six men this afternoon," the reporter said, "for attempting to break into the home of fashion designer Gigi Gateau. The men also tried to block the car that her spouse from Husbands, Inc. was driving, with her in the passenger seat—"

"This can't happen!" Venus snatched up her phone and dialed GiGi. A busy signal blared in her ear. "Who gets busy signals anymore?"

"A disabled number," Gus said. "Maybe she was getting harassing calls."

Venus watched the screen, which showed protesters

attempting to climb GiGi's fence.

"Venus," Gus said, "I recommend we hold security drills with our staff and clients twice every day, starting tomorrow."

She nodded.

"Morning and evening," Gus said. "We'll brief everyone on what to do during an emergency and how to evacuate. And we'll run the alarm in test mode."

"Good," Venus said. "Tonight, I want you to speak briefly at the dinner-dance as a reminder about security. Announce that the alarm will ring twice daily, starting tomorrow morning."

"Will do." Gus nodded.

"This is crazy!" Kimberly stared in disbelief at her phone and computer. "I'm getting bombarded with calls, texts and emails from across the country—"

"Kimberly," Venus said, bolting up and pacing by the fireplace, "go meet with Zahra and Eden to compose a text message, an email, and a voicemail message, to tell our clients what to do if they're harassed."

Kimberly typed notes.

"Tell them how to protect themselves," Venus said. "And for the email, attach a voucher for two free nights at the nearest Butterfield Hotel, so clients and their Husbands can escape until the mayhem dies down."

Kimberly nodded.

"Issue a statement to the media about how we're handling this. Then," Venus said, "summarize everything so I can review it before I address our clients and franchisees tonight at the dinner-dance."

As Kimberly dashed out, Venus heard the hiss of the shower, and her phone rang.

"Vee!" Raye sounded furious. "The bullshit on the news right now is Neanderthal's last hurrah at being diabolical."

Venus sighed. "Whittaker still hasn't restored the

video—"

"I've moved on to Plan B and Plan C," Raye said. "First, get ready to watch John Barker get led away in handcuffs very soon."

"How?"

"The SEC will be all over his ass," Raye said, "because I called in a favor with someone who has some very bad dirt on how Detroit's favorite lawyer handles his investments."

"Excellent," Venus said. "What's Plan C?"

"He's trying to use teamwork to make his dream work," Raye said, "so we can do better. I called in a team of women who say John Barker either sexually harassed them in the workplace, or had extramarital affairs with him while married to you and Tia."

Venus grasped her sour stomach.

"I also know a former stripper," Raye said, "who says she used to work for Gregor Nikolai as a prostitute — with John as a steady customer."

Venus shot to her feet. "Raye, why have you never told me this? And when was he screwing hookers?"

"Don't worry, she met him after you divorced," Raye said, "when Neanderthal expanded his network to include international gangsters."

Venus felt nauseous and dirty.

"I got your back, girl," Raye said. "I know you've been slammed left, right and center with all this pandemonium."

Venus closed her eyes. "Thank you, Raye."

"One way or another, we're slaying the beast," Raye said. "A sex tape, an SEC investigation, sexual harassment and prostitution. I should've done this long ago, but we were having so much fun—"

"Speaking of," Venus said, "how's Buck?"

"Buck Briggs is good," Raye said, breathlessly. "Too good. Girl, I'm 'bout to lose my mind under this man. Help!"

Venus smiled. "This is a first."

"And last," Raye snapped. "This man is giving a Herculean effort to knock Raye Johnson off her game—"

"No, don't let him. Ever!" Venus was suddenly consumed by an overwhelming yearning for Rex. It surrounded her like a soft cloud; she could almost feel his hands on her back, pulling her close, his hot lips on her mouth, his deep voice vibrating through her.

But he's probably doing all that with a brunette seductress right now...

The hiss of the shower went silent; a hot wave of lust consumed her.

"Raye," Venus said, "think back to your first marriage, and how awful it was when Tremaine had all the power over you."

"Smack!" Raye laughed. "Thanks, Vee. That knocked some sense back into me. But Buck feels different, like I've met my match. I can't even describe it, because I've never felt this way—"

Venus closed her eyes, hating that Raye was echoing her own thoughts about Rex.

"Let me stop," Raye said, "before Buck gets back from the kitchen. Has Mr. Literary given you an answer yet?"

"ManGuard did," Venus said somberly.

"He's gay?"

"No, a hot-blooded heterosexual man, possibly doing what they do best."

"That motherfucker," Raye said. "You might be right about him being a henchman for Neanderthal. That crossed my mind about Buck. Our enemies would love to get us where it would hurt the most — in our beds — by tricking us into believing all the lovey-dovey bullshit that's the antithesis of what we do."

The bathroom door opened. David was so big and muscular, his shoulders almost touched the sides of the doorway. He wore only a white towel around his hips. His wet hair dripped over his glistening muscles.

"I'm about to get thrashed back to *my* senses," Venus whispered. "David is here to help me get my power-glow back before the dinner-dance."

"Oooh, you and me both. See you in a few hours, Vee."

Venus devoured David with her eyes, aching to luxuriate into the orgasmic essence of this extraordinary world that she and Raye had created.

Chapter 55. Slipping Into Orgasmic Oblivion

Raye loved times like this, after a short break from hours of sex. Sprawled nude on the bed, she pressed her palms to her thighs to feel her muscles jumping.

Sex with her first real husband had never made her tremor like this. But her first lover after the divorce — a gorgeous, mahogany hunk of smiles and muscle from the Islands — had introduced her to how a real dick thrashing was supposed to leave her: as a quivering mass on the bed.

Buck hadn't just learned at that same school of lovemaking; he was proving that he'd actually written the textbook for its most advanced degree. So he knew that now, after four hours of fucking, that her body's sex parts were so sensitive and swollen, that any more touching or licking or thrusting would set off orgasms with the power to lobotomize.

As in, disconnect an important part of her brain that enabled her to make decisions, such as what she would wear to the costume party.

He can try his hardest. But I will not be defeated. Cleopatra will make her grandest entrance ever at Masquerade at Sea Castle, with Mark Antony on her arm...

She cast a triumphant glance at the red cheerleader

costume on the floor, where it would stay. She couldn't wait for him to come back from the kitchen and make love like his pride depended on it. They still had a whole hour before it would be time to shower for the dinner-dance.

"Baby," Buck said, bounding into the bedroom with a tray of food and champagne. "I guess Quinn knew what would be goin' down, 'cause he left us all this."

He set the tray on the bed, then placed a round cracker heaped with herbed seafood salad into her mouth. She did the same for him as he poured two glasses of bubbly.

"Mmmm," Raye said, feeding herself and Buck little wedges of brie on slices of French bread.

He handed her a glass and raised his. "Cheers to making every minute blow our minds with sexy shit like this!" He clinked her glass.

She sipped, but only to wash down the food, because she hated his toast. It was missing something — his usual proclamations of love. Instead, he'd kept it nitty-gritty, unemotional—

Like I told him to...

But I'd rather have the upper hand of hearing how he's head over heels "in love," while I'm "in control."

She smiled slightly, studying his eyes for a sign that he'd offer a second toast about something more than sex. But Buck was too busy feeding himself mini mounds of roast beef on rye. Raye savored another seafood cracker, watching him attack the spinach dip and a cluster of green grapes, occasionally feeding one to her.

"Damn, this roast beef is good," he said, using a tiny spoon to dab horseradish sauce on a piece before he held it to her lips. "Open."

She did, but closed her eyes to savor all the flavors and textures, as opposed to looking at his self-satisfied smirk.

He thinks he laid it on so good, I'll change my mind about the costumes...

Buck laughed. "My stomach was growling like, 'Feed

me!' With all this hard work, lunch is long gone."

Raye winced inwardly. *Now he's describing our lovemaking as "hard work" — as if he's been hauling bricks on a construction site all afternoon!*

She hated that Buck was actually playing by the rules that she'd laid out yesterday, including: *don't talk about real love.*

"Mmmmm," Buck moaned. "Baby, have some more meat. You still look hungry."

Shit. He wasn't talking about hunger for food. Or sex. He could see in her eyes that she was hungering to hear his romantic proclamations.

She nibbled a cluster of grapes, glancing at the clock. "We should start getting ready."

He looked up, alarmed. "No, baby, we got an hour left!"

Raye slid to the edge of the bed and placed her feet on the floor. The movement caused delicious friction on the hot slick between her legs; her nipples turned rock hard.

"Enjoy your food," Raye said. "I'm going to shower now—"

Buck shot up from the bed and stood in front of her. Then, with a move as powerful and graceful as the touchdowns that had made him a superstar on the football field, he picked her up by the waist, kissed her passionately, laid her on the bed, and thrust into her, deep and hard.

Oh hell yeah... She smiled up at him, thrilled that he'd succumbed to her power play.

"Raye, baby, you still haven't told me what you want me to do to you tonight," Buck said with a sexy-gruff tone.

As his lower body moved with superhuman speed and force, every stroke of his cock against her hypersensitive canal sent a million more tingles through her. Closing her eyes was like looking up at purple fireworks against a black sky. And opening them revealed a stunning, intriguing man who was by far the best lover she had ever had.

I have met my match. God help me...

As Buck continued to thrust with bionic brawn, he stared down into her eyes with the determination and intensity of an Olympic athlete. He was sprinting toward victory, using every ounce of muscle and mind power to win the gold.

"You love this shit like you never loved some dick," Buck said with his sexiest swagger yet. "You're gonna be cravin' this cock. Beggin' for it—"

Raye wanted to say something like, *No, I don't have to beg.* But she couldn't even string words together to form a *thought.*

Because an orgasm of cataclysmic proportion was trembling up from the deepest depths of her soul. It exploded between her legs, sending shockwaves of pleasure down her legs and up her body. It electrified her skin, making every cell feel like it was popping up and dancing. It turned her insides into a molten flow that flooded her mind and heart. And it imprinted the beautiful face of Buck Briggs forever in her mind as the man who could carry her into the kind of end zone that she'd vowed never to enter.

A sound, like a sob, escaped her mouth. Tears welled in her eyes.

"Yeah, baby." Buck flashed a sexy smile as he watched her convulse and cry. "Yeah, I got your ass now."

She squeezed the tears from her eyes — were they pleasure or pain? — as she stared up at him.

"I told you what would happen if you fulfilled my fantasy as a cheerleader," Buck said. "I'd fulfill yours, like this." He thrust even harder, and he wasn't even out of breath. She was hardly hearing him, because her ears were ringing from cumming once again.

"But if you won't wear the costume—" he suddenly stopped thrusting "—then I won't go all the way Buck wild on you."

All she could do was moan in protest, because she hadn't finished orgasming.

"I'll take that as a yes," Buck said, fucking her hard and fast once again, as she continued to cum. "Yeah," he said triumphantly. "I'll take that as a big, loud yes that Raye Johnson will be Buck Briggs' cheerleader at the Masquerade Ball."

His words registered somewhere in her mind, as his dick rocked her body like the global earthquakes that were supposed to come at Armageddon.

Because this is clearly the end of the world as Raye Johnson knows it...

Chapter 56. Under Siege, Inside and Out

As David scooped her into his arms, Venus was determined to escape into orgasmic oblivion for the next hour. Hearing Raye's new strategy to strike back at John had filled her with confidence, but she still gripped her phone, hoping to hear good news about the video.

"Business can wait," David said, casting a disapproving look at her phone. "We got another kind of work to do, so I can get you back to normal."

He carried her into the bedroom, which contained only her huge, round bed atop three white marble steps. Evening sunshine cast a golden glow over the gauzy silver sheers hanging from the metal canopy of swirling purple metal. Two tall candelabra of the same design flanked the white bed. Above it, the unlit ceiling dome appeared shadowy.

Venus couldn't stop imagining that David was Rex, carrying her toward the bed, and gazing at her like he wanted to spend forever and a day making love to her.

"When I get through with you," David promised, "you'll have that cocky look back in your eyes. Literally."

Venus tried to smile. Oh, how she had delighted in focusing on David's handsome face during so many glorious orgasms when he was her first Husband, then her lover between subsequent marriages.

But now her mind was playing tricks —projecting Rex's face over David's. How would Rex be in bed? Rough? Gentle? Boring, exciting? Would he say poetic things? Or would he say nothing and speak pure eloquence with his eyes and his body?

"I got my work cut out for me tonight," David whispered. "Looks like you're a million miles away."

David kissed her. The only way she could respond was by fantasizing that his full, warm lips were actually Rex's mouth, plying hers with perfect pressure and precision.

Was Rex kissing that long-haired vixen right now? Was she just an easy fuck, or did he have feelings for her? Was he wishing that he were here, rather than there?

No, he's playing you for a fool, and John may have put him up to it. He's fucking that chick to his heart's content, right now, and everything he pledged on the yacht, and in the Moroccan Lounge, were just lines from his deceitful script.

Venus kissed David fervently. Urgently. She clawed at his giant shoulders. Lust surged through her, re-igniting that hot ache between her legs.

"Take me outside," she said. "To the cabana."

He carried her through the gauzy sheers and French doors, onto the terrace, where Gus and Mario stood guard, overlooking the bustling grounds and lake.

The full moon hung in the fiery orange sky. Security boats whizzed back and forth near the beach, while pleasure cruisers and tankers traversed the darkening lake. Below the terrace, clients and Husbands were splashing in the pool, sitting on benches nestled in the bursts of flowers and lush greenery, and playing sunset volleyball.

"Gorgeous night," David said, kissing her forehead. "For a gorgeous lady."

Venus smiled, but felt exposed. Anyone on the lake could see them over the banister and between the hibiscus trees.

"Take me inside," she said, nodding toward the draped cabana.

As David took one step, her phone vibrated in her hand. Excitement welled in her; maybe it was Kimberly calling to say that Whittaker had restored the entire sex tape.

We can use it to stop John in his tracks. Tonight!

But the phone flashed "X." It was John.

She remembered that adage, *"Keep your friends close, your enemies closer."* She answered.

"Enjoy Hercules while you can," John growled. "'Cause you won't see the likes of him when I get you locked up in prison for life!"

Panic prickled through her.

He's watching me...

"Divorcing me and becoming a world-renowned pimp was the worst mistake you could ever make, Venus Barker." His tone was cold and sharp; a deep hum and wind in the phone indicated that he was on a boat.

David scowled; John's voice was loud enough for him to hear. With chivalrous urgency, David carried Venus back into the house.

"Just know this," John threatened. "You will be out of business, wrecked, ruined, and condemned on all fronts, by week's end. And you'll wish you had never, ever, relinquished the privilege of being my wife."

Click.

"Call the police," David said. "That's stalking."

She made a three-way call with Gus and Zahra, told them what happened, and instructed them to report this to authorities.

Stiff and painfully tense, she cast a pleading look up at David; he kissed her passionately, unzipping her dress, and removing her bra and thong. That began to quiet her mind and relax her muscles.

He laid her on the bed; sexy music boomed from unseen speakers.

David dropped his towel, standing before her with a huge erection that would last all night if she wanted, and a look in his eyes like he'd rather be here with her than anywhere in the world.

"You look like you want to get right to it," he whispered, leaning toward her across the bed, then trailing his fingers over her wet slit. "And you feel like it, too." He sucked his fingers, then applied a condom.

As he knelt before her, she savored this symbolic moment: an infinite supply of pleasure at her beck and call, with more than enough to share with all the women of the world.

This is my mission, and nothing, no one will stop me!

David's dick was like a giant exclamation point after that thought, as he rammed inside her.

She closed her eyes in anticipation of feeling goose bumps tickle across her face and every inch of her skin, to set the stage for too many orgasms to count. Normally the face-tingle was immediate, with the first thrust, but perhaps her extreme state of stress would require her to relax a bit first.

She grasped the small of his back, loving his smooth, hot skin over solid muscle as his hips thrust ferociously.

Her body went limp as she received this magic elixir. She tried to focus on how fortunate she was, having this astoundingly sexy, skilled lover in her bed.

But I could lose it all. The evil cast of characters trying to destroy her danced in her mind like goblins. John. Ted. Frank. The protesters. Whoever hacked the computers.

And the maniacs who want to kill me.

As for Rex, was he a lover or a hater? An authentic soul mate, or a convincing imposter? Would he step forward and agree to marry her? Would she stand firm and shout a resounding "no," or would she succumb to his beguiling allure and let him serve as her Husband, starting six days from today?

Venus felt numb.

My face didn't tingle... Oh my God...

Eight years ago, David had set the standard for that sensation as the benchmark for good dick.

Now I'm too stressed to feel it.

This was unprecedented. Totally unacceptable!

Venus pushed David's shoulders up slightly. He bent back onto his knees, hoisting her hips up. He pressed his fingertips to her clit, where he stroked while ramming her hard and fast. He cast a lusty smile down at her.

"Yeah," she moaned, eager for pleasure to ripple through her. But she felt like she had received an epidural — the injection that an anesthesiologist had shot into her back before she gave birth to J.J. and Christina. The powerful drug had deadened her lower body to the pain of labor.

"No," Venus gasped.

"What?" David looked worried. "You okay, baby?"

"Yeah." She closed her eyes. But she envisioned Rex fucking that temptress. And she heard John saying: *"Enjoy Hercules while you can... 'cause you won't see the likes of him when I get you locked up in prison for life!"*

A hot, burning sensation rose in her throat.

"I'm sorry," she said, moving to get up. David pulled out. She ran to the bathroom and closed the door.

"Oh my God," she cried at her reflection in the mirror. She had not seen such a haunted, horrified look in her eyes since the night she decided to divorce John.

Then, as now, her father's voice echoed in her mind, as he shared his favorite Scriptures: *"It's always darkest before the dawn;"* and *"Weeping may endure for a night, but joy cometh in the morning."*

But how dark would it get? And how long would this proverbial night last? She sobbed into her hands.

A knock on the door. "Venus, baby, you okay?" David asked on the other side.

Suddenly an ear-splitting noise made her freeze.

The alarm... Why the hell is it going off?

No siren test was scheduled for this evening; it had already occurred this morning, and the new schedule wouldn't start until tomorrow. She held her breath, waiting to hear Gus' recorded voice saying, *"This is only a test..."*

But the deafening siren continued to blast.

"Fire!" announced the electronic female voice. "Evacuate immediately. Fire!"

Venus did not smell smoke. But this was a huge mansion.

Oh my God, is the house on fire?

Or being attacked?

Threatened by a bomb?

The door flung open. David, wearing the shorts that he'd worn under his costume, dashed in, followed by Gus and Mario, whose guns were drawn.

"We have to get out," Gus shouted.

Venus stared at them, dazed.

Evacuate. Fire. Bomb. I'm naked...

David grabbed a robe from the nearby stand and wrapped it around her. He picked her up, carrying her behind Gus and Mario, who moved toward the bedroom door in ready-to-shoot stance.

"Venus?" David yelled over the siren, as concern roiled in his eyes. "You okay?"

No, I'm not okay. I'm under siege...

ELIZABETH ANN ATKINS

Elizabeth Ann Atkins writes and speaks from the spectacular human spectrum that she embodies as the daughter of an African American judge and a former Roman Catholic priest who was English, French Canadian and Cherokee.

She began writing *The Husbands, Incorporated Trilogy* about a decade ago, to explore her observations about love, romance and marriage.

Elizabeth has a master's degree from The Journalism School at Columbia University and a bachelor's degree in English Literature from the University of Michigan. As an Okemos High School student, she studied French through Collège de Rivière-du-Loup in Quebec, Canada.

She has written more than a dozen books, including *White Chocolate, Dark Secret,* and a love story penned with actor Billy Dee Williams called *Twilight.*

Elizabeth made her acting debut in the inspiring feature film, *Anything is Possible,* released in theatres and on DVD in 2013.

She also composed an original screenplay, *Redemption,* a suspenseful drama about a struggling writer and a repentant gangster.

As an electrifying speaker who shares messages that promote human harmony and celebrate writing, Elizabeth is represented by The American Program Bureau. She elicited a standing ovation as keynote speaker at an NAACP banquet and for her performance of her autobiographical poem, *White Chocolate,* at a prominent church.

She has lectured at GM's World Diversity Day, Gannett, Columbia University, Levy Home Entertainment, Comerica Bank, the Association of Multi-Ethnic Americans, the University of Michigan, the American Library Association, a National Human Rights Conference,

Beaumont Hospital's Diversity Symposium and the Oakland County Employment Diversity Council.

Elizabeth is planning to introduce and teach a new series of writing classes for fiction and non-fiction. She has taught seminars at colleges, companies and conferences, as well as courses at Wayne State University, Oakland University and Wayne County Community College District.

She is a health and fitness enthusiast whose 100-pound weight loss was featured on *Oprah*. She has also discussed race and writing on *Montel, Good Morning America Sunday*, BET, *The* CBS *Evening News*, and many national television shows. NPR and many radio stations have interviewed her.

Her journalism career began at *The Michigan Daily*, and she has worked at *The New York Times, Fox 2 News, The San Diego Tribune, The Lansing State Journal*, and *The Detroit News*. The former president of Detroit's National Association of Black Journalists chapter has also written for *Ebony, Essence, Ms.*, HOUR *Detroit*, BLAC *Detroit*, and a tribute to Rosa Parks.

Elizabeth has served as a writer for many fascinating people, including business leaders, a surgeon, an intuitive medium, a popular minister, and a quadriplegic man who owned a record company. She also wrote *Fat Family, Fit Family: How We Beat Obesity and You Can, Too*, the memoir of a family featured on NBC's *The Biggest Loser*.

Her novellas have appeared in two anthologies: *Take It Off!* in *Other People's Skin*, about women's self-love; and *The Wrong Side of Mr. Right*, in *My Blue Suede Shoes*, about overcoming abuse.

Elizabeth meditates, practices yoga, runs, cycles, lifts weights and rejoices in nature. She enjoys speaking French and indulging a daily "breakfast 'til bedtime" writing schedule.

CPSIA information can be obtained at www.ICGtesting.com
Printed in the USA
BVOW04s0439080514

352870BV00005B/6/P

9 780982 141526